# PHOENIX UNBOUND

# GRACE DRAVEN

ACE

NEW YORK

ACE
Published by Berkley
An imprint of Penguin Random House LLC
375 Hudson Street, New York, New York 10014

Copyright © 2018 by Grace Draven
Penguin Random House supports copyright. Copyright fuels creativity, encourages diverse
voices, promotes free speech, and creates a vibrant culture. Thank you for buying an authorized
edition of this book and for complying with copyright laws by not reproducing, scanning, or
distributing any part of it in any form without permission. You are supporting writers and
allowing Penguin Random House to continue to publish books for every reader.

ACE is a registered trademark and the A colophon is a trademark of
Penguin Random House LLC.

Library of Congress Cataloging-in-Publication Data

Names: Draven, Grace, author.
Title: Phoenix unbound / Grace Draven.
Description: First edition. | New York: Ace, 2018. | Series: The fallen empire; 1
Identifiers: LCCN 2018018971 | ISBN 9780451489753 (paperback) |
ISBN 9780451489760 (ebook)
Subjects: | BISAC: FICTION / Romance / Fantasy. | FICTION / Fantasy / Paranormal. |
GSAFD: Fantasy fiction.
Classification: LCC PS3604.R385 P48 2018 | DDC 813/.6—dc23
LC record available at https://lccn.loc.gov/2018018971

First Edition: September 2018

Printed in the United States of America
1 3 5 7 9 10 8 6 4 2

Cover illustration by Arantza Sestayo
Cover design by Adam Auerbach
Book design by Elke Sigal

Phoenix Unbound *is dedicated,
in loving memory, to Lora Gasway.
I am Grace Draven because of you.
Thank you.*

# PART ONE

# EMPIRE

# CHAPTER ONE

For Gilene, spring was the season neither of rain nor of planting, but of suffering.

She waited beside her mother, sister, and brothers as the caravan of shackled women plodded down Beroe's market street toward the town square. The slavers of the Empire guided the line, shoving their cargo forward with harsh commands and the occasional warning crack of a whip.

She had already exchanged farewells with her mother and siblings. Each had embraced her, dry-eyed and grim-faced. This wasn't their first parting, and for good or ill, it wouldn't be their last.

Her eldest brother, Nylan, squeezed her shoulder. "We'll be waiting for you in the usual spot," he said in low tones meant for only her to hear. Gilene nodded, reaching up to pat his hand.

Her eyebrows arched when her mother sidled a little closer, her fingertips brushing Gilene's sleeve in a hesitant caress. "Come back to us when it's over."

Gilene kept her reply behind her teeth. It was never over. Not for her. Despite her mother's half-hearted gesture of comfort, she wouldn't defend her daughter. Gilene would endure this every year until her age and her scars crippled her so badly, she could no longer wield her magic well enough to fool the Empire, and her burden became another's. Her resentment served to blunt her fear.

She gave a quick nod before turning her back on her family and striding toward the line of captives.

People hemmed either side of the dusty road. Their gazes, as she walked past them, were fearful, hopeful. Ashamed. A few villagers, however, wore expressions of warning instead of pity on their faces.

*Yes, come back to us,* they seemed to say. *Or else.*

Their stares shifted briefly past her shoulder to where her family huddled together to watch her leave.

Not all shackles were fashioned of iron.

Some of the villagers reached out to touch her, their fingers drifting across her sleeves or skirts like dead leaves. Gilene shrugged them off and made her way to the motley group at the end of the path.

One of the slavers snarled an impatient "Get in line!" and shoved her to the end of the queue. A few of the women stared at her empty-eyed; others wept and wiped their noses on the backs of dirty hands, their chains rattling as they raised their arms.

Another slaver approached her, a pair of manacles dangling from his fingers. He gave her a black-toothed smile as he snapped them around her wrists and tethered her to the woman next to her.

"Pretty jewelry," he said and shook the shackles to show there was no breaking them.

The vision of the slaver enrobed in flames and shrieking in agony almost made her smile, but she kept her expression blank and dropped her shoulders in a defeated sag. She had learned years earlier that a broken captive didn't incite the whip as often as a rebellious one did.

Beroe was the last stop on the slavers' route to retrieve the living tithe the Krael Empire imposed on its subjects for the annual celebration known as the Rites of Spring. Gilene was the last tithe to join the others before they set off for the capital of Kraelag. She settled into the lurching rhythm of the chained line, dreading the four-day march ahead of her and its final destination even more.

Except for the chain rattle of shuffling feet and the bark of orders from a slaver, all stayed silent, fearful of the stinging flick of the whip.

Their journey was as miserable as it had been the previous year and the year before that: relentless marching under a spring sun that beat down on them with the promise of a brutal summer, nights spent huddled together for warmth as the remnants of winter rolled in with the twilight and whittled through clothing and skin like a knife.

The night before they reached the capital, Gilene curled into the back of her chain mate, a prostitute named Pell, and closed her eyes to the lullaby of chattering teeth and the soft sobs of her fellow prisoners. Her feet throbbed, but she dared not remove her sandals for fear of peeling away layers of skin from the many blisters.

She smelled the city's reek long before she saw it. When the great walled capital of the Krael Empire came into view, some of the women cried out their relief at the sight. The slavers laughed, yanking on the chains hard enough to make some of their captives stumble and fall. Gilene helped a fallen Pell to her feet before the man fondest of bestowing the whip's kiss strode toward them. Her fingers burned hot, earning a startled look from the prostitute before Gilene let go and stepped away as far as her chain length allowed. She forced down her fury before the tiny sparks bouncing between her knuckles grew to flames.

*Patience*, she silently admonished herself.

The slavers herded the women onto a wide, paved road that

led to the colossal main gates. The space around them disappeared as they were hemmed in by a milling throng of people, carts, and animals. The noise was deafening, and the combined smells of sewage and unwashed bodies made her eyes water. She lifted her hands to cover her nose, the clink of her chains lost in the cacophony of shouting people, bleating livestock, and creaking wagon wheels as the masses heaved and rocked toward the gates.

Guards perched at their watches high in the two towers flanking either side of the gates, idly watching the crowd—many of whom had come to attend the Rites of Spring—as it squeezed its way into the city's confines. They casually dropped garbage and other offal on people as they passed beneath them, their raucous laughter carried on the fetid breeze.

A guard leaned out of a tower and shouted down to the crowd. "Any pretty flowers this year, Dolsh?"

The slaver closest to Gilene yelled back. "Does it matter? One roasted hen looks much like another."

Laughter followed his reply, along with faint weeping. Gilene growled under her breath. A roasted cockerel looked like any other as well. She wanted to burn them all, every last one of them, but she was only one woman with limited power, a power she'd drain to the dregs just so she could survive this madness and keep her compatriots from suffering.

They were whipped, shoved, and cuffed through the narrow closes that branched off the main road like strands on a debris-littered spiderweb. At the web's center, a man-made hill rose, its top crested with the emperor's palace. Temples, manors, and bathhouses marched up its sides, and at its base, the arena crouched. A circular, roofless amphitheater whose sole purpose was to entertain Kraelag's citizens with blood sport and brutality, it was known as the Pit, and to it the slavers herded their charges.

They reached the Pit's outer walls and an entrance closed off by a barred gate manned by more guards. The sunlight faded as the procession descended several flights of slippery steps, through passages dimly lit by torchlight. The walls narrowed, forcing everyone into a single line. All snaked through the labyrinthine maze until they reached a low-ceilinged chamber in the city's catacombs.

Gilene inhaled a stuttered breath as she crossed the threshold, knowing what awaited them in the chamber. Fresh from the Pit, covered in gore and reeking of sweat and butchery, the gladiators of the Empire lounged at the chamber's opposite end and eyed the newcomers.

They didn't approach, but the weight of their leers pressed down on her as she and the other women huddled together. She pretended not to see them. These were the men who had survived the day's games, and their reward would be the sacrificial victims known as the Flowers of Spring. As one of those unfortunate blooms, Gilene would whore for her village tonight and burn for it tomorrow.

The girl on the other side of Pell shuddered and chanted a desperate prayer in a foreign tongue. Gilene leaned past her chain mate and grabbed a stretch of links attached to the praying girl's manacle, giving it a quick jerk. The girl gasped, prayer forgotten as she stared wide-eyed first at Pell, then at Gilene.

"Shh," Gilene instructed her in a soft voice. "Be still. Be silent. Some lust for beauty, others for fear. Don't show them yours."

The other woman nodded, her lips moving in a now-soundless chant. Gilene gave her a brief smile of approval. She could offer little else, at least for tonight.

Pell leaned down to whisper in Gilene's ear. "Her prayers are in vain. She's too pretty, even under all the dirt. She should pray the one who chooses her will be gentle." Her words were blunt rather than merciless.

Gilene sighed. "Gentleness has little meaning when one is unwilling." She stared at Pell, wondering at the woman's practical calm. Gilene had made this horrific trip four times before this one. She knew what to expect. The only unknown was how terrible each year would be compared to the one before it. "What will you pray for, Pell?"

The slattern's calculating smile deepened the lines around her mouth and those fanning the corners of her kohl-lined eyes. "I haven't prayed in years, girl. Wouldn't know how to go about it even if I tried. I'll be happy to get one of those fine stallions with the blood washed off him and enough skill between the blankets to make it worth spreading my legs for free."

Gilene admired Pell's bravado. The woman knew what awaited her with the dawn yet still held on to a cynical wit.

Pell made to say more but stopped when a short, muscled bull of a man strode into the chamber. Dressed in mismatched armor and carrying both whip and dagger, he was a formidable sight. Blue markings decorated his skin, sleeving his bare arms. The marks curled over his shoulders and crept up a thick neck to cap his bald head. Some of the women in line cowered away from him, and he grinned.

Hanimus, gladiatorial master trainer, still presided over this event each year with relish. Like Pell, Gilene didn't pray, but if she did, she'd beseech the gods for Hanimus's death. He represented all that was rotten about the Empire.

He walked the long row of women, pausing at times to lift the chin of one with his whip handle or fondle the breast of another.

His fighters called out encouragement and vulgar suggestions for what they wanted to do to their chosen prizes.

"They sent us a good crop this year, lads," he proclaimed. "Too bad you only have them for a night." Groans and ribald laughter filled the room, drowning out the softer weeping.

"We'll all grow old before we can choose," one impatient fighter protested.

The trainer's eyes narrowed, and he spun to glare at the men. They snapped to attention. "You'll wait your turn," he warned. "Azarion is still fighting. If he lives, he'll have first choice as Prime."

As if on cue, the boisterous cheers of the arena's crowd vibrated against the stone walls of the catacombs, sending dust raining down on everyone's heads. The death bell pealed a sonorous song—tribute to the victor, a dirge to the slain.

"Lot of good it'll do him," someone muttered. "Herself will summon him like always. She rides that cock every chance she gets." A chorus of *ayes* answered him.

Hanimus shrugged. "He still has first pick."

Gilene bowed her head to hide her anger. Most of the women in chains had been separated from husbands and children, parents and siblings. Brought to Kraelag for the sole purpose of dying, they shouldn't have to suffer this final degradation.

A part of her recognized they were alike in some ways—the condemned women of the villages and the enslaved gladiators of the arena. They had once been beloved sons and brothers, maybe husbands and fathers. Now they were all fodder for indifferent gods and the entertainment of the Empire, their deaths more valuable than their lives to those who ruled. Still, she couldn't find it within her to pity these men who would subjugate them.

An expectant silence descended on the group as the crowd's triumphant chant swelled to a thunderous bellow.

"Azarion! Azarion! Azarion!"

Hanimus smacked his whip handle against his thigh and grinned. "Ha! I knew he'd take the fight. The Margrave of Southland owes me a goodly sum now."

The march of feet soon sounded on the steps leading down to the catacombs—the last victorious gladiator and his entourage of guards. Gilene watched the doorway from the corner of her eye, her stomach knotting itself in dread of seeing the man who would come through the entrance.

Like the other gladiators already here, he'd be dressed in blood-spattered armor. Unlike the others, he'd suck the air out of the room with his presence. She remembered Azarion from her previous annual treks to the capital. Worse, Azarion seemed to remember her.

Boot heels scraped across the dirt, and the Gladius Prime made his appearance. He bent to avoid hitting the lintel and entered the chamber. Stifled gasps from the women and bows from the men greeted him—this slave who commanded the deference reserved for kings.

He'd changed little since she'd seen him the previous year. A tall, solidly built man with wide shoulders and long, muscled arms, he exuded a presence that diminished the men around him. He was disarmed now, but she had no doubt he could kill as easily with his bare hands as he did with the weapons he carried into the arena.

His dark hair was shorter than she remembered, resting on his shoulders in sweat-dampened tendrils. She refused to look at him directly, choosing instead to watch him from the corner of her eye. She'd met his gaze before and regretted it.

He was handsome, with the high cheekbones and light eyes characteristic of the nomadic clans that roamed the Stara Dragana. The cold expression he leveled on the room's occupants turned his green eyes flinty. Gilene hunched her shoulders and tucked herself as far back from the line as her chains allowed.

One of the gladiators broke the expectant silence. "Was it a good fight, Azarion?"

Azarion glanced at him before returning his attention to the women. "Aye. Damiano fought well and died honorably."

Gilene shuddered. She'd forgotten his voice. Low and gruff, it carried to all corners, challenging, as if he dared anyone to make light of his victory or the death of the man he'd fought.

Hanimus tapped him on the arm. "We've been waiting for you. Best make your choice quick before Herself calls for you."

Azarion slowly moved down the line, and Gilene's heart joined her stomach in trying to squeeze itself into a corner of her rib cage. He paused before each woman, staring at her with a prolonged gaze. Beside Gilene, chains clanked as Pell patted down the snarled mess of her hair and adopted a pose to show off her attributes.

Gilene clenched her hands in her skirts, trying not to panic. Surely, he couldn't recognize her. She'd returned to the capital time and again with a different face. Her skills with illusion were as refined as they were with fire. The slavers never knew they brought the same woman from Beroe to Kraelag year after year. No slave fighter from the Stara Dragana should have the talent to see past her veil of enchantment.

Fear coated her tongue at a memory from the previous year. Azarion's green gaze had locked on her and narrowed. Neither lustful nor leering, he'd stared at her for several moments as if seeing not a freckled redhead with wild, frizzy hair, but her true self: a plain, dark-eyed brunette.

"Do not know me," she muttered under her breath. It wasn't a prayer. She'd ceased believing in gods long ago. Still, she chanted the plea silently. Her heart slammed against her breastbone when he halted in front of her.

*Do not know me.*

This year she was round-faced and cross-eyed, with lank brown hair and sunburned skin. She'd bound her breasts and wore layers of sweltering wool to mask her shape.

*Do not know me.*

The prayer that was not a prayer pounded in her head, and she swallowed a whimper when he lifted her chin with one finger. Her gaze slid past his face to a dent on the pauldron protecting his shoulder.

"Look at me." His deep voice, so quiet, carried the resonant command of a general.

She refused to take her eyes off the dent.

"Look at me," he repeated in the same tone. His fingers curled around her jaw and pressed. She dragged her gaze to his, the drumming of her heartbeat making her chest hurt. He leaned closer, gripping her chin even harder to keep her still, eyes blazing in triumph.

"I know you," he whispered.

# CHAPTER TWO

Azarion peered through the small barred window of his cell door and waited impatiently for the guards to deliver his companion for the evening. A decade of slavery, of fighting, killing, and biding his time had finally paid off. Skilled though he was, Damiano hadn't stood a chance against him in the Pit, not when the prospect of freedom awaited him in the dank catacombs below the arena. The emperor and empress had been disappointed by the speed with which he dispatched his opponent, but the crowd roared its approval and chanted his name to thunderous applause.

He'd offered up a silent prayer to the goddesses for the fallen gladiator before striding from the Pit to the catacombs. The familiar pungency of manure and animals, of mold and stagnant water, was nearly overwhelmed by the stench of the unwashed guards who followed him to the common room where Hanimus waited with the unfortunate women chosen as this year's Flowers of Spring.

Not until he spotted the tall, plain creature among the dejected row of victims did he realize how hard his heart pounded in both anticipation and the fear she might not return this year. He shouldn't have worried. She returned to Kraelag every year to face the fires. A different face, a different body, the same dogged perseverance.

Azarion didn't know why she subjected herself to the Rites

time and again, or why he saw through her spells when others didn't. At this moment, he didn't care. She was the key to his escape.

Footsteps sounded from the main corridor leading to the barracks, one heavy-footed, the other light and hesitant. A voice bellowed its presence. "I've brought Azarion's bit o' cunt. Unlock his door."

The guard stationed near Azarion's cell answered, scorn dripping from his words. "This is her? Not much to look at. Slim pickings from this year's crop of kindling?"

"Nay, plenty of fine pieces to choose from. You never know with these savages. I hear they fuck their own mares, even when their women aren't scarce."

"The mares probably aren't as ugly."

The two men shared a round of smirking laughter. Azarion waited, ignoring their insults, his gaze trained on the flickering shades of torchlight in the corridor.

During the first years of his captivity, he would have charged the door, determined to rip the guts out of the men who insulted him and his people. Now, their words were nothing more than a fly's annoying buzz. The slight shadow that glided along the curving wall and finally solidified into the mousy woman who'd first refused to look at him, and then gaped at him in horror, interested him far more than they did.

She stood next to her escort, hands clasped in front of her, shoulders slumped and head bowed. He wondered how long she'd maintain such a demeanor once he revealed his knowledge of her deception and how he intended to use it. He stepped away from the door and leaned against the far wall, arms crossed. The guard's warning to move back was unnecessary. They'd done this many times. Keys jangled on their metal ring, and the lock ground until it released on a snap. The door opened, revealing the two guards, one holding a loaded crossbow aimed at Azarion's chest, the other gripping the woman's arm.

The second guard leered at Azarion. "Best make it a quick tup, bull. Rumor has it Herself will be wanting you tonight and soon."

He shoved the woman into the cell and slammed the door behind him. The guard with the crossbow flashed him a grin through the bars and turned the lock before disappearing from view.

Azarion contemplated his new cellmate, seeing what the guards didn't—an unsteady shimmer surrounding her, like rain spilling over the surface of a polished shield. It blurred and wavered, finally fading under his continued scrutiny until her true self was unmasked.

She wasted no time assuming her role. Nimble fingers worked the ties at her high collar, loosening them so that the outer tunic gaped to expose more layers of cloth, and below those, a threadbare shift. The single candle in the cell flickered over waxen skin and the slight curve of her breasts above her binding as she lowered the garment from her shoulders.

He came away from the wall, darkly amused at her stoic manner. She might be selling him chicken feed for all the eagerness and interest she showed in bedding him. He expected nothing different. She wasn't here of her own accord, and she'd done this before. He recognized the behavior, had acted in the same manner in similar circumstances. When the struggle only pleased the torturer and made the torture worse, you stopped fighting and learned to endure. To endure was to survive.

He halted her before the shift drooped lower. "Don't bother," he said softly. "You heard the guard. The empress will send for me soon, and I want you for something other than fucking."

Her gaze flashed up to his, and he was struck by the guarded hostility in her eyes. Ah, it was as he thought. She was suspicious and feared him for far more than the threat of physical abuse.

"How many years have you burned at the Rites of Spring?"

It was the nature of people to look away when they lied, but this woman's eyes remained steadfast. "I don't understand."

She possessed a lyrical voice, her accent almost aristocratic.

He closed the space between them. Her breath hitched, and she went rigid, though she didn't give ground at his approach. Despite its lank appearance, her hair drifted thick and soft through his fingers as he lifted it away from her neck. "Your hair is black, your eyes are brown, and you aren't as well-fed as these clothes make you look."

He stood close enough to feel her limbs quake. Before she could escape, he imprisoned her wrist and raised her hand. Under the illusion, her palm was smooth and pudgy, the hand of a merchant's pampered daughter perhaps. To his eyes, it was slim and work-roughened, and bore a telltale color. "You have green hands, woman. Stained by the sap of the long nettle. I'd wager a herd of breeding mares you're a Beroe dyer."

He'd never seen the village of Beroe itself, but it was common knowledge the popular green dye used to color the rugs and clothing of wealthy Kraelians was made there.

A whimper escaped his companion. She closed her eyes, her arm suddenly limp in his grip. He released her and stepped back. He had her. It was time to bargain. An uncomfortable twinge settled under his ribs when she opened her eyes once more and gave him a bleak stare.

"How can you see this?" Her voice had flattened to a dull monotone.

He shrugged. "I don't know. I only see it with you. I've watched you for five years. Each year the same woman with many faces walks to the pyre, is burned in the arena, and walks away untouched by the flame, with none the wiser. My people would call you an *agacin*, spirit of the goddess Agna made flesh."

Desolation turned to desperation. She clutched his arm. "Please, I beg you. Have mercy. Say nothing. Other lives depend on this deception." He stared at her, then at the hand gripping his arm, letting his silence play out. It unnerved her as he had hoped. She dropped her hand in favor of curling it into a fist. "I have nothing to offer for your silence." She admitted this failure between clenched teeth.

"You can give me my freedom."

Her jaw sagged, disbelief lifting her eyebrows. "What?"

Again, he'd shocked her. "You can change faces."

"Yes." The guarded look masked her features once more.

"Tomorrow, after the burning, you'll come back to the catacombs as Hanimus and unlock my cell door."

She gave a croak of laughter. "You are mad. We'll be discovered. They'll kill us both before you can step outside this cell."

He hadn't survived ten years and the savagery of the arena to die in the dark at the hands of guards no more intelligent than their own shit. Death wasn't an option. Not now. But she didn't need to know that. "Better dead than held here any longer."

"Good for you," she snapped before lowering her voice. "I don't have that choice. I can't die. Not yet. Beroe depends on me, on this lie. Find another to help you. I help enough already." Bitterness poisoned each word.

"There is no other. You'll do this." He'd expected her resistance and planned for it.

Her face hardened. Finely cut cheekbones stood out, and though shorter than he was, she managed to stare down her nose at him as if he were one of the filthy puddles dotting the floors.

A subtle shift in the air lifted the hairs on his nape, and he straightened, arms hanging loose at his sides. This woman was no match for his prowess. Still, that inner alarm put him on guard, growing louder when she lifted her hands, palms cupped. Within the cages of her fingers, a blue-tinged flame burned brightly.

She was indeed an *agacin*—a fire priestess—and watched him with an imperious disdain worthy of the goddess who bequeathed her such power. "I'm not only safe from fire, gladiator," she said, her fury as hot as the fire she held. "I can burn you to ash where you stand."

Azarion laughed aloud. No helpless martyr here. She was as fierce and stubborn as any Savatar woman. Her initial passivity was no more real than the illusion of her crossed eyes or plump body. His admiration for her grew, as did his sense of purpose. She'd help him or he'd kill her.

Undeterred by her threat and the flames leaping in her hands, he stalked her until he backed her against the wall near his pallet. Her shallow breaths warmed his neck as he braced an arm on either side of her head and leaned closer to nuzzle her ear. Heat glazed his sides, warning that her fingers still blazed.

She might be as fierce as a Savatar, but she lacked the honed instinct that signaled danger. This close and he could snap her neck before a single hot ember touched his skin.

His mouth drifted lower until he reached her neck. She flinched when he grazed his teeth across the long vein below the skin and felt the heavy pulse of her blood surge under his lips. "Another knows your secret and will only keep it as long as I'm alive. Burn me," he murmured, "and you seal your fate and the fate of Beroe."

His heart beat as hard as hers did as he waited to see whether she'd sniff out his lie and call his bluff.

Rage bubbled in her voice, deepened it until she was almost growling. "It would be worth it."

She didn't break easily. A woman who willingly suffered through the Rites of Spring each year for half a decade wouldn't. Strands of her hair, fine as silk threads, tickled his nose. "Would it?" He drove the point home. "Do you want Beroe to become another Midrigar?"

Midrigar. The township that once refused to tithe its women and grain to the Krael Empire and paid a terrible price. Even for those who thrived on watching the violence and bloodshed of the arena, the destruction of Midrigar was an abomination, its name spoken only in whispers.

For a moment, the heat strengthened, searing his sides before disappearing altogether. A soft sob broke the tense silence as gladiator and witch stood together. To other eyes, it might seem as if they embraced, his face hidden in her neck, her hands now resting against his ribs.

"You bastard," she said in a defeated whisper.

Azarion kept her trapped, determined to gain her cooperation and content to taste her skin. "What say you, *Agacin*? Help me and none will ever know the village of Beroe has made a fool of the Empire."

She leaned away from him so that her gaze met his, and in the dark depths of her eyes a calculating hatred settled. "What do I have to do?"

Triumph nearly made his knees give way. The plan he had

strategized for the last three years, with this *agacin* at its heart, had only a slim chance of working, but it was at least a chance. Without her consent, extorted via threat, it had no chance at all.

He had only moments before the guards came for him, and he kept her trapped against the wall as he spoke, the wandering caress of his hand over her shoulder and breast in sharp contrast to his pragmatic instructions. Anyone watching might think the Gladius Prime wooed his plain companion to his bed.

She listened with a close ear and barely checked anger. "It won't work," she muttered when he finished, and swatted his hand away from her hip.

"It will." He cupped her buttock to pull her into him and buried his nose in her hair. "It must."

The clatter of keys and a thump on the cell door signaled visitors. He kept his back to the door, but the girl's face had gone a sickly pale shade as she stared past his shoulder at the barred window. Azarion casually turned to find a face leering at them.

"Time's up, bull. If you haven't tupped the bitch yet, it'll have to wait. Herself is wanting you. Now."

The *agacin* retreated to a corner as far from him and the guards as she could get. She busied herself with righting her tunic and retying the laces.

The guard gave Azarion a puzzled look. "I saw this year's offerings. You could have done much better than her."

Azarion didn't reply. He almost never spoke to the guards, and they had learned long ago he was far too dangerous to tease without risk. He kept his attention on the second guard, who trained the crossbow on him and held the hated shackles.

That first guard motioned him forward. Azarion held still as the iron collar encircled his neck, growing heavier—tighter—when the guard snapped it closed. A length of chain hung from the iron ring bolted at its center, the links kept short so that he was forced to hunch when the guard attached it to the chain connecting the shackles that bound his wrists and the ones that gripped his ankles. Trussed in irons, he shuffled after his escort as they led him through the door and into the corridor—a broken beast of burden. It was how the empress liked to see him when he first entered her apartments.

He sighed inwardly when no cup of drugged wine was forthcoming. It seemed the empress hadn't yet had her bloodlust appeased, even after witnessing a full day of slaughter in the arena. He wondered whom he'd be forced to fight and kill for her pleasure before she bedded him.

And kill he would. Again and again. With his freedom at the tips of his fingers, he'd do whatever it took to stay alive and fulfill that dream. He glanced at the *agacin* huddled against the wall. She stared at him, eyes wide. Frightened. Hostile.

"She'll still be here for you to enjoy when you return, stud," one guard said. "That's if Herself doesn't take it into her head to geld you just for fun."

The taunt elicited snorts of laughter. Azarion paid no heed and concentrated on keeping his feet as they navigated the slimy floor toward a set of steps that ascended to street level.

They exited the underground labyrinth and entered an enclosed bailey. The guards shoved Azarion toward a waiting wagon. He half fell into the back and was joined by the guard with the crossbow and another who gripped an ax. The driver whistled, and the wagon lurched forward into the city's narrow streets.

Night had descended on Kraelag as they traveled toward Palace Hill. Lamplight illuminated signs advertising pub houses and brothels. Revelers made drunk on wine and made poor by pickpockets spilled into the streets, continuing the weeklong celebration of the Rites of Spring.

The hill overlooking the city blazed with light, a beacon of brightness that hid a corruption far fouler than the worst of Kraelag's middens.

The wagon rolled up the hill, leaving behind the closes for the wide, cobbled avenues lined with gates attended by guards.

Behind the gates, the Empire's wealthy and noble enjoyed the fruits of their riches. The closer they drew to the hill's peak and the palace that crowned it, the larger and more lavish the manors became. And the greater the number of soldiers guarding these sanctuaries.

Azarion found it all suffocating. Even with the wider streets, the buildings seemed to loom above him, sometimes blocking the moon from view. Trees grown as privacy barriers were clipped into shapes that defied nature's hand. Like the manor houses and temples, they towered above him, a green wall threatening to collapse on top of him.

A decade spent as a slave in the Empire's capital hadn't dulled his memory of the open steppe, with its wild grasses bent to the ceaseless wind. The Sky Below was an unforgiving land, nor were the nomadic clans that roamed its expanse peaceful, but he missed it. Fiercely. He went to sleep each night with its image behind his eyelids and woke up each morning to its memory. If his plan succeeded, he would ride across its grasslands once more, a free man.

The road finally leveled out as the wagon reached the hilltop and turned onto a paved avenue even wider than the one winding up the slope. More of the ubiquitous trimmed trees lined the way toward the royal palace.

Azarion's first sight of it when he came to the capital as a slave had stunned him enough that he momentarily forgot his rage. Until then, he'd lived within a culture of wagons and tents, where the biggest shelter was the *qara* belonging to the chief of the largest Savatar clan, and that was still smaller than the meanest outbuilding surrounding the palace.

They rolled to a stop in front of a plain door that opened to a maze of hallways. Azarion could find his way to the empress's apartments blindfolded by now. He'd been brought to her more times than he could count or want.

Palace guards took over his stewardship and escorted him up flights of stairs and down corridors lined with statues of the Empire heroes, past galleries whose walls were crowded with portraits of the royal tyrants who had ruled for centuries.

Music and laughter drifted from various rooms along the way, accompanied by the cloying scent of perfume or the acrid smoke of incense.

At last they reached a pair of carved doors burnished in gold leaf that shimmered under torchlight.

Unlike the men who guarded the arena, those who guarded the palace gazed past him as if he were an invisible spirit, their expressions blank masks behind their helmets' face shields. A pair dressed in full armor and heavily armed stood sentry at the doors. One nodded to the soldier on one side of Azarion before he and his companion pushed the doors open to allow entry.

One of the guards shoved Azarion forward, hard enough to make him stumble.

He straightened as far as the shortened length of chain at his throat allowed, and raised his head to take in his surroundings. The apartments belonging to the most powerful woman in all of the Empire were everything that defined luxury.

A painted ceiling arched above him to create a dome, its curving joists carved and painted in bright colors and more of the gold leaf. Silks and velvets imported from the south graced the walls inset with windows made of real glass. More of the costly fabrics spilled over tufted couches and the grand bed occupying one corner of the room. Animal pelts shared floor space with carpets woven by Velian weavers rumored to shed the blood of their shredded fingers into the very knots of the fibers they warped and wefted.

Jewel-encrusted chests and boxes took up additional space, the largest, as big as a horse trough, footing the great bed.

Such opulence would have brought any merchant to his knees in drooling awe. It had ceased to amaze Azarion long ago, except for one thing. Suspended from the joists by chains, the colossal bones of a draga encircled the entire room in a skeletal coil.

All of the Empire knew the tale of how the empress's great-great-grandfather had slain the last living draga and dragged its corpse back to Kraelag, where he offered its blood and bones to the emperor. His feat, and the gift of such treasure, had earned him and his family a place of power within the ranks of the Empire's nobility.

Azarion still marveled over the creature's size, its majesty undiminished by death as it spiraled up to the dome's center, only to swoop down in a serpentine arch that ended in a massive skull hovering over an ornately carved chair set on a dais.

The draga's eye sockets, larger than doorways, looked blindly upon him, its gaping jaws filled with a forest of teeth the length of tree limbs and sharper than swords.

A petite woman, made even more diminutive by the draga's hulk looming above her, lounged in the chair, a silk-clad leg draped over one of the arms. A dainty, slippered foot tapped the air in careless rhythm as Azarion shuffled toward her. He dropped to his knees before the dais in wordless obeisance, watching her through locks of hair that fell in front of his eyes.

Dalvila, empress of the Krael Empire, was a worthy mate to its emperor. As cruel, merciless, and power hungry as her husband, she was even more feared by her subjects.

Tonight she wore an open tunic and trousers of indigo silk. Delicate strands of gold encircled her neck and spilled between generous breasts fully bared to the room's other occupants. Gold cuffs, mockeries of his own iron shackles, banded her wrists, the jewels worked into the soft metal catching the torchlight to flash in colors of blue, crimson, and green.

Kohl outlined her large eyes, enhancing their shape, and she watched him with a serpent's hypnotic focus. Her tongue darted out to lick her lower lip, and all the hairs on Azarion's nape rose in response.

Hard experience had taught him that such an action heralded pain. That her tongue wasn't forked never ceased to surprise him.

The tiny diamonds woven in her upswept hair sparkled in the light as she tilted her head. "I think you become a better slayer of men every time you enter the arena, Azarion. Either practice and time have improved your skills, or you now enjoy spilling blood as much as I do."

He dared not answer her. The one time he had spoken out of turn, the punishment for his transgression almost killed him. He had pissed blood for days.

Dalvila motioned to one of the silent handmaidens flanking her chair. The woman rushed forward until she stood beside the empress, head bowed and shoulders hunched. Like Azarion, she held her tongue and awaited her mistress's command.

"Have the guards bring the other bull. The festivities in the arena today were fine, but I've decided I'd like a little more." A lascivious smile curved her lips. "The winner will be rewarded, of course."

The handmaiden bowed and darted toward the doors. Azarion

wondered which poor bastard besides him had been dragged up from the catacombs for the empress's entertainment.

Dalvila gestured at the guards. "Unchain him. He can't adequately fight or fuck while trussed up like a pig."

He stared into the distance while one of the guards unlocked his shackles and pulled the chains aside. He wanted to rub his throat and wrists but stayed as he was, his hands clasped together between his knees, his head lowered.

The empress stared at him with reptilian interest.

She repulsed him at every level, yet his cock stiffened at the sight of her nubile body and the lust in her gaze.

Beautiful, soft, and perfumed, Dalvila of Krael could raise an erection in a corpse, and Azarion wasn't immune to her physical charms. He couldn't be. He'd learned quickly that to displease her in bed courted imminent death.

He returned from every encounter either light-headed from the euphoria of having survived or bloody and nearly retching from the agony of her attentions. Who knew what this night held for him?

An image rose in his mind's eye, of a dark-haired woman—the tall *agacin* with her condemning gaze and bitter fury. A woman filthy from the road and the catacombs, yet still far cleaner than this predator in her perfumed silks, perched before him on the makeshift throne like a spider.

He blinked away the memory and the hope the reluctant *agacin* offered. Distraction now could get him killed, and he had no intention of dying tonight, even if it meant taking the life of another for the pleasure of a queen whose touch made his cock throb and his skin crawl.

Dalvila swung her leg down and rose from the chair. The sense of threat made every hair on Azarion's body stand at attention the closer she sashayed toward him. The soldiers on either side of him tensed. His skin prickled when one of her fingers skated over his shoulder before sliding down his arm. The cloying scent of flowers, underscored by the musk of aroused woman, made his nose twitch. Her round breasts bobbed, sheened in perspiration.

"The private games are much superior to the public ones," she purred.

As if on cue, the doors opened once more to admit another cluster of guards surrounding a man two hands shorter than Azarion and twice his size in mass. No doubt a fighter brought in from one of the numerous gladiator schools and transported to the capital for the empress's pleasure.

Dalvila always referred to her gladiator lovers as bulls, and the one striding toward them lived up to the name. His close-cropped hair rose on his round skull like hackles, and the veins in his thick neck throbbed under his skin. The beefy shoulders bulged, as did his massive arms, and he moved with a lumbering gait that, while ungraceful, spoke of immense strength and speed.

"Lovely," the empress said and clapped her hands, her delighted smile avaricious. She curled a lock of Azarion's hair around one finger. "Time to please your mistress, bull." She nodded to his guards, who hauled him to his feet.

Blood roared through his veins, and his heart thundered a beat in his chest that echoed in his skull. For one moment, he met Dalvila's gaze. His stomach clenched, as it always did when he looked into her eyes.

Bards had written and sung odes to the empress's beauty, including her blue eyes. Azarion was sure none had ever peered into their depths. Behind the blue lurked . . . nothing. Only an abyssal emptiness, as if the goddesses had created a child and forgot to bequeath it a soul. His gaze flickered away, back to the less lethal fighter waiting to break him in half. The sight of his opponent didn't make Azarion's spirit shudder the way the empress did.

He toed off the simple sandals he'd donned in his cell. The chill of the marble floor made his feet flex. His breeches and tunic followed, leaving only the loincloth knotted at his waist. Now he matched the other man, almost bare and weaponless except for his own strength and cleverness.

The guards enclosed them in a makeshift circle, swords drawn to deter any notion about breaking through the living wall to escape.

The empress clapped her hands together. "Begin!"

Azarion dropped into a crouch, forgetting Dalvila, forgetting the guards, and especially forgetting the *agacin* waiting in his cell. All that mattered now was the man facing him, as intent on winning this fight as Azarion was.

The gladiator charged him, his strategy obvious. Brute strength to conquer his adversary. Azarion's counter was just as straightforward: keep away from those grasping hands and stay on his feet long enough to wear his opponent out, then go for the death blow.

He spun out of the way, but not fast enough. The man's shoulder caught him high in the chest, throwing him off balance. He stumbled but kept his feet, pivoting in time to take a direct blow from a head-butt. The hit took him to the floor, knocking the breath out of him as his adversary landed on top of him. His hands wrapped around Azarion's neck and squeezed.

Neither as heavy nor as muscular, Azarion used the leverage of his long legs to break free, swinging one over his opponent's shoulder and wedging it against his throat, pushing back until the other man was forced to loosen his suffocating hold to keep from falling backward.

They clashed again, wrestling and grasping in a tangle of sweating limbs. The man went for Azarion's neck a second time. Again, Azarion dodged him, repeating the move several times. His plan was working until the empress added an unexpected challenge. The crack of a whip sounded close to his ear before a hot pain tore down his back in a scorching line. He flinched away from it, directly into the gladiator's deadly embrace.

The fighter whooped in triumph, only to shout his surprise when the whip kissed the back of his thighs, bringing him to his knees, Azarion still in his grip.

"Stop boring me," the empress snarled, and struck again, this time catching Azarion across one shoulder with the lash. He glimpsed her face, pink with fury, spittle glossing her full lips.

The fighter wrapped himself around Azarion, his bulk belying his ability to act like a constrictor squeezing its prey. Azarion writhed in his grip, managing to free one arm. He curled his fingers into a tight fist and clubbed his adversary on the side of the head, hard enough that he rocked sideways. It wasn't enough to dislodge him, and Azarion struck him again, this time full in the face.

There was a crunch of bone, and the other man jerked back as blood gushed from his nose and split lip. He let go to take a swing, his knuckles plowing into the underside of Azarion's jaw.

Both men tore into each other, exchanging blows and crashing together like two bulls caught in the mating rut. The empress followed their movements, calling out encouragement or curses, and inflicting pain with the arbitrary flick of her whip.

The marble floor within the makeshift arena was slippery with sweat, blood, and saliva. Tired from a day battling for his survival in the Pit, Azarion's muscles screamed for rest. He staggered from a brutal blow and felt a vague pop in his left side. The agony that followed turned the breath in his chest into a wash of fire. If he didn't end it now, he'd lose this combat.

A surge of power, fueled by desperation and sharpened by pain, pumped through his battered frame. He broke free of his opponent's persistent grip, twisted behind him, and caught him around the neck with one leg. His position and the hard grip of his thigh defeated the fighter's efforts to break free.

Azarion tightened his hold, squeezing until he thought the veins in his leg would burst. He stared down at his captive, who thrashed in his hold, arms grasping uselessly at Azarion's elbows. His eyes bulged even as his sweating face darkened to a dusky red, then purple, and his mouth opened and closed in a futile effort to breathe.

The empress lowered her whip and crept closer, her gaze avid as she watched Azarion choke his opponent to death.

He stared at her even as the fighter's struggles weakened until they halted altogether, and he slumped lifeless in Azarion's grip.

They stayed that way a few moments longer, until Dalvila smiled her approval. "Well done, my pet! I do believe you're the winner tonight." She gestured for him to rise.

A pair of soldiers pried the dead fighter out of his hold and dragged the body out of the room while two more hauled Azarion to his feet. The moment they let go, he fell, clutching his thigh as the muscles there knotted into an unholy cramp. The pain was as bad as the one in his side, and he groaned between clenched teeth, uncaring that he might have incurred Dalvila's wrath over his inability to stand at her command.

"Bring him to the bed and strip him," the empress ordered.

The guards lifted him to his feet a second time, their aid ungentle and unforgiving. The earlier agony in his leg was now overshadowed by that in his side. He'd cracked a rib; he was certain of it. And if he was lucky, it was only a crack. He pulled his arm free from one guard to tuck it against his side as he staggered to the massive bed.

Silken sheets shrouded him as he collapsed onto the mattress. Every breath was a knife between the ribs, and he didn't move when rough hands ripped away his loincloth, leaving him naked. Perfume mixed with the scent of gore filled the bed's draped interior, accented by the smell of beeswax from candles nearby.

Dalvila crawled onto the bed, bare from the waist down. She straddled him, slim legs spread wide to nestle his cock between them. Her eyes looked black in the half-light, her nostrils flared wide like a wild horse's.

She braced a hand on his chest, laughing in delight at the tortured hiss that escaped his lips. "You performed well for me tonight, bull." Her delicate hand slipped down to grip his cock. "Keep doing so, and you might live to see the morning."

The pain was making him light-headed, and still his erection surged in her hand, ready to sink into the empress's wet heat. He'd learned.

Her hand glided up and down his engorged shaft until, impatient with her own teasing, she rose, positioned herself above him, and sank down hard, taking him to the hilt.

Azarion's back arched, and he groaned, both from the agony in his side and the hard ride of the empress's passions. Each gasp was a torture, every thrust a lash that tore up his torso and blasted into his skull until he thought he might exhale a gout of flame. The black stars exploding across his vision were as much from his injury as from the sudden shock of his climax.

Caught in the throes of her own orgasm, Dalvila rocked hard atop him, carving bloody crescent moons into his collarbones with her nails.

He slipped out of her as she tumbled off him and onto the

rumpled sheets. Her raspy breathing echoed his as she sprawled beside him.

"Get him out of here," she called to her waiting guards. "He's destroyed the bedding, and I need a bath."

They jumped to do her bidding, and Azarion found himself dragged once more, out of the bed and into the hallway outside the royal bedchamber. The guards waited impatiently while he stood on trembling legs to dress before shackling him for the march through the palace corridors.

He kept his gaze on the moon, partially hidden behind a scuttle of clouds, as the cart that had transported him to his assignation with the empress brought him back to the catacombs. The bone-rattling ride took on new and more painful depths as he struggled to sit as straight as possible. To slump meant to suffer, and he already exerted what will he still retained not to howl his misery into the silent night.

Never before had he been so happy to return to the grim reality of the catacombs and the cage he'd called home for ten years. The sight of the hollow-eyed *agacin* crouched in one corner as his guards shoved him inside revitalized his hope.

She was the wide grass plains of the Sky Below, the horse herds grazing under the sun, the Savatar women singing as they felted, the flap of the clan flags atop the *atamans*' tents. She was freedom made flesh, and in that moment, she was the most beautiful thing he'd ever beheld.

# CHAPTER THREE

Gilene gripped the cage bars for balance and surveyed the crowd in the arena seats as the cart navigated the uneven expanse of stirred sand. Drunk on wine, spring heat, and a day's worth of brutal blood sport, the spectators shouted for more, eager to witness the immolation that closed the annual Rites of Spring. Her fellow victims either clutched the bars and stared at the scene in horror or huddled in pairs and hid their faces.

Beside her, Pell tucked a skein of matted hair behind one ear and straightened her dress as if preparing for a street-side tryst. "If any of our worthless gods are willing to trouble themselves, may they be merciful and make this death swift."

*The gods have nothing to do with it.* Gilene didn't voice her acerbic thoughts. She touched the prostitute's hand briefly. "It will be."

The look Pell gave her held both doubt and amazement. "You have such faith then?"

Gilene's dry chuckle lacked any humor. The cart transporting them rolled toward the pyre built of dried kindling, carcasses of animals killed in arena battles, and dead gladiators. A great wooden pillar, wound with thick rope, stood at its center—the final destination for the women sacrificed to the gods in exchange for their goodwill toward the Empire.

She had no faith in deities who found glorification in senseless butchery, nor did she believe they understood the concept of mercy. But she had faith in herself and her talent for wielding fire. She answered Pell in a sure voice. "Yes, I do."

They said no more as the cheers grew to a deafening roar. The cart halted at the base of the pyre. The stench of blood, fear, and death filled her nose.

Guards gathered around the cage, their sun-creased features leering and cruel behind their helms. One unlocked the cage door and reached inside. Gilene was the first to tumble out. The crowd roared with laughter. Another guard hauled her to her feet and shoved her toward the pyre. The frightened cries of struggling women and curses from the guards accompanied her as she climbed over the dead piled around the waiting pillar. Flies swarmed about her head, their buzzing as loud in her ears as the crowd's shrieking exuberance.

The soldier who pushed her onto the pyre bound her to the pillar with a length of rope, cinching it tightly so she wouldn't escape when the flames licked at her feet.

"I hear the Prime picked ya last night." A puzzled note entered his voice. "Odd, considering the look of ya." He shrugged and left her to ponder his words.

Azarion had selected her for a purpose, not her appearance. She had little faith in the idea his plan for escape would work, but she had no choice in acting as his accomplice. His threat to reveal her deception had ensured that. The expression he'd worn while they bargained had been resolute. When the guards came to deliver him to his royal mistress, hatred had cast a shadow over his handsome features and flattened the color of his eyes to a flinty gray, and she had wondered whether this was the look his opponents saw when they faced him in the Pit.

She had retreated to a corner when the door opened and three guards crowded into the cell. They shackled Azarion's hands and feet, securing the short lengths of chain to a collar snapped around his neck. The fetters forced him into a subservient hunch, and he shuffled instead of strode.

He had left the cell bound and returned the same way, except for the reek of perfume and the musk of sex. In the small hours before dawn, the catacombs' dim torchlight revealed a faint limp and shoulders held more stiffly than proudly.

She'd awakened from a fitful doze at the first creak of the cell door and watched as Hanimus himself accompanied Azarion into the cell and removed the chains. The tattoos on his cheeks twisted into macabre shapes as he scowled at his champion fighter.

"You'll not be fighting tomorrow with those injuries. You'd go down in the first melee." He took a bucket of water and washcloth from one of the guards and set it at Azarion's feet. "Have your bitch help you clean up." He shook his head and exhaled a disgusted sigh. "I don't see any other broken bones, but if you hurt too bad to stand it, tell the guard to summon a leech."

Gilene almost believed Hanimus held some infinitesimal regard for his best fighter until she heard his last muttered comment as he exited the cell.

"Stupid cunt. She'll end up killing him, and I'll lose a fortune."

Quiet returned to the cell once the guards left, except for Azarion's staccato breathing. "Woman, are you awake?"

She'd hugged the tattered blanket he left with her. "Yes."

"Help me with my shirt."

His voice was no less commanding for its softness. Still, she heard its weary strain, the hints of pain suffered in silence.

He loosened the lacings in preparation and smothered a gasp when she eased the shirt off his broad shoulders. She winced as new scabs tore away with a crackle. A crosshatch of lashes ran the length of his back and disappeared into his trews.

She tossed the bloodstained shirt to the ground and stepped back for a look at his injuries. They stood out among the mural of old scars carved into his back, glistening a crimson-black from the oozing ribbons of dark blood that trickled down to stain his trews. Gilene forgot her reluctance to touch him. Her fingers glided a hairbreadth over the wounds. He must have sensed her near touch. Gooseflesh pebbled the bronze skin.

"Did the empress do this to you?"

He spoke to the wall. "Aye, and other things. You'll need to clean the wounds and wrap my chest. I've a cracked rib or two as well." He eased out of the trews, pausing to lean against the wall and take shallow breaths. More blood had dried in rivulets that ran the length of his thighs. More whip marks decorated his buttocks.

Empress Dalvila's particular carnal preferences were fodder for gossip and sly laughter throughout the Empire. The reality of those preferences robbed any humor from the conjectures. Gilene wondered in which arena Azarion faced his deadliest enemies.

The tepid water had turned scarlet with the first rinse. He remained quiet as she cleaned the torn skin on his back and washed away the blood on his legs. There were no poultices to prevent the wounds from poisoning. He'd lived years as a Pit fighter; she suspected he'd suffered much worse than these and survived to fight again. Unwelcome sympathy welled inside her. He was lucky to still be standing. By the look of him, the empress enjoyed doling out a good flaying as much as she did a fucking.

Azarion helped her tear the moth-eaten blanket into strips, pausing only once to hold his side as he took a deep breath. His nostrils flared, his lips went white, and sweat beaded his forehead.

Compelled to compassion by such obvious suffering, Gilene rested her hand on his arm. "Do you want me to call for the leech?"

He shook his head. "No. I've had my fill of the Empire's gentle touch for the night."

The flesh along his left side sported a darkening bruise. Azarion favored that side, careful not to raise his arm too high.

She held a cloth strip in her hands. "It will pain you, but you have to raise your arm higher so I can wrap the bandages tight enough."

He did as she instructed, emitting a soft groan when she tied the first strip snug around his chest. Despite her resentment of his extortion, she didn't wish to visit more cruelty on him.

"Forgive me," she said. "This is necessary."

He accepted her apology with a grunt, remaining docile beneath her ministrations until she had swaddled his chest in a layer of makeshift bandages. Gilene surveyed her handiwork. It was a fair enough job considering what she had to work with and the fact that she wasn't a trained healer.

Azarion gingerly tapped the bandages and gave a nod of approval. "This is good."

She told herself she couldn't care less if he lived or died. A small inner voice whispered that she lied. "A temporary measure to lessen the pain a little. If you wear it too long, you'll bring on lung sickness."

His scrutiny sharpened. "Are you a healer as well as a dyer?" He didn't mention her ability to wield fire.

"I knew a man in our village with a similar injury. Our healer gave him the same instructions."

His prolonged scrutiny made her tense. "You can take the bed. Sleep. I'll breathe better sitting up."

She had avoided his pallet earlier in favor of a seat on the floor. Since her arrival in his cell, he'd shown no interest in bedding her. Still wary, she had accepted his offer and stretched out on the bed, careful to keep the cell door and Azarion in her view. Sleep was an indulgence she couldn't afford. The catacombs were a dangerous place, her cellmate a threat despite his injuries and reassurances he wouldn't hurt her. But she fell asleep as soon as her head rested on the straw-filled mattress, the image of Azarion sitting straight-backed against the wall next to her the last thing she saw.

She had awakened to a comforting warmth and the tickling vibration of a voice whispering in her ear. A heavy body pressed against her back, long legs entwining with hers. Panic roared through her, scattering away any vestiges of sleep as she lunged to break free. A muscular arm tightened around her midriff, and the legs tensed, trapping her as effectively as any cage.

"Be still," Azarion ordered, his tone gruff, his grip unyielding. "The guards are coming to get you, and your illusion has faded."

Unlike fire magic, which she could summon by will, illusion required true, incanted spellwork. Gilene spoke the words her mentor had taught her to revive her illusion, hoping she'd gotten it right. The guards' voices echoed in the distance as they ordered gladiators awake for their breakfast and retrieved the sacrificial tithes from some of the cells.

Her stomach churned, and she forced back a hard knot of tears. She hated the Empire. Hated the power, the debauchery, the care-less disregard for its citizens and vassals. She traveled to the capital each year, suffered degradation, burned in the Pit, and returned home scarred in both soul and body. She shifted, and Azarion's hold loosened just enough so that she could turn onto her opposite side and meet his gaze. She and this slave fighter shared a common truth. He dealt death with sword and ax, and she with fire. Neither commanded their fates.

As if he heard her thoughts, his hand left her waist to stroke her jawline. He was sickly pale, and she wondered how much pain he was in as he lay beside her in a position that no doubt made his ribs ache. "Do we have an agreement?" he said.

They weren't words of encouragement or gentleness. Gilene brushed his hand from her cheek. "Do I have a choice?"

"No."

"Then we have an agreement."

His eyes warmed. "I know why Beroe sent you, *Agacin*. Even beyond the fire." He levered himself carefully off the pallet, leaving her puzzled by his enigmatic remark. He groaned under his breath and pressed a hand to his side, head hanging low for a moment before he gained his feet.

Doubt and compassion had risen within her. Even with her help, she didn't think he'd escape Kraelag alive. The fact he'd survived the rigors of the Pit this long testified to his prowess in combat. Still, cracked ribs left even the toughest warrior vulnerable, and Azarion's movements lacked their casual grace from the night before. If he had to fight his way out of the city, he was dead.

When the guards opened the cell door, Azarion's shoulders slumped, and he shuffled to one of the cell's far corners, his movements as hesitant and slow as an old woman's. Astonished, Gilene caught his quick, warning glance. He might be injured, but this show of weakness was merely an affectation.

She didn't look back when they took her from the cell to rejoin the condemned women in a common cell closer to the Pit.

They had passed the day in the stifling prison, serenaded by the applause and jeers of the crowd, the howls of injured and dy-

39

ing animals, and the clash of sword on shield as gladiators fought to the death.

Now, with the crowd swelling the seats ringing the arena, baying for their blood, the women wept and prayed to indifferent gods.

In their awning-covered balcony high above the masses, the emperor and empress lounged on couches in the shade, attended by a small army of servants. They were too far away for Gilene to make out their expressions, but she saw the emperor raise and lower his hand, signaling the final Rite of Spring—the immolation of the women—to begin. The guards tossed lit torches onto the pyre and fled from the arena floor.

Each year this nightmare played out the same way. The signal, the torches set to the kindling, the crowd's roar of approval, the cries for mercy from the women struggling against their tethers.

Tears washed Gilene's cheeks. She found sanctuary within herself, the call to fire that ran through her spirit in rivers.

*Witch-fire*, the villagers named it. An ancient magic woven into the flesh and fabric of a single girl child born each generation in Beroe. No one knew from whence it originated or why only one woman from every generation in a small village inherited it, but the village elders had kept its secret close and had deceived the Empire for decades.

Gilene summoned witch-fire to join the flames consuming the kindling surrounding her. She breathed the acrid smoke of charring wood and the burning dead. Deaf to the victims' laments and the spectators' applause, she concentrated on the internal river of magic, captured its flames, and swelled it to a ravenous creature that bit and clawed at the cage of her will. Smoke and heat swirled around her. She ignored both, bound by the rise of power.

She shrieked as the fire erupted around the pillar's base, then shot skyward in a column of white flame. It fountained back to the ground, servant to her silent bidding, incinerating within and around it in an instant. The sacrificed women, the pillar to which they were tied, the dead upon which they stood—all turned to ash in the space of one breath to another. Flames shot toward the stone firebreak surrounding the Pit and protecting the spectators in the lower seats. Still, many of those fled, not trusting that the wall would contain the hellfire tide that clawed at its unyielding surface.

Only Gilene stood untouched within the conflagration, now cloaked in another illusion. Freed, she leapt off the burning platform and sped through the fire, nothing more than flame herself to the eyes of the exuberant crowd. Spirits of the newly dead fluttered past her. She thought she glimpsed Pell's vaporous features before the hot wind generated by the fire shredded the apparition.

Power leached from her like oil from a broken lamp. By the time she reached one of the deserted entrances to the catacombs, she was stumbling and bent with the urge to vomit. The cool interior offered respite, and she collapsed against it, sloughing off her disguise.

Her trial wasn't over. Gilene wiped the sweat and tears from her face and straightened from the wall. Fire exacted a steep price for its subservience. She didn't have much time left before that price left her helpless. She exchanged one illusion for another and descended into the underground. The clusters of guards ignored her, uninterested in an old slave who clung to the shadows as he went about his daily tasks.

Azarion occupied the last cell at the end of one of the long corridors branching off the underground's main hub. Once more Gilene incanted a spell and became the much-despised Hanimus.

Her vision turned hazy at the edges. She flattened her palm against an archway to stay upright and concentrated on the illusion. The chief handler's appearance proved the most difficult she had ever attempted.

A solitary soldier monitored the hallway. When he saw Gilene lumbering toward him as Hanimus, he straightened from his indolent pose and saluted. Her luck held when she gestured for his keys. He dropped them into her waiting palm without question.

Azarion regarded her from the cell's narrow window. Gilene unlocked and opened the door, stepping aside just in time as the gladiator rushed the opening. The guard had no chance to cry out before Azarion grabbed his head and snapped his neck. He dropped to the ground without a sound. The years of traveling to Krael's capital and witnessing its casual cruelties had left Gilene hardened to many such sights, but her stomach still roiled at the sound of cracking bone.

Unfazed by the killing, Azarion stripped the soldier of his breastplate, helmet, and weaponry and tossed the body into the cell. He caught the keys Gilene tossed him with a nod of thanks.

Torchlight cast his sublime face in sharp relief, transforming it into a skeletal mask made even more macabre by bestial-bright green eyes. Gladiator, Pit fighter, he'd probably shed enough blood to fill a dozen washtubs.

A jagged ache pressed needles into her right thigh, hip, and lower back—the first warning of the agony to come. She flinched and surrendered her illusion of Hanimus with a moan.

"Woman?" Azarion gave her a puzzled look.

She ignored him, intent on escaping the city before the price of her magic brought her to her knees. She assumed the illusion of the old slave again and turned her back on Azarion. "Our agreement is met, gladiator," she said over her shoulder.

"What is your name?"

Fresh air and the promise of escape gave her tired feet wings. "Forgotten," she murmured as she hurried away from him.

His gaze burned holes between her shoulder blades as she fled back the way she came. An invisible fire licked at her leg and back, slowing her stride and making her whimper. She cast off all illusion just as she escaped the catacombs. By the time she merged into the flow of foot traffic on the narrow streets, she limped.

Sanctuary, personified by her two brothers and a pony cart, waited at the nearby Fell Gates. Nylan's face twisted into a fierce frown when he saw her. She was so close. Each year she fell into his arms and sobbed on his shoulder as he and their younger brother, Luvis, settled her into the cart for the trip home. This year would be no different.

Sick with pain and desperate to reach her siblings, she barely heard the thunder of hoofbeats or the panicked shouts of the crowd behind her. Nylan's horrified expression and Luvis's shouted "Gilene, look out!" made her pivot.

Time slowed. Road dust hung in the air in a choking miasma. Pedestrians stood flattened along shop walls or leapt into the shallow safety of doorways. A soldier bore down on her at full gallop, his mount's hooves pounding out a relentless beat as he consumed the distance between them. Gilene glimpsed the rider's eyes—as green and hard as sea glass. Familiar.

"No," she whispered and spun away in a futile bid to avoid him.

Too late. He leaned from the saddle, arm outstretched toward her. A terrific force wrenched her upward, almost garroting her with the collar of her own shift as the fabric pulled tight. She landed belly down across a pair of muscled thighs. Air gusted from her lungs in a hard *whoosh*.

It was nothing compared to the crippling shock of pain that

torched her back and thigh. Reduced to emitting only breathless grunts, she arched and twisted in her captor's imprisoning grip.

The world careened in all directions as the horse balked at her struggles, and Azarion fought to bring it under control. Snarled curses, her brothers' diminishing shouts, and the mount's protesting whinnies all blended into a mad cacophony while Gilene thrashed even harder on the gladiator's lap.

A sudden crack of agony blossomed across the side of her head. Her vision went dark, and she knew no more.

# CHAPTER FOUR

The captive *agacin* twitched across Azarion's lap like a dying trout. His mount, stolen from one of the cavalry stables, snorted in protest at the strange movements and jerked against his rider's guidance. With a hand on the fire witch's back and another holding the reins, Azarion maneuvered the horse across the narrow bend of a feeder stream that traveled down the mountains and merged into the Holstet river. Kraelag lay behind him, hidden by a cloud of wind-stirred dust and the blinding rays of the setting sun. He kept an ear tuned for voices, the bays of hunting hounds, even the *thwang* of a bowstring as an archer loosed an arrow to bring him down.

This was a temporary reprieve. He'd barreled through the city's crowded streets and out the main gates without raising a single warning cry from his guards. Some of the soldiers he passed had even laughed and cheered him on his way at the sight of the unconscious woman draped in front of him across the saddle. No one was the wiser that the Gladius Prime, a priceless slave and a favorite toy of the empress, had just escaped his prison. Dressed in the military garb of the Empire, he was only a soldier, hot for a woman and eager to tup her, willing or not, in the nearest straw heap.

He needed to put as much distance as possible between him and the capital before the alarm sounded and a contingent of trackers hit the trails to find him. They wouldn't kill him—only return him to the Pit and the arms of the empress.

East and north of the stream lay the belt of Krael's farmland, its fertile plains fed by the silt drained from the river. Two days' ride on a fast horse and he'd reach the northern edge of the capital's immediate land holdings—from there, a dangerous trek across the vassal lands of the Nunari and finally to the steppes of the Sky Below. If he was lucky, he'd manage to evade capture while crossing open fields, avoid being shot by Nunari clansmen for trespassing, and keep the witch from escaping or setting him alight when his back was turned.

"Be my protection, Fire Mother," he prayed to Agna. "Be my strength."

For once, the vicious games so loved by the Kraelians played to his advantage. No one cared if a Pit guard lay dead in the catacombs, and Azarion's handlers would assume Herself's favorite had once more been summoned to her chambers. He had until the small hours, when the celebrations and street parties ended, before the hunt began. He might even have until dawn if Hanimus was too far gone in his cups or the arms of a whore to notice no palace guard returned his best gladiator to his cell.

Capture wasn't an option. He had learned to cut a throat long before his cousin sold him into slavery, and he had lost count of the number of men who had choked on their own blood from the slide of his knife in the arena. He would drown in his before he let Kraelian hunters drag him back to that cell.

Many years had passed since he'd been on a horse, and he felt clumsy in the saddle. The invisible daggers stabbing his side didn't help. The *agacin*'s wrap eased some of the discomfort, but every beat of the galloping horse's hooves against the earth was a punch to the side. He gritted his teeth and did his best to ignore it. He had three things to accomplish: stay in the saddle, keep hold of the *agacin*, and find shelter for them in a place far enough from the capital that he could rest for a few hours before taking to the road once more.

The sun had dropped far below the horizon, and night filled the sky with stars when the tired horse finally topped a small rise and slowed to a walk. The witch had regained consciousness, but only enough to give a small moan. She didn't open her eyes. Azarion frowned as he glanced down at her, laid across his thighs. In his bid to keep her from tumbling them both from the saddle, he'd accidentally clipped the side of her head with his knee, hard enough to knock her out, but not for this long. This torpor of hers stemmed from something else.

"*Agacin*." He tapped her lightly on the back. She moaned again but didn't wake. He was tempted to stop the horse and lift her off his lap for a better look at her. She might well be sick. Her face had been ghostly under the mask of her illusions when she unlocked his cell door. Shadows painted crescent moons under her eyes, and her lips had lost what little color they possessed. His hands tightened on the reins to slow the horse to a stop when a sound reached his ears that turned his blood to ice: the baying of hounds.

Someone had discovered his escape.

He slammed his heels into the horse's sides, and the animal leapt forward, galloping toward the jagged silhouette of a woodland in the distance.

They rode at a dead run, the echo of the hounds and the horns of hunters pursuing them. The horse labored valiantly up a gentle incline where a line of evergreen trees began their march down the opposite side of the slope.

Azarion slowed their wild ride to a nervous pace once they reached the ridge, as much to rest the tired horse as to gain his bearings. They couldn't stay long. The moon's light slanted away from them to illuminate the trees and cast him and the *agacin* in shadow. It wouldn't last, and the hunters closing the distance would see them.

At the bottom of the slope, where the trees parted on either side of an overgrown path, the remains of a city lay in darkness. Not a single flame from an oil lamp or candle could be seen, and the silence pulsing from its heart was a palpable thing, a waiting hush that tainted the breeze. No song of night birds, no drone of insects. Not even the watery call of frogs.

Azarion stared down at the dark city, pondering what to do. He was nearly cross-eyed with exhaustion, one arm numb from keeping the *agacin* from sliding off the horse. The animal was worn out by the hard, steady pace and the labor of carrying two riders. Its sides swelled and shrank like hard-worked bellows.

He could run the horse into the ground until it dropped from under him. It would put more distance between Azarion and his pursuers, but he'd then be without a horse and forced to leave the *agacin* behind while he fled on foot. Injured as he was, his chances of hiding from or outrunning a hunting party were nonexistent. Below them, the abandoned city crouched, offering a roof over their heads and a place to hide for a short time while the horse rested.

Still, Azarion hesitated while an uneasy feeling crawled up his spine. Surely even the hunters, driven by duty, a promise of bounty, or fear of the empress, would hesitate to follow them into this place. They would think him mad for hiding there. All made wide berths around the haunted city of Midrigar.

The *agacin* herself had capitulated to his demands only when he threatened her with the possibility of seeing her village destroyed like Midrigar if the rulers of the Empire found out they had been deceived.

Midrigar sprawled across the landscape in its unnatural silence, repulsing and beckoning him by turns. Hiding behind its walls guaranteed him safety from the Empire's trackers, but what lay beyond the shattered gates, waiting for the unwitting or foolhardy traveler?

He tapped the horse's sides, coaxing the animal down the slope before guiding it to a spot not far from the western gate. Not far for an uninjured man unencumbered, but an interminable distance for one with cracked ribs and carrying supplies as well as the dead weight of an unconscious woman. It couldn't be helped. He needed the horse, and he needed Midrigar, and the two would not meet, no matter how much he might wish otherwise.

Within the shelter of evergreens, he found a place for his mount to graze. It happily ignored his actions in favor of eating and stood docile as Azarion eased himself off its back and paused a moment to lean against the saddle to take shallow breaths. The bloodbath in the arena followed by the brawl in the empress's chambers and a round of fucking in her bed had drained the life out of him. The pain in his side, while piercing and burdensome, reminded him with every breath that he hadn't died yet.

With night fully on them, the air had turned chilly, still carrying the last vestiges of old winter. Azarion shivered from the cold as he looped and tied the reins around the branch of a young fir. He pulled the supply satchels free of the saddle rings and dropped them to the ground before lifting the *agacin* from the horse's back to lay her gently on the grass. He left the animal saddled in case he had to abandon Midrigar and ride away fast.

The *agacin* had rolled to her side and curled in on herself. Azarion knelt beside her, staring at her features, pale in the moonlight. A bruise marred her cheekbone, the skin puffy under her eye. He hadn't meant to strike her in his struggle to keep them both in the saddle. He didn't blame her for fighting to get free. In her place, he'd have done the same and more.

Were she a Savatar woman, she would look for the first opportunity to sink a knife between his shoulder blades or set him ablaze. Even so, he hadn't failed to notice her resolve or the abhorrence of him in her gaze. He would do well to stay on his guard when she revived. The deadliest adversary wasn't always the fiercest, and he suspected that, like him, this woman would do whatever was necessary to obtain her freedom.

He stroked her cheek and found it hot to the touch. Fever. Her eyes snapped open, and she cringed away from him. The movement made her cry out, and she gripped her leg, rolling back and forth on her side.

Caught off guard, Azarion covered her mouth with his palm and held her still. "Shh, *Agacin*," he whispered. He didn't think the hunters would hear them yet, but they grew closer every moment. No need to help them in locating their prey.

Had she been injured during their flight from Kraelag beyond the blow from his knee? He remembered her in the street, moving purposefully through the crowd toward a wagon and a man who beckoned to her. Azarion hadn't noticed at the time, but when he thought back on it, she had limped.

"*Agacin*," he said. "Can you stand?" They couldn't stay here. Midrigar's questionable sanctuary was their best hope, and Azarion needed the fire priestess to walk there on her own.

"Wake up, *Agacin*." He shook her shoulder but got no response. He recalled another man by the cart, his expression as horrified as the first one as they caught sight of Azarion riding toward the witch. He had shouted a word that had made her turn and face what pursued her. Gilene. "Gilene," he said and shook her harder.

She peered at him with a confused gaze. As memory and awareness seeped in, her eyes widened. She struggled to sit up. Grass and the remnants of dead leaves rustled as she scooted away from him on her haunches. Whatever injury plagued her was forgotten for a moment.

Azarion stayed where he was, waiting for her to settle. He kept a wary eye on her hands, looking for the warning bloom of flame to ignite in her palms.

"Filthy bastard," she spat at him. "I should have known better than to believe a Pit fighter might keep his word." Her hand came up to touch her cheek, and she flinched. "You struck me."

He rose and followed her movements, noting she still hadn't risen, and the tightness around her mouth spoke of pain as much as it did fury. "Where else are you hurt?"

Her hand went involuntarily to her thigh before she pulled it back. "My face, where you hit me."

Azarion sighed, his patience thinning even as his unease rose. "It was an accident. Gilene . . ."

"Don't call me that."

"Is it your name?"

"No."

"What is your name?" he asked for the second time since he met her. Her mutinous silence told him he wouldn't get that piece of information from her anytime soon. He shrugged. Unless her name held magical powers and could transport them from here to the Sky Below, it didn't matter what she was called.

"*Agacin*," he said. She went still at his warning tone. "Tell me if you can walk. If you can't, I'll have to carry you, but we aren't staying here."

"I'm not going anywhere with you." She rolled to her hands and knees and paused, hands curling into fists in the grass, head hanging low between her shoulders. He empathized with her; his own pain made him dizzy, but what care he might be able to give her would have to wait. He bent and scooped her into his arms.

She thrashed in his grip, back arching away from him. He had all he could do to keep a hold on her as she did her level best to climb up him and out of his arms.

"My back," she said between gasps. "My back is on fire."

Had anyone else said the same thing, Azarion would have assumed they spoke figuratively, but this was a fire priestess. He set her down, looking for any flames that might be dancing up and down her spine.

She swayed, and her hands shook as she reached for him to steady herself. "Mercy, please, I beg you. Don't touch me."

He stared down at the witch's pale features. If he didn't need her to gain back his place in Savatar society, he would abandon her. Her injuries, combined with his, put him in jeopardy, slowed him down. Even now, they should be inside Midrigar instead of here at the tree line struggling to walk. They were a pathetic pair—the half dead defeated in their goal to rest among the long dead.

"Which hurts worse? Your leg or your back?"

She blinked at him through a fall of tears. "My back."

"So be it." He crouched, ignoring the splinters shooting through his side and the tearing of scabs on his back. The *agacin* gasped when he flipped her neatly over his shoulder, growling through the agony of holding her weight, even on his uninjured side.

Her hands clutched at his tunic. "Put me down! I'm going to be sick!"

"Then be sick and have done with it." He bent once more to retrieve the supply satchel he'd taken from the saddle. It held a water flask and road rations to last half a day between two people.

She squirmed in his grip, which made him hold on to her even tighter. "Be still," he warned in his most threatening tone, and her struggles subsided.

Black spots swarmed his vision, and he feared he might pass out before he took his first step toward the west gate. The moment passed, and he trudged to the dead city.

"Where are you taking me?"

He didn't answer. It hurt to talk, to walk, to breathe. The last two were unavoidable actions, but the first he set aside. She didn't harangue him for an answer but fell silent, her hands still buried in his tunic. Azarion thanked the Fire Mother that his captive didn't retch.

By the time they reached the gate, he thought his chest had cracked open and his lungs had caught fire. Though the night was cold, sweat slicked his skin and dripped into his eyes. The *agacin*, tall and slight, was an anvil on his shoulder. He halted and tipped her down until she found her feet. "We're here. You must walk the rest of the way," he said, holding his side as he breathed hard and tried to stay conscious.

She braced a trembling hand on what remained of the gate. "What is this place?"

She'd figure it out sooner than later, so he didn't bother lying. "Midrigar."

The *agacin* jerked back as if bitten. Her wide eyes nearly glowed in the dark. "You would shelter in a grave."

"We'll shelter from the Empire." He captured her elbow. "Don't fight me. You have more to fear from me than any spirit still trapped behind these walls."

He expected more resistance from her and was surprised when she only stood tense beside him. Her expression spoke more than any words of her loathing for him, even greater than her terror of Midrigar. "I hope whatever waits in there devours you."

"Pray it finds me tastier meat than you, since you'll be in there with me." He tugged her along behind him as he stepped over the rubble partially blocking the entrance to the shattered gate.

The *agacin* edged a little closer to him, shivering hard enough to make her teeth audibly clack together. Azarion turned, signaling for quiet with a finger to his lips. Every hair on his arms stood at attention. The dead didn't sleep in Midrigar; they listened, and they heard.

If the ruins stretched before them gave truth, then he and the fire witch were the only living souls in the city now, and the hush hung like a shroud over its crumbling ramparts. He'd hear the tracking party from Kraelag long before it ever reached the gates. For now, the silence reigned, unbroken except for the occasional gust of cold wind that swirled through the gaps in the wall.

The city gradually revealed itself in a jumbled sprawl half lit by the moon's rays, half obscured by the night's shadows. Scorch marks licked up the outer walls of roofless buildings, testament to old fires that must have raged through Midrigar when the Empire chose to punish her for her rebellion. Even now, when the stench of burnt bodies had long since faded and the fires were nothing more than the memory of ash, Azarion fancied he caught the acrid scent of smoke.

He half dragged, half carried the witch across the courtyard toward a temple, ears straining to catch the sound of their pursuers drawing closer. A lone howl caught on the wind, and Azarion didn't dare hope it was a wolf. The witch added her own voice to the wind's mournful tune in a wordless hum inspired by pain and misery.

He'd made the same sounds more than once as he nursed injuries obtained in the arena. He hummed so he wouldn't scream as the pain swelled and ebbed and swelled.

He halted at the temple steps when she fell to one knee. The *agacin's* features were drawn as he crouched and tilted her chin up with his thumb for a better look at her. Lines bracketed her tight mouth and furrowed her forehead. The humming continued unabated.

She favored her leg and flinched away when his fingers edged closer to her back. He saw no blood on her clothes, no signs of attack, no singe marks from the conflagration she had called forth in the arena. "What causes your pain?"

Her eyes swallowed him whole in a gaze dark as the shadows that crawled down the temple steps. Her breathing was labored, her words short. "I burn. I burn."

He frowned, recalling her telling him in his cell that she was impervious to fire.

She remained docile while he helped her stand and turned her until her back was to him, hissing softly when his fingers clasped the hem of her tunic to lift it. The humming resumed, rising in pitch as he inched the garment past her waist, toward her ribs and higher. He caught only a glimpse of red, blistered skin—some of it overlaid across a patchwork of old burn scars—before she jerked away from him.

"Enough," she said in a shaky voice. Her gaze swept the shattered cityscape before settling on Azarion. "We shouldn't be here," she said in a trembling whisper.

His own senses thrummed warnings. In this dead city, they weren't alone. He could feel it. "We have no choice," he said in low tones to match hers. He tried to distract her. "I thought you couldn't burn by fire."

Her jaw flexed with the failed effort to hold back a pained whine. He didn't think she'd answer until she inhaled a careful breath. "It isn't fire that burns me; it's the magic I use to summon it. It comes with a price."

"And you pay each time you summon it?" She nodded, and he touched her arm, a poor offering of comfort. She pulled away. "Come," he said. "We'll shelter there." He pointed to an undamaged section of the temple's portico.

She didn't argue or resist his light nudge to her shoulder, choosing instead to hobble along just behind him as they picked a narrow path through the rubble to the cracked stairs that led to the portico.

The heavy feeling of being watched only deepened as stars gleamed above them. Azarion kept a hand on his knife and an eye on his surroundings. The shadows cast by the gutted buildings were odd. Instead of cutting across the ground in sharp angles, they seemed to undulate, their edges undefined and ever shifting, as if they were alive.

He reached back for the *agacin*, capturing her cold fingers in his. "Up the stairs."

She paused, teeth chattering, either from fear or pain or both, and peered at the black chasm in the temple's archway. No light penetrated that darkness. "I'm not going in there," she stuttered.

Injured he might be, but she was no match for him physically. If he chose to force her into the temple's shelter, he had only to lift and carry her up the steps and through the archway. But even in the straits they found themselves now, he wasn't that desperate. The longer he stared into the fathomless murk, the more certain he grew that something stared back. Waiting.

"Neither of us is," he replied. "We'll rest outside, against the wall there." He pointed to a spot away from the archway but still under the temple's roof overhang. The deep angle of a corner and the girth of a massive pillar offered a little shelter from the chilly breeze and a small bit of concealment from any who might come searching for them. They'd be cold and uncomfortable, but they wouldn't freeze.

She nodded and freed her hand to clasp her arms in a futile bid for warmth. "Walk up the other side. I don't want to go near that door."

If something decided to hurtle out of the temple and attack them, taking the steps at a different spot wouldn't make much of a difference, but he did her bidding and helped her climb stone treads cracked and blackened by fire until they reached the spot he chose for their rest.

"Tuck into the corner," he instructed. "I'll sit in front of you and block the wind."

She gave him a puzzled look before hobbling to the place he indicated. Her lips pressed flat against her teeth as she carefully folded to the ground and lay on her side.

Azarion watched as she curled into a semi-fetal position. The wounds on her back made her hiss a protest when she curved too far, and she straightened with a groan. She closed her eyes, her lashes lying dark against her pale cheeks, and shivered.

He dug into one of the satchels and found a cloak. Made of coarse-woven wool that reeked of sweat and sour wine, the garment was standard issue to every Kraelian soldier, given to him along with a water flask, a tin plate, and a knife. Azarion tossed the cloak over the *agacin*'s shaking form. Her eyes opened. Startled by his solicitude, she clutched the cloak, nose wrinkling at the smell, and tucked it closer around her. Her hesitant thanks surprised him. He sat down beside her and reclined back against the marble wall. "Get some rest, *Agacin*."

"Not likely," she muttered. "Even the dead don't rest in Midrigar."

He smiled, relieved that for a brief moment they were in accord. His gaze flickered back to the blanket covering her. He might well have to tear a strip from it and gag her with it to keep her from warning the hunters if they chose to follow them into the city. He prayed they weren't nearly as foolish as he was desperate.

He turned his attention to the ruined city. All knew the history of Midrigar. Once a thriving town and vassal to the Empire, it had rebelled when Krael demanded the vicegerent's daughter as a Flower of Spring. The man refused, raising a revolt among the citizens, who already resented sending their wives and daughters to burn in the Pit.

The emperor's wrath had been boundless, and the example he made of Midrigar ensured no other city risked suffering the same fate. Scribes recorded and storytellers whispered in hushed tones the tale of Midrigar's fall, the wholesale slaughter of its people from the oldest crone to the youngest babe. The streets had washed red with rivers of blood, and the buildings burned for days, lit by a fiery glow that could be seen as far south as the islands of Lohar and as far west as the river port town of Dulvaden.

Even when the Kraelian soldiers had butchered everyone and everything down to the last rat, the Empire wasn't done. The emperor sent in his sorcerers with their spells and curses so that even in death, the souls of Midrigar would be punished through the centuries for their rebellion. No wonder the witch's defiance had crumbled in the face of Azarion's threat that Beroe would meet the same doom as Midrigar if she refused to help him. At the time he meant every word. Now, seeing the remains of the city's destruction and breathing the despair carried on every draft of cold air that swirled around him, he doubted he could follow through with so heinous a threat. Herself and the Pit had done their best to twist his soul into a reflection of the Empire's own corruption, but even they hadn't hardened him enough to consign another town and its folk to this terrible fate.

He glanced down at the *agacin*. Despite her claim that no one slept in Midrigar, she did. Huddled under the cloak, only the top of her head and a strip of her forehead were visible. She still shivered from the cold, but Azarion no longer heard her teeth chatter.

His own skin pebbled, the clothing he wore not much protection against the night's chill. He ignored it. The elements rarely bothered him. As one of the Empire's many gladiators, he sometimes traveled to other cities, fighting for the pleasure of whichever of Hanimus's patrons chose to pay for the entertainment. They rode in rough carts or walked under a blistering sun, in the pouring rain, and sometimes in driving snow. Hanimus believed such hardships made his gladiators tougher fighters. Azarion gave an internal shrug. The master trainer might well have been right, but Azarion wished his companion had the strength to at least summon a small campfire.

What had she said about her magic? *It comes with a price*. The wounds were one thing, but she hadn't tried to escape him by burning him. Not even a blister on his finger. Had she used up her power? If so, did it return sooner or later? The thought made him uneasy. He needed her abilities. Without them, he'd have a difficult time reclaiming his birthright.

He sighed and dragged the second pack closer. Inside he found a full flask and prayed it held water instead of the foul wine that scented the cloak. He unstoppered the flask and sniffed. Water. It was flat but cold and soothing against his dry lips and throat.

"I'd like some, please."

The *agacin*'s voice was hoarse. Azarion shifted, careful not to twinge his left side too hard, and held out the flask. Fingers that had been cold a little earlier burned now as they grazed his knuckles. She took the flask and brought it to her lips for a quick swallow before handing it back.

Azarion frowned, certain the flags of color on her cheeks hadn't been there earlier, only the bruise from his knee. She watched him with glassy eyes. "What?"

She drew away when he reached out, trying hard to avoid his touch and failing when he lay his palm against her forehead and then her uninjured cheek. "You need to drink more. You've a fever."

She pushed away his second offer of the flask. "It will pass. It always does."

Magic and its price. "And the burns?"

A shrug. "They'll heal and leave their mark." Her too-bright eyes narrowed. "Why did you take me? I'm no use to you now. In fact, I'm a burden."

He tucked the cloak more snugly under her. "You're even more valuable to me now. You're an *agacin*, and *agacins* are revered by my people."

"What does that have to do with anything?"

*Agna*, he prayed silently to the goddess. *Please let her loss of magic be a temporary thing.* Aloud, he told the witch, "I need an *agacin* to reclaim my birthright. I need you."

The heat of her glare matched the heat of her fever. "Pig," she spat before yanking the cloak over her head to shut him out of her sight.

He heard no more from her, and soon her breathing slowed and deepened as sleep claimed her once more. The following hour passed in thick silence as Azarion listened for the hunters. He no longer heard the hounds, and prayed they had strayed in an opposite direction, misled by a lead dog's faulty nose or an instinctive fear of Midrigar. They might be safe from the Empire for the moment, but he and the witch weren't out of harm's way. The prickling sensation of being watched didn't abate, though it had blunted, either because whatever observed them lost interest or his own exhaustion dulled his senses. They sharpened to full alert when something moved in the shadows of the buildings across the bone-littered avenue.

Azarion straightened from his slouch against the wall and unsheathed the knife at his hip. Stolen from the guard he killed in the catacombs, it wasn't much in the way of weaponry but better than nothing.

More movement rippled through the darkness before a ribbon of vapor unfurled itself from the shelter of a broken column to float above the street's cobblestones. Azarion possessed a newly discovered and puzzling talent for seeing through illusion, but whatever hovered in midair before him wasn't an illusionary mask cast over a person. Nor was it a mist. The night was cold and clear, and dry enough to sting the lungs with each breath. And mist didn't move the way whatever this was did. As insubstantial as a cloud, it bore the vague outlines of a person, its borders solidifying until Azarion could make out the ghostly form of a man.

He wore the clothes of another age and stared at Azarion from a face half hacked away by a sword or an ax. The grotesque visage didn't take away from the intensity of the one-eyed gaze that rested on Azarion. A mournful keening, separate from the wind's own dirge, rose along the street, and soon the wraith was joined by a throng of other wraiths.

Men, women, and children, young and old, they poured out of doorways and windows and bled through the scorched walls. Their keening turned to hollow wails that crescendoed and ebbed over and over until Azarion's ears rang. He stood, blocking the feverish *agacin* from their gazes. None approached them, but their numbers swelled, spreading through the city streets to surround the temple where he sheltered.

"I told you," the *agacin* whispered behind him. "This is a grave, and we're desecrating it."

He didn't dare take his eyes off the ghostly crowd to look at her. "They've done nothing so far except deafen me with their wailing." He had far more to fear from the living than the dead.

"Not just wailing." The witch's tone firmed. "Can't you feel it? They're calling to something. Beseeching it to come."

Her words, more than the shifting spirits and their wretched cries, sent a spike of ice water down his spine. He didn't ask her to explain. Those who worked magic, any magic, possessed a sense that others didn't for the odd and unnatural. His shaman mother often sensed things otherworldly and strange when working her rituals. If the witch said this was more than the grieving of the suffering dead, he believed her.

He bent to empty the satchels, finding only rations, utensils, and a bone needle and thread. A small bundle tumbled out last, and his fingers made short work of the binding. He crowed in triumph when bits of charcoal for starting a fire spilled onto the portico floor.

"What are you doing?" The *agacin's* wide eyes were fever-bright, her gaze frightened.

"Drawing a circle of protection around us. My mother taught me this." He set to work, using the charcoal to sketch a circle around himself and the *agacin*. Sacred words of power, taught to him and his sister when they were children, spilled from his lips, and the soot-stain arc he'd drawn shimmered faintly in the darkness.

"It's coming," the witch said, her warning almost drowned as the ghosts' wails pitched to ear-ringing shrieks.

Azarion eyed the circle, searching for any gaps. His hands

trembled as he filled in the spots he'd missed. There could be no gaps, or whatever the ghosts had summoned would break through the meager protection.

The mob of wraiths pulsed with a kind of ravenous eagerness for whatever horror approached. Their wailing halted with an abruptness that made Azarion jump. Midrigar's spectral prisoners thinned like fog before a sunrise, fading from a vaporous army crowding the streets to shredded wisps of smoke that sank into the cobblestones and walls or darted away, quick as moths chased by bats. In moments, the city emptied, leaving only the suffocating silence that had first greeted them at the gate.

It was a false serenity.

They didn't have long to wait for the thing summoned by the dead. Azarion spotted a strange warping of the stones along the side of one of the buildings facing the temple where he sheltered with the *agacin*. At first, it looked like the masonry oozed in spots, as if the moonlight glimmered so hot, it melted the mortar used to hold the stones in place. He squinted for a better look and noticed the melting was simply the watery movement of a translucent creature as it crawled down the structure like a long-limbed crab.

Three times the length of a man, with two arms and two legs, it scuttled along the surface of the building until it reached the street. Long fingers—seven on each hand—detached from the wall and stretched out to skate across the cobblestones. The thing had no face, only the watery outline of a skull atop a neck and shoulders whose shape rippled, collapsed, and re-formed as if made of melting ice.

Free of the wall, it paused to crouch, rocking one way and then the other, head tipped up as if to sniff the air with a nose that wasn't there. Azarion dared not breathe. Behind him, the witch was as silent as the dead.

Suddenly, it pivoted on its haunches, its faceless head whipping toward Azarion. Spindly limbs tucked into themselves before snapping apart as the creature hurtled toward them, eating the distance in disjointed leaps.

Azarion spoke over his shoulder. "*Agacin,*" he said. "If you have fire, now's the time to use it."

The creature kept coming, limbs rippling like the thrashing of a worm as it crossed the avenue and clambered up the temple steps. Azarion's skin crawled as the thing's head ratcheted from one side to the other in spasmodic jerks. Whatever it was, it didn't belong in this world.

Azarion stepped farther back in the protective circle, careful not to scrape away the charcoal's flimsy barrier. Spidery fingers reached for him. Blue sparks crackled off its hands when the otherworldly predator touched some invisible wall. It recoiled, emitting a shrieking buzz like that of a disturbed hornet's nest. Azarion glanced down at the circle's drawn barrier, noting it now glowed a hot yellow.

The thing paced back and forth, agitated fury in every line of its misshapen body. Azarion was reminded of the caged cats the Empire imported for fighting in the Pit. Given a choice, he'd rather fight a clowder of those than one of these monsters.

It hurled itself against the invisible obstruction created by the charcoal and the Savatar incantations. A shower of sparks lit the darkness once more, followed by the angry buzzing. Gnarled fingers clawed at the resistant magic, the creature desperate to grasp the prey it could so clearly see but couldn't reach.

Azarion spared a quick glance for his companion. She had gained her feet, and her wide eyes glittered with terror. "I'll kill us both before I let that thing take us, *Agacin.*"

She turned even paler, thin fingers clutching the blanket as if it were a shield. "No," she whispered, gaze darting back and forth between him and the monster. "Please. No one should have to die inside Midrigar."

Her obvious horror made him pause. She was right. His own soul cringed at the idea of joining the imprisoned dead.

The creature suddenly halted its frenzied attempts to breach the spell wall. Its head slowly swiveled on its spindly neck. The featureless visage split apart in the space where a mouth might have been, creating a lesion from which a fleshy tongue, red as pulped meat, unfurled to taste the air.

"What's it doing?" the *agacin* whispered.

Azarion studied it. Even without a face, its body language revealed much. Something had drawn its attention, and like a serpent, it tested the air for the scent of other prey.

Midrigar's unnatural silence clung to its walls and buildings, but beyond it, the living world still spoke and whispered, hooted and chirped, rustled and fluttered. And howled.

For all that the creature attacking the spell wall to reach them made Azarion's skin crawl, it didn't twist his gut into knots the same way as the baying of hounds.

The sound carried on the night, growing louder and more frenzied as the tracking party closed in on the city. Azarion flicked another glance at his captive. Her eyes had narrowed as she, too, heard the dogs' approach, accompanied by the thunder of horses' hooves.

Starshine cast an otherworldly glow on the monster's pallid skin, highlighting the rippling movement of flesh over skeleton as it dropped into a crouch. Its faceless skull continued to turn, the long, thick tongue tasting. Tasting.

Voices joined the chorus of barking dogs and galloping horses. The barking changed to reluctant whines, some escalating to pained yelps following the crack of a whip and a rider's angry shout.

Equine whinnies and snorts mimicked the dogs' wordless protests. The ruckus originated from a place on the other side of Midrigar's north gate. Azarion imagined the chaos, a mob of dogs, horses, and trackers facing the cursed city, the animals showing more sense than their human masters by refusing to go any farther.

The creature continued its odd swaying back and forth as if deciding whether to take the hunt to the new, unwary prey or stay with the ones it had cornered but couldn't yet reach.

A telltale soft inhalation made Azarion spin around, yank Gilene in his arms, and clap a hand across her mouth. "Don't," he ordered.

She glared at him over the edge of his palm. Against his callused skin, her warning cry came out as nothing more than vibration and heat. She remained undeterred, drawing in another breath through her nostrils to try again.

Azarion shook her, disrupting the breath so that she coughed into his hand instead, wetting it with a spray of spittle. He lowered his head until his nose almost touched hers. "Those men and their dogs are here to capture me, not rescue you. Do you understand the difference?"

She was desperate, and desperate people did foolish things. His colossal mistake in choosing Midrigar as a sanctuary was testament to that.

She stood rigid in his arms, and the breath from her nostrils gusted across the back of his hand, but her gaze turned thoughtful. Her eyes slid to the side where the creature continued to hover. It stretched out a misshapen arm to casually rake its talons across the spell wall, trailing sparks in its wake.

"Do you understand?" Azarion repeated. She nodded slowly,

and he eased his hand away. "If you lie . . ." He left the threat implied.

"I won't scream," she assured him in a whisper.

"You give your word?"

"No, but I give you my understanding."

It would have to do for now and was the thing he wanted from her most.

A voice rang clear in the chilly air, furious and frustrated. "What is wrong with those fucking mutts?"

Another voice answered. "It's Midrigar, Captain. "Theys knows it's haunted. So do the horses. You'll not get 'em past the gate neither."

"Then we go in without them. Load your crossbows. First sight of the gladiator, shoot to wound, not to kill. Herself wants him alive."

"No mercy in that," another voice chimed in.

"Not our problem," the captain replied. "And if any of you lily-livered fucks refuse like the hounds and horses, I'll shoot you myself, and it will be to kill. Now move!"

More sounds from the north gate traveled to Azarion's ears; the tramp of boots, curses, and prayers as the tracking party entered Midrigar on foot.

The monster's tongue writhed like a worm impaled on a hook as it slurped a path up its own skull as if in anticipation of a feast. It slapped the spell wall a final time—a wordless promise that it intended to return—before loping down the rubble-strewn avenue toward the invaders.

Azarion watched it dwindle out of sight before releasing the *agacin*. She shuddered and tossed the blanket aside. Azarion kicked the packs out of the way. He didn't need extra weight to slow him down. He was impaired enough by his own injuries as well as those the *agacin* suffered. He held on to the knife. A blade might not work on the otherworldly hunter, but it was effective against a human adversary.

Listening for the chanting of ghosts or the monster's distorted buzzing that signaled its approach, he heard nothing except the voices of the men drawing ever closer to their hiding spot.

A strange popping bludgeoned his ears as he stepped across the charcoal circle. The *agacin* gaped at him when he held out a hand to her and gestured for her to follow him.

"How did you do that?" She glanced down at the circle and back at him, befuddled.

"It's a simple ward. Protects us from demons and wights who try to get in and traps them if they try to get out. We're neither, so we can move in or out of the ward as we please." He crooked his fingers to signal her. "Come, we can't linger."

"What if it comes back?" Her eyes darted toward the path the creature had taken.

Guilt plagued him, along with the harsh lash of self-recrimination. He'd thought Midrigar a tragic example of the Empire's worst brutality, a dead city populated by harmless ghosts. How wrong he was.

The *agacin* had accused him of sheltering in a grave, and he had shrugged off her fear. He wasn't afraid of ghosts. The Sky Below was dotted with numerous barrows in which his people sometimes took sanctuary with their livestock during dangerous storms and kept company with the occasional lingering shade.

Midrigar wasn't a barrow or a necropolis; it was something much more. Something infinitely dark and malignant. Both prison and gateway, it trapped its dead and allowed things like the faceless hunter to cross over, find a different hunting ground from the one it stalked in some other, strange world.

"Oh, it will come back," he said softly.

His declaration gave her feet wings. She flew past him, pausing briefly to shake her head when she crossed over the warding circle's invisible barrier.

Azarion caught up with her. "We run for the gate we entered. No stopping, no crying for help." He suspected those pleas would come from the opposite direction at any moment.

The trackers still called commands to each other, their voices fanning out in a widening arc as they searched for him. The monster had yet to attack, but it was only a matter of time.

As if it heard his thoughts, a piercing scream rent the quiet accompanied by the eerie buzzing. The witch blanched, her eyes black and wide.

Azarion gave her a none-too-gentle shove. "Run."

Her back arched away from him. Whether from his touch or her response to his command, he didn't know, but she bolted down the steps and into the street, toward the gate. Azarion loped beside her, looking back every few paces to see if they were followed.

More screaming threaded the wind, human made inhuman by an indescribable torture. In the distance, the dogs had gone silent.

They passed in front of the broken temple's grand entrance with its impenetrable darkness. A final prolonged shriek rose and fell in hideous rhythm before abruptly dying. Azarion lengthened his strides, grabbing the witch's hand and nearly lifting her off her feet as they ran.

The buzzing returned, a wetter, more saturated sound that came from their left. The hunter now hunted them. Azarion forgot the pain of his cracked ribs and the way his lungs burned with every panting breath.

The gate. The gate was so close and the creature eating the distance between them even closer. He gripped the knife in the hand not holding on to the *agacin*. There might well be armed survivors outside this gate, waiting with their arrows and their dogs. His chances of winning a fight against such odds were non-existent, and the witch's fate grim, but better that than death by Midrigar's monster.

That wet, gurgling buzz filled his ears. The *agacin's* hair whipped behind her like a flag as they hurtled through the gate and whatever new threat awaited them in the shadowed tree line. The creature emitted its own shrieking fury behind them but didn't follow. Azarion didn't stop to look back but continued to run with the witch toward the forest.

A figure suddenly emerged from a clump of shadows cast by the trees. A Kraelian tracker, his bloodless features twisted in horror, raised his crossbow and aimed at Azarion. The witch gasped and wrenched herself free of Azarion's grip.

He didn't stop, didn't hesitate, and flung the knife. The blade caught the man in the chest, hard enough to make him stumble back a step before falling to the ground. The loaded bow landed in the grass beside him.

Azarion slowed and skirted the fallen tracker before retracing his steps. The dead man stared at the forest canopy above him with sightless eyes. Azarion jerked the knife free and wiped the blade on the grass before resheathing it. He retrieved the bow, along with the quiver of quarrels beside the tracker, and gave a quick reconnoiter of the tree line, looking for another Kraelian tracker to materialize. None did so, and he turned his attention to the *agacin*.

She hadn't run far on her own. He spotted her on her knees, leaning against the trunk of a sapling, her eyes closed.

The abomination behind Midrigar's walls had ceased its screeching, and Azarion gave silent thanks to whatever deity listened that it was trapped there like the dead who had summoned it.

He limped toward the witch. With their race over and their safety assured, at least for now, the pain in his side nearly took his breath away.

The *agacin* opened her eyes when he crouched in front of her, dark pools reflecting moonlight and fever. She ran her tongue across her lower lip, and her graceful throat flexed when she swallowed. "What if I had fallen or couldn't keep up?"

He glided a fingertip along a valley made by the folds of her skirt. "I would have carried you."

She continued to stare at him, saying nothing, until her eyes closed again and she sagged against the tree. Azarion caught her before she hit the ground. He lowered her gently to her side before taking a seat beside her. Sweat dripped into his eyes, steam rising off his skin in the cold air. He wiped his face with the hem of his tunic and pressed a hand to his side to ease the stabbing pain there.

Safety was a fleeting and a variable thing, but for now, they were safe from the horrors lurking in Midrigar and not far from where he had tied the horse. Azarion checked the witch and left her where she lay. He had no choice. If he tried to lift her, he'd collapse. He prayed to Agna for protection of her handmaiden and set off to retrieve his mount.

Misfortune still held him in its grip. The horse was gone, leaving behind a pair of broken reins hanging from a tree branch like stripped strands of ivy. Sometime during their deadly stay in Midrigar, the animal had spooked and freed itself by breaking its tethers. A trampling of grass and hoofprints created a half-moon around the base of the tree. Azarion suspected the otherworldly creature's hideous screeching, along with the screams of murdered men, had carried far into the wood, frightening the horse so much it managed to snap the reins and escape.

Without the satchels he'd left behind in the city and the horse, they lacked transportation and supplies, and somewhere on the other side of Midrigar, a pack of hunting hounds likely still lingered, waiting for their masters to return.

Still, the Empire hadn't yet caught him, he had escaped a thing that had wiped out those who hunted him, and he had his knife, along with a crossbow and quarrels. A stream ran not far away for water, and the trade road nearby was bound, at some point, to yield a traveler on horseback. It was just a matter of patience and time before he could replace the mount he lost.

For now he'd rest. Weariness had him seeing double, and pain made his stomach roil. The *agacin* lay unmoving next to him except for steady, shallow breaths. He wished he could stretch out beside her, but it hurt too much to lie down. Instead, he nudged her carefully into his lap and reclined against the sapling. His eyelids drooped. Every bruise and cut inflicted by the empress, and the fighter he killed for her entertainment, ached. The forest surrounding him turned fuzzy in his vision. He blinked hard to stay awake and finally surrendered to an exhausted sleep.

Voices and a mule's braying snapped him awake. Azarion straightened from a slouch and rubbed his eyes for a better look at his surroundings. Morning sunlight spilled through the trees' newly leafed canopy, dappling the *agacin*'s sleeping features. High color dusted her cheekbones, and her lips were dry and cracked. Sure signs the fever still raged through her body.

The voices grew louder, and the creak of wheels, clank of bells, and steady clop of hooves joined the mule's racket. Travelers on the trade road, just as he expected, and from the sound of it, part of a caravan.

He stayed where he was, hidden in the tree line until the caravan came into view. Seven wagons pulled by a mix of horses, oxen, and the single mule. The brightly painted wagons and garlands of bells strung on their sides marked the group as free traders. Unbound by the rules and laws set by the Trade Guild, they plied their trades along the offshoot roads of the Golden Serpent without Guild approval or protection. Most of the lower rungs of society and the towns perched at the edges of Krael's hinterlands bought their goods from the free traders.

The Guild barred them from working the more lucrative Golden Serpent, which wrapped around the borders of the Empire and stretched into the lands of Usepei and Ardin, but it didn't stop the wily traders from getting their hands on items as cheap and ubiquitous as clay pots or as rare and expensive as purple silk. Some things were obtained through means that didn't always include the exchange of coins, but no one reported the traders to the garrisons that squatted in the remote regions, and if they did, the garrison commanders turned a blind eye, finding the benefits of trade with such people far outweighed the petty crimes they might commit to provide those benefits.

The crew driving these wagons or walking beside them were a motley lot, a mix of men, women, and a few children. Every adult was heavily armed, and while their scruffy clothing marked them as not the most prosperous group, they looked well-fed and clean enough—something neither he nor the *agacin* could claim at the moment.

She twitched in his lap, hotter than a bonfire. She needed succor he couldn't give and was far too valuable to leave behind. And he owed her much. Revealing himself—and her—to the traders was his only choice.

He carefully moved the witch off his lap and onto the grass

before creaking to his feet. The crossbow and arrows would have to stay with her. Walking out of the trees with it in his arms guaranteed him a quick death. He kept his knife sheathed to show he meant no harm, stiffened his back, and stepped onto the road in front of the lead wagon.

Before the wheels rolled to a halt, he found himself once again in the lethal sights of not one but six crossbows, their nocked arrows pointed at various spots on his body.

"Help us," he said and waited.

A man garbed in mismatched layers of ragged wool and bits of expensive silk sauntered from behind the lead wagon and approached him, a short spear held casually in one hand. He wore his graying hair clubbed at the nape, and the gimcrack beads draped around his neck sparkled in the sun. His gray gaze, flat as unpolished steel and just as hard, settled on Azarion. "What happened to you?"

The witch had named him a liar and a thief, and in this moment, Azarion hoped he lived up to the first insult by spinning the most convincing of tales, otherwise he'd be shot full of arrows before he could take a single running step. "Thieves set upon my wife and me," he said. "We were traveling to the Silfer markets to sell our dyes and were attacked. They stole everything, including our horse." Thank Agna the *agacin* sported green hands from dyeing the long nettle. That, more than any words from him, should convince them he spoke truthfully.

The caravan leader's eyes narrowed, his gaze suspicious. This wasn't a man who let sympathy overwhelm caution. "Why did they let you live?" He peered beyond Azarion's shoulder into the woods. "And I see no wife."

Azarion shrugged. "She's injured. I left her just within the trees there." He gestured with a tip of his chin to where the *agacin* lay hidden. "I don't know why they let us live. They didn't share their reasons or their purpose. Not all murderers are thieves; not all thieves are murderers." A quick glance behind the leader at the trader folk nodding their heads and murmuring told him his words had struck a chord.

The man himself remained unconvinced. His flat gaze flickered down. "You still have a blade on you. What manner of thief doesn't take a weapon?"

"Not a very good one or maybe one who doesn't think a common knife is worth dying for. I used it to defend us. I have a crossbow as well that fell from one of their saddles. I left it beside my wife."

"Bring this wife to us. Only the wife." They waited on the road until Azarion returned, the unconscious *agacin* heavy in his tired arms. He hadn't wanted to leave the bow, but in this scenario, negotiation served him best, not force or threat.

The leader's hard gaze settled on the witch. "Is your woman sick?"

In an instant, the fragile rapport Azarion had established with the traders vanished. Fear of plague burned away compassion in even the most softhearted person. His own heartbeat trebled as fingers on the crossbows' triggers tightened. "Injured," he assured them. "One of the thieves pushed her into the kettle of water she was boiling for our dinner. It spilled on her. She's been scalded and is fevered from the wounds. Can you help her?" he repeated.

The *agacin*'s burn marks looked worse than a scalding, but telling this lot he held a fire witch injured by her own spells might get them both killed as quickly as if he confirmed the traders' fears of plague.

A young woman emerged from behind the second wagon. Shorter than the *agacin* with lighter hair and sweeter features, she had the same color eyes as the caravan leader, only kinder and faintly melancholic. "Let me help her, Uncle." She reached the man's side, stretching up on her toes to speak softly in his ear.

He frowned, said something to the girl, shook his head at her reply, and finally gave a sigh and a roll of his eyes. He turned to Azarion. "You can travel with us as far as Wellspring Holt, but I'll take that knife you're carrying as payment for food and care of your wife, along with the crossbow." He gestured for one of his men to retrieve the bow Azarion had left in the forest.

Azarion didn't hesitate and turned his hip so another of the traders could remove the blade from his belt. He was now both injured and unarmed. He shifted the *agacin* in his arms. "It's a good knife," he assured his new host.

The other man took the blade, hefting it in his palm to test its balance, turning it this way and that to inspect the edge. "It is. I'll use it well." He gestured to his niece and an older woman who joined them during their bargaining. "Put your woman in Asil's wagon. Halani there can see to her. You'll have to walk like the rest of us."

Azarion nodded. He could do that, welcomed it, in fact. Sitting hurt. Lying down was agony, running an exercise in torture. The pain of his cracked ribs might finally subside if all he had to do was walk. "My thanks."

The girl called Halani motioned for him to follow her. Her uncle and the older woman Azarion assumed was Asil fell into step on either side of him.

Asil offered him a sweet, vapid smile. "What's your name?" She possessed a young voice, at odds with her aged features.

"Valdan of Pran." That lie spilled as easily from his lips as all the others before it. Soon, he wouldn't be able to tell the difference between lies and truth if he kept this up. He didn't regret it.

His real name might be noted and possibly recognized. It was common enough among the Savatar, not so much in the Empire, and the Gladius Prime known as Azarion had achieved great notoriety among the populace who attended the fights in the Pit.

Unlike Asil, the caravan's leader didn't smile, and his gaze raked Azarion from head to foot. "You've the look of the nomads from the Sky Below about you."

Azarion almost stumbled at hearing the Savatar words used in describing the Stara Dragana. It had been a long time since anyone he knew called it the Sky Below. Homesickness, buoyed by newfound hope, swamped him. He held the *agacin* a little closer.

"My mother was a Nunari clanswoman, my father a Kraelian soldier."

Halani, striding ahead of them, spoke over her shoulder. "And your wife? How is she called?"

Azarion glanced down at the witch's flushed features, recalling once more the man standing by the cart in Kraelag, shouting a name as Azarion galloped toward her. She had snarled at Azarion when he used it, refusing to claim it as hers.

"Gilene," he said. "Her name is Gilene." And for the first time since he'd broken free of his bondage to the Empire, he was certain he spoke the truth.

# CHAPTER FIVE

Gilene's first thought when she regained consciousness was that someone had spoon-fed her a bowl of sand while she slept. The gritty burn in her throat hurt each time she swallowed, and her tongue felt stuck to the roof of her mouth. She tried to lick her bottom lip only to stop at the dry scrape of chapped skin. She cracked open an eyelid to a blurry view of shapes and colors. One shape, made of shades in red and yellow and black, moved toward her. "Thirsty," she croaked.

A gentle hand gripped the back of her neck and lifted her enough to sip from a cup held to her mouth. "Sip," said a soft, female voice. "Slowly or you'll be sick."

Gilene did as instructed, controlling the urge to gulp as cool water filled her mouth and slid down her throat in a soothing tumble. She mumbled a protest when her nurse took the cup away, and reached for it with a trembling hand. "More."

A hand stroked her hair. Once more the soothing voice spoke. "In a moment. Let your stomach get used to having something in it. Rest for now."

She was lowered back to a soft pillow, a covering that smelled of bay leaves instead of stale sweat tucked around her shoulders. Her vision remained blurry despite her best effort to blink it clear. Another shape joined the first one.

"She has pretty hair," a younger voice said.

"She does, Mama. Now leave her be. She's injured and needs rest." A cool palm curled over Gilene's hand and gave it a squeeze. "Shh. Sleep. When you wake again, your man will be here with you."

Gilene frowned, confused. Man? What man? The spell sickness turned her mind into a mud puddle. She had no man. None wanted a fire witch made barren by her magic and fated to "die" every year, doomed to both physical and emotional ruin by the time her unfortunate successor assumed her role as Beroe's savior. She fell asleep to the soft croon of a woman singing and the ache of resentment in her belly.

She awakened again—hours or minutes or days later, she couldn't tell—to the glow of an oil lamp and the curve of a painted night sky above her.

Her gaze traveled across an enclosed horizon, pausing at points to note neatly stacked chests and barrels set against slat walls washed in shades of teal and amber. The sound of voices penetrated their barriers. Men and women talking and singing, children laughing, all accompanied by the bleat and bray of livestock. The bed on which she lay rocked beneath her in a rough cradle's sway. Where in the gods' names was she?

"You're awake."

The familiar sound of the deep voice sent a cascade of memories tumbling past her mind's eye: the floor of the Pit consumed in fire; the spirits of the sacrificed women departing; the painful lurch toward her brothers, who waited with their cart for her; and most of all the gladiator who extorted her cooperation and repaid her help by abducting her.

Gilene's gaze snapped to the large figure folded into a cross-legged position near her knees. Azarion. She would remember his name until the day she died and not with affection. His green eyes caught the ambient light of the lamp, and the somber expression he wore highlighted the high curve of his cheekbones. A beard shadowed his jaw. She tried to sit up, but the blankets tucked around her felt heavier than iron, her muscles weaker than a crone's on her deathbed.

Azarion rested three fingers on her shoulder and effortlessly pushed her supine once more. "Halani says your fever's broken, but you need to rest a little longer. The poultice she used on your back and leg worked wonders. Without it, you'd still be feverish and lying on your side."

Gilene's thoughts spun. She had so many questions, with only memories made hazy by fever to find her answers. She lay very still, searching for the hot agony of the burns left by her magic, and felt nothing except an extra bit of padding against her back. Her fingers sought and found the bandage on her thigh, discovering as well that, under the blankets, she was as bare as a newborn.

She accepted the flask Azarion offered her without comment, took a careful swallow, and handed it back to him. "Where am I?"

"In a free trader's wagon. The caravan master's niece and sister have been taking care of you."

Gilene recalled the voices of two women, one calm and soothing, the other girlish and sweet. "How long have I been ill?"

"Three days with fever." She gasped and tried to sit up once more, only to fall back again as muscles sore from lack of use cramped in protest. Azarion frowned but didn't touch her. "Lie still. You're not helping yourself by doing that."

She rubbed a hand over her cheek, wincing at the ache still lingering where Azarion's knee had struck her. Her skin felt clammy, and her scalp itched. Memories fluttered like moth wings through her mind, fragile and fleeting. The pain in her back, begging her captor to let her go, the scent of despair blanketing cursed

Midrigar, and the living darkness hovering just beyond the threshold of the ruined temple, watching as she and Azarion climbed the steps to the sheltered portico. The recollections made her shudder.

"How did we escape Midrigar?" She remembered the thing summoned by the dead, her own panic overriding the fever as Azarion searched frantically for something to draw a protective circle around them.

Azarion's features sharpened, and she caught the glimmer of true horror in his eyes. "The sacrifice of a tracking party and a sprint to the gate," he said. His gaze flickered away for a moment before returning to her. "You were right. Midrigar is no sanctuary for anyone. More than the dead linger there."

She blinked at him, stunned by his ready willingness to admit his error. It even had the vague ring of apology. Crowing over it served neither of them, so she simply nodded and went back to her questions.

"How did we end up with traders?" When he recounted the tale, it was her turn to frown. "Do these people know who you are?"

His relaxed manner disappeared, replaced by the implacable demeanor. His eyes darkened, gaze harder than emeralds. "They know I'm Valdan of Pran, traveling with my wife, Gilene, to the Silfer markets to sell dye. We were attacked and robbed on the road. You were burned when the pot of water you were boiling spilled on you during the struggle." He bared his teeth at her when she opened her mouth to protest. "The fever clouded your memory, wife. I traded my knife and a crossbow for help."

More terrifying memories surfaced: the thing screeching at them from the gate's threshold, the lone tracker raising his crossbow to fire at them, and his quick death from Azarion's blade. She shivered.

"We'll be near the town of Wellspring Holt by tomorrow evening."

Wellspring Holt. She had visited the town as a child with her family for the summer wedding of a distant relative. It would be simple to find her way back from there to Beroe. She just had to escape the gladiator. She eyed him, her renewed anger burning away her lethargy. "What's to stop me from telling them you're an escaped Pit slave known as Azarion?"

He shrugged, the easy gesture belied by the narrowed gaze. "Nothing except whatever sense of responsibility you carry. If you tell them, you sentence them to die. I'll be forced to kill every one of them so they won't sell me back to the Empire. That includes the woman who nursed you and her mother, who is like a slow-witted child."

If the power she wielded hadn't been drained dry in the Pit, she'd set him on fire and worry about reparations for the wagon later. "What has the Empire made of us that we both kill innocents without hesitation?"

Another shrug. "Survivors."

Her rage sapped what little strength Gilene had left. Her eyelids grew heavy even as she struggled to stay awake and bargain with her captor. "Will you let me go when we reach Wellspring Holt?"

"No."

She refused to let the bastard Savatar see her weep. "Why not? That your people revere fire witches is all well and good, but I don't want to be abducted and worshipped. I just want to go home."

Azarion leaned forward and placed a finger against her lips. "Shh," he ordered in a tone that brooked no argument, no matter how softly spoken. The look he leveled on her was curious. "Why haven't you burned me to escape?" Her mutinous silence didn't deter him. "Because you can't," he said, answering his own question. "At least not yet. You're like a lamp that's burned away its oil. You need time to replenish as well as to heal."

He was a loathsome snake and a liar, a thief, and a butcher, but he was most definitely not stupid. Gilene seethed and pulled her blanket up to cover her face and shut him out of her sight. "Go away," she muttered.

She waited for him to say something else, but he stayed silent and did as she asked. The wagon rocked when he stood and creaked on its struts as he hopped out of the shelter.

He left the door open, and Gilene peeked out from the covers to see sunlight gild the door frame. Azarion's deep voice echoed back to her, along with the soft voice of a woman—the one Gilene associated with slender hands and a soothing touch.

A shadow filled the opening for a moment, and the wagon swayed again, this time under the feet of a woman wearing dusty skirts and a reassuring smile. Gilene guessed her similar in age to herself. She wore her brown hair in an intricate plait that fell over one shoulder to her hip, its end tied with a beaded ribbon. She assumed Azarion's previous place by the bed.

"Your husband said you were awake. How are you feeling?" The woman had gray eyes, velvety as a dove's wings, somber as a pall monk's prayers.

Gilene swallowed back the denial that she was married, and certainly not to her captor. She licked dry lips, wishing she'd partaken more from the flask Azarion had handed her. "Much better. Are you Halani?" At the other's affirmative nod, she continued. "He said you nursed me. Thank you."

The trader woman's smile widened. "My mother, Asil, helped

83

too, though she offers company more than help. I've poulticed your back to ease the pain and speed healing and done the same with your leg. I'm not much of a healer, but it should work."

Gilene's erstwhile nurse didn't give herself enough credit. The pain in her back and thigh was almost gone, hardly a sting remaining to remind her that fire magic wielded a whip against its user. "It's wonderful and hurts very little now. I'm grateful." Azarion had neatly trapped her into silence. There was no way she'd reveal his true identity to these people, if only to spare Halani, whose kindness had eased her suffering.

Halani laid her hand over Gilene's forehead. "Your skin is still cool. No more fever. Do you feel well enough to eat?"

Gilene's stomach rumbled in answer, and both women laughed. Halani stood. "I'll be back with some broth and a little bread."

The scent of herbs filled the wagon's small space when she returned and set down a bowl of warm broth and a hunk of bread on a tray atop a storage chest. She helped Gilene sit up, tucking pillows behind her as a back rest. "If you're too weak, I can feed you."

Keeping her hands as steady as possible, Gilene reached for the bowl and spoon Halani offered. "I can do it." She hated the aftermath of her magic use as much as the reason for using it. Left weak as a babe for several days, and just as pitiful, she had to rely on her family's help. Coming from strangers, it was even worse. She'd eat the soup on her own if it half killed her.

The first sip made her eyebrows lift. "This is better than good. Did you make it?"

Halani chortled. "I only wish I possessed such skill with a cooking pot. That's Marata's doing. He's the caravan's cook and used to run the kitchens on a Kraelian nobleman's estate. If my uncle had to get rid of all of us save one, he'd keep Marata."

"Your uncle is the caravan leader?" The chime of small bells sounded outside, the mark of those who refused to join the Trade Guild and obey its stricter laws.

Halani straightened the blankets at Gilene's feet before offering her a napkin. "Aye. When it's safe enough and there isn't a war or two going on, our caravan travels most of the hinterland roads. Our best profits come from the garrisons." She frowned. "I'm sorry to hear the thieves took your horse and goods. Your husband said they even stole your dye pots."

Gilene tried not to choke on her broth. Azarion—Valdan, whatever he chose to call himself at the moment—spun a false tale better than a spider did a web. And she was forced to validate his lies. She dabbed at her lips with the napkin. "All can be replaced. We're just lucky to be alive." The last, at least, was a hard-won truth. Between the Rites of Spring and the predator in Midrigar, it was a wonder neither of them was dead yet.

She surrendered her now empty bowl to Halani, who nodded. "Indeed. Some who thieve think nothing of murdering their marks. You're fortunate your husband knew how to fight." A wistful note entered her voice. "He's a handsome man who obviously cares for you. That's a treasure none can steal."

Gilene was saved from replying to that profound misconception by the arrival of a woman older than Halani but with similar features. The space in the wagon grew a little more cramped as she lingered at the entrance and grinned, eyes bright with a child's curiosity.

Halani gestured to her. "This is my mother, Asil. Mama, this is Gilene, Valdan's wife."

Asil waved, and again Gilene had the notion that she faced a child wearing an adult woman's face. She recalled Azarion's earlier threat to kill their hosts if Gilene revealed his identity. He had said Halani's mother was simple.

Even Asil's voice was that of a much younger girl, high and sweet. "Hamod says come to the front, Hali. He wants to talk to you."

Halani sighed. "Hamod is my uncle," she clarified for Gilene. "I'll return soon. Mama, can you help Gilene if she needs it while I'm gone?"

As soon as Halani exited the wagon, Asil scooted closer, and her smile turned beseeching. "Can I braid your hair? It's very soft."

Gilene wondered what had happened to Asil that made her the child and her daughter the parent. There was an engaging appeal about the older woman, an innocence in her interactions that most people had lost by the time they were nine or ten years of age.

Gilene's hair felt stuck to her scalp, in need of a good washing and thorough combing. She welcomed Asil's request. "Of course, though I don't have a comb."

The other woman practically bounced where she sat. Her hand dove into a pocket of her colorful apron, emerging with a prized comb. "I do," she crowed, her smile growing larger. "And I'll be gentle; I promise."

She fluffed the pillows higher behind Gilene, tucked the blanket under her arms, and set to unraveling the locks of hair that had tangled themselves into mats. Asil was still working at her task with gusto and regaling Gilene with anecdotes regarding the caravan and its close-knit members when her daughter returned.

Halani sighed, though her features were soft with affection as she gazed at her mother. "You are the worst sort of gossip, Mama. What nonsense have you been pouring into Gilene's ear while I was gone?"

Asil laughed, the sound one of such joy it almost brought tears to Gilene's eyes. She couldn't recall the last time she heard anyone laugh in such a way. "All true, Hali. You know I don't lie. You remember when Supan's breeches fell down around his ankles while he was courting that girl in Silfer?" More peals of laughter, and Halani and Gilene joined her.

"We're a ridiculous lot sometimes, Gilene, but it makes for good stories," Halani said.

Gilene hid a wince when Asil's comb snagged on a particularly nasty knot. "I like Asil's stories. They speak of family and love between you." Something thin and frayed in her own family. There was duty and devotion, both driven by guilt, and not much else.

She wondered what her mother and siblings were doing at the moment, whether they fretted over her and worried for her safety. The village as a whole, she knew, would be in a state of panic. Someone had taken their fire witch, the one person they relied on to protect the other village women from the Rites of Spring each year. She shook away the growing darkness of her thoughts. They had no place here with two women who knew her as nothing other than Gilene, wife of Valdan.

"I tell funny stories, but Hali tells the best ones," Asil bragged of her daughter. "One each night after supper if she isn't sick or the rest of us too tired."

"Or too bored," Halani quipped back.

Asil's expression creased into an indignant pinch. "No one is ever bored with your stories, Hali."

Halani bent and kissed the top of her mother's head. "If you say so, Mama." She straightened and gave Gilene a wink. "When she's done combing out your hair, we can help you dress and leave the wagon to get some air. It will do your legs good to walk about. That's if you're up to it."

Gilene leapt at the offer, achy from lying down for so long and desperate to see the sky. "Oh yes, I'm well enough for that."

Halani bent to a basket wedged between a chest and a wagon bow. "I washed your clothes while you healed." She pulled a neatly folded tunic out of the basket and shook out the wrinkles. "We're near a stream and will camp close by for the night. Valdan says he'll take you there so you can bathe. You can wear this tunic for now, and take your clothes with you to dress once you're done."

The offer of a bath excited her, and Gilene swore she could hear the trickling murmur of the stream. Still she hesitated. Her reason warned her that to go alone was far too dangerous, even for a healthy woman fleet of foot, and at the moment, she was neither of those. The thought of Azarion acting as her watchdog seemed just as threatening. "I don't want to bother . . . my husband." The word stung her tongue, and she did her best to hide her distaste. Halani's puzzled look hinted she might not have succeeded.

"I'm sure he won't mind, and it would be best if your man went with you. We're not far off the traveler road, and it's mostly safe, but not all those who travel it are."

To argue would undoubtedly raise suspicion. Gilene let it go and occupied the remainder of the time Asil worked on her hair in idle chat with her and Halani. When Azarion came to fetch her, her hair was combed smooth, and she wore the tunic Halani gave her. Someone had brushed her shoes free of dust and even mended a hole in the side where her small toe had rubbed through the worn leather. Outside, the temperature carried the snap of an early spring chill, and she shivered in anticipation of an unforgiving bath in an icy stream.

Still, she breathed in the fresh air gratefully. The wagon bed was far more comfortable than the hard portico floor of a broken temple in a haunted city, but her muscles craved movement and her lungs the green scent of the forest around them. Brightly painted wagons formed a circle under an oak grove's newly leafed canopy, and through the spaces between the tree trunks and the wagons she caught sight of the ribbon of dusty road that marked the caravan path.

Curious members of Halani's trader band came up to introduce themselves, some to offer her good health, others to do no more than stare for a moment or nod and move on to whatever task called their attention. Hamod, the man Halani called uncle and Asil called brother, was one of the ones whose gray gaze bore holes into her before he gave a cursory tilt of his head and walked away. He reminded Gilene of Azarion in a way.

When the gladiator arrived, he eyed her up and down before finally speaking. "You're feeling better, wife." The term spilled easily off his lips. He bowed briefly to Halani and Asil. "You're in fine hands with these two." Asil giggled and blushed while Halani gave a small bow before tugging her mother away from them.

"You can keep the soap cake if there's any left, Gilene," she called back over her shoulder.

Gilene hugged her laundered clothes and gift of soap to her chest and returned Azarion's stare with a bland one of her own. "As much and as easily as you lie, how do you remember what the truth is?" She shouldn't goad him. He hadn't yet used violence against her physically, only threatened to hurt others if she didn't cooperate, and that was bad enough. Still, he was more than capable of killing her with no more effort than it took to kill a chicken. She didn't want to die. She couldn't die. Not yet at least.

Her insult rolled off him. "I remember because I must. There's always a grain of truth embedded in a lie." He gestured for her to walk beside him as he headed toward the stream Halani mentioned.

"I am not, never have been, and never will be your wife," she snapped as she fell in step beside him.

His exasperated snort sent a vapor cloud streaming out of his nostrils to dissipate in the cold air. "To these people you are. Thus, a truth." His green gaze flickered to her. "How are your burns?"

His unexpected inquiry almost made her stumble. Had that truly been a question of concern or one of self-interest? He was so unpredictable. Threatening and cold one moment, solicitous the next. "Healing," she said, wary of this conversation. She noted the way he walked, the concentrated rhythm of his breathing. "Your ribs?"

He gave another one of those annoying, indifferent shrugs. "Hurting but I'll live. I've dealt with worse."

Of that, she had no doubt, though something in his tone made her glance at him twice, a jagged splinter of emotion that spoke of more than just physical pain.

He snagged her hand in his and held on, even as she tried to pull free. He tightened his hold. "Half the caravan is watching us. Act as if you at least like me."

"But I don't like you, and I'm not the gifted liar you seem to be."

"Is that so? Tell that to the Empire, Flower of Spring."

His mouth twitched at one corner at her wordless growl, even as she allowed her fingers to relax in his palm and cursed his name under her breath.

They reached the stream without further argument, and Azarion let go when Gilene yanked her hand out of his clasp hard enough to nearly lose her balance and fall into the water. She refused the steadying hand he offered and hugged her folded clothing even closer. Water rilled over the tops of her shoes, soaking through the leather to chill her feet. Getting clean trumped the desire to stay warm, but this would be unpleasant bathing at best.

She scowled at Azarion, who eased down on a flat swath of

stone at the stream's edge. Unlike her, he looked clean and re-freshed, his hair thick and soft where it grazed his shoulders. A burnished glow sheened the brown skin of his face and arms. Even the places where bruises and healing cuts mottled his flesh didn't detract from his looks. Unbothered by the damp stream spray, he turned his face up to the sun, eyes slitted nearly closed against the golden light spilling through the clouds.

If she didn't despise him so much, she might appreciate his beauty.

He slanted her a look. "Are you going to bathe or just stand there all day staring at me?"

If she didn't need the soap, she'd throw it at him. "Turn your back. I'll not have you watching me bathe."

"You possess nothing I haven't already seen a hundred times," he said. "And you may need my help."

"I need you to free me so I can return to Beroe."

He stood again and approached. "So you've said. Often." He tapped his left shoulder. "Lean on me. I'll help you remove your tunic."

As much as she hated to admit it, she did need his help. After three days in a bed, her legs were unsteady, and she tired quickly. The short walk to the stream had drained what energy she still had from earlier, and the clothes she held felt more like an armful of rocks than skirts and a tunic. Azarion relieved her of her burden, letting her keep the soap, and put her clean garb on the rock he'd abandoned.

"Raise your arms," he instructed. "I'll ease the tunic over your head." She followed his command, her back protesting the move-ment, the place where her magic had marked stretching tight the higher she lifted her arms. But there was no pain, just the stretch-ing. Halani's poultices had worked a magic of their own.

She put aside her crumbling modesty upon noting Azarion's lack of interest in her naked body. Instead, his gaze locked with hers. "You may be healing," he said. "And I may be injured, but I can still run you to ground and bring you back if you try to escape. And I will tie you to me if necessary."

Cold and nakedness forgotten, Gilene worked up a froth of saliva and prepared to spit in her opponent's face.

"Do it, and I'll just spit back," he warned.

"So much for fooling others into thinking I like you," she snarled. "What will they think seeing me tethered to you?"

"That you're a faithless shrew deserving of a beating once I toss aside my pride and admit I caught you trying to return to your lover." He grabbed her hand and dropped the soap into her palm. "Take your soap and get to washing. We can't be here all day. Keep your shoes on. There might be sharp rocks in the water."

The temptation to reach down, grab a handful of those rocks, and pelt him with them was almost more than she could resist. Instead, she clambered through the calf-high water to sit partially submerged in the icy stream. Her teeth chattered hard enough to make her head hurt as she soaped her body and then her hair, giving both a thorough scrubbing. By the time she finished, her toes and hands were numb, and her breasts ached. There was nothing left of the soap.

She tried to stand on her own, only to find Azarion suddenly in the water with her, blessedly warm hands under her shoulders and knees to lift and carry her back to the sun-heated rock. He waited while she dried off, then helped her dress. She tried not to dwell on the soothing touch.

Her feet were still cold in their wet shoes, and her damp hair left a soggy trail down her back, but the rest of her was soon thawing out in the familiar layers of her clothing.

"Your burns look much better," Azarion observed. "They shouldn't scar like these others. Did you get these from the magic as well?"

She was reluctant to tell him any more about herself than he already knew. He had a talent for turning information to his benefit and against the person who gave it to him. "Yes." At least he showed no revulsion for her scars. Many who saw them did, as if she were somehow to blame for them. "Halani didn't ask me about my other scars. Did she say anything to you?"

Azarion shook his head. "Don't be surprised by that. These people are prudent with their curiosity. The less they ask about you, the less you'll ask about them."

As they walked back to the camp, he continued questioning her. "Do you feel well enough to leave the wagon and sleep outside?"

Even if she didn't, she'd follow his example and lie that she did. Halani and Asil had given up their home for a sick stranger. Gilene didn't know if they bedded down in other wagons with family or friends, or slept under the open sky, but it was time they got their home back. Her back and leg no longer hurt, and while she was tired from lingering illness, she didn't need to sleep in their bed.

"Halani and Asil have been more than kind, and I miss seeing the sky at night. Maybe I can beg a pallet and a blanket from them. It would be nice to sleep under the stars."

She frowned at the pleased expression that settled over his face. "Good. You can sleep outside with me. Hamod's given me a pallet and several blankets to serve us both." He cocked an eyebrow. "Trust me, the hospitality of these traders has been bought with the knife I used on that Kraelian tracker. Halani and Asil are good women, but don't make the mistake in thinking the same applies to the rest, especially Hamod. You'll be safer sleeping next to me, and as you're my wife, it's expected."

His reason was as maddening as his threats. "The evil I know versus the one I don't?"

He nodded. "Something like that."

The caravan leader met them at the edge of camp. The camp itself was alive and loud with people setting up for the evening, preparing supper, and admonishing the half dozen shrieking children who tumbled through the chaos, chasing the caravan dogs or each other. Hamod spoke to Gilene this time, though his gaze was no less penetrating than before. "My niece has taken good care of you, mistress?"

Gilene spotted Halani among the crowd, talking to a stout man cutting onions on a makeshift table under one of the oaks. "She has. You're fortunate to have her. She's a gifted healer. I thank you both for helping us."

Hamod gave a quick nod. "Your husband traded a good knife. It was a fair bargain." He tipped a quick nod to Azarion. "Our cook will make good use of the game you trapped today. We'll eat well tonight."

Gilene watched him leave before turning back to Azarion. "You're hunting for them?"

Azarion's gaze remained on Hamod's retreating back even as he answered. "I learned how to lay a trap when I was a child. It's a useful skill on the Stara Dragana and an appreciated one when taking shelter with others."

Gilene initially thought her captor was only good at fighting in the Pit. It was easy to forget that, like her, there was more to him than the life forced upon him by the whims of the Empire. The notion didn't endear him to her, but it did make her wonder what he had been like before his enslavement.

People noticed them standing at the camp's perimeter and quickly drew them into its circle. With Halani's and Asil's help, Gilene learned the names of everyone in the caravan, lamenting to herself she'd only remember half at best by the next morning. The temperature dropped as afternoon waned, and a woman brought her a shawl while another offered a pair of slippers to wear until hers dried. She protested Halani's insistence that she sit on a blanket set not far from one of the fires, only relenting when the woman handed her two half-woven baskets.

"Can you weave a basket?"

Gilene clutched the baskets as if they were bags of gold coins. "In my sleep if need be." It wasn't a boast. Like Azarion and his game trapping, she'd learned the art of basket weaving while barely free of her mother's lead strings. Her nimble fingers worked the strands of blackberry vines stripped of their thorns, and she sniffed appreciatively at the fragrant steam rising out of two cauldrons suspending over a fire nearby. Behind her, Asil sat and combed out the few tangles Gilene had gotten from her hair washing, before braiding the strands into a neat, simple plait.

Firelight illuminated the camp in flickering patches that chased shadows across the tree trunks. Gilene sat, facing away from the road toward the forest's interior. The ever-flitting light exposed for brief moments the hulking shape of something tucked farther back into the trees. She turned a little to address Asil over her shoulder. "Do you know what that is behind those trees?" She pointed in the direction of the unmoving silhouette.

Asil's fingers smoothed out her braid. "Hamod says it's a grave. I don't remember it from last year when we traveled this way. He and Halani have gone to take a look."

Gilene hadn't seen either of them leave, though when her gaze found Azarion, she noticed he stared into the wood's gloom in the burial mound's direction, his brow knitted into a faint frown.

Graves were meant to be left alone, not explored. After the terror of Midrigar, she planned to avoid any and all as much as possible.

She returned her attention to the basket, listening with half an ear as Asil rambled on about everything from who in the caravan had lost a tooth to what they all ate a week earlier. Still, Gilene couldn't help but cast glances toward the mound and a few more at Azarion, whose scrutiny was not so obvious now but no less intense.

When Hamod and Halani returned to the camp, Hamod wore a pleased expression and Halani a dour one. What had they discovered at the burial site of some local village leader?

Such questions were risky ones, and Gilene kept her curiosity to herself, noting that Azarion made no comment to Hamod either. She worked the baskets, finishing one and almost the other by the time the stout cook Marata called them all to supper.

They ate in a communal circle instead of separate family gatherings, enjoying bowls of stew made of the rabbit Azarion had snared and the wild onions and parsnips foraged by some of the caravan women and their children. Everyone drank cups of thick ale from a barrel perched on a platform at the back of one of the wagons or from water carried in buckets from the nearby stream.

Gilene sat beside Azarion, trying her best to act as if his nearness and casual touches on her knee and shoulder were a natural thing between them. She didn't talk to him, listening instead to the easy banter he exchanged with the other men and the occasional laughter that spilled from his lips at someone else's ribald joke.

Across the fire, Halani sat with Asil and stirred the contents of her bowl with little enthusiasm. Her features only lightened when, after supper, someone called for a story.

"Tell us a story, Halani!" one man yelled from his perch on the steps of his wagon.

Another joined him. "Yes! Tell the tale of how Kansi Yuv slew the last draga and gave it to the emperor!"

Halani, who was putting away the recently washed bowls in a chest by one of the wagons, straightened with a groan. "I've told that story a hundred times! Wouldn't you rather hear about the sea maidens of Latchep? Or how Soriya caught lightning in her basket and gave it to men to turn into fire?"

A chorus of "No!" sounded through the camp, followed by a single voice that yelled, "The draga! We want the draga!" It was taken up by the others, who made it a chant until Halani plopped down on a fallen log that had been dragged near the fire as seating.

"Very well," she said. She smoothed her skirts over her knees and leaned forward. Azarion's huff of smothered laughter teased Gilene's ear as the crowd mimicked Halani's actions. "Golnar was the last great draga that besieged the lands of the Empire, stealing cattle and treasure alike. He burned villages with the fires that spewed from his nostrils, and his wings were so large that, in flight, they blotted out the sun."

The audience caught their breaths when Halani paused. Gilene did the same, despite knowing the tale.

"Many had tried to kill Golnar," Halani continued. "But the draga was old and wise and far too clever. If he didn't kill them, he used his sorcery to escape, back to his hidden cave with its treasures greater than all the wealth of the world." She raised her arms and spread them wide to encompass an imaginary world before her.

"But one man understood that for all a draga's many strengths, it had one weakness: a lust for treasure. The great hero Kansi Yuv asked the emperor to have a statue made. That of a beautiful woman cast in gold."

Several in the crowd chimed in then. "The Sun Maiden."

Halani scowled. "Who's supposed to be telling this story?" The group settled down once more, and the storyteller resumed her tale.

"Kansi Yuv planned to use the statue to lure Golnar into a trap and kill him, turning his prize over to the emperor for honor and glory." Whistles and hoots from the enraptured audience punctuated her words.

"He and his men hid ballistae loaded with spears in a ravine too narrow for a draga to swoop in and carry off its prize. At the bottom, they placed the gold-covered statue."

"The Sun Maiden!" one child shouted.

Halani nodded. "Given such a name because her gold shone like the sun.

"Kansi Yuv and his men waited for four days in the ravine. Finally, a great shadow passed over them." Halani stood and spread her arms, tilting right to left in imitation of soaring wings. "And when they looked up, they saw the draga." She wove in and out of the crowd, her mock flight captivating her audience as if she truly flew above them. "Golnar landed on the edge of the ravine and stared down at the Sun Maiden, suspicious." Halani halted abruptly. "Remember, what is the draga?"

Several voices tossed out an answer.

"Smart!"

"Clever!"

"Wise!"

Halani snapped her fingers for emphasis. "Exactly. Golnar

knew this was strange, likely a trap. Still, he lingered and watched. Why?"

Gilene answered. "Because dragas are greedy."

Asil joined her. "And lust for treasure."

Halani nodded. "And the draga couldn't resist the Sun Maiden. Instead of flying away to safety, he folded his wings and climbed down into the ravine. Kansi Yuv readied the ballistae. Golnar was enormous, with a mouth full of sharp teeth that could snap an ox in half with one bite!" The crowd gasped. "His eyes were as red as the rubies in the Sun Maiden's hair."

She stalked through the crowd. "No one made a sound as the draga crept toward the Sun Maiden, his great feet making the earth shake beneath them. He stretched out his claws to snatch up the Maiden and flee. Do you know what happened next?"

One of the children leapt from his father's lap, waving a toy sword in his fist. "Kansi Yuv shot the draga!"

"Yes! The great spear cleaved the draga's breast to pierce his heart. Golnar roared, and fire shot from his mouth. He tried to spread his wings and fly, but there was no room. He clawed at the spear in his chest. But the point had gone deep, too deep. He fell to the ground, dead, still reaching for the Sun Maiden."

Gilene blew out the breath she'd been holding. She spared a quick glance for Azarion. Unlike the others, he didn't look at all entranced but bleak instead. She could puzzle for days over what thoughts lay behind those enigmatic green eyes and never learn the most inconsequential thing about him. She turned her focus back to Halani.

"Kansi Yuv and his men waited, making certain the draga was dead before they ventured from their hiding places. When they knew for sure the monster no longer lived, they used ropes and pulleys, axes and swords to butcher the corpse and heave it out of the ravine for transport to the capital, a magnificent gift for the emperor and an end to that which had terrorized the countryside for so long."

Enthusiastic applause and whistles filled the air when she ended the story. "Another, another!" the crowd chanted, clapping their hands even harder.

"Not tonight." Halani remained unmoved by their disappointed cries. "Besides, there's always tomorrow night and another story." She glanced at Hamod, who stepped into the firelight.

"It's late. We've a long day of travel tomorrow. See to your chores and go to bed." No one argued with the leader's commands, and soon the group dispersed, filing away to their wagons or the sleeping pallets laid out on the ground beneath the trees.

Gilene left Azarion to seek out Halani. "You're a born story-teller, though I've always found the tale of 'The Draga and the Sun Maiden' tragic in a way."

Halani's pretty face looked haggard, as if the zest with which she told her tale had drained her. "I hate that story," she said in a flat voice. "But it's popular with everyone. Sometimes when times are lean and trade is sparse for the free traders, we'll travel to a town, and I'll earn supper for us by telling stories to the crowds in the pubs or in the town squares if the weather is fine. 'The Draga and the Sun Maiden' always brings the most coin and the better suppers."

"You're a bard then."

The other woman shook her head. "I play no instrument, and I'm terrible at verse."

"Your instrument is your voice," Gilene argued. "You had those people enthralled, though they know the story by heart."

Halani's eyes took on the melancholy shadow Gilene had noted when they first spoke. "Thank you." Her gaze shifted to a spot past

Gilene's shoulder, and her mouth tightened. "My uncle summons me. You're welcome to stay in the wagon again tonight."

Gilene glanced back and found Hamod watching them from a short distance. She turned to Halani. "I've kept you out of your shelter long enough. Thanks to your poultice, I'm much better and can sleep outside with . . . Valdan."

Distracted, Halani gave her a quick bow. "Good night then," she said before striding toward her uncle.

Gilene called after her. "Good night."

She found Azarion by a pallet under one of the big oaks. Made of layers of blankets and furs, the makeshift bed looked both comfortable and warm and big enough for them to sleep without fighting for the covers. All very enticing except for the fact that she'd have to share it with her captor.

Azarion took off his shoes and slid gingerly between the layers of bedding, fully clothed. He stretched out on his back, one arm crooked behind him so that his head rested in his palm and acted as a pillow. He watched Gilene, who stood at the foot of their bed.

"Your ribs don't trouble you now?" Just days earlier, he'd been unable to sleep lying down, the pain in his ribs too sharp to stay in such a position. Cracked ribs took weeks to heal, yet he lay there, looking peaceful and pain-free.

"Don't sound so disappointed," he said, and his eyes narrowed with a silent amusement that made her back snap straight. "They still ache, but Halani used a salve for bruising, and it's taken much of the pain away."

Gilene looked to where Halani stood talking with her uncle and three others. They spoke too softly for anyone beyond their immediate circle to hear, but whatever was said elicited argument from Halani and excitement from Hamod and the others.

The trader woman possessed a gift or two worthy of note: that of storytelling and of healing. The second was remarkable in its effectiveness, and Gilene suspected there was more to her poultices and salves than just a skilled hand with herbs and beeswax.

"You can't stand there all night, wife. Come to bed." Azarion's teasing interrupted her musings, and Gilene growled at him.

"Don't call me that," she said.

"Gilene then."

"That either." She sat down on her side of the blankets and pulled off her borrowed slippers, wondering whether anyone would question things if Valdan was found dead of suffocation the next morning. Such a plan was doomed to fail as she didn't think she could summon enough false tears to convince even the most sympathetic soul she was a grieving widow.

Like him, she slid under the blankets fully clothed, trying not to sigh her pleasure that the heat generated by Azarion's big body already warmed the space between the covers. She lay on her side, back to him, and pulled the blankets up to her jaw.

"Did you like Halani's tale of Kansi Yuv and the draga?" he asked.

Gilene flipped to her other side so she might face him. "I liked her telling of it, though I think the ending sad." Why was she even carrying on this conversation with him?

Tiny lines fanned at the corners of his eyes, as if he heard her thoughts and found them funny. "The dragas, they say, were once many, and only became destructive when the Empire hunted them for trophies and glory. The Sun Maiden's draga was the last of its kind."

That was the element of the story she found tragic. "It must have been something to behold when it lived."

"It's still something to behold in death. Golnar's bones hang as decoration in the empress's chambers. They circle the entire room at least twice."

She gasped. He'd seen the actual draga's bones? Part of her only half believed in the story. No one she knew had ever seen one draga bone, much less an entire draga skeleton. They seemed more myth to her than history—until now. That made the story even sadder.

The dying flames from the nearby fire cast shadows that hollowed out the spaces under Azarion's cheekbones and turned his bright gaze dark. "You told Halani you'd sleep with me?"

"Aye, though she offered her wagon to me for another night."

"If you try to escape . . ."

Whatever faint truce existed between them for that transient moment died with Azarion's implied warning. Gilene bared her teeth at him. "If I promise not to repeat several times a day how much I loathe you, can you do the same and stop threatening me? I'm aware I'm a mere woman and you are the great warrior who can catch me at any time."

He didn't mock her, and his expression turned intense. "I will return you to Beroe when I no longer need you, *Agacin*," he said in an oddly fervent voice.

Her heart leapt at his words, yearning to believe him yet not daring to. His tone brought forth a vague recollection. She had asked him a question in the forest adjacent to Midrigar, and he had answered with the same fervency.

*What if I had fallen or couldn't keep up?*

*I would have carried you.*

Had that exchange been real or a figment of fevered delirium? Her heart wanted to believe the first, believe that there was more to this man than threats, and violence, and relentless resolve. Her mind shouted down her heart, and she frowned. "Why should I trust you when you've lied so often?"

Azarion stretched out his hand as if to touch her, stopping when she drew back. "Because in this, I'm not lying."

His declaration had no more substance than a puff of smoke from the nearby fire. And even if it did, there were ways of interpreting it that made the hairs on her arms rise in warning. "Then the question remains," she said. "When you no longer need me, will you return me to my people dead? Or alive?"

# CHAPTER SIX

They remained with the free traders until the wagons rolled up to the market square of Wellspring Holt. A thriving town populated by merchant farmers who dealt mostly in produce and livestock, it welcomed the caravan with its stock of unique goods obtained from the hinterland garrisons where free traders met and traded with each other in spices and dyes, wool and silk thread, copper jewelry and painted pottery. All of it was paid for via barter or the exchange of silver from the Savatar silver mines protected behind the legendary Fire Veil.

They had arrived during the height of the weekly market day, and people crowded the streets. Vendor stalls lined the main avenue and stretched into the side lanes radiating from the town square like the spokes of a wheel. Judging by the numerous shouted greetings and the large group of townspeople surrounding the wagons, Hamod and his folk were popular in Wellspring Holt.

Azarion walked next to one of the slow-rolling wagons, Gilene beside him. He held her hand, and to any who glanced their way, the two seemed like nothing more than an affectionate couple. None could see her fingers curled like a fist in his palm or that her nails carved half-moons into the skin there.

"You may as well give up," he said close to her ear. "I'm not letting you walk freely. Not in this crowd." She hissed at him and carved deeper.

He'd be a fool to take his hand off her; she would bolt the second he did. When she wasn't throwing glares that threatened to flay him, her eyes traveled over the crowd, pausing to stare at the various gates leading into and out of the town, the small alleyways that disappeared into the cluster of buildings away from the teeming town square. She watched, noted, measured—hunting for the best avenue of escape, waiting for the right moment to take it.

He lengthened his stride, tugging her with him as they shouldered through the crowd to reach the lead wagon. Hamod rode as passenger, calling out greetings to various vendors as his driver, a woman named Ona, guided the oxen pulling the wagon through the street.

The caravan leader glanced down from his high perch, his stern features for once almost jolly. "Valdan, you're welcome to camp with us another night."

As much as Azarion wanted to say yes, it wasn't to be. The free traders had been generous with him and Gilene, offering food, shelter, and nursing. The knife and crossbow Hamod took in trade paid for Halani's care of Gilene but not much else. Azarion made certain his hunting skills and help with the wagons took care of the difference and bought both time to recover from injuries and distance from the Empire. They hadn't come across any more tracking parties while they traveled. Such might have been luck, Agna's blessing, or Hamod's own wish not to be noticed by scouts working on the Empire's behalf. He had his own secrets to keep, and that need for covertness played into Azarion's wish to remain hidden.

He shook his head. "Our thanks, but we're off to find lodgings with a cousin." The lie fell as smoothly from his lips as all the others before it. "Gilene and I are grateful for your help. May the knife stay sharp and bow shoot true."

Hamod and Asil each raised a hand in farewell. Gilene dragged her feet as Azarion guided her away from the wagon and into the crowd. "I want to tell Halani and Asil goodbye!"

A troop of Kraelian soldiers marched toward the square from one of the offshoot streets. Azarion hunched to make himself smaller and bowed his head. The beard he let grow over the past week obscured half his face, but he was a tall man, taller than most, and men of great height were always noticed by others.

"You said your goodbyes yesterday," he muttered, and yanked her into a doorway. The troop marched ever closer. Azarion crammed himself and Gilene into the shallow space, positioning them in such a way that his back was mostly to the street while Gilene faced it. He cupped her face between his hands, glimpsed the shocked expression that widened her eyes and made her lips part, and kissed her.

As kisses went, this was a shambles of one—nothing more than the pressing of lips back against teeth. Azarion trapped Gilene in the unyielding cage of his arms and watched the soldiers from the corner of one slitted eye. Except for a few amused snorts, they ignored the passionately entwined pair in the doorway and continued their way through the square toward the main gate.

The moment they were out of sight, Azarion broke the kiss and dodged the slap Gilene attempted to deliver.

"I don't care that there are Kraelian troops prowling the streets. Never do that again," she said, the words almost garbled by the snarling fury in her voice. Had he still carried his knife, no doubt she would have tried to use it against him.

He kept a wary eye on her hands. "Woman, your value to me doesn't sit behind your lips or between your legs." Her fury lessened a fraction at his words. "We need to get out of Wellspring Holt with two horses and a day's worth of supplies. Horses without army brands on their hindquarters. There's bound to be a nearby stable with the like for the taking."

Gilene's gaze lit with another fire, one of calculation. "Take one horse and go your way. Whether or not the Empire gets you back is of no concern to me. You'll reach the Stara Dragana a lot faster if you go alone."

He shook his head, amusement blending with his exasperation. "You're valuable enough to make it worth the effort and the delay, *Agacin*."

"If you're caught because you're too slow, all your plans with me at their center will be for nothing."

"We won't get caught."

Her upper lip lifted the tiniest fraction in a faint sneer. "*I* won't. *I'm* not the one running from the Empire."

With the threat of killing the caravan folk no longer an issue once they had parted ways, she was back to fighting him and doing so even harder now that her burns were healed and she felt better. Azarion scowled. "You think so? You, more than many, know of the Empire's mercies. Do you really think they'll believe their Gladius Prime decided to take a woman on a whim during his escape? They'll think you helped me. *I will tell them you helped me.*"

She paled at his words, the rebellion that flared in her eyes burning out. Her shoulders slumped, and she leaned back against the sliver of wall where it edged the closed door behind her back. "Let me go."

"Not yet."

With the most fragile of truces between them, they left the shelter of the doorway to merge once more with the milling crowd. Azarion kept a grip on Gilene's arm, though she offered no resistance to his touch this time. Her head was bowed, shoulders slumped. Hamod's caravan was nowhere to be seen, but it wasn't the traders Azarion searched for as he and Gilene navigated their way through a sea of people.

Every town the size of Wellspring Holt had a public stable yard—a place where visitors to the town could leave their horses for a few hours or a night while they visited or shopped or did business. The stable offered a variety of services at escalating prices, from a spot at a hitching post to a full grooming by a team of stableboys.

He spotted a group of a half dozen mounted men—scholars and monks instead of soldiers—and followed them as they rode through the town at a casual pace. Gilene remained silent, even when Azarion picked up their pace to keep up. He paused when the stable yard came into view around the corner of a bustling tavern.

Horses crowded the space, tied to hitches or placed in stalls, depending on their owners' means. Grooms wove in and out of the lines of their equine charges, some hauling water, others hay or feed, and still others carrying saddles and tack or grooming tools.

From his vantage point, Azarion had a clear view of several of the animals, many of them lacking the brand that marked them as army ponies. There were a number to choose from, but his gaze settled on two that looked sturdy and quick.

He pulled the silent Gilene along with him, circling the perimeter of the yard in a meandering path, pretending to find the contents of some of the vendor stalls nearby interesting enough to stop and take a look. Always his eyes shifted back to the yard, noting the entrance in one corner, the two exits at opposite ends, and the door by which the grooms came and went to the stable and where the three guards who were paid to watch that no one made off with the horseflesh had set up their sentry.

Stealing two horses in broad daylight guaranteed a hanging from the gallows or a spearhead through the belly. Doing so at night was no less dangerous but had a marginally better chance of success. He'd wait until then, and in the meantime scout the various stalls in the quieter part of the town, far away from the brothel alleys where the Kraelian troops were most likely to quarter and while away an afternoon. He didn't have the skills of a pickpocket, but he was quick enough to snatch bits of food from hawkers busy with other customers.

The bustling crowds worked in his favor, both to hide him in their midst and to provide cover while he pilfered pieces of fruit, a small sack of oats enough for a road breakfast, and a wedge of cheese wrapped in cloth. He slipped the fruit into a small satchel he stole from the back of a cheesemonger's stall and tucked the oats and cheese wedge into the pockets of Gilene's apron. Her disapproval hung about her like a storm cloud, though she didn't resist when he filled her pockets with the items.

They were tracking back toward the stable yard when a warning shout went up next to them. A wagon, overloaded and overbalanced with crates full of grain sacks, tipped to one side with an agonized creak, falling toward the street. People screamed, and the throng as a whole surged backward as those nearest the wagon tried to flee and avoid being crushed. Some lost their balance and fell underfoot to be trampled by others. In the pushing, shoving mayhem, Azarion lost his grip on Gilene.

The crowd instantly swallowed her up, obscuring her in the flail of arms and elbows and the choking haze of grain dust as the sacks from the fallen wagon burst open. Even knowing she wouldn't answer and likely couldn't hear above the noise, Azarion still roared her name.

"Gilene!"

He battered his way through the mob, tossing anyone in his path aside like chaff in his bid to reach the spot where he last saw her. She was a tall woman but slight. If she didn't keep her feet and stay upright, she was dead. He searched for the dark crown of her hair, ubiquitous among so many others with hair as dark as hers.

A flicker of motion caught his eye, and he spotted her as she broke free of the crowd to pause at its edge and look right, then left. She glanced over her shoulder and saw him staring at her. Her eyes widened before she lifted her skirts to her knees and dashed toward the town's interior, fleet as a hunted deer and just as desperate.

The years spent fighting in the Pit served him well. Brute force freed him from the prison of too many people packed together in one place, their frenzied scrabbling for grain turning them into a multi-armed entity with clutching fingers. Unlike Gilene, he didn't stop once he got free but hurtled after her down the street. She was nowhere in sight. That didn't slow him.

His newly healed ribs twinged a warning at him with every breath, but still he ran, dodging the flow of more townsfolk who streamed toward the mob, curious as to what aroused it.

He checked under parked carts, sought out shadowed doorways, even barreled through two taverns and dodged vegetables thrown by an outraged scullery wench as he tore through the tavern's kitchen and out the back door.

A beggar, crouched at a street corner, urinated on himself in terror when Azarion stopped and loomed over him. "Have you seen a woman . . ." He described Gilene, emphasizing her height as well as the fading bruise on her cheek. Those, more than the nondescript clothes she wore or her facial features, would be things people remembered about her. At least he didn't have the challenge of her illusion. Like her fire, that magic had yet to return. While Azarion could see through her conjuring, others couldn't.

The beggar pointed with a shaking finger down the length of an alley garlanded in clotheslines hung with laundry, and Azarion sprinted down the dim close, dodging wet garments and blankets that flapped and showered water droplets onto the street. He spotted movement ahead—the whip motion of a clothesline pulled or dragged as someone passed under its hangings—and picked up his pace. The snap of a skirt rounding a corner sent him running down a wider street. A dead end and, at its farthest reach, his quarry.

Her back was to him for the moment, and she was surrounded on three sides by the leaning heights of mud-brick buildings. She whirled to run back the way she came, skidding to a halt when she saw him.

Azarion slowed to a walk. "It's done, Gilene. No more running."

Her hands opened, and she raised her arms, palms facing him. Her eyes closed as she turned her attention inward.

Azarion paused, poised on the balls of his feet to flee if she managed to call up any of her drained magic and summon fire. He had no doubt that, if she succeeded, she would do her best to roast him like a butchered pig.

Tears spilled down her cheeks in silvery rivulets as she concentrated to no avail. Nothing so much as a candle flame lit her fingers, and she soon gave up, her arms dropping to her sides. She retreated from him until her back hit the wall that trapped her in the alley. She refused to look at him when he stood in front of her. "You have no right to take me," she said in a flat voice.

"No, I don't," he replied. "But I need you."

"My village needs me, and they're more important than you are."

Right or wrong, he had no intention of arguing with her any longer. This wasn't a good place to be, for either of them. Azarion swooped in, lifted her rigid body in his arms, and jogged away from the entrapping alley. He had no comfort to offer, only the repeated assurance—which she didn't believe—that he'd return her to her people whole and hearty when he no longer needed her.

She murmured something against his chest. He leaned in closer. "What did you say?"

Her voice was quiet, warbling, but no less vitriolic for its softness. "I curse you. May you suffer, and strive, and never succeed."

A faint shiver danced along his arms. As curses went, this one lacked the drama of torture and epic death. But what it lacked in extravagance, it more than made up for in longevity and thoroughness.

His sigh ghosted the top of her head. "Best hope that doesn't take, *Agacin*, or I'll never be able to send you home."

They said no more to each other until Azarion found an alcove created by the intersection of two garden walls not far from the stable yard and a good distance from the teeming market. A fountain burbled nearby, and he drank its water from cupped hands. Gilene did the same, her throat working hard as she sipped down several handfuls of water.

She followed him to the shaded alcove and sat, too tired to fight him. For now. She tilted her head back until it touched the wall, and closed her eyes. Her hands, still wet from the fountain, rested easy in her lap. No hint of the bleak, frightened woman remained. In that quiet moment, Azarion could almost convince himself she was his companion for the day, enjoying the weather and his company.

It was a good dream, albeit a fleeting one. He had just chased her through half of Wellspring Holt and, had her magic worked, would have been burned to a cinder for his trouble. He didn't have much hope that the truce between them now might last long enough to at least get out of the town.

His gaze skimmed her, noting the graceful length of her neck, the way her collarbones created a straight ridge under her skin, curving at their ends to highlight the hollow of her throat. He'd seen her naked at her bath, goosefleshed from the cold, her long legs bent so close to her torso, she could have pressed her cheek to her knee.

He hadn't leered at her. It was true he'd seen and embraced many women, some prostitutes, but mostly Kraelian noblewomen who lusted for a gladiator fresh from the Pit and covered in blood. Gilene didn't stand out among them, except for her height and the many scars she bore from her magic. Were she something other than an *agacin*, he might have overlooked her. Those scars puzzled him mightily, though it was obvious to him she expected revulsion instead of puzzlement.

Now, with the sunlight bathing her upturned features and her closed eyelids hiding the hatred in her expression every time she looked at him, she was almost pretty. Driven by a strange combination of bitterness and devotion, she was as intent on returning to Beroe as he was to the Sky Below. It was unfortunate their goals conflicted and the places they most desired to reach lay in opposite directions.

She shifted a leg to get in a more comfortable position, and Azarion heard a soft plopping sound before the wedge of cheese he'd stolen earlier fell out of her pocket. Surprised and delighted that, despite the chase, she still carried it and hopefully the small stash of oats, he rescued the cheese from the dirt and tucked it back into place. He'd eaten well, as had Gilene, before they bade Hamod and his folk farewell. Eating again would have to wait until nightfall, when they were horsed and on the road far from Wellspring Holt.

"We'll eat tonight on horseback," he said. "The stable yard is housing two horses that will serve our purpose and put a few leagues between us and the town before anyone knows they're gone."

Gilene turned her head a fraction, her gaze merciless in its judgment. "You lie. You steal. Have you no guilt over the things you've taken? Someone's horse. Someone's goods. Someone's daughter or sister?"

She was relentless in her bid to shame him. He sloughed it off. Survival had no use for shame. "Ten years ago my cousin stole my birthright and my freedom by selling me to the Empire. Trust me, I understand the pain of having something valuable taken from you by someone else."

Curiosity brightened her gaze. She sat up straighter and faced him more fully. "You survived the Pit for ten years. You must be very good at slaughter."

"Very good." It wasn't a boast. He'd spilled enough blood in the arena to float a ship.

A line appeared between her eyebrows as a thought occurred to her. "Why is it I've only seen you the past three years during the choosing of the women?"

Her question was a fair one, and he had nothing to hide in that matter. "I had no interest in taking part until then." And sometimes not even the opportunity. The empress had favored him for a long time, delighting in degrading him, whether by means of combat, rape, or false hope. So while there had been nothing he could do to help the Flowers of Spring or change the fate that awaited them, he sympathized with their plight. The Empire spared no one, man or woman.

Gilene's question brought him back to the present. "What changed your mind?"

"You did." He allowed himself a small smile when her eyebrows rose. "I saw you the first time when the guards were taking me to Herself. At first I thought your illusion a trick of the light or maybe a leftover from a blow to the head when I fought a bout in the Pit. I thought nothing of it, but I remembered and made sure I watched the Flowers arrive the next year. Tricks of the light aren't that predictable. Nor are the visions caused by head wounds. Hanimus gave me a boon the second and third year, allowing me to watch the immolation. I couldn't believe it at first—an *agacin* wielding fire right under the Empire's nose, and they, all blind to your deception."

Her mouth curved down. "You began to plan."

He nodded. "And here we are." He had told her he still needed her to regain power in his clan but never explained the why or how of it. If she asked, he'd tell her, though she'd balk at his explanation. No one liked being used.

The streets around them were quiet. A few people traveled these more isolated avenues, though none seemed to notice the couple sheltering in the tucked-away alcove. Still, Azarion kept an eye on their surroundings, watching for Kraelian soldiers or any passerby with an overdeveloped curiosity and underdeveloped sense of survival.

Gilene continued with her questions. "Why do your people worship fire witches?"

"They aren't worshipped, but they are esteemed. *Agacins* are the spirit of Agna made flesh. She's the goddess we worship, the holiest of all the gods worshipped by the Savatar."

"I don't know this Agna, and I don't worship her."

He shrugged. "It doesn't matter. You're one of her handmaidens. She's chosen to bless you with the gift of fire."

She gave a derisive snort. "Is that what you call it? A blessing? She can keep her blessings."

Azarion tensed. Gilene's irreverent ingratitude bordered on blasphemy. He hoped Agna wasn't listening to one of her priestesses decry her gift.

The biting tone of her replies emphasized the resentment she carried for her role as a Flower of Spring. He'd learned quickly enough during their brief negotiations that she loathed the role she played every year. Who wouldn't? Yet still she did it, and even now had done her best to escape him so she might return to Beroe and do it all over again in a year's time. "Why do you shoulder this burden for Beroe?"

Her gaze took on a farseeing aspect, as if she no longer saw him but instead some memory. "Because I have to. It became my duty once the witch before me became too crippled to attend the Rites. Sometimes you do the thing you hate so others don't have to, whether it's from love, guilt, or blackmail." She paused to level a condemning stare on him. "No other woman in Beroe is safe from fire. It would be wrong and cowardly of me to let them burn when I can go in their place and survive. It doesn't mean I have to like it just because I'm willing to accept it."

Her actions made more sense now. He admired her commitment as well as her bravery. What she subjected herself to was a horror few would want to suffer once much less several times. "Does your family know how you feel? Beroe itself?"

Her sardonic smile lacked any humor. "Of course they know,

and it doesn't matter. I'm not the first fire witch born in Beroe, and I won't be the last. The village fathers protect Beroe." Her pinched features drew even tighter. "By whatever means they must."

A terrible legacy, an ominous hint. "The witch who came before you, she taught you how to summon fire and create illusion?"

Gilene rubbed a hand across her eyes. "Yes, just as I'll teach the girl who will come after me." Her eyes focused more sharply on him once more. "Do you understand why I have to go home? If I'm not in Beroe by next spring, the slavers will take another woman to burn in the Rites, and she will die. The village elders will punish my family if I don't return and give the Empire my sister or one of my nieces."

His captive was a prisoner of her birthplace, bound by the chains of familial devotion and threat. He almost regretted taking her. Almost. "I will return you to Beroe before that happens."

She slapped her thighs and growled her frustration. "My gods, are you not hearing what I'm telling you? I can't go with you to the Stara Dragana!"

"Keep your voice down." She glared but stayed quiet. "I heard you, and I understand why you need to go back, but it doesn't change the fact you have to come with me." He ignored her angry snort. "My father is a clan chief," he said. "An *ataman*. As the *ataman*'s only son, his leadership would pass to me when he died. When he became ill, my cousin had some of his friends attack me, beat me until I passed out, and sell me to Kraelian slavers. All so he wouldn't have to challenge me for the chieftainship if my father didn't survive. I intend to reclaim my birthright, and to do so I will need an *agacin* by my side. The Savatar recognize succession through blood tanistry—worthiness of a successor based on combat. If my cousin weren't the coward he is, he would have challenged me to combat for the right to rule the clan. With me gone, he needed only the approval of the clan *atamans* and the *agacins* to become an *ataman* himself. However, if I return with an *agacin* who supports my claim to take back the chieftainship, they will be forced to allow me to challenge my cousin, because it comes with Agna's blessing. I can demand the right of combat to retake the chieftainship."

She hunched away from him and turned her head so she wouldn't have to look at him. "I want no part of this struggle between you and your relative."

He coaxed her back to him with a finger on her chin. "Help me regain my place as *ataman*, and I swear on the spirits of all my ancestors I will return you to Beroe before the slavers arrive next spring."

Disbelief was stamped on every part of her body and face. "And why would you keep your word once you've gained your prize?"

"Because, despite what you might think, I have honor."

Acerbic laughter greeted that statement. It died as quickly as it erupted. "Do I truly have a choice?"

"If you want to see Beroe again? No."

She shook her head. "Honesty for once. There's hope for you yet."

He swallowed back a cheer at the thread of agreement in her voice. "Will you help me?"

"As I really have no choice, then yes."

"Do I have your word you won't try to escape again?"

"Absolutely not."

He hadn't expected a promise, so her reply didn't surprise him. "Then we know where we stand with each other." He settled back against the wall, feeling the hard thumping of his heart calm a little. "You're a brave woman," he said. "A bitter one, but brave."

She didn't acknowledge his backhanded compliment. "What will you do to your cousin when you see him again?"

Ten years of smothered rage threatened to boil up inside Azarion. He pushed it down, back to the cold, dead place that had kept him alive for so long. "Kill him and mount his head on a pike outside my tent."

He cocked an eyebrow when she tilted her head and gave a shrug of her own. "That seems only fair."

This time, Azarion didn't bother hiding his grin. "You may not look like a Savatar woman, *Agacin*, but sometimes you think like one."

# CHAPTER SEVEN

Stealing horses was easier than Gilene imagined. Either Azarion was as good a horse thief as he was a gladiator, or the drunken sentries and grooms paid to watch the stable yard and take care of the animals had imbibed enough wine and ale to drown an army. It might have been both, as she soon rode away from Wellspring Holt on a stolen chestnut mare, heading toward an unknown future.

Azarion rode beside her on a bay mare with white fetlocks. While Gilene had to use all her concentration to stay on her horse's back and not fall off, he rode with ease. The Savatar were known throughout the world as excellent horsemen, and obviously ten years fighting in the Pit weren't enough to make him forget how to ride.

A pouch containing the foods he'd stolen earlier at the market as well as rations and leftovers uneaten by the drunken stable hands was tied across the back of his saddle, and he was armed with a crossbow, a quiver of arrows, and two knives—courtesy of one of the sentries, who didn't see Azarion creeping stealthily up on him until it was too late.

Gilene didn't ask whether the sentry was dead or merely knocked unconscious, and Azarion didn't offer an assurance either way.

They rode east and north through the night and by dawn had passed out of the heavily forested territories belonging to Krael and into more open terrain where the trees grew in solitary majesty or clumped together in small clusters. Fields of waist-high grasses brushed the horses' bellies as they galloped toward the distant silhouettes of the Gamir Mountains.

Azarion pointed to a set of hillocks that marched east under a rising sun. "We'll stop there and take shelter in one of the barrows to rest the horses and sleep through the day."

"Another grave?" she grumbled. "What is this desire of yours to sleep among the dead?" She covered her mouth to stifle a yawn. She was saddlesore and irritable, and unprepared to spend hours in a tomb, no matter how much she might want to get warm and fall asleep.

"One of those barrows will be big enough to house even the horses. We'll be warm, out of the wind, and with a roof over our heads." He nodded toward the sun. "That's a blood dawn rising. We'll be in for storms later and can wait them out until nightfall."

His reasoning was sound enough. Still, she remembered a similar argument before they stepped through the shattered gate and into Midrigar. What had lurked there made standing in the middle of a savage gale seem safe.

Her expression must have revealed some of her thoughts, because Azarion guided his horse closer to hers. "These are old barrows, scoured clean of spirits and anything of worldly wealth. And they were built to honor the dead, not imprison them. Midrigar is an abomination. Barrows are simply resting places—mostly for the dead, sometimes for the living."

"Barrows sometimes house wights," she argued.

"True. Those ahead don't. Just the occasional mouse or a colony of bats if grave robbers cut their entry hole into the roof."

Her hands felt frozen to the reins, and the two shawls Halani had given her before they parted ways did little to ward off the cold. She was tired and far from home, with a stranger who kept her for purposes of which she wanted no part. They had escaped a demon thing in a cursed city and found solace with free traders who dealt in questionable goods. The idea of sleeping the day away in a barrow next to the bones of the departed didn't seem all that strange at the moment. She just hoped her fear of a lurking wight didn't come to fruition.

Azarion took her silence for agreement and tugged on her mount's bridle to get her moving again. They reached a gradual rise just as the sun's lower edge cleared the horizon to spill morning light across a flat landscape that purled and swayed in a tide of tall, pale-plumed grass. She gasped at the sight. "Have we reached the Stara Dragana?"

Azarion spared her a glance, his attention mostly on the barrows before them. "Within its western borders. This part of it belongs to the Nunari, vassals of the Empire. The city of Uzatsii sits about a league from here."

The grasses parted on either side of a shepherd's road that led to three hills clad in a flowering carpet of sweet vernal. Made by the hands of men instead of the whimsy of nature, the middle hill was the largest barrow. A rectangular doorway built of stone was framed into one side. A stele, twice as tall as a man, stood sentry to its right, and as Gilene rode closer, she spotted pictograms carved into the stone. Arcane and enigmatic, they decorated the stele from top to base. She could only guess their meaning and prayed they weren't curses to warn away any who might wish to enter the grave mound.

Azarion halted his horse at the stele and motioned for Gilene to do the same. He dismounted for a closer look. Gilene waited, silent, until her curiosity got the best of her. "What does it say?"

He traced the carvings' outlines in the air with one finger. "It tells a story. This is the youngest of the three barrows, built for a Nunari chieftain named Gisrin and his family. According to these carvings, he was a great warrior who slew a thousand men and sired twenty-seven sons with five wives." His mouth curved in a smile at Gilene's snort. "Keeper of the fastest herds, blessed by Agna, the Great Mare."

Gilene shifted in the saddle. "That's all very impressive, but is he cursing anyone who enters his barrow?" She wanted out of the cold but didn't want to fight off a wight defending a grave just to find a little warmth.

Azarion nodded. "Aye. According to the stone, if we enter, we'll suffer baldness and sores, and our cocks will fall off." Amusement glittered in his eyes. "Not that the last should concern you."

A bubble of laughter rolled into her throat and threatened to escape. She disguised it with a cough, refusing to let her captor see how his commentary delighted her. They were adversaries working under an uneasy truce. Friends shared laughter. She and Azarion were not friends.

"Come," he said and gestured for her to dismount. "Lead your horse in behind mine. This grave mound is tall. The ceiling will be high enough for the horses to enter." He patted his mare's neck and gave Gilene a wry look. "Horses are herd animals with a strong sense of themselves as possible prey. If there's danger in the barrow, they'll know it long before we will."

In the end, her need for warmth overrode her fear of angry spirits. She nearly fell out of the saddle, stiff from hours of riding. She pushed away the helping hand Azarion offered. "Lead on," she said and took up her horse's reins.

The animals didn't balk as they passed through the barrow's tall entrance. Wide enough that she and her mare might have walked side by side across the threshold, the barrow doorway was edged with stacked stone and cut birch timbers mortared into solid earth. A shallow depression in the soil outside the entrance marked the place where a stone had once been wedged to seal off the entrance. Its remains spilled in a pile of broken rock stacked against the mound's base.

Gilene expected darkness thick enough to weave inside the grave and was stunned to discover a high-ceilinged chamber illuminated in gradually brightening shades of gray. The source of anemic light came from a hole near the top of the roof's vault, just big enough to allow a man in. Grave robbers had visited this tomb many times, breaking in from the top and from the door.

The clop of the horses' hooves echoed softly in the barrow as they walked toward the chamber's center. Gilene paused, and the mare paused with her as she peered into the shadows that clung to the curved walls and edged the packed earth steps that laddered toward the roof, stopping not far from its narrowest point and supported at regular intervals by a framework of more birch logs.

The lower step levels were a ruinous mess of broken clay pots, rotted blankets, and bits of riding tack. Among the detritus she saw bones of humans and animals. Some of the skeletons remained intact, half buried in yellow and red ocher. Beside them, a horse skull kept watch from large, empty eye sockets. Nearby, more skeletons were not so fortunate. In their search for valuables, looters had destroyed whatever careful placement relatives had arranged for their dead. Human skulls lay among the rib cages of sheep and the jawbones of dogs.

Gilene shivered and leaned against her mare. She wondered what the long-dead Gisrin might think of such desecration to his family's gravesite. She hoped wherever his spirit resided now, it had given up such worldly cares long ago. The barrow was a macabre place to shelter, but it lacked the suffocating malevolence that shrouded Midrigar. Here, the shadows were just shadows.

Azarion led his horse to one side of the barrow, kicking aside bones and pottery shards. "Bring your mare to stand with mine. They'll stay put, and they can graze outside tonight before we leave."

As they had few supplies, it didn't take long to settle in. Gilene carefully cleared away debris from the spot they'd chosen to sleep, whispering words of apology to any lingering ghost as she placed bones back on the lower step.

Azarion used the horse's thick blankets as pallets and set them side by side. He sighed at Gilene's dismayed expression. "I've had plenty of opportunity to lift your skirts, *Agacin*. You even raised them for me back in my cell." Her face heated at that reminder. "If I wanted to tup you, I would have done it by now. All I desire right now is rest and warmth. I know you do too. Sleeping together is the best way to do it."

The memory of Azarion's body heat curved along her back certainly swayed her. Despite her best effort not to fall asleep and to keep some distance between them as they shared a pallet in the traders' camp, she awakened in the mornings huddled under borrowed blankets and tucked against Azarion's chest and midriff, his arm heavy on her waist. He was a light sleeper and sensed the moment she woke, rolling away to slide out from under the covers and make his way to the communal fire one of the traders had started. She had been slower to follow, content for a short time to soak up the pleasant warmth and pretend she was indeed a wife and not a captive.

Their circumstances now were far more reduced, with only the horse blankets for bedding and her shawls to ward off the chill. The barrow's earthen walls kept out some of the cold and all of the wind, but a draft still sneaked into the entrance or whistled down from the hole in the roof. Azarion's assurances of his disinterest in her were both a comfort and, in an odd way, an insult.

Gilene chose not to think too long on the last and crawled across the makeshift pallet to lie on her side with her back to him. Her stomach growled. She was hungry but also tired, and willed away the gnawing at her belly.

Azarion curled around her, tucking her into the cove of his body. Gilene stifled the soft groan that danced across her lips at the feel of all that lovely heat, and kept her body stiff. Already her eyelids felt as if they were weighted with stones. The whuffles and snorts from the horses nearby soothed her like a lullaby, and her limbs loosened, sinking farther into the thick horse blanket.

Azarion's low voice revived her a little. "The sun will heat the barrow soon enough. I don't dare light a fire. Anyone will be able to see the smoke rise from the top for leagues."

She wrapped the edges of her shawls around her hands and tucked them under her chin. "Do you think the Empire would track you this far?"

He shrugged against her. "It depends on whether or not they think I'm worth the amount of bounty they've put on my head. The Empire might not send its soldiers after me this far into the steppe, but the Nunari won't hesitate to capture outlanders and sell them as slaves. It was to them my cousin sold me, and Uzatsii is where I was put on the auction block."

Her drowsiness evaporated. She rolled to face him. "If they catch us, they'll sell us both." The realization made her shudder. Her lot in life was a grim one, her fate determined the moment her magic manifested, but she had never suffered the degradation of slavery or the humiliation of the auction block.

His long lashes shadowed his eyes. "Or they'll keep you if one of their warriors takes a liking to you."

That made her shake even more, and Azarion's arm pressed a little harder on her waist as if to soothe her. She pictured the Stara Dragana outside the barrow, with its swaths of flat land carpeted in plumed grasses, and sparse clumps of stunted trees dotting the landscape as it purled out to the distant mountains in the east. "So much open space." She all but breathed the words. "And no place to hide."

"There are barrow towns like this one along the way, laid out in a line like a road. For the most part, people avoid the places of the dead, considering them sacred. We'll keep doing as we are now. Travel at night and shelter in a barrow during the day until we reach Savatar territory."

Her gaze went beyond the curve of his shoulder to the laddered walls with their many skeletons and grave goods. Bones upon bones, like chaff on a threshing floor. "Never did I imagine I'd rely so much on the dead for my safety." She rolled back to her original position, wondering at the vagaries of fate that had put her here in a grave next to a man both brutal and gentle, desperate yet unbroken.

His lack of reply to her comment meant he'd no rebuttal to offer or had fallen asleep. Gilene didn't turn to check, choosing instead to cover her head with her scarves and warm her ears. Azarion loomed large behind her, hot as a hearth fire. The thought of a merry flame made her miss her magic. It would return in time. It always did, this thing she called a curse and Azarion named a blessing.

She slept and dreamed, not of the Empire but of her sister standing beside her as they boiled long nettle in copper vats to extract the green dye Beroe sold to the Trade Guild for their merchants to barter with on the Golden Serpent or to ship out of Manoret. Ilada said something Gilene couldn't hear and laughed, waving her verdant-stained hands to emphasize her remark. Kraelian slavers suddenly appeared behind her to whisk her away in shackles. Gilene cried and clutched her sister's skirts, pulling and pulling but to no avail. She called out Ilada's name, and the girl turned, eyes wide but features calm.

"It's my fate to burn, Gilene," she said, and walked away with the slavers into a blinding, bloody sunset.

Gilene twitched awake with a strangled gasp. She blinked, bewildered by the blurry sight of horses and circular steps and bones. So many bones. Something lay heavy across her hip, and she glanced down to find a sun-browned hand flat against her abdomen. She tried to jerk away but was trapped by the pressure of that hand.

"Shh, *Agacin*. Be still. Be quiet. We don't know if anyone is outside."

Azarion. Ever present at her side. Relentless in his purpose. He was taking her farther and farther away from her village, farther and farther away from her ability to save Ilada and all the other women living in Beroe.

"I wish I were home," she whispered.

A shift of long limbs and she felt his face press against her head. "We're too far from your village to just set you on your horse and send you west. You'd be caught by the Nunari before you got half a league."

She sniffled. "You'll be the death of someone I love."

He tensed behind her, and the steel in his deep voice returned. "I've been the death of many people others have loved, *Agacin*. I can carry the burden of one more."

Gilene closed her eyes and willed back the tears, seeing once more the dream image of Ilada and her strangely tranquil features as the slavers led her away to burn as a Flower of Spring.

Whatever somnolence lingered when she had first opened her eyes burned to ash with the anger bubbling in her blood. She was in difficult straits now with only a slim hope based on a promise made by a man she didn't trust. Alone on the steppe, and she'd be in worse danger from multiple sources. For now, her best hope in returning to Beroe lay with her captor.

Neither of them spoke as they both abandoned their bed, he to leave the barrow and scout the immediate vicinity, she to tend to her body's demands. Her mare nickered a greeting as she passed, and Gilene paused long enough to stroke the necks of both horses. Fading sunlight pouring through the roof's hole gilded their hind-quarters, and nearby a puddle of rainwater had gathered in a shallow dip in the dirt floor, carved there by countless rainfalls.

Azarion had warned her they'd have rain during the day, and his prediction proved correct. She'd slept so deeply, she never heard the storm move in, though the air in the barrow smelled fresher than when they first entered.

She was laying out their meager food stores when Azarion returned. His handsome features were even grimmer than usual. "Campfires to the west of us. Likely a Nunari patrol or scouting party."

The hollow feeling of hunger swirling in her belly gave way to the hollow feeling of fear. "Are you certain?"

He shook his head at her offer of an apple. "Certain enough not to linger. Eat and pack. I'll lead the horses out to graze for a short time. I wanted to leave at twilight, but that camp smoke changes things. There's another barrow town not far from here. We ride hard and hide there."

She rose, appetite gone, despite his encouragement that she

fill her belly. "What if they're looking for us?" The food went back into the satchel, and she checked their sleeping spot to make sure nothing remained of their presence.

Azarion tossed the blankets over the horses' backs, cinched saddles, and tied headstalls while he spoke. "They probably are. The rain has muddied our tracks or washed them away altogether, which is a boon for us, but the Nunari are good trackers."

She followed him as he led the horses out of the barrow. Late-afternoon sunlight washed the steppe golden, and the wind was sharp and biting. Azarion pointed silently to the west, and she spotted smoke and the faint, far-off glow of fires.

"Are you sure we should wait for the horses to graze?" she asked, almost under her breath, fearful the wind might carry her words across the open landscape.

He tied the satchel she handed him to his saddle while the horses bent to graze on the silvery sagebrush growing amid the taller plumed grass. "We don't have much of a choice. They'll fight us the whole way if they're too hungry. I can tell by the way you ride, you aren't used to the saddle. A struggle between you and the mare? The mare will win. Let her eat. We can make up the time once we ride."

To the east, she saw nothing but more of the open steppe with its occasional stand of trees. Whatever barrow town they rode for now, she couldn't see it.

Azarion leaned over her shoulder and gestured to one of the larger clusters of woodland. "There, behind those trees, is the barrow town. Pray the Nunari don't track us there."

Gilene never prayed. "I thought you said most people avoid the gravesites."

He gave another of those shrugs she found so annoying. "These are men with purpose and motivation. They'll check the barrows."

She shivered. "We're targets in the open and prisoners in the barrows."

He nodded. "Aye, but they won't find us helpless." He patted the two knives tied to his belt and raised the crossbow he held. "Unfortunate that I can't kill them and take their horses. They would make fine gifts to the Savatar, who would be more willing to welcome us, but they'd slow us down."

"You mean there's a chance they won't welcome a long-lost son with smiles and open arms?"

The hint of a smile flitted across his mouth, though his eyes remained somber as he watched the campfires. "You've a sharp tongue."

Nerves and fear made her that way. "I'm surprised you haven't yet cut it out."

His expression turned severe. He gathered up the reins and coaxed the horses away from their feed with soft clicks of his teeth. "You're safe with me, *Agacin*."

She let him hoist her into the saddle, gritting her teeth at the ache in her protesting thighs. The reins felt heavy in her hands, her mare's gait unforgiving as they galloped toward the next barrow town. And farther from home with every hoofbeat.

# CHAPTER EIGHT

They traveled the night at a gallop, resting the horses with brief periods of steady trotting. The ground was a quagmire in spots, softened by the hard rain earlier in the day, and through these they picked their way at a slug's pace as they searched for drier ground. Azarion kept Gilene in his sights at all times. He'd seen the panicked look in her eyes as they packed their meager supplies and prepared to leave. That look harbored more than fear of the Nunari. She'd awakened from the throes of a dream that had her twitching in her sleep, crying, and calling out a name in anguish.

He shook off the pinpricks of guilt that had ridden him since they escaped from Midrigar. He sympathized with her fury, her resistance, even her hatred. She had helped him when he needed it most, even if she'd done so under duress. Abduction was no way to pay back a life debt, but his need for her hadn't ended with his escape from the Pit. He needed her even more now, and as long as he could keep her from escaping him or plunging a dagger in his back the moment his guard was down, he'd deal with her hostility.

At the moment, she sat slumped in the saddle, holding the reins as her mare kept pace beside his own horse. She looked as ragged and beaten as he felt. He didn't trust her any more than she trusted him, but he admired her. She persevered; she planned, and she negotiated at every opportunity, even when they both knew the odds were overwhelmingly in his favor. She might be subdued, but she wasn't yet conquered. What little he knew of her character, he suspected such a thing might well be impossible.

Darkness was slowly retreating from the steppe when they reached the knot of trees obscuring more of the burial mounds. They stopped long enough to water the horses and refill the single flask at a wet weather stream swollen with rain that flowed through the middle of the woodland. Azarion kept one hand on his horse's reins and the other on the loaded crossbow he carried. So far, the only sounds to reach his ears were those of bird whistles and the rustling of small creatures waking up to forage for their daily meal.

These barrows were smaller than the ones they left behind, and there were seven instead of three, set in a semicircle. Packed earth pathways led to a low doorway in each. A crumbling altar squatted in the middle of the semicircle, its stones black with the vanished remains of burnt offerings.

They left the mares ground-tied in a narrow lea between two of the barrows. The barrow entrances were too low for the horses to enter. Even their riders would have to crouch to keep from hitting their heads on the timber lintels.

Leaving the horses visible presented numerous problems, but it couldn't be helped. At least if the Nunari found them, they'd have to enter the barrows on bent knees and one at a time, making the graves easily defendable—as long as no one broke through the roof or tried to smoke them out.

The barrow he chose for himself and Gilene followed the same construction style as its bigger counterpart. The witch hesitated at the entrance, taking a reluctant step to bend and peer inside. "Are you sure this is safe? What if there's a wight hiding in this barrow? Just because the other one didn't have one doesn't mean they're all unoccupied."

She was right. He unsheathed both his knives and passed her in two swift strides. Her quick inhalation echoed behind him as he bent and entered the grave's dim interior.

His shaman mother had taught him and his sister the value of protection circles against demons and the effectiveness of iron against wights. If one lingered in here, he'd know it soon enough and would make it think twice before trying to attack him.

Gilene's pale features sharpened with annoyance when he emerged and blithely announced, "Empty. You can go in."

"You didn't have to scare me to death to prove your point," she snapped.

Azarion tilted his head to one side, surprised by her irritation. Had she been frightened for him or just frightened in general? He mentally admonished himself for the frivolousness of the first notion. He shrugged. "You would have demanded no less from me to believe it. Come. We need to get inside."

They set their meager belongings and tack just inside and to the left of the entrance, out of sight from any who might peer into the barrow's interior. Enough wildlife, such as marmots and ground squirrels, populated these lands that he could easily trap enough to make a hearty meal, but he didn't dare start a fire to even get warm, much less roast meat or boil water in one of the clay pots that still remained unbroken next to their deceased owners. They'd have to make do with the road rations he'd stolen. His stomach gurgled, the sound echoed by Gilene's belly as she came to stand beside him at the barrow's entrance.

Azarion fished an apple out of one of the packs, cutting it in half to share with her, along with the flask of cold water. "Eat and drink your fill," he said. "There isn't much, but cooking means smoke, and smoke is a signal, as you saw when we spotted the Nunari."

She gnawed listlessly on her share of the apple for a moment. "Do you think they'll find us?"

"Hard to say. We covered a good distance since last night, and it's still early. Those whose campfires we saw are just now getting their camp in order and seeing to their mounts."

"What about our horses? Surely, their hoofprints are easy to track." Her eyes, heavy-lidded from lack of sleep, glittered with worry.

"Horse herds are plentiful here, as they are in Savatar territory. There isn't a patch of ground on the steppe that doesn't have a hoofprint on it, whether from one made by a riderless horse or one with a rider on its back. If the Nunari are looking for me, they're searching for a man traveling alone. Two sets of tracks will puzzle them a little, though it won't stop them."

He made quick work of his share of their rations. His belly still growled, though the hunger pangs weren't as sharp. Once they got closer to Savatar territory, he'd trap game and fill both their bellies. His companion finished her last bit of food, drank from the flask, and sat down just inside the entrance. She leaned her head back against the wall and closed her eyes.

"I didn't think I'd miss the traders so much," she said. "Halani and Asil had a fine wagon."

Azarion chuckled. "Hamod, for all that I wouldn't trust him not to rob me blind and sink a knife in my gut for extra measure, takes good care of his folk." He turned his gaze from the necropolis grounds outside to the barrow's interior. "I suspect they'd know the value of every grave good still in here."

Gilene frowned. "Do you think them grave robbers as well as free traders?"

"I know they are. Wooden beads and clay pots don't fetch much at the markets, at least not enough to make it worthwhile fending off an angry wight. Free traders have an eye for what grave goods bring in a lot of coin. Hamod or any of his folk could tell just by walking this barrow exactly how much they'd get at market if its dead still wore their jewelry."

Her expression turned contemplative. "I thought they seemed unusually prosperous for trading outside of Guild support."

"It's common knowledge that free traders live on the edge of starvation. Without the Guild, they can't ply their trade on the Serpent, and to trade, you need goods. The barrow of a wealthy man can yield enough to feed a trader band for a month if they're good barterers."

"It makes sense. Hamod and his company were well-fed, their wagons and livestock in good order and healthy. And a starving band of free traders couldn't afford to help us and share what little they had, even if they wanted to."

"You disapprove?" He knew her to be resentful. It seemed she might be judgmental as well.

She sighed. "No," she said, surprising him with her answer. "You do what you must to survive, and the dead have no care for such things anymore. Whom does it hurt if some long-dead chieftain's wife no longer possesses her favorite earrings?"

He suppressed a smile, not wanting her to think he mocked her. She was a puzzle—prickly-sharp and unforgiving, devoted to her village to the point of blind obsession even as she resented them for forcing a terrible burden on her. Yet she was polite and grateful to those who helped them. Her mercy for her fellow victims at the Rites of Spring had prevented them from suffering by delivering a quick death, and she wore the marks of that mercy all over her body as reminders.

She had another question for him. "The new grave mound we saw when we camped with Hamod and his caravan . . . do you think they looted it?"

The image of Hamod's avaricious expression and Halani's dour one rose in his memory. There had been whisperings and meetings in the shadows, and the dull glint of moonlight on the steel scoop of a shovel. "I'd bet a good horse on it," he said.

"It seems odd." Azarion arched one eyebrow, and she clarified. "I remember Halani's face when we first came across the grave. She looked like I feel every time the slavers come to Beroe for the tithe."

He didn't ask her to expand on her statement. He didn't have to. She had told him in his cell in a voice thick with acrimony, *I help enough already.* That told him all he needed to know about her feelings regarding the annual journey to Kraelag.

"Have you any pain in your back or leg?"

Gilene pressed her palm to her thigh, her expression one of relief mixed with admiration. "I always heal from the price I pay to wield magic, but I've never recovered this fast. Halani's healing skills are better than most." She glanced down to his side. "I see they weren't wasted on you either. Those cracked ribs should still be troubling you."

The poultice Halani had applied to his ribs was meant only for the bruising yet went deeper than skin and sore muscle. He swore he had felt the bones knit themselves together. And Gilene was right. He should still be in agony with every breath he took. Riding would be a torture and sleeping on his back an impossibility. Yet he had done all three now with only a twinge to remind him of his injuries.

"I know little of healers and their ways," he said. "But the trader woman knows what she's doing. Should Hamod decide to stop robbing graves and whatever else he does to obtain his goods, he could sell Halani's salves to keep them fed."

Silence fell between them again, and Azarion turned his attention back to watching the steppe and listening for the sound of hoofbeats. For now, there was only the whisper of grass bent to the wind, and the lively buzzing of insects interrupted by the occasional birdcall.

"Tell me something," she said. "The empress is known throughout the Empire for her cruelties, but you were a valuable slave. Hanimus said you were her favorite, so why inflict such punishment on you?"

Gilene's unexpected question, asked in a voice soft with compassion, made his gut twist.

Over the years, Dalvila had done far more to Azarion than just beat him. His mind shied away from the worst memories, the worst degradations. The carnage in the Pit, with its blood-lusting crowds screaming endlessly for more slaughter, was gentle play compared to the brutality of the woman all of the Empire feared. The last six years of his captivity had been the most trying, and that horror he would lay at the empress's dainty feet. The only thing that had stopped him from killing her long ago was his absolute resolve in regaining his freedom. To kill her was to die himself, and he wasn't ready to die. Not yet.

"The empress," he said slowly without looking away from the sunlit steppe, "enjoys pain. Sometimes of those she beds and sometimes her own. But most of all she enjoys humiliation, risk, death, blood."

He glanced at Gilene. The burial chamber was too dim to make out subtleties in expression, but Azarion thought he spotted the brief flicker of sympathy—of knowing—in her eyes.

"Not so different from her subjects then."

He snorted, amused by her wry remark. As a surviving Flower of Spring, she'd certainly see it that way. "No, I suppose not."

"You must hate her."

Somehow, that seemed too mild a word for what he felt for the empress. "I do."

"I hate them all. Were the Krael Empire wiped off the face of the world, I wouldn't weep."

He didn't blame her. As the day waned, Gilene slumped sideways, eyes closed, lips partially opened to emit a soft snore.

Azarion watched her for a moment, noting her smooth skin, the curve of her cheekbone, and the shape of her mouth. Her features, softened in sleep, lost the pinched sourness stamped there when she was awake. She was long legged and slim, with forgettable curves and memorable scars. And a will the Empire had not yet broken and likely never would.

He left her in the barrow to check the horses and survey the necropolis. So far, he'd heard nothing beyond the natural music of the steppe, but he had caught a faint whiff of smoke. It was too wet and too early in the season for a grass fire, so that meant a campfire. If the Nunari drew no closer, he'd have to decide whether they should leave the barrow at nightfall and chance being spotted or heard, or stay one more day and risk losing the distance they'd gained earlier. Neither option pleased him.

The *agacin* was still asleep when he returned to sentry duty at the door, and he took a moment to ease her to her side and drape one of her shawls over her back. The sun beating down on the grave's threshold and several hours of no sleep made Azarion drowsy. He occupied himself with recollections of his home and family: horse herds stretched as far as the eye could see, and Savatar women, dressed in their long tunics and flared trousers, dancing to the music of flute and mouth harp. He was so close to the Sky Below now, he could almost taste it on his tongue.

At nightfall, the gathering vibration of hoofbeats rose up in the earth to tickle his feet through his shoes. The vibration was soon joined by the sound of those hoofbeats and the distant pitch of voices.

Gilene jerked upright when Azarion shook her shoulder. He pressed a finger to her lips. The whites of her eyes shone in the dark like sickle moons. "Shh," he whispered. "Get up. They're coming."

She scrambled to her feet, snatching up her shawl to toss it against the adjacent wall where the rest of their gear was hidden from view. Azarion guided her to the opposite side and tucked her behind him. To see them, their visitors would have to enter the grave instead of crouch at the threshold.

The voices grew louder, along with the hoofbeats of horses. Azarion eased the longer knife he carried out of its sheath and waited.

While he couldn't see the riders from his hiding place inside the barrow, he could make out the various tones of their voices and counted three different ones. There might have been more who didn't speak, but if his questionable fortunes held, then he'd have to deal only with a trio of Nunari.

The voices changed, rising in pitch with their excitement when they discovered the two mares ground-tied between the barrows before falling ominously silent. The Nunari were on the hunt.

Azarion imagined the scene: a slow, careful dismount from their horses and silent hand signals communicating instructions and commands. Were he coordinating the hunt, he'd have at least one man outside, bow drawn and arrow nocked, in case his quarry barreled out of the grave ready to fight.

He and Gilene waited in the darkness, hardly breathing as the Nunari systematically visited each barrow, saving the one they sheltered in for last. Azarion took the time given to push Gilene a little farther away from him to allow him room to move. All his senses centered on the sounds outside—a carefully placed footfall, the nicker of a horse, the scrape of cloth on cloth as those who hunted for them stepped closer to the barrow's entrance.

The first man to enter approached from the side that wouldn't cast his shadow in relief on the stacked stones of the inset doorway. Azarion sensed his presence by the sudden pungent odor of sweat and wild onions that seeped into the barrow. He lingered at the threshold, close enough to let his eyes adjust to the darkness, far enough back to leap out of reach if someone or something tried to grab him and drag him inside.

A small, lit torch soon hurtled into the barrow's center from the doorway. It rolled once before coming to a stop, its flames large enough to reveal the lower levels of the burial platforms and the arched expanse of the opposite three walls. In their hiding spot next to the door, Gilene went up on her toes in an attempt to keep her feet out of the illumination that edged the space where she stood behind Azarion.

The scout crept across the threshold, sword drawn. Torchlight bounced off the blade, giving Azarion a good view of the weapon he carried. The man was past the threshold and turning right, away from them, when Azarion snatched him by the back of his tunic, yanked him into the shadows, and cut his throat in one clean swipe.

He held the twitching body as blood bubbled up from the

open gash to spill down the man's chest. A few gurgling gasps and he slumped in Azarion's arms.

Azarion slid him gently to the ground and eased the Nunari's small shield off his arm. More a buckler than an aspis, the shield didn't offer much protection from arrows but worked well in conjunction with a sword. He sheathed his knife and retrieved his victim's sword where it had fallen in the dirt with a dull thud.

The silence remained unbroken outside until a second set of steps reached the doorway, followed by a third, then a fourth. Azarion recalculated. Either the man with the drawn bow had defied an order and joined his companion at the doorway, or there were more than three Nunari searching the barrows.

This last kill had been by ambush. These would be by combat. Three entered the barrow, one at a time, on cautious feet. They spotted the body of their fallen comrade the moment they straightened inside the barrow's interior.

Azarion rushed out of the darkness, and chaos erupted. The scouts were adept fighters but no match for a Pit gladiator.

He dispatched one of the men with a thrust under the ribs that pierced his heart, and was in the middle of killing another when a howl rent the air. He spun, blade slick with blood, to discover the last to enter the barrow staggering toward him and clutching the gashed ruin of his face. Azarion made quick work of killing him before searching frantically for Gilene.

She no longer stood in the shadows but closer to the barrow's center, her hand curled in a fist around something that oozed blood between her fingers. Her eyes were huge and bright with terror. They rounded even more, and she gasped out a word, pointing to something at the barrow's far side with a shaking finger. "Wight." Her breath steamed in front of her in the suddenly icy grave.

Azarion pivoted and confronted a visage out of a demon's nightmare. A mottled, twisted thing scuttled down the earthen steps, scattering bones and grave goods in its path. It hurtled toward him and Gilene, fanged mouth open wide on an unearthly screech meant to freeze its prey in place from terror.

Azarion lunged for Gilene, hauling her toward the barrow's opening at a dead run. He cleared the short flight of steps with a leap, lifting the *agacin* behind him off her feet as he went. He managed to raise the buckler just before an arrow struck its metal face and bounced off. Cleared of the barrow and the howling wight, he dropped Gilene's arm and charged the lone archer frantically nocking his next arrow.

Azarion plowed into him just as the arrow loosed from the bow. The two men skidded across the grass in a tumble of limbs. A hard fist smashed into the side of Azarion's head, and he saw stars before managing to get a grip under his opponent's chin and one behind his head. He used the leverage of his body and, with one quick yank, broke the scout's neck. He leapt to his feet, dreading the last arrow had found its mark in Gilene's body.

She stood, uninjured, next to where the arrow had planted itself in the ground by her foot, and watched the shrieking wight claw at them from the barrow's entrance. Her hair haloed her head in a frazzle of strands that had come loose from her braid, and she still clutched the thing in her fist that bloodied her fingers and spilled an occasional crimson drop on the ground.

Once assured she was well and that the wight couldn't leave the confines of the barrow, he quickly scouted the rest of the necropolis for the enemy. Only their horses stood at the perimeter, their ears laid back at the sounds coming from the grave guardian.

Battle fury still coursed through him, leaving him in a momentary fog. He shook it off. He had to keep his wits about him. These

Nunari were from the camp whose fires he'd spotted earlier. The five who came looking were dead, but that only meant others would search for them when they didn't return to their clans.

He found the *agacin* farther away from the barrow but still eyeing the wight lingering in the doorway. The creature stared back, no longer shrieking, but snapping its jaws as if eager to gnaw on their flesh. Gilene's frightened gaze settled on Azarion. "Will it be able to come out?"

The wight whined at the sound of her voice, as if starved. "No," he said. "Its purpose is to guard the grave and its sanctity."

Her expression changed, became baffled. "Its sanctity? That barrow has been looted several times, and I'm sure others besides us have slept in there for whatever reason. Surely, there's nothing left which is sacred."

He looked to the wight, who looked back from crimson eyes that burned with malevolence. "Different acts awaken wights. Sometimes it's the looting, which is what makes it so dangerous. I think this time it was the spilling of blood. I desecrated the barrow when I spilled Nunari blood in there."

Gilene stared at him for a moment before striding to the dead archer. She knelt beside him. "I spilled blood in there too," she said. She rose and approached Azarion, opening her hand to show him what she clutched in her bloodied fist—a pottery shard. Its edge, darkened with blood, was sharp as any knife in some spots. "The last man to enter the barrow saw me." Her fingers played over the shard's surface and the broken lines of lost engravings etched into the clay. "For now I am a captive. I refuse to be a slave."

Azarion stared at her with new respect. At some point during their time in the barrow, she had found the shard, recognized it as a possible weapon, and hidden it. "I've underestimated you, *Agacin*. You're as dangerous without your fire as you are with it."

She dropped the shard and kicked it aside with her foot before using her skirt hem to wipe her hand clean. "If you tell me again it's a blessing, I will find a way to feed you to that wight."

He believed her. "When will the fire return?"

She shrugged, tucking a windblown strand of hair behind her ear with a bloodied hand. "It usually takes weeks, though after my first time, it was longer." She tilted her head to one side. "You believe me when I say I can't use it yet?" He nodded. "Why?"

Gilene wielded her power with skill; he'd seen that with his own eyes, and if she still had any left to summon, the perfect opportunity to exploit it had just presented itself.

He coaxed her toward the spot where their own horses huddled with those belonging to the dead Nunari. "Because if your power were fully returned, you'd be on one of those horses and riding for home. The barrow is as much a trap as it is a defense. You could have burned me and the men I killed and walked out untouched."

She halted, her expression dark. "I don't like being so predictable. Nor am I a murderer."

If that pottery shard in her hand, and the Nunari she had disfigured with it, were anything to judge by, she was anything but predictable. "You aren't, but you're driven and as intent as I am on surviving."

The sour look was back, along with the shadow of sorrow. "This is why I hate the Empire most of all," she said. "Because it's twisted us into people we despise."

The wind whipped her tattered skirts around her long legs and bent the grass to her feet in supplication. Moonlight silvered her hair, and those dark, dark eyes watched him, bleak and despairing.

# CHAPTER NINE

After five more days of hard riding and sleepless hours worrying over pursuit by more Nunari, they topped a low rise whose sweeping views encompassed more of the swaying plume grass and a shimmering orange line in the distance.

Azarion pointed to it. "There. That's what we ride toward."

Gilene stared at him, bleary-eyed and exhausted. "Will they know you when you return?" Ten years was a long time of separation, and the boy taken had changed into a man she suspected none of his clan would recognize now.

"Maybe." His voice was muted, thoughtful. "Maybe not. It doesn't matter. The Sky Below is the land of my spirit. It's where I belong."

She turned away. She envied her captor and his obvious love for his land. Gilene had been born and raised in Beroe. It was the village she lived in, yet she felt no connection to it beyond the guilt-ridden obligation, ingrained in the history of its existence, to protect its denizens and most of all her family. The gift of her magic came with a terrible price. She could grieve for the women who died in the Pit each year, endure a night with a gladiator who might not live through the next afternoon, and persevere through the pain of the magical backlash created by wielding so much power at once. But the crushing guilt of knowing Beroe expected her to pass on her knowledge and her burden to another girl cursed with fire magic ate at her.

She envied Azarion because he'd broken free of the shackles the Empire had put upon him. Though she had been one of the Empire's many victims, Gilene had never been one of its slaves. She belonged to Beroe instead, and those chains would hold her until she died.

"I may curse your name for dragging me here," she whispered, "but I shall never forget this place. I shall never forget you."

She turned back to meet his gaze, admiring the way the rising sun gilded him in the colors of morning: bronze and gold, hints of fiery red, and the last fading lavender of night. His eyes glittered with a thousand untold secrets. "Then you will have made me immortal, *Agacin*." The corners of his mouth lifted a fraction. "At least for a little while."

They continued to stare at one another while her stomach did somersaults under her ribs. She shook off the feeling and clucked to set her horse in motion toward the glowing horizon. "Let's get to it then. It looks another day's ride, and I'm sick beyond words of being in this saddle."

The landscape changed as they rode, rising subtly. The plumes of the tall grasses lightened from pale linen to snow white and grew in haphazard clumps now, dotting the steppe amid the fringed sage that had deepened from a silvery green to an ash blue.

The orange thread of light they rode to widened and brightened the closer they got, and soon Gilene gasped, stunned at the sight before her. Azarion wheeled his horse in front of hers, and they slowed to a stop before a colossal wall of flames.

The wall stretched high above them, far too high for a horse to jump clear to the other side. The flames didn't crackle; they roared, pulsing upward as if the land itself had captured a slice of the sun and tethered it to earth, where it strained and stretched to break free and return to its origin.

"The Fire Veil." Gilene had grown up hearing tales of the Veil. Never in her life did she think she might see it for herself. If she managed to return to Beroe, she'd have quite the story to tell her family.

Raised by nomadic spellworkers generations earlier to shield the Stara Dragana from invasion by the Krael Empire from the west, the Fire Veil worked in tandem with the distant Gamir Mountains in the east to protect the Savatar clans that claimed this part of the Stara Dragana as theirs.

Azarion stared at the endless length of fire that stretched to either side of them as far as the eye could see. "On the other side is the land of the Savatar, the Sky Below. For all its power, the Empire still hasn't found a way to tear down the Veil and take it from us." The reverence in his voice matched hers.

Gilene's stomach fluttered at the yearning in his features, the near disbelief in finally returning to something he'd lost long ago. Were she here as a friend and not a captive, she'd congratulate him. Instead, she turned her gaze back to the majestic Veil.

"Is this why your fire witches are of such importance? They built and hold the Veil?"

Azarion's faint smile was wry. "It's one reason. An important one. Agna is the goddess of fire, of birth and death, of horses. We call her the Mother of All, the Great Mare. She gifted fire to men so that we would keep warm during the winter of the world." His gaze raked her, as if he expected her to scoff at him. She didn't, and after a moment he continued. "*Agacins* are holy to the Savatar. You're one of Agna's handmaidens, even if you don't worship her."

"And to claim such a handmaiden lends you power." He had made no secret of needing her to reclaim his place in his clan. Obviously, these *agacins* lent status to those with whom they were aligned. "They won't care that you took me captive?"

His horse paced in front of hers, uneasy before the Veil, even at this distance. Azarion shook his head, and his mouth quirked a little more. "My people will see it as a rescue. I freed us both from the Empire's grip."

Gilene frowned. "Convenient. No wonder you've sworn not to hurt me." She knew nothing of the Savatar but was grateful for their beliefs and the value they placed on their witches. Azarion refused to free her but so far hadn't physically harmed her. She touched her cheek. Not intentionally anyway.

His expression turned cold. "I'm better than those who called themselves my masters."

She had insulted him and suffered regret for doing so. She shook it off. What did she care if she bruised his feelings? He'd forcibly taken her from all she knew, and while he promised to return her to Beroe, she didn't really believe him.

The echo of hoofbeats made Gilene jump, certain she'd find Nunari horsemen bearing down on them. The steppe behind them was empty.

She turned back to find Azarion peering hard into the flames. "Savatar patrol," he said. "They ride the Veil's boundary. Krael can't penetrate with its armies yet, but marked spies and traitors can get through."

Gilene stared hard into the Veil, finally seeing the shadowy outline of riders coming toward them. "The fire is obvious in its protection, but surely it can be defeated? A protective shield wall, wagons that can withstand the flames long enough to break the Veil and drop Kraelian soldiers onto Savatar territory."

"They've tried all those things. The wagons will make it through but carry nothing but men turned to kindling. This isn't flame made with flint and fatwood. It's god-fire like you cast. Water doesn't quench it, and any person who touches it is instantly burned, no matter how well protected."

She swallowed hard and edged her mount farther back from the Veil. Gilene knew herself to be impervious to the flame built by men and to the fire she summoned in the Pit each year, but who knew if this was the same? Despite Azarion's insistence that she was his goddess's handmaiden, she didn't think herself beyond risk.

"How do you expect to get through?" she asked. "How do you expect to get your horse through?" The shadows of the riders on the other side grew clearer as they rode closer to the Veil.

Azarion watched them, his brow furrowed in thought. "The *agacins* who raised the Veil understood the need to protect but not to trap. This fire allows animals through as well as those who are marked by Agna's blessing. I'm marked." He pulled aside the neckline of his tunic to show a small starburst pattern etched into his flesh just under his collarbone where it met his shoulder. Gilene had noticed it when she helped him wrap his ribs in his cell but hadn't thought it anything more than some self-inflicted scarification the gladiators practiced. Azarion straightened the tunic. "At their first year and naming day, every Savatar is given Agna's mark by an *agacin* as protection against the Veil's fire. As one of her handmaidens, you're already protected from Agna's fire by her blessing. You don't need the mark."

He sounded so certain. She wished she could believe him. "What if my witchery isn't born of Agna? I will burn in her fire."

He shook his head. "You won't." He guided his mount closer until both horses stood side by side, and Azarion's leg pressed to hers. "You have to trust me, *Agacin*. I can't leave you on this side of the Veil, and I can't stay, but if I thought you'd burn, I'd figure out another way." Again that wry smile flitted briefly across his mouth. "You aren't much good to me as a pile of ash."

"Ride through on my own, or you'll carry me? That isn't much of a choice. I risk death by fire no matter which I choose."

He refused to bend. "You won't burn."

"Such faith in your goddess and her blessings," she scoffed. The Veil simultaneously roared and whispered, its fire crackling, its flames blinding. "I'll ride. At least if I die, I'll do so knowing *I* made the choice."

"We'll blindfold the horses and lead them through. They won't balk so much if they can't see the flames."

"What about the patrol on the other side? Will they be friendly to us or put us to the sword the moment we cross?" The irony of surviving the Pit, Midrigar, Nunari trackers, and an enraged barrow wight only to die at the end of a Savatar sword point would have made her laugh if it weren't so frightening.

"It'll depend on who they are and if they recognize me." Azarion sounded supremely unconcerned.

She briefly closed her eyes. "I will die on this journey."

They prepared the horses, using Gilene's shawls to cover their eyes. Azarion held the reins of both mounts. Gilene stood next to him, staring at the horsemen who waited on the other side.

Azarion's green eyes flared in his sun-bronzed face. Eagerness, triumph, confidence. All the things Gilene didn't feel. Her stomach lurched this way and that, an internal dance of fear, and she knew the steps well.

"We'll walk through together, *Agacin*," he said.

She frowned. "I will haunt you until you die should you be the cause of my death. You'll know no peace."

He didn't mock her threat as she half expected. Instead he offered her a brief bow and a solemn expression. "I haven't known peace in a long time." He gestured with a hand toward the Veil. "Come. It's time."

# CHAPTER TEN

Their pass through the Veil was less of a rush and more of a crawl. Azarion held the reins for both horses in one hand and walked slowly through the fire. Gilene followed, her palm pressed against his back as the flames swallowed them. He could hear the staccato rhythm of her breathing. He knew she'd cross the Veil without incident. Knew it down to his bones. She didn't, and she didn't fully believe him.

"Can we not go any faster?" Her voice trembled.

He wished he could grant her request and rush them both through the Veil, but he risked spooking the already anxious horses. "Just keep walking, *Agacin*, and don't look at the fire. We'll be through soon enough."

Her fear was justified. As a young boy, he and other boys in his clan would ride out with the patrols, learning the roles they'd assume as men and warriors. They often went back and forth through the Veil—as much to numb themselves to the fire's intimidation as to train their horses not to fear it when they crossed into Nunari territory on raids. It didn't matter how many times he crossed; the first sight of the roaring, crackling beast always made his stomach drop to his feet.

"Shouldn't you be holding your sword instead of the horses' reins?" she said, the words muffled as she spoke them into his tunic. Her steps shadowed his from behind as he led them through the Veil.

"Only if I want to be shot full of arrows the moment we reach the other side." The fiery wall towered above them, blinding but oddly lacking any heat. It was a trap for the unwary and the unknowing who assumed that such an absence meant it was harmless. "There are at least four Savatar archers watching us with their bows drawn and their arrows nocked. If they see me holding steel, they'll kill us once we emerge."

"Remember what I said. My spirit will haunt you all your days."

Magic and fire spiraled and pulsed around them, flames licking at their clothes, skin, and hair. Nothing burned. Behind him, Gilene gasped in wonder at the brilliance around them.

The great fire, summoned by *agacins* now long dead and fed by those who came after them, generation upon generation, cavorted in a chaotic dance all around them.

"I'm not burning!" Relief rang through Gilene's exclamation.

Fire coursed over and around them, leaving only the resonance of its magic behind to lick their skin. Azarion's prickled with the sensation: a low hum more felt than heard as if the magic fueling the god-fire sang to his blood instead of his ears. The sensation was similar to when he lay beside the sleeping Gilene in the barrow's darkness. Her own magic thrummed like this, only not nearly so strong, and he was certain he'd felt its presence near the somber Halani when they traveled with the free traders' band. He even felt it around his mother sometimes. A stray thought occurred to him. Did others feel this sensation as he did? Or was it unique to him, like his unexplained ability to see through illusion?

The blindfolded horses followed Azarion's tug on the reins, their ears flicking left, right, and back as they listened for a predator. They didn't fight the lead, and soon the little group walked out of the Veil, unhurt and untouched by the divine fire.

Azarion tensed at the warning creak of a saddle as a nearby rider adjusted his seat on his mount. The four archers who waited for them on this side of the Veil faced him, bows drawn as he had predicted.

They wore garb similar to that of the Nunari—long-sleeved quilted tunics woven of wool and edged in fur, woolen breeches held tight to the lower legs by leather stocking boots cross-strapped at the calf and tied off at the ankle. Leather armor overlaid their clothing in a protective covering, and all wore either caps or helmets. Their swords and knives remained sheathed, but the arrows nocked to their bows and aimed at Azarion and Gilene posed more than enough of a threat.

Three of the four men were young, not many years beyond their first beard. The fourth was older, closer to Azarion's age, if he were to guess, and it was this one who guided his horse forward to confront them. Azarion recognized none of them, which was a relief in itself. He had feared one or more of the Savatar waiting for them to cross might be one of his cousin's henchmen.

"Who are you?" The older Savatar spoke in Savat, his suspicious gaze flickering back and forth between Azarion and Gilene, noting their appearances, Azarion's armament, and the distinctly Nunari tack on the horses. Behind Azarion, Gilene stood silent, her hand no longer buried in his tunic, the space between them much greater. He mentally applauded her. She'd given him the room he needed to raise a fast defense.

"Azarion," he replied in the same tongue. "Son of Iruadis Ataman and Saruke. Kestrel clan."

The Savatar's eyes narrowed, and his hand on the bow grip tightened. "Iruadis Ataman died six years ago. His son before that. You are a liar and a spy."

All four bows lifted a notch as the archers prepared to fire.

Gilene's faint but fervent "Oh gods" echoed his own silent prayer to Agna for deliverance.

That deliverance arrived on the thud of hoofbeats and a hard voice bellowing, "Hold! Don't shoot him yet."

A man dressed like his comrades, but carrying a sword instead of a bow, trotted up to Azarion on a chestnut mare. His gray hair, tied in a top knot, matched the color of his beard, and he studied Azarion and Gilene with a hard, flat stare. His beard was decorated with tiny beads tied off at the ends of braids that dangled from his chin, and he wore a red sash wrapped around his trim middle, the badge of a Savatar *tirbodh*, a captain of archers.

Azarion's gut wrenched. This man he knew. Memories of childhood, of better days and hard bruising, of pragmatic wisdom and endless patience. Agna continued to rain good fortune on him by sending the one archer captain who would stay his hand at killing him.

"You're wearing Kraelian garb and Nunari weapons but walked through the Veil. Let me see your mark."

Azarion dropped the reins and pushed aside the tunic's neckline to expose his shoulder. If anything, the *tirbodh*'s gaze hardened even more. "You're Agna-marked, so likely a spy. You and your woman. Where's her mark?"

Gilene huddled behind him, trying to make herself as small as possible. "She doesn't bear one. She doesn't need it."

The captain's eyebrows rose. "Is that so? You look Savatar; she doesn't, yet she walked through the fire. If I wasn't curious about that, you'd both be dead right now."

The archer closest to him spoke. "He says his name is Azarion, son of Iruadis Ataman."

That revelation snapped the *tirbodh* rigid in the saddle. His weathered features paled for a moment, and the tiny beads in his beard clicked together. When he spoke again, he almost spat the words between his teeth. "Iruadis Ataman had only one child, a son with the name you claim."

Azarion shook his head. "No. He had three children. Another son before me who died in infancy and a daughter younger than I am named Tamura. You know I speak the truth, Masad." They all visibly startled at his use of the *tirbodh*'s name. "You delivered her of my mother in a pasture when she'd herded goats too far from the encampment to make it back in time for a midwife's help."

Masad's eyes glittered, and his jaw clenched. "Disarm and toss your weapons on the ground. Then you sit." He gestured to Gilene. "Both of you."

The implacable command carried an implied threat. Refuse and die. Azarion slid his forearm out of the shield's straps and flung the shield on the ground.

"What did he say?" Gilene's mild tone didn't quite disguise her unease.

He untied his sheaths, sending his sword and both knives the way of the shield.

"He wants us to sit down, *Agacin*. We do as he says. Our lives depend on it." He dropped to the ground, pulling her down next to him.

Masad regarded them from the high place atop his horse. "The last time I saw Azarion, he was as tall as you but without the breadth of shoulder or the muscle. That beard of yours can be hiding any face." He pointed to one of the knives Azarion had surrendered. "Have your woman use that to shave you, so I can see what hides behind the hair."

Azarion froze. Gilene, extorted and compelled, was unwilling to be here but unable to leave, and he was supposed to hand her a knife and offer his throat? She returned his shuttered stare with a wide-eyed one of her own.

"What? What did he say?"

He might still die this day, even if it wasn't by Masad's hand. "He wants you to take one of those knives and shave me so he can see my face better."

Her mouth dropped open, and she rocked back on her haunches. A calculating spark lit the black of her pupils before her gaze slid from him to the waiting Savatar, then to the knives. He wanted to remind her that once her fire returned, she'd have the ability to murder him at any time. Now, though, was not the time.

Gilene rose and made her way to where the knives lay in the grass, keeping a wary eye on the Savatar. She bent to pick up one of the blades and unerringly picked the sharper of the two. At least if she shaved him, she wouldn't nick him too badly, and if she cut his throat, his death would be swift.

She returned, weapon clutched in her hand, to crouch before him. Dark humor flickered in her equally dark eyes. Sunlight winked off the blade as she lifted it and moved closer to his face. He held his breath.

"So tempting," she murmured.

"So foolish," he replied just as softly, his stare never wavering from hers.

"Trust me."

Those two words, spoken by her this time instead of him, punched him in the gut. Azarion understood helplessness and the vulnerability of having your entire life—your fate—in the hands of someone who considered themselves your master. In those instances, he wasn't expected to trust nor asked to believe anything others told him. Still, he had blinded himself to Gilene's point of view, far too focused on his own goals and his surety that he'd never hurt her to truly understand her disbelief in his assurances. Trust was earned, not freely given.

Every instinct urged him to snatch the blade out of her hand and put space between them. Instead he sat motionless while she carefully cut away the thick beard and scraped the bristle until he was clean-shaven and nick-free with his jugular intact. Her fingertips on his jaw and cheeks made his skin tingle. A light, capable touch, but something about it heated his body in a way that the most sensual caress never had. When she finished, he remembered to breathe.

Gilene knee-walked a short distance from him and carefully set the knife in the grass in front of her, signaling the watching Savatar that she wasn't a threat. A half dozen stares rested on him; Gilene's thoughtful, the archers' curious, and Masad's stunned.

"You are your mother's son," the *tirbodh* said on a disbelieving exhalation. "Agna's mercy, I thought you dead these many years." He dismounted, strode to where Azarion still sat, and stretched out his hand. Azarion took it and was yanked to his feet, then into a hard embrace that sent shards of pain through his newly healed ribs.

The other archers stared at them, astonished, and slowly lowered their bows. Masad released Azarion, his craggy features wreathed in smiles. "Come back from the dead. This is a good day. A good day! Where have you been?"

The smile fell away when Azarion told him. "Enslaved by the Empire." He glanced at the archers listening behind their captain. Now was not the time to reveal details. "I've much to tell."

Masad nodded, understanding Azarion's unspoken message. "And much to hear." He turned his attention to Gilene. "Who is your woman?"

Azarion gestured for Gilene to stand by him. She came willingly, obviously deciding that he was, for now, the safer alliance. "This is Gilene of Be . . ." He almost said Beroe, but the fleeting shot of alarm across her features as she guessed what he was about to say stopped him. "Krael," he amended. "She's an *agacin*. Blessed by Agna but without our marks. As you saw, she didn't burn in the Veil."

Gilene made a distressed noise when the gazes resting on Azarion suddenly fell on her. "What did you just tell them?"

"That you're an *agacin*." He turned back to Masad. "Speak in trader's tongue so she can understand."

Masad raised an eyebrow, then shrugged. "You're both blessed then," he said in the language understood by any who lived in or near the Krael Empire and the Golden Serpent. "Come. You've traveled a long way and over Nunari territory to reach us. The encampment isn't far, and many will be happy to see you again."

Masad ordered his men to stand down and introduced them to Azarion by name. Azarion remembered the three younger ones as small children, now grown to early manhood. He didn't recognize the archer close to his age, a man Masad proclaimed had come to Clan Kestrel through marriage to a Kestrel woman.

Assured now that any danger from this patrol was past, Azarion gathered up and belted on his sword, and retrieved his knives. Gilene removed her shawls from the horses' eyes, shook them out, and wrapped herself in their layers. She stood next to her mare, features tense. "What now?"

He gestured for her to mount. "Stay next to me and hold your tongue. You'll learn much by listening. I'll make sure Masad speaks in trader's tongue so you can understand."

"They aren't planning to kill us then?" Her voice was steadier now.

"We won't be dying yet." He tipped his chin to the *tirbodh*. "That's Masad. He's my mother's brother, the man who trained me up as a Savatar warrior. My clan's encampment isn't far. He'll lead us there."

Her hands clenched the reins, tightening so that her horse backed up a step in response to the inadvertent signal. "Then this ordeal is just beginning."

Part of him—the part eager to see his remaining family again, eager to confront an old enemy face-to-face—wanted to refute her statement, but he didn't. Were she not an *agacin*, she'd be shunned by the Savatar as an outlander, a Kraelian outlander at that. Even her status as one of Agna's handmaidens didn't guarantee friendly overtures and instant acceptance.

He leapt into the saddle and guided his horse to walk beside his uncle's. Masad ordered his men to ride ahead of them. After learning the news of his father's death, Azarion dreaded Masad's answer to his question. "Are my mother and Tamura still alive?"

Masad chortled. "Your mother and sister are well and thriving. Saruke rules the clan from her favorite rug." His features turned dour with a touch of sorrow. "Your father would have been overjoyed to see you again." His mouth curved down. "Karsas is the *ataman* of Clan Kestrel since Iruadis died." He eyed Azarion. "You're not surprised."

Azarion's casual shrug belied the fury cascading through his veins. "I would have been had you named another." His cousin had plotted long ago to assume the role of Clan Kestrel's chieftain, even if it meant stealing it from the rightful heir.

Masad's attention shifted to Gilene. He spoke in the trader's tongue. "You can truly wield fire?"

She nodded and kept her reply succinct. "Yes."

He eyed her a little longer before turning to Azarion. "The Fire Council will want her to prove it. Seeing her walk through the Veil will give truth to your story, but they'll want more. The Ataman Council will want to speak with you as well."

Azarion had waited ten long years for such an opportunity. "I want to speak with them." His cousin Karsas sat wrongly as head of Clan Kestrel, and Azarion wanted justice. Killing your relatives through ritual combat was accepted by the Savatar. Selling them into slavery was not. Karsas had taken the coward's way in getting rid of his rival.

Masad edged closer to him, his voice barely above a murmur. "Even with an *agacin* by your side, you'll still have to face Karsas in ritual combat for the chieftainship."

He truly hoped so. The chance to challenge his cousin to a fight had been a dark dream that had kept Azarion alive for so long as a gladiator.

With the four other archers ahead of them but still close enough to hear everything spoken in a normal voice, Azarion didn't badger Masad for details regarding Karsas and his leadership. And while Masad had been his teacher from childhood and was, in many ways, a second father, he was fiercely loyal to the clan. Karsas was *ataman* of his clan; therefore, Masad was loyal to Karsas. Azarion didn't want to put the man into an untenable position of divided loyalties. He would make a stronger ally if not forced to choose between his chieftain and his newly resurrected nephew.

He steered their conversation toward less dangerous subjects. "Tell me what has happened since I've been gone these many years."

They rode at a leisurely pace for several hours as Masad recounted the ten years Azarion was enslaved within the Empire's borders—the ever-shifting status of the Savatar clans, births and deaths, marriages and raids, the seasonal migration from the Novgarin foothills to the sweeping pasturelands of the east and back again.

All these things Azarion remembered, unchanging, as predictable as the sun's rise and the wind's ceaseless breath over the grasses. Yet Masad's narrative hinted at less welcome changes. There were others besides him who'd embrace the chance to fill Azarion's ears, namely his mother, Saruke.

Masad left Azarion and Gilene behind and joined the archers ahead of them. The Sky Below stretched before them in a flat swath of swaying grasses and the rolling shadows of scudding clouds.

"You've been gone a long time," Gilene said. "Your family will be overjoyed to see you."

He hoped so. An image of his mother rose up in his mind's eye, her features creased by her gap-toothed smile. Tamura was a vaguer memory. Pretty, fierce, and one of the clan's finest archers. According to Masad, she hadn't married, and Azarion was grateful that Karsas hadn't taken her to wife. Such a familial connection wouldn't stop him from killing the man, but he'd regret hurting his sister if her husband meant more to her than just an elevation in status.

"Karsas is the cousin who sold you?" Gilene kept her voice low.

"He is."

A thoughtful expression settled over her face. "But if you're here, alive and recognized by many as the *ataman*'s son, why do you need me to claim your place as *ataman*? It belongs to you by birth, does it not?"

He wished it were that simple. "I've been gone too long. There's a point where claim by merit overrules claim by birthright. I've nothing in the way of experience and rule to justify my challenge to retake the *ataman*'s seat without something beyond my bloodlines. No council decisions, no enriching the clan through trade or raids. I haven't married another clan's daughter to strengthen ties or the line of families. You are the only link to the chieftainship that means something now. As my woman, you're a direct blessing from Agna, a sign of her approval of me."

Her mouth pinched. "I'm not your woman."

"For your sake, pretend you are. It puts you under my protection. Say I have no claim to you, and I'll have to fight off those who would take you for themselves. You might never see Beroe again." That threat had become the weapon he employed to force her cooperation, and he was growing heartily sick of using it. He'd much rather coax than threaten her to stay.

"Why would you let me go if they won't?"

They'd argue this until he delivered her to her doorstep. "Because, as I said before, you saved my life. I'm in your debt, and I've made you a promise."

The disdain faded from her expression; the distrust did not. "Do all Savatar keep their promises?"

"This one does."

"Won't you lose your place as *ataman* if I leave?"

He glanced at the men riding ahead of them. Gilene's question was a dangerous one, spoken from the stance that he would inevitably reclaim his birthright from his cousin.

"No," he said. "Once Agna's blessing is recognized by the councils, it's permanent, even if the *agacin* chooses to marry into another clan or, as with you, leaves the Savatar." That, and he planned to kill his cousin. Karsas wouldn't live to work his treachery a second time.

Gilene arched a doubtful eyebrow. "There have been *agacins* who left?"

"Not in the memory of the people."

"I thought not." She huffed a frustrated sigh. "Where will I stay while I'm in your camp? With you?"

"Yes, and it's anyone's guess where I'll lay my head. Likely in my mother's *qara*, though she's subject to Karsas's will now, and he might not allow it." There was no reason for his cousin to forbid it except from pettiness, but he was *ataman*. His clansmen wouldn't question so small a thing.

"He may try to kill you." Gilene's voice lacked any glee at the possibility, and he fancied for a moment that it actually contained a hint of worry.

Azarion smiled. "I've no doubt of it. He failed the first time. The Karsas I remember never accepted failure well."

They went quiet when Masad trotted back to them. "Do you want me to send those foolish boys ahead to cry the news? Or should we ride in and surprise them all?"

The shrewd look his uncle leveled on Azarion told him he already knew the answer. Azarion's reply was simply for the benefit of other listening ears. He was happy to oblige. "Surprise them," he said, letting his voice carry on the wind. "I long to see my mother's and sister's faces after all this time." And to keep a shocked Karsas from planning an unfortunate accident.

They picked up their pace after that, traveling at a gallop until Azarion caught sight of colorful flags fluttering atop the peaks of *qaras*. The round structures squatted on the steppe in loose clusters. Carts stood next to several of them, and horse and sheep herds grazed nearby.

He wanted to stop, just for a moment, to take in the tableau before him. Vengeance against his cousin wasn't the only dream to sustain him through the long years of slavery. This one did as well—the gathering of Clan Kestrel, encamped on the white-plumed sweep of the Sky Below under the sky above. Blood, pain, degradation. Nothing had broken his will to live or his desire to escape when the promise of returning to this still bloomed behind his closed eyelids at night.

A few clansmen from the camp rode to meet them. Masad

called out to those approaching. "Someone find Saruke and Tamura and bring them here. Hurry!"

They were swarmed by Savatar before they even reached the camp's perimeter. Curious faces peered at Azarion from the ground and from horseback, crowding closer until his and Gilene's horses were hemmed in by a press of bodies. He made out bits and pieces of conversation flying around them.

"What's Masad doing with two Kraelians this far into Savatar territory?"

"Agna's grace, I recognize him!"

"Who's the woman?"

There were so many people around them, he had a hard time picking out individual faces among the crowd. They all blended into a sea of humanity that parted as two women cleaved through the throng to reach him.

He swung off his horse to stand amid the Savatar and quelled the nearly overwhelming urge to rush forward and scoop up the weathered crone swooping down on him like a crow and the much taller woman with the fierce eyes of a hawk.

Both halted abruptly in front of him, both scowling as if they wanted nothing more than to rip out his guts. The crone had not been so aged when Azarion was sold ten years earlier. A life spent under the hot sun and harsh wind had weathered her, but she'd been straight-backed then, her hair brown and shot with gray instead of the silvery white it was now. Lines of sorrow carved furrows into her face, but her gaze was still sharper than any blade, still capable of slicing a person down to their soul with a single look. Right now that gaze searched his face, searched hard. Her eyes watered, and her chin shook with the stuttering breath she took.

"Azarion?"

A chorus of gasps followed her question, and the younger woman next to her dropped her hand to the pommel of the sheathed sword she carried. She glared at Azarion, disbelief hardening her face.

His chest felt as if one of the horses stood on it. He remained where he was, desperate to embrace his mother and sister, but familiar enough with them to know such a move courted danger. "I've missed you, *Ani*," he said, using the informal Savat word for "mother." He glanced at his sister. "You, too, Mura. Do you still chew your hair when you're nervous?"

Tamura stepped back, as if to ward off any more surprises Azarion might lob at her. Saruke, on the other hand, stumbled forward, arms outstretched, hands trembling as she reached for him. "My son," she sobbed. "My son."

This time he didn't hesitate and gathered her into his arms, lifting her off her feet. She felt light as a bird and just as fragile. Azarion wanted to crush her close and bury his face in her neck as he once did as a young boy long ago, but he dared not, too afraid of breaking every bone in her body with the force of his affection.

Tamura eased a little closer, wary as a wolf circling wounded but dangerous prey. Her eyes, as green as his and as cutting as their mother's, grew glossy, and she blinked to clear them. "You're much bigger than I remember," she said in a hoarse voice.

Azarion grinned at her over Saruke's head. "You're still a midge fly, Mura," he teased, remembering fondly how she tried to pummel his head in every time he called her *midge*.

The term forced a sob past her lips, and she halted another by compressing her mouth so tightly, her lips virtually disappeared. She blinked several times and reached out to curve her hand over his where it rested against Saruke's back.

Azarion was halted from pulling her into the same embrace

with their mother by another rippling surge of the crowd and a voice he so reviled, he remembered every nuance of its timbre.

"Azarion, we all thought you were dead."

Azarion gently set Saruke aside so he could face the person he hated even more than the empress. He offered the barest hint of a bow. "Not yet. *Ataman*."

Karsas of Clan Kestrel had been his adversary since they were children. Older than Azarion by only a few years, he had coveted the role of clan chieftain since he was old enough to draw a bow. His father, Gastene, had been Iruadis's younger brother. Unlike his son, Azarion's uncle had never craved the role of leadership and never challenged his brother for the seat. Karsas resented his father's lack of ambition, and that resentment had festered over time, fed by jealousy and the certainty that he was the best candidate to take Iruadis's place as *ataman* when Iruadis died.

Azarion didn't hold his cousin's ambition against him, only his cowardice. That, and his treachery, made him loathe Karsas. Azarion had sworn to himself years earlier that he would live long enough, no matter what it took, to exact revenge on his cousin.

Unlike Saruke, who had aged and turned stooped, and Tamura, who had matured from awkward juvenile to majestic woman, Karsas had changed very little. Tall like Azarion, but leaner, he cut a notable figure, every bit the proud chieftain in his bearing and the richness of his clothing.

If one looked close enough, though—past the rich fabrics and priceless gold—they could see the dissipation around Karsas's mouth and eyes, the jowly droop of his jaw, and the tiny spiderwebs of broken blood vessels that blotched his cheeks and nose.

The two men stared at each other. Azarion hid his contempt behind a carefully neutral facade. Karsas wore a similar expression, one that didn't quite conceal the shock and wariness flitting through his eyes as he gazed at his nemesis.

The crowd quieted as the staring match lasted beyond a natural pause and into something awkward. And dangerous. Hands dropped to knives sheathed at the waist and swords sheathed at the hip. Karsas broke the rising tension when his regard shifted to Gilene, who sat frozen on her horse.

Karsas arched an eyebrow, his faint smile more a sneer. "Who is this?"

Azarion glanced at Gilene, who returned Karsas's stare with a steady one of her own. "My woman, Gilene." He paused, savoring the anticipation of the moment and what his next statement would mean to his cousin. "She's an *agacin*."

More surprised gasps from the crowd rose, and they exclaimed among themselves over the idea of a Kraelian *agacin*. Who had ever heard of such a thing? Their net tightened even more as they edged closer for a better look at this handmaiden not born and raised behind the Veil.

Had Azarion blinked or looked away for a moment, he would have missed Karsas's reaction to the revelation, but the signs were there, slight and subtle to the casual observer, obvious to Azarion. His cousin flinched, and there at his left eye a tic started in his eyelid, the fold of skin twitching in a haphazard pattern as he stared at Gilene.

Karsas's voice remained unchanged except for another level of chilliness. "There are no *agacins* beyond the Veil, nor any who aren't Savatar."

Masad spoke up. "I saw with my own eyes as she walked through the fire untouched."

Karsas cut him a glare. "Empire sorcery."

To emphasize his words and demonstrate his claim on her for

the witnesses gathered, Azarion placed his hand on Gilene's knee. She accepted his possessive touch, though her thigh muscle was so tense, it might have been a slab of rock under her skirts. "She's blessed by Agna, as am I since she chose me."

Karsas's hand dropped to the pommel of his sword. "So you say," he replied, and there was no mistaking the snide disbelief in his voice. The crowd grumbled, uneasy at his faint mockery of a woman declared a handmaiden of Agna.

Sensing their unrest, his demeanor changed. He donned a cloak of friendly welcome and spread his arms in a gesture meant to encompass them all. "A long-lost son of the Savatar has returned to us. We will celebrate and call council afterward to learn what happened to him during the long years he was gone!" The crowd's mood swung from disquiet to jubilance, and they cheered. Karsas bared his teeth at Azarion in a sham of a smile. "Until then, I think your mother will be pleased to have you and your . . . woman stay in her *qara*." He spun away to return to the encampment, an entourage of grim-faced warriors following him as he cut through the throng.

Gilene bent down from her perch to whisper in his ear. "Obviously not all are happy to see you. And take your hand off my leg."

He gave a short laugh and moved away from her to pull Saruke close to him again. "Off your horse," he told Gilene. "We'll walk from here to my mother's home. We can eat, rest, and sleep warm by a fire. There will be a celebration tomorrow night and probably a council gathering the day after."

Her expression brightened and darkened by turns at the mention of food and rest and then celebration. She dismounted and came to stand before the staring Saruke and Tamura. Her low bow was respectful without being obsequious. "It's an honor to meet the family of Azarion," she said in formal Kraelian.

Unlike Azarion, the two women didn't speak the language and glanced at him for translation. He obliged, telling both, "She's addressed you in Kraelian high tongue as a sign of respect. Speak trader's tongue, so we can all understand each other."

Saruke's face softened into a cautious smile; Tamura's did not. She watched Gilene with a raptor's focus as if trying to see the magic inside her that made her one of Agna's handmaidens.

Saruke took Gilene's hand. "Come, we'll walk together while my son is remembered to his friends." They strolled leisurely toward the encampment, leaving Azarion to face a swarm of well-wishers who embraced him, slapped him on the back, and passed around skins of fermented mare's milk in an impromptu celebration of his return.

By the time he broke free of old friends and new acquaintances, his head buzzed from countless swigs of the potent milk. Masad showed him the way to one of the seasonal creeks, now swollen with melted snow and spring rain.

"Saruke won't let you into her *qara* smelling like you do." Masad wrinkled his nose and promised to return with a change of clothes. Azarion used the time to dig up a fist-size bulb of soaproot not far from the creek. All around him, other holes were made, signs the women had been here earlier, harvesting the wild root for either roasting to eat or crushed into a poultice for infected wounds or a sickly stomach.

He pulled away the tough fibers from the bulb and peeled back the sticky layers. The water was so cold that it burned his skin, and his teeth chattered hard enough to make his jaw hurt as he washed his body and hair, sending islands of soaproot lather careening down the creek's fast current. By the time he was finished, he was numb, and he dressed in the clothes Masad brought him with fingers made stiff from the cold.

He followed his uncle toward his mother's *qara* in the fading afternoon. Masad led him through the maze of felt-covered shelters whose placement might look chaotic to an outsider but made perfect sense to a Savatar. The *ataman*'s home occupied the camp's center space with all others radiating out from its point. Those subchiefs and families of high status raised their *qaras* closest to the *ataman*'s, while those of lesser rank pitched closer to the camp's perimeter.

Azarion was surprised to discover his mother's tent not too far from Karsas's, still in a spot that denoted her status as the widow of an *ataman* but below that of the subchiefs who helped Karsas lead the clan. One day, very soon, she'd take her place in or right beside the *ataman*'s *qara* if his plans still found favor under Agna's gaze.

Masad patted him on the shoulder at the entrance. "Spend time with your mother and sister. Tup your priestess tonight, and tomorrow seek me out. We'll hunt, and you can tell me all that happened while you lived within the Empire's borders."

He left Azarion with a promise to retrieve him before dawn. Azarion stared at the low doorway that, like some of the barrows, forced a person to bow or hunch to enter. Azarion had been raised in a *qara* but hadn't seen the inside of one in a decade. So many recollections crashed down on him—the filtered sunlight spilling in a column to the floor from the *qara*'s crown, bedding and cook pots stacked against lattice-framed walls held up by steam-bent timber ribs and wheels that his people traded silver and livestock for with the Goban clans to the east. The heady scent of cooking food drifted to his nostrils, and the sound of women's voices talking teased his ears. He bent and swept into the *qara*.

The sight that greeted him gladdened his heart. Saruke sat on a rug near a fire, stirring something fragrant in a pot he remembered from his childhood—a gift given to her by his father on the birth of the brother who didn't live past infancy. Tamura sat across from her, against the felt and timber wall, hands busy at building a bow. She stilled at her work to watch him from the shadows.

Gilene sat not far from Saruke, weaving her dark hair into a braid. At some point, while he drank with the men outside and caught up with their lives over the last decade, she had bathed and washed her hair. The dim light from the cooking fire caught strands of red in her locks, creating a shimmering net that haloed her head. She no longer wore the Kraelian clothes almost reduced to rags from their journey. Instead she sat garbed in the typical dress of Savatar women—a long-sleeved wool tunic that fell to her calves over loose trousers tucked into ankle-high goatskin boots.

She raised tired eyes to watch him as he made his way to Saruke and sat down beside her. His mother squeezed his arm with one hand and continued stirring the contents of the pot with the other. "There is tea and stew. You must be hungry."

He kissed her gnarled fingers. "Speak the trader's tongue, *Ani*. The *agacin* doesn't yet understand our language."

"Is she truly able to wield fire?" Tamura asked in Savat, disregarding his instruction.

He nodded. "Yes, though she pays a price for it that our handmaidens don't when she uses it." He accepted the cup of hot tea and the bowl of stew Saruke handed him. "Did you eat?"

She nodded. "Aye. Your woman looks as if she'll blow away with the next stiff breeze." She gave Gilene a brief smile that was returned. "We thought it best to put something in her belly before she flew away from us."

Azarion had finished most of his bowl when Saruke spoke again, her eyes glossy with tears. "What happened to you? They said you were separated from the hunting party. None could find you. All they brought back were your horse and your cloak, both bloodied. Your father was inconsolable."

"Is that what they told you?" His hand clenched around his spoon. "It was the hunters who took me. I was beaten until I passed out. I woke up in Uzatsii, waiting my turn on the auction block."

Tamura sprang to her feet, the half-finished bow held in such a way that Azarion expected her to nock an arrow and draw. "Who did this to you? I will cut out their hearts!" She still hadn't spoken in trader's tongue, but Gilene's quick scuttle back told Azarion she understood perfectly Tamura's outrage. And her threat.

He waved her back down. "Peace, midge," he consoled her. "I'll have my revenge soon enough." He squeezed Saruke's hand as tears tracked down her cheeks. "Yerga, Zabandos, and Gosan all had a hand in my enslavement. They were the ones who beat me and sold me to the Nunari. But they did so on Karsas's orders."

Tamura paced, pausing once to point at her mother. "I knew it." This time she used trader's tongue. "Didn't I say those piles of sheep shit had something to do with his death? I knew they were lying!" Her nostrils flared, and her pacing threatened to wear a bare spot in the rug under her feet. She stopped again, hands on hips, to glare at Azarion as if he were somehow as responsible for his own abduction. "All three are dead, by the way. Yerga broke his fool neck from a fall out of his saddle. He was always too stupid to learn how to ride properly. Zabandos took a spear to the gut." Tamura's humorless smile stretched wide. "Got caught tupping a *tirbodh*'s wife in his own *qara*."

Azarion didn't know whether to cheer or curse. He had hoped to mete out justice to Karsas's henchmen as well as to Karsas himself. It seemed fate had done it for him. "And Gosan?"

"Drowned in a spring flood." Tamura's waspish smile faded. "I don't think anyone mourned him much. We all felt sorry for his wife. She's a kind sort. Deserved better than him."

There were more than a few widows and fatherless children in every clan camp. Some women grieved their men, others did not. If Karsas was married, Azarion would soon make his wife a widow and his children fatherless. "When did Karsas become *ataman*?"

Saruke answered him. "Right after your father died. He courted the Ataman Council long before that, and as the closest living male relative to your father, they considered him the next in line to succeed."

It was as he expected, though hearing it made him want to howl his anger. "The Fire Council agreed?"

"Yes. There were none to challenge him and no *agacin* to naysay the vote of the Ataman Council."

Azarion turned to Gilene, who listened with a confused expression. "The *agacins* have their own council separate from that of the *atamans*, and even more powerful. When an *ataman* is chosen by the other clan chieftains, they still must get approval from the Fire Council. If they don't, then another must be chosen."

Her eyebrows climbed toward her hairline. "You have a council of women more powerful than that of your men?"

Tamura's sharp laugh filled the *qara*. "The Savatar value their womenfolk. Unlike Kraelians." Her voice lost a little of its edge. "My brother says you are an *agacin*, even though you aren't Savatar."

Gilene nodded. "I can wield fire, yes, and I don't suffer its burn."

"Show us," Tamura challenged. She pointed to the cook fire. "Strengthen the fire here."

Gilene shook her head, refusing to rise to Tamura's obvious baiting. Azarion was tempted to end it but sensed this was a play of dominance between these two, one where his interference wasn't welcomed or helpful.

"I can't," she said. "Not now, anyway. I don't know how it is with your *agacins*, but my power doesn't draw from an endless well. I drained it weeks ago. I need time to replenish."

Tamura snorted and shot Azarion a disdainful glance. "She told you she was *agacin*?"

"No. She didn't even know the word until I told her. I've seen her summon and control fire with my own eyes several times."

Saruke put more water on to boil for tea. "The Fire Council will want her to prove it to them."

Azarion's eyes met Gilene's. Hers were dark, anxious, weary. "She can. That she doesn't burn should be enough to satisfy them until all her power returns."

For all that she had aged twenty years in the ten he'd been gone, Saruke rose nimbly to her feet and without aid or complaint. She motioned to Gilene and gestured to a pallet of blankets and furs. "Come. You and Azarion can sleep there tonight. For now you can rest unless you want to attend tonight's celebration." Gilene gave an adamant shake of her head, and Saruke smiled. "I didn't think so. Go on. One of us will wake you if you're needed."

Gilene accepted the offer without protest, not even questioning Saruke's assumption that she and Azarion shared a bed. For all practical purposes, they had done so since their sheltering with Hamod's traders, always out of necessity and often for warmth. He inwardly cheered her lack of resistance to the notion of sharing this particular pallet with him. She didn't like him, but she had begun to trust him a tiny bit, at least in this matter.

She slid under the pile of covers, still fully clothed, and turned to face the *qara* wall. In moments she was asleep, the curve of her shoulders drooping as slumber overtook her.

Saruke returned to her place and gave her full attention to

Azarion, slipping back into Savat. "Now you will be truthful with me. What did you suffer at the Empire's hands?"

He was reluctant to tell her, reluctant to recall those things that left a scar on his soul each time. "Everyone suffers at the Empire's hands," he said shortly. He did offer up one fact and left out the worst details. "I was the Gladius Prime."

Tamura gasped and Saruke's eyes narrowed. Tamura leaned forward, gaze shrewd. "A useful skill then, if you intend to regain your birthright," she said in a low voice meant only for him and their mother.

He took the tea Saruke passed him. "I do. It's the thing that's kept me alive all this time."

Tamura slapped her knees. "I want to help. Karsas is a toad. Our clan has been lessened in the eyes of the other clans while he's been *ataman*."

The question lurking at the back of his mind since he first arrived at the clan camp surfaced to his lips. "Why didn't he make you his wife?"

She bared her teeth. "Because he knew I'd kill him in his sleep."

Saruke rolled her eyes. "She won't marry anyone. I have no grandchildren."

Tamura mimicked her mother's expression. "We live well enough without a husband underfoot. And I hunt, and herd, and fight as well as any man."

Azarion chuckled. "You always have." Tamura had always held her own with him and the other boys her age, riding, fighting, and shooting as well as any of them and better than most.

"Whatever child I bore wouldn't live to see its first year completed," she declared, and refilled her cup with steaming tea. "Karsas would see to it. He wants no contender for his role as *ataman* or anything that will endanger his son's chance at inheriting it."

Azarion growled. For now, the role of Clan Kestrel's *ataman* belonged to Karsas and his progeny unless the Fire Council revoked it. "I've much to learn and even more to avenge."

Some of Tamura's ferocity faded. For a moment, she looked as careworn as Saruke, her back bent with worry. "A lot has happened since you were taken from us. Much of it not good. Trade has thinned on the Serpent's eastern flank, and our wool and horses fetch only half the price they used to. Only the silver holds its value, but our best mines are playing out. Raiders from the Gamir Mountains are wreaking havoc in territories belonging to the Goban, who in turn flee into our lands and ask us to help them against their enemies. I'm afraid if we don't, they'll turn to the Empire for support, though some suspect it's the Empire supplying the raiders and encouraging them to harass the Goban."

His thoughts reeled with this revelation. He'd been wrong to think most things hadn't changed since he was sold to the Empire. The Savatar were no longer the powerful people they had been ten years earlier. "If the Goban can't hold off the Gamir raiders or turn to Krael for help, Krael will use that to invade our lands. The Veil requires a lot of power from the *agacins* to keep it standing. There aren't enough of them to add a second one."

Tamura snorted. "Trust me, nothing you've just said hasn't been discussed to death in council meetings. The *atamans* talk and talk but come to no decisions. Karsas isn't the only one guilty of that failing."

Saruke stirred the coals of the fire to redder life. "We send warriors to help the Goban fend off a raid or two, mostly during trade exchanges, but it isn't enough."

"The clan council and the Ataman Council will ask you the same thing we did, Brother." Tamura drained the last of her tea before continuing. "They'll want to know everything that happened to you to glean information. If you want a strong claim to challenge Karsas for the clan's leadership, you will need to offer something to gain their favor. Knowledge of the Empire will help toward that."

She wasn't telling him anything he didn't already know. He only hoped what little he could offer as a Pit gladiator with his wits about him and his ears open would be enough. "I wasn't a statesman there. I was a slave, so I won't know Krael's plans, but I know the layout of the capital and how it places its regiments. Some of the gladiators were once Kraelian soldiers, commanders even, who displeased the emperor for some reason and were punished by having their freedom taken. They talked sometimes of their exploits. If you listen hard, you can learn while in the practice arena."

Saruke's hand on his arm made him turn. His mother's eyes, a more faded green than his, were dark with grief and sympathy. "Then you'll have something useful to tell them. Maybe they'll listen."

He glanced at the sleeping Gilene. "I have an *agacin*. They'll listen."

Tamura gave another one of her sardonic snorts. "An *agacin* who can't light a candle at the moment. You'll need luck as much as Agna's blessing, Brother."

He had no argument to deny that.

PART TWO

# THE SKY BELOW

# CHAPTER ELEVEN

Gilene turned her face to the sun, grateful for its light and warmth. She'd been in the Stara Dragana for five days, finding her footing among a people whose ways and language were unfamiliar to her. Behind her, the roofs of the black felt tents the Savatar called *qaras* rippled in the wind.

The clan camp was a hive of activity. The wedding of a Kestrel man to a Marmot woman was to take place in three days' time, and several women from the Kestrel families had banded together to create felt rugs for the groom to present to the bride's family as gifts. It was backbreaking labor, and Gilene joined in, welcoming the hard work.

When they started the first rug, Gilene offered her services as a skilled dyer to dye baskets of wool rovings in the colors requested. Once they dried, they'd be separated into more baskets while the women worked in teams of four or five to felt the white and gray rovings that made up the foundation of each rug.

One of the older clan matriarchs had eyed Gilene suspiciously, as if the offer to oversee the dyeing process would somehow endanger everyone handling the wool. With Saruke acting as translator between them, the matriarch peppered Gilene with questions.

"What do you know of dyes?"

Gilene hid a smile. "My village is known for its dyes. We extract the green out of long nettle and sell the dye powder throughout the Empire."

"But do you know how to dye cloth? Making dye and using dye aren't the same."

Gilene didn't argue that. The woman was right. "I've been dyeing cloth for a long time."

A small crowd of women had gathered around them now, curious about this outlander's purported skills. Still skeptical, the Savatar elder pointed to the kettles of dye set up nearby. "Show us what you can do."

While the Savatar used plants that rendered colors in shades of yellow and red instead of the green she usually worked with, the process of dyeing the wool was much the same. Several dunkings with a hand rake and spoon and drying time on the racks produced rovings in the expected vibrant shades. Gilene, however, had added her own twist to the process, and the rovings looked like a sunrise or a sunset, graduating in shades from pale yellow to crimson. The many gasps of delight and approving nods told her she'd won the crowd. But had she won the critic?

The elder stared wordlessly at the rovings before flicking a quick glance to Gilene and then to Saruke. "She can dye the wool," she said and walked away.

After that, the task was hers, and she watched from her place at the kettles while the other women designed and felted the rugs for the new couple. A few of the younger ones approached her, and in trader's tongue asked her if she'd teach them some of her techniques.

"It's mostly practice," she said. "But I'll teach you what I've learned." She was trapped on the Stara Dragana for at least another month, if not more. Sharing a skill with her reluctant hosts might make things a little easier for her. She wasn't looking for acceptance, but tolerance was just as valuable and as useful.

This morning she sank a bundle of rovings into a kettle of bright yellow dye and stirred it with her rake. The felters spun and laid out yarn while arguing incessantly with each other, no doubt over how the design should be laid down. Loud whistles and a series of shouts from one side of the camp interrupted their squabbling.

Gilene didn't dare leave the kettles unattended, but craned her neck to see what had given cause for such commotion. Soon, a line of wagons, like the ones parked throughout the Kestrel camp, rolled toward them, accompanied by an escort of mounted riders.

As one, the felters paused, then hurriedly stood, wiping wet hands on their aprons. They spoke in animated whispers, several glancing at Gilene. Because she didn't speak Savat, their excitement over these visitors puzzled her. Their focus on her made her uneasy.

Saruke came to her aid as she watched the wagons approach. "News travels fast," she said in trader's tongue.

Gilene spared her a quick glance. "What do you mean?"

"That is the Fire Council. They've heard the Kestrel clan has an *agacin*. They'll want to speak to you. Leave the kettles and go back to the *qara* to change. I'll follow in a moment."

Gilene's stomach dropped at the news. She did as Saruke instructed and hurried to the *qara*. Azarion met her en route, leading one of the horses he'd taken from the Nunari he'd killed. He was dressed in the garb of the Savatar, with bits of his hair braided at the temples, and wore a felt hat to keep the rest tamed. A bow rested across his back, along with a quiver of arrows at his waist.

Except for his clean-shaven features, which were already shad-owed with a beard, any hint of Kraelian about him was gone.

He carried a brace of marmot in one hand and fell into quick step beside her. "You saw the Fire Council arrive?"

She nodded. "Your mother sent me back to change, though I don't know what else I'm to wear." Her wardrobe was limited to her Kraelian clothes, which were no more than rags at this point, and the tunic and trousers borrowed from Tamura. Those she now wore, and despite the apron, they were splotched and stained.

"She or someone will bring you something to wear." Azarion left his horse outside the *qara* and followed Gilene inside.

The interior's warmth eased the stiffness in her cold fingers but didn't stop the chattering of her teeth. She was nervous as well as cold. She strode to her sleeping pallet and sat down to remove her shoes and trousers. The tunic's length hid most of her body except her calves, and while Azarion had once seen her fully na-ked, she wasn't inclined to strip in front of him a second time.

He was busy with his own disrobing until he was down to a loincloth that left very little to the imagination. Gilene knew what he looked like dressed only in skin and bloody welts. She'd seen the whip marks and slashing scars that decorated his back, shoul-ders, and sides. His chest and abdomen bore more of the same— souvenirs of his time as a Pit gladiator. He wore them with neither pride nor shame, just as she wore hers.

Years training as a gladiator had made their mark in more than just scars. Azarion was tall, but so were many of his clansmen. Lean and toughened by life on the steppes—much of it spent on horseback—they lacked Azarion's muscular bulk.

His broad shoulders flexed as he reached for a tunic, muscles rippling on either side of the deep indentation that highlighted the length of his spine and the narrowness of his waist. The men he had fought with and against in the Pit had all been shaped and honed to survive it, to please the crowd, to fight with sword and shield for long periods without tiring or slowing. Azarion had risen to the elevated rank of Gladius Prime not only by clever strategy but by brute strength, and it showed in every line of his body.

As much as she hated to admit it, he was breathtaking to behold, clothed or not. And she wasn't the only to think so. More than a few Savatar women viewed him favorably, and Gilene assumed some of their unfriendliness toward her stemmed from a touch of jealousy at the idea that she, and not one of them, was his concubine. If they knew the truth, she had no doubt he'd be mobbed at Saruke's *qara* door by a crowd of enthusiastic, unwed maidens.

Unaware or uncaring of her silent scrutiny, he stepped into trousers and was donning a tunic when Saruke strode in, arms loaded with a stack of clothing. She dropped them into Gilene's lap. "Dress quick. Karsas has summoned you both to his *qara*. The Fire Council waits there."

Azarion strapped his stocking boots to his newly clad legs. "I'd rather hunt wolves than eat with his ilk."

"Better they eat with you than eat you," Saruke rejoined. "Besides, I didn't say anything about them feeding you." She gestured for Gilene to hurry it along.

Gilene cast a quick glance at Azarion. He was busy with his belt and knife, and she took advantage of the moment to shrug out of her stained tunic and pull on the one Saruke brought her. The trousers followed before Saruke handed her a pair of shoes free of dirt or mud.

Gilene glanced down at herself and gasped. The outfit she wore now was obviously meant for special occasions instead of everyday wear. Heavily embroidered and beaded at the neck and over the chest, the tunic was made of felt so soft, it rivaled the feel of silk on her bare skin. Wide, bell-shaped sleeves edged in luxurious fur draped down her arms to almost cover her hands. More fur lined the hem, and colorful embroidery decorated the trousers.

"This is lovely," she breathed. Saruke smiled. "Who was so generous to loan such a fine garment to me?" She tried not to succumb to the terror of possibly spilling something on it.

Saruke's smile turned sly. "It isn't a loan; it's a gift. Suitable for an *agacin* who is about to meet her sisters of the Fire."

Gilene's heart sank. She plucked at the tunic. "This isn't meant for one such as I. I'm not Savatar. I don't even think I'm *agacin*." She glanced at Azarion, whose shuttered expression revealed nothing. "I can't accept such generosity. I have no means of repaying it."

Saruke's smile fell away, and her eyes narrowed. "A gift is just that. Given with gladness and without expectation of repayment. If you refuse it, you'll insult the giver in the worst way."

Embarrassed heat flooded Gilene's cheeks, along with guilt. She resided among Azarion's people under duress, here only until she helped him fulfill his ambition to reclaim his inheritance. What she wore now was meant for someone who wanted to be here, who wished to be Savatar and all that such a thing entailed. She was not that person.

However, she had no wish to give offense. Not here, among people she barely understood and knew so little about. "Will you not tell me their name so I can thank them myself?"

Saruke shook her head. "You don't know them, not really. You wearing their gift will speak of your appreciation."

The gift giver would remain mysterious, and Gilene set aside her curiosity over Saruke's enigmatic statement to concentrate on the situation at hand. She faced Azarion once more while Saruke re-braided her hair before winding it into a bun at the back of her neck.

"What will the Fire Council do when I face them? Are there questions I should expect? A trial I must endure?" That made her heart lurch a little. "You know my power hasn't returned and won't for at least another month or two."

She didn't lie. Her abilities took time to return, and it had been less than a month since the Rites of Spring in Kraelag. Hints of her ability to cast illusion had shown themselves, but not the power to summon or control fire. The waiting never bothered her before. Now, she had to exercise patience. No amount of wishing or anger would hurry it along.

Azarion's gaze swept her from head to foot. If he was impressed with her appearance, he hid it well, and an odd niggle of disappointment lodged itself under her breastbone. She blamed the unwelcome feeling on her alarm at facing the Fire Council.

"You'll be questioned and tested by nine priestesses, including the chief priestess, whom the Savatar call the *ata-agacin*. We address her as *Ata*." He frowned a little. "It would be better if they witnessed you wielding fire, but I'll tell them you summoned it to help us both escape the Empire, and it drained you. That's no less than the truth."

She gave a wry laugh. "But hardly the whole story."

He cocked an eyebrow. "Do you really want to tell them the whole story?"

"Not unless I have to. You realize the chance of them declaring me an *agacin* is slim at best, even though there were witnesses to me walking through the Veil unburnt."

His broad shoulders lifted in a brief shrug. "Maybe, but your reasons and those witnesses will be enough for them to return for a second consideration once your power does show itself."

Gilene shuddered. Two council sessions. She dreaded the first one and didn't want to imagine having to deal with a second one.

Azarion escorted her through the camp toward the *ataman's qara*. She was grateful for his company. Her success in this endeavor was as important to him as it was to her. His unwavering faith in her ability to recapture her magic surprised her. There was a steadfastness to this man that, at times, annoyed her but now helped calm her fears. The press of his hand on her lower back as he guided her through the makeshift alleyways created by the *qaras* comforted her.

The *ataman's* tent was the largest in the encampment and, at the moment, the most crowded. Someone had removed the felt covering at its peak, allowing a column of sunlight to spill downward and illuminate the floor layered in decorative rugs. The lit braziers set in various spots provided more light and warmth as well.

Karsas and his subchiefs sat on the floor in a half circle that hugged the *qara's* perimeter. In front of them, nine women dressed in Savatar finery and intricate headdresses that sparkled with beads also sat, facing the newcomers. More people, whose rank and status Gilene could only guess, stood against the *qara's* walls. All eyes settled on her and Azarion, and the buzz of idle chatter fell silent.

Azarion bowed to the women as well as to the *ataman* and his subchiefs. "*Agacins*," he said in an admiring voice. His tone flattened. "*Ataman*," he said, addressing Karsas behind them.

Even in the dim light cast by the braziers, there was no mistaking Karsas's thin half smile at his cousin addressing him as chieftain. His eyes, green like Azarion's, shifted to Gilene. She offered him and the priestesses a quick bow as well.

"*Ataman. Agacins*," she said in smooth Savat. Two words she knew in the language of the steppes, important words. She was learning more every day but still relied on trader's tongue to communicate, as well as translations offered by Azarion, Saruke, and occasionally Tamura.

She didn't wish to antagonize the clan's leader, though the role she assumed as his adversary's concubine guaranteed he'd see her as a threat, especially if the fire priestesses proclaimed her one of Agna's handmaidens like themselves. His hostile gaze crawled slowly over her. Gilene quelled the urge to scratch or swat away an invisible pest.

He'd yet to address her directly since her arrival to the camp, but she often caught him watching her as she went about the tasks Saruke assigned her. Azarion's scrutiny could pierce armor and freeze one's bones, and the natural way he carried himself warned anyone with any sense of self-preservation that he was a force to be reckoned with. Yet he lacked a certain slyness that his cousin possessed. Nor did his gaze make her skin crawl the way Karsas's did. In a way, the *ataman* reminded her of the faceless abomination in Midrigar, and had his tongue flicked out to test the air, she wouldn't have been surprised.

Karsas spoke in Savat, and Azarion translated for her in the same flat tone. "You've both been summoned here to prove Azarion's claim that you, Kraelian woman, are actually a handmaiden of Agna." A twitter of muffled laughter circled the *qara* at the faint mockery in Karsas's voice.

Gilene schooled her features into an impassive mask. His was a well-aimed shot. He'd addressed her not by her name but by her origin. To those watching these proceedings, she was no longer Gilene or Azarion's concubine. She was the Empire, an enemy of the Savatar. Anything she said now would be suspect.

"Yes, *Ataman*," she replied in trader's tongue, and said no more.

She glanced at the *agacins* facing her. They varied in age, young and dew-faced to elderly and gnarled. The one in their center, wearing the most ornate headdress, was a woman in her middle years, and judging by her place and the deference paid to her, the *ata-agacin*. Like the priestesses on either side of her, she hadn't laughed at Karsas's calculated jibe. She turned her attention to Azarion.

"Tell us why you believe this woman is blessed by Agna." Unlike Karsas, she was willing to speak in trader's tongue. Gilene caught Azarion's brief smile of triumph. He'd just scored a minor victory over his adversary.

He bowed a second time and recounted his tale of first meeting Gilene a few years earlier and discovering her talent for summoning and controlling fire, albeit, the recounting contained a great deal of fabrication, espoused with the utmost sincerity. By the time he was finished, even Gilene almost believed the slave gladiator and the Kraelian fire witch were united in mutual affection instead of blackmail and bargaining. Azarion might not have been as overtly sly as his cousin, but he had a true talent for deception.

Silence reigned in the *qara* after that, except for one attempt by Karsas to speak. The *ata-agacin* raised a hand in wordless command, and he quieted. She shifted her attention to Gilene. "He says you walked through the Veil without burning, and there are witnesses here now who can verify it. I don't think any of us have seen the like before from a person not of the Sky Below, and I hesitate to name you one of Agna's handmaiden's despite Azarion's tale."

Karsas injected his opinion. "He could be lying." This time he spoke in trader's tongue.

The priestess's eyes narrowed. "He could be." She snapped out an order in Savat, and the crowd leapt to do her bidding, filing reluctantly out of the *qara*. Even Karsas and his subchiefs rose to exit, though the *ataman* scowled and glared at both Azarion and Gilene as he passed. Only the priestesses stayed seated.

Gilene turned to Azarion, panic curdling in her belly. He grasped one of her hands and brought her fingers to his mouth for a quick kiss. His new beard tickled her knuckles, and his lips were light as a butterfly's wings. He squeezed her hand briefly before letting it go. "They wish to speak with you alone. Remember what you face every year, what you would willingly face again next spring, and know this is nothing so hard as that."

His words bolstered her courage, and she gave him a quick nod before facing the *agacins* again. She didn't hear him leave but immediately felt his absence once he departed.

The chief priestess rose gracefully from her seat on the floor and began to circle Gilene. It was hard to do so, but Gilene remained in place, staring at the *qara*'s walls.

"The son of Iruadis speaks highly of you. He says you can wield fire, though your role in helping him escape his masters has robbed you of your power."

"True on both counts."

Nine stares measured her worth.

The priestess continued her interrogation. "And you are also his concubine. This is true as well?"

Gilene hadn't missed the suspicion in the woman's eyes as Azarion spoke of his attachment to her. Had he said too much or too little? Her captor hadn't yet demanded more from her so far other than her patience and her collusion, but she did live with him in his home and shared his bed if not his body. It was, in a way, the definition of *concubine*, and she didn't have to lie about that. "Yes. I'm his concubine."

She returned the priestess's steady gaze and wasn't the first to look away.

"A handmaiden of Agna has great influence among the Savatar. We approve alliances and marriages, battles, and new leaders of the clans. Azarion knows this. A chieftain's son returned from the dead might well wish to claim what's been lost to him. The support of an *agacin* would be very useful."

Gilene considered remaining silent but thought better of it. The *ata-agacin* didn't outright ask a question, but she did imply her want of a response. This was treacherous ground upon which Gilene stood. Who knew what alliances formed among the Savatar leadership? Who served whom in their ambitions? Who owed a favor or bowed to a threat? She searched for a reply she hoped wouldn't compromise either Azarion or her.

"I can't speak for Azarion's wishes, but if that were true for him, would it be wrong to strive for such a thing if it helped the clan?"

The priestesses still seated glanced at one another, and one of the *ata-agacin*'s eyebrows did a slow climb. The corner of her mouth twitched up for just a moment. "No, it wouldn't be wrong." She motioned to one of the priestesses who brought her the basket. "You say you have no power to draw from now, but we'll test you anyway. Let's see if you're as good with your magic as you are with your words."

"You want to test me inside the *qara*?" Gilene took in her surroundings. Wood, felt, baskets. From its peak to its floor, Karsas's home, like every other tent in the encampment, was potential kindling for an uncontrolled flame to become a devouring inferno.

The *ata-agacin* raised that questioning eyebrow once more. "To put your doubt to rest . . ." She gave a wordless gesture at one of the braziers. The coals flared a vivid orange before an arc of flame burst from the brazier's confines to follow the movements of the *ata-agacin*'s hand. It hovered in midair before twisting around itself into an interlocking figure like a serpent swallowing its tail.

A wave of heat cascaded down Gilene's body as the flame whipped around her, coiling up her frame but never touching. The priestess gave a final, sharp gesture, and the fire raced across the *qara*, where it plunged into another brazier, making those coals snap and spark while smaller flames licked the grate in a merry dance. Not even a hint of burnt cloth tainted the air.

"Your turn now, outlander," the priestess said.

Gilene didn't know whether to laugh or applaud, the first because she knew her efforts would come to naught. The second because the *ata-agacin*'s control of flame had been impressive to witness.

She didn't protest when they fished out candles from the basket and set them around her with instructions to set them alight, either one at a time or all at once. Nothing happened. The candles remained unlit. A cold brazier was brought forth, and under Gilene's hand, it remained dark and cold. An oil lamp. A handful of fatwood. A square of charcloth. Nothing caught flame in her hands.

"I said from the beginning," she told the priestesses, "I may be able to summon fire and force it to do my bidding, but not yet. What power I possess, I've used up for now."

The *ata-agacin* stretched out her arm. "Give me your hand."

Gilene did so, and a bubble of blue fire burst across their clasped fingers. The priestess's grip tightened as the flames traveled up both their arms, but Gilene didn't struggle. She returned the other woman's stare with one of her own as the flames danced along her shoulder and neck and cascaded down her chest until she and the priestess were engulfed. She felt the fire's heat, but only its heat, and squinted her eyes against the bright illumination. Soon the brightness faded, as did the heat. The flames died away, leaving both women unscathed.

The *ata-agacin* let her go and took a step back, her expression puzzled. "You don't burn, just as we don't. That is indeed the hand of Agna there." She returned to her sisters, and they gathered together in a huddle to talk in whispers.

Gilene didn't move, a small kernel of hope that even without a demonstration of fire summoning, her resistance to burning might be enough proof to get them to declare her one of Agna's handmaidens. If so, then achieving her goal of returning to Beroe was that much closer.

The *agacins* finished their discussion and, as one, turned to Gilene. The *ata-agacin's* words sent Gilene's stomach plummeting to her shoes. "We recognize your ability to not burn and believe you when you say your power is depleted for now. However, it isn't enough to declare you a handmaiden. We need to see you summon and see you control the gift that Agna bestows on her priestesses. When your magic reawakens, have Azarion or the *ataman* send a message to us. We'll return and test you again."

Tears welled on Gilene's lower lids, and she blinked to force them back. Despite her best intentions not to hope too much for a different outcome, the *ata-agacin's* refusal to recognize her was a crushing disappointment. It meant more weeks living among strangers, viewed either as an outlander by the clan members or as a threat by their *ataman*. All she wanted was to go home. Her resentment for Azarion, dulled a little these past few days, sharpened once more. She wanted no part of his machinations, and she followed the priestesses out of the *qara*, dry-eyed and grim.

They were met by a crowd of curious clansmen, with both Azarion and Karsas waiting on either side of the *qara's* entrance. When the *ata-agacin* shook her head, the crowd lost interest and slowly dispersed. Karsas lingered, a gloating smile twisting his vulpine features. Gilene turned away and followed a stoic Azarion back to his mother's tent.

They were met by a dour Tamura and a more sympathetic Saruke, who offered cups of tea as consolation. Their *qara* was quiet, with only the clink of the teapot against a cup to break the silence as Saruke administered refills.

Azarion's gaze looked beyond the *qara*'s lattice frame and felt covering to some invisible horizon, his face forbidding. The unaccountable urge to apologize to him hovered on Gilene's lips, and she bit them nearly bloody to stop the words. She had nothing to apologize for. This was his failure, not hers. Saruke had told her earlier that upon Iruadis's death, the *agacins* had voted unanimously to make Karsas *ataman*. Until that vote was challenged by another *agacin*, it trumped Azarion's right to reclaim the chieftainship through ritual combat.

Gilene's spirits fell even more, and she suspected she wore the same disappointed scowl as Tamura across from her.

Azarion set aside his cup and rose to rummage through a set of trays that acted as Saruke's pantry. He returned to their circle around the brazier with a flask. "This calls for something stronger than tea." He thumbed the top off the flask and took a swallow before passing the flask on to Gilene. "Not unexpected," he said. "But still not a good day."

"No, it isn't," she agreed and swallowed a mouthful of the drink as sour as her mood.

# CHAPTER TWELVE

Azarion led two horses toward the outskirts of the camp as the women and children dismantled the *qaras* and packed the felt coverings and framed into waiting wagons. Clan Kestrel prepared for its summer move east and deeper into the Sky Below where pastures untouched by sheep waited to be grazed. All the Savatar clans did the same, staking their claims to ancestral grazing lands and reviving the annual summer trade markets with the Goban people at the base of the Gamir Mountains.

He spotted his sister not far from the camp, astride a gray mare, talking to other riders. They had argued good-naturedly earlier in the day over who would help the drovers move the sheep herds and who would capture the wild mares and foals to replenish the camp's milk supply before they decamped.

They had resorted to a child's game of slap-knuckle to decide who got first choice of tasks, and Azarion won. Tamura had grumbled over her loss but set out to meet up with other riders and join the drovers bringing in the sheep. Azarion whistled sharply as he walked the pair of horses past their little group and gave Tamura a cheerful wave. She responded with a rude hand gesture and stuck her tongue out at him before tapping her heels into her mount's sides to gallop away with her companions.

The *ataman's qara* would be the last one dismantled and the first to go up when they arrived at the new camp spot. Karsas had announced the plan to move three days prior, and since then the camp had been a frenzy of activity and noise as wagons were lined up and *qaras* broken down into stacks of lattice, poles, and folded felt. Karsas had watched it all in indolent splendor from his seat on a rug in front of his *qara*'s door.

As if conjured by Azarion's thoughts, the *ataman* suddenly stepped out from the shadow of a still-standing *qara* and blocked Azarion's path. He wore a tunic in need of washing, and his eyes held the glassy sheen of inebriation. The strong fumes of fermentation drifting off his breath made Azarion turn his face away and cough.

What Karsas's gaze lacked in sober clarity, it more than made up for in malice. "Did you really think that little trick you pulled with the Fire Council would actually work?"

Azarion didn't try to pretend he didn't understand his cousin's question. This confrontation had been a fortnight in the making, ever since Gilene had failed to garner status of *agacin* from the Fire Council. Ever since Azarion had first passed through the Veil and returned to the Sky Below and the clan of his birth.

"Gilene walked through the Fire Veil and didn't burn. She may have failed the test, but Agna has noted and blessed her."

Karsas snorted. "Sorcerous trick from some renegade wizard taught to a Kraelian whore in exchange for her favors. Agna doesn't bless those who don't worship her."

Azarion's hand settled on his knife handle where it rose from its sheath. Gilene wasn't a whore, and even if she were, she possessed more character and bravery in her little finger than this piece of filth did in his entire body.

He kept his expression neutral, recognizing Karsas's insult for what it was: a calculated move meant to give maximum offense and incite the predictable response.

"As *ataman*, you speak for the clan, but you are still only *ataman*, or do you believe yourself more now and speak for the goddess as well?"

Karsas blanched at the question, couched in the vague accusation of blasphemy. He glanced skyward for a moment as if expecting a lightning bolt to crackle out of the blue and strike him. His lips drew back in a snarl. "You should have stayed dead. You no longer belong in the clan. Your place should be forfeit. The Sky Below is not your home, nor is it your concubine's, even if she can set the steppe ablaze with her power. The Fire Council will never name her as an *agacin*, and the chieftainship will remain mine. You gave it up ten years ago."

He spoke in a low voice so that only Azarion could hear him. They faced each other in the shadow of the *qara*, backed by its frame on one side and that of the two horses Azarion led through the camp on the other.

Azarion's quiet tones matched Karsas's, though he seethed inside with the urge to gut the man right there and pay the consequences for the impulse. "I gave away nothing. You had three men ambush me on a hunt, beat me until I was unconscious, and sell me to the Empire. You took the coward's path, Cousin, by not killing me yourself." His lip curled in a sneer. "You shame your sire; you shame your ancestors, and one day, everyone will know it."

Karsas lunged for him, and Azarion met him halfway. They slammed together. Azarion pressed his blade's edge against Karsas's throat. A sharp sting in his side warned him that his cousin wielded a blade of his own and threatened to slide it between his ribs.

The two men gripped each other in a lethal embrace as the camp's occupants eddied and flowed nearby, unaware of the confrontation between their current *ataman* and the man from whom he had stolen the title.

"Finally," Azarion said, nearly nose to nose with his cousin. "You grow a spine and would fight me." He didn't flinch when the tip of Karsas's knife pierced his tunic and flesh, sending a trickle of wet heat sliding down his side. His own blade pressed a little harder as well, leaving a shallow cut on Karsas's throat that welled with blood.

Karsas jerked his head back and shoved Azarion away. "No one will believe you, and the men who sold you are dead."

Azarion shrugged. If Gilene's power returned and she passed the Fire Council's tests in her second try, they didn't have to believe his accusations. He would challenge Karsas to ritual combat, and his cousin would have no choice but to accept. "Don't think I didn't notice that. Reward for their misplaced loyalty. At least in that, you were thorough and saved me the trouble of killing them myself."

Red-faced, Karsas glared at him before wiping the cut on his neck with his sleeve. A scarlet smear joined the numerous other stains on the garment. "The clan is mine," he snapped before whirling away and disappearing around the *qara* from where he'd first appeared. Azarion stood there a moment longer, knife held at the ready in case one of Karsas's lackeys suddenly made an appearance and challenged him. When none did, he checked the wound Karsas had left and pressed his tunic to it until the trickling of blood stopped, then gathered up the reins of his patient mares and led them toward his original goal, the patch of ground where his mother's *qara* had stood.

He found her, Gilene, and two more women loading rugs, blankets, braziers, and cooking pots into one of two wagons parked nearby. The other wagon was already full with the dismantled *qara*.

Saruke saw him first and waved him nearer. "Where are you off to?"

He felt Gilene's gaze on him, though she didn't greet him. "To capture some of the wild mares for milking. There's a herd not far from here with a lot of foals. Bornon and his sister are to meet me there."

His mother nodded and passed Gilene a rolled rug to place in the wagon. "Why do you have two horses?"

"One for Gilene if you can spare her, and if she wishes to go."

Gilene slowly pivoted away from the wagon to face him. The delighted smile blossoming on her face before she hid it behind a bland look surprised him and sent a pleasant warmth coursing under his skin. That smile hinted at a woman fashioned of more than strong will and sharp edges, and he resolved in that moment to coax another one out of her in the near future.

Saruke's eyes slid from him to Gilene and back before she bent to gather a basket of onions and carry them to the wagon. "Good. She can help with the milking." She indicated the other two women with a lift of her chin. "I have enough help here."

"But . . ." Gilene stood by the wagon, obviously wavering.

Azarion held up one pair of reins. "It's up to you. I've picked a mare with a comfortable gait and good disposition, and milking a wild mare is much like milking a tame one." If you didn't mind a few more kicks and bites.

Despite the interested spark in her eyes, she hesitated, until Saruke gave her a light push toward Azarion. "Go. I've seen how you work hard to learn our ways. This is part of who we are. Learn that too."

With that, Gilene reached for the reins Azarion offered to her.

"Thank you," she said and swung into the saddle on the horse he'd chosen for her.

They rode out of the camp toward the open swaths of steppe where the grasses hadn't been flattened by *qaras* or grazed down by livestock. The wind blew the scent of budding wildflowers on warm currents, and Azarion admired Gilene's profile as she rode beside him, face lifted to the sunlight, strands of hair escaped from her braids fluttering across her cheeks.

They found the herd at the base of a low-sloping hill. Four other Savatar waited for him and Gilene, raising their hands in greeting as they gathered together. They'd already set up a milking line with supplies of rope, pails, and halters stacked in a nearby cart.

Bornon clutched two slender birch poles, each twice the height of a man, with a loop of rope secured at the end. He handed one to Azarion and offered a quick bow to Gilene. "Does the *agacin* know how to catch the mares and foals?" he asked in Savat.

Azarion repeated the question for her in trader's tongue.

"I haven't the first notion of how to do it," she said, casting an uneasy eye at the herd that watched them from afar. "I thought I was here to help with the milking."

Azarion grinned. "You are, but if you want to give the other a try, just tell me. I, or Bornon, or his sister Juna there, will show you what to do."

Gilene glanced at the long poles the riders carried couched under their arms and said, "I'll watch first, then we'll see."

He left her with a Savatar woman named Lemey, who had come to help with the milking once the mares were captured and tied to the line. The sun beat hot on his head as they drove the herd closer to the milking station and harnessed the foals, who whinnied for their dams while Gilene and Lemey tied them to the line.

The real work began with the mares themselves. Fast and skittish, they dodged the poles and loops before being cornered by the equally fleet-footed driver mares. More than once Azarion was nearly yanked from the saddle by a frantic mare fighting the loop.

By midday, they had the mares tied to the milking line. Soaked in sweat and streaked with dirt, Azarion joined Gilene where she crouched under a mare with a milk pail. The strike of a hoof against the pail made her leap back with a curse. Milk sloshed onto the ground as she set the container down to shake one hand before clutching it with the other.

Azarion skirted the annoyed mare and another well-aimed kick. "Did she get you?"

Gilene glared at the horse before holding up a hand to show red fingers and the arc of a shallow scratch across her knuckles. "This is a lot harder than milking a cow."

Nearby, Lemey laughed. "They barely tolerate their foals stealing a sip, much less us."

Azarion motioned to Gilene. "Let me see."

She offered him her hand, hissing when his thumb glided over the scratch. Such a fine-boned hand, despite its calluses and scratches. He'd seen her hands hold fire, felt their weight on his injured back and their grip on his arm. Capable and strong, much like the woman herself.

"Nothing broken," he said. "But you'll have to be faster with the milking, or you'll end up with a broken finger or two before we're done. Come, I'll show you a few tricks for keeping clear of a hoof."

He was as good as his word, and Gilene filled the rest of her pails without mishap. When they were done, the milk was poured into tall, narrow-mouthed jugs and loaded onto the cart along with the pole lassos. After that, they set the mares and foals free.

Gilene pulled the harness off a foal that nibbled curiously at her tunic cuff. "What happens to them now?"

Azarion freed a mare and leapt out of the way as she kicked at him before bolting off, her foal's gangly form stretched out beside her as it raced to keep up. "We'll leave them be. These herds are numerous on the steppes. We'll come across another one at the new pastures and do the same thing again. Until then, we'll rely on the sheep for the unfermented milk and curds."

Once all the horses were freed and the cart was packed, everyone rinsed away the grime of their tasks and compared the bruises they'd earned. Azarion declined the invitation to join the others in their afternoon meal. He'd brought Gilene out here for a reason.

"I want to show you a place you might be interested in, and we can eat there. I've brought food." He gestured to the satchel tied to a ring on the saddle of the mare Gilene had ridden.

One eyebrow rose in a speculative expression. "It isn't a barrow, is it?"

He laughed. "It is, though I will swear on anything you wish, there's no wight waiting inside. And we can stay outside if you want."

She worried her lower lip against her teeth for a moment before deciding. "Take me to this barrow."

They said goodbye to the other drovers and headed toward a flat stretch of steppe where a single mound rested amid a field of purple and pink wildflowers.

Once they had their mounts unsaddled and left to graze nearby, Azarion laid out the horse blankets for seating not far from the mound's perimeter and the low entrance that faced east. Gilene dug into the satchel he handed her, setting down barley cakes, dried curds, and flasks of tea and barley water.

She sat cross-legged on one of the blankets and passed Azarion a cake when he reclined beside her, his legs stretched out so that his feet disappeared in the thick carpet of early-summer grass. He closed his eyes and nibbled at the cake while savoring the silence, the sunlight, and the company of the woman beside him.

"You're a good rider," she said. "More so than I realized until today."

He cracked open one eyelid to gaze at her. "I used to be better and was unmatched by any who fought in the Pit, but we were rarely on horseback during those fights. I'm still remembering the feel of a horse."

She pointed to a spot at his side. "What happened there? Hoof nick you?"

Azarion glanced down and saw that the small amount of blood inflicted by Karsas's knife had seeped through his tunic's heavy layers and left a stain. "Nothing so noble as a horse's hoof. Karsas and I had a . . . talk this morning. It went well enough." Gilene's worried look made him smile.

"Good conversations don't usually end in bloodstains."

"We're both still alive. It was friendly."

She flicked a crumb of barley cake at him. "I didn't think he was capable of 'friendly.' Your sister hates him."

Azarion stiffened. "Has he threatened you?" His cousin was lazy, double-dealing, and murderous. He wasn't stupid. To threaten a woman who might well be an *agacin* bordered on madness. *Ataman* or not, his entire clan would turn on him if he dared such a thing.

Gilene shook her head. "No, just looked at me as if he wished me dead or thought me a pile of sheep dung. But then I've seen him look at many people that way, including his wife."

He had no intention of sharing with Gilene the details of his conversation with Karsas. It served no purpose. He still wanted to rip out his cousin's guts, but again suppressed the anger, letting it cool and feed his desire for vengeance.

Gilene handed him a flask of the tea. "May I ask you something?" He nodded. "If Karsas were a good *ataman*, if the clan thrived under his leadership, would you still challenge him?"

Her question made him pause. It was something he never had to consider. Karsas as *ataman* put Clan Kestrel in danger. Once a stronger, bigger clan when Iruadis ruled it, it was diminished now. Azarion didn't need to hear the mutterings and discontent of his fellow clansmen over Karsas's governance to see how much the clan had fallen in wealth, status, and influence. It was obvious to him since the first day he returned. But while those things justified his reasons for wanting to oust Karsas as *ataman*, they weren't the only ones that drove Azarion toward his goals. "What good is there in a man who is a coward and sells his relative into slavery?"

She shook her head. "I didn't say he was a good man. A person can lead well and still be awful."

That was true. Brutal men had raised up powerful kingdoms in the past. A brutal woman co-ruled one now. "I don't know," he said. "I want back what was stolen from me, and Karsas makes it easy for me to justify my challenge. If he were as you say, a good leader with the clan's welfare his first concern, I might give it up. It would be a hard choice to make." He gave her a wry smile. "You ask difficult questions."

She smiled back, and Azarion forgot to breathe. "You give good answers." She paused, then continued her interrogation. "If you become *ataman* . . ." At his scowl, she amended her statement. "*When* you become *ataman*, what will you do for your clan? What will raise their status in the confederation?"

It was unfortunate no one on the Ataman Council had subjected Karsas to such questions years earlier, or if they had, he'd done a fine job of deceiving them into believing he would be a good leader for the clan.

This time Azarion had a ready answer for her, though one he knew would shock her. "I plan to take the entire Savatar nation to war against the Empire."

Gilene dropped the flask she held, only to snatch it up before all the tea spilled onto the blanket. The smile was gone, replaced by disappointed dismay. "You would drag your people into a war they can't win?"

That made him bristle. "The Savatar have grown too dependent on the Veil to protect them," he said. "They think only the Nunari are their enemy because they're the Empire's vassals closest to the Veil. We can actually see them through the flames when they test the Veil for weaknesses. The clans have forgotten about the east and its vulnerability.

"The Empire is invading there, not with a charge but with a slow creep. They're building more and more garrisons along the Golden Serpent, clawing their way into Goban territory one road, one garrison at a time. If they get through the Gamir Mountains and put a garrison there, there will be no stopping them. The Goban will fall first and then the Savatar. The Empire won't have to breach the Veil or even go near it to conquer us."

Her consternation faded as he spoke, replaced by an arrested expression that told him she considered his explanation. "The Empire is vast," she said. "There aren't enough of you to defeat her armies. How could you possibly succeed in such a plan? How could you convince the clans it would work?"

Azarion hadn't been idle while he waited for Gilene's magic to strengthen. Karsas had barred him from attending his council meetings with the clan's subchiefs, a petty move that earned him more than a few speculative looks and side-glances. It didn't stop

Azarion from gathering information about the status of the clan, of the confederation, of the Savatar nation, and the worries of their Goban neighbors to the east. A plan had formed in his mind, ambitious, risky, and dangerous, and the only way he could begin implementing it was to take back the chieftainship.

"You're right. It isn't possible to attack all of the Empire, but we can stab it in the heart, and its heart is Kraelag."

"Attack the capital?" Gilene tapped her chin, contemplating. "The Savatar would have a distance to travel to reach her gates, and every general would call up his units to defend her."

Azarion smirked. "I'm counting on it."

She was quiet after that, her mind working through all he had said, though she kept her thoughts to herself. He stretched out on his side to face her and propped his head on one hand. "My turn for questions. Why did you look surprised when I asked if you wanted to come with me to this drive?"

Over the past weeks, he'd caught her several times watching him with a thoughtful expression, as if she tried to puzzle him out. That same look settled on her features now.

"Because I think it's the first time since I met you that you haven't ordered me, threatened me, or bargained with me to do something."

Azarion's mouth dropped open, then snapped shut at Gilene's silent amusement. He tried to recall all of their interactions since they met, and scowled when he realized she didn't exaggerate. He'd never considered himself a tyrannical person. It was hard to be so when you were a slave who served many masters, but maybe he'd adopted their habits during his servitude even as he despised them for their ways.

His relationship with Gilene had been contentious from the start, not unexpected considering their circumstances. Still, they were no longer on the run from Kraelian trackers, Nunari clansmen, or Midrigarian demons. There was no reason to command instead of ask.

"You're right," he said. "I will ask more often."

A spark of something flickered in her eyes before disappearing. "I'm glad." She gave him another of those engaging smiles.

Her fingers danced restlessly across the pattern woven into the horse blanket on which she sat, and her forehead creased as she glanced at him and then away, only to do it again.

"Go ahead," he coaxed her. "Ask another one. I can see you want to."

"Why haven't you told anyone you can see through illusions?"

"I don't see any reason to do so. Maybe I was born with some slim thread of my mother's magic that's somehow knotted." He shrugged one shoulder. "Even if someone knew why I could see through illusions, it doesn't change the fact that I can. Saruke's magics are small. Warding circles, charms for health and protection against evil spirits. They're useful, as you saw with that thing in Midrigar, but she and other shamans like her don't wield the powers the *agacins* do, and the *agacins* don't wield illusion. I doubt they'd have any more idea than I do as to why I possess this talent. For all I know, half the clan might be able to see through your spells. They just aren't aware of it yet." He watched the wind seduce a lock of her hair into a dance. "And as you well know, sometimes a thing kept secret has power."

She acknowledged that with a quick tilt of her chin. She had given up much to help him, even when that help had been extorted at first. It was small repayment to let her keep this one secret of her magic until *she* chose to reveal it.

"How does a woman become an *agacin*?" she asked.

During her stay with his clan, Gilene had settled into the daily rhythm of the camp with only a few moments of awkwardness. That assimilation was partially due to his mother's subtle, guiding hand, but also to Gilene's natural inclination to listen more than she spoke and an active curiosity that inspired her to learn.

The *agacins* were enigmas themselves, though they were held in both awe and admiration by the Savatar. "Agna chooses a handmaiden to bless according to her whim," he replied. "No one clan is favored, no one family bears a line of *agacins*. A girl with the blessing doesn't even know she has it until after her menses start and the fire manifests in some way. One family almost burned to death in their *qara* when their middle daughter set it alight in her sleep."

Gilene's gaze focused on the horizon, though Azarion thought she looked inward instead of outward. "That's similar to the witches born in Beroe. The magic doesn't pass from generation to generation in a single family, and it never manifests before the girl has her menses." She frowned. "But why only Beroe? Why don't other villages have their own fire witch?"

He didn't have an answer. There might well be other witches, and like Beroe, those villages kept such knowledge a well-guarded secret. With the destruction of Midrigar by the Kraelian army and the Empire's most powerful sorcerers, the emperor then had recognized the implicit threat of those born with magic and who were trained in using it. The reward for those sorcerers who did the emperor's bidding and laid waste to what remained of Midrigar was execution, followed by the wholesale slaughter of every person in the Empire's boundaries suspected of possessing even the smallest magic. That had been well over a century earlier, and the Empire still didn't abide magic. If another village like Beroe sheltered a witch like Gilene, they were as vigilant as Beroe in keeping it secret.

"Your magic is different from the Savatar *agacins'*," he said. "Not in the way you wield fire but in the aftermath of the summoning. They don't suffer the wounds you do when they use their magic."

She sighed and raised her knees to clasp her arms around her legs and rest her cheek on her kneecaps. "That must be nice."

They sat in silence for several moments after that, watching the horse herd they'd worked earlier appear on the top of a small hillock before racing down its slope to a dip of pastureland.

"Why aren't you married?" Azarion asked. Her snort of laughter made him raise an eyebrow.

"Who says I'm not?"

He sat up. Her rebuttal made his heart seize for a moment, a reaction that startled him. A darker emotion chased the heels of his surprise—jealousy. He reeled inwardly at the revelation. A cascade of questions rushed to his lips, but he held them back.

*What is his name?*

*What excuse for a man would willingly surrender his wife to the horror of the Rites of Spring, not just once but many times?*

*Why isn't he tearing apart all of the Empire to find you?*

*Do you love him?*

At that last thought, he felt the blood drain from his face.

"Azarion?" Gilene reached out to touch his arm, her amusement replaced by faint concern.

He revised his question to be more direct. "Are you married?"

A bleakness chased away all humor in her features. "No. I will die young and disfigured, with no children to comfort me. What man would bind himself to a woman doomed to such a fate as mine? One made barren by her magic?" She spoke the words without a shred of self-pity, only a flat acceptance of a desolate future.

*I would.* Azarion crushed the thought as quickly as it blossomed in his mind, and sought frantically for some part of her statement that he could reply to without revealing his own turbulent emotions. "Our *agacins* aren't barren." She visibly startled at that declaration, and he continued. "Some are married. The *ata-agacin* is widowed. I think four or five of them have children. One or two have grandchildren. Why do you think your magic has made you barren?"

"Because I'm no innocent and should have had at least one child by now."

Azarion didn't carry the argument further. He'd seen the doubt of her own assumption flare in her eyes when he told her the *agacins* had children. And the hope. If Gilene were truly barren, then it was something other than her magic that made her so.

Once more, quiet reigned between them, and this time, it was Gilene who ended it with a question that might well have been a punch to his gut. "Why have you never used me? Without my magic to defend myself, I couldn't stop you."

Painful memories battered him. He allowed them their abuse, then pushed them away. He might one day be able to face them and not flinch, scatter them into nothing because they no longer meant anything to him, but today was not that day.

Gilene watched him, curious but also patient with his delayed response. While not a slave to the Empire as he had been, she had been its victim. Understood firsthand its cruelties and debasements, had suffered them and walked away bitter but still unbowed. If anyone might understand his reasoning, it was she.

He stared down at one of the patterns stitched in the horse blanket on which he sat. "Because I know what it is to be used. By one. By many. The empress likes an audience when she plays with her toys, and sometimes she likes the audience to participate."

When had his voice become so hoarse? His throat so tight? "The worst injuries I ever suffered—those that almost killed me—weren't earned in the Pit but in Dalvila's bedchamber. I might not have been able to help a Flower of Spring escape the fire when I was a gladiator, but I never made them, or any woman, suffer rape. I never have. I never will."

He didn't know if his words reassured her or if his revelation regarding his own tortures at the empress's delicate but merciless hands repulsed her, just as they repulsed him. But he no longer felt so burdened.

Gilene knee-walked from her spot to sit directly in front of him. Compassion, not pity, softened her gaze, and there was a warmth there that hadn't been present before when she looked at him. Behind those softer emotions, a banked fury glowed. She didn't touch him, nor did he reach for her, but her nearness filled all of his senses, and he leaned closer.

Her voice was as soft as the look in her eyes, her sentiment as unforgiving as her anger. "If I could, I would turn Kraelag into a scorch mark on the landscape."

They stared at each other until Azarion offered her a small smile. "I believe you."

Her gaze slid to a point beyond his shoulder. "Why did you bring me to this barrow?"

Grateful for the change in topic, he gained his feet and helped her stand. The barrow was a simple mound, lacking any decorative steles to describe some dead *ataman*'s military exploits or brag about his vigor and the many children he had sired. The only ornamentation lay in a carved disk set in the entrance's stone lintel—a kestrel with outstretched wings.

"My ancestors are buried here, including my father." He traced the kestrel. "I was born in front of this barrow. My mother insisted on it. She said the shared blood of mother, father, and child would bind me closer to my ancestors. To my grandfathers who ruled before my father. Their spirits would guide me when I assumed the role of *ataman*." He stroked the rough stone. "I wanted to show you that not all barrows are hiding places for the hunted or nests for wights. If fortune favors me, I'll be put in there to lie alongside my father when I die."

They walked half the barrow's perimeter before climbing to its peak. The elevation afforded them an even better view of this part of the steppe. Below them, their horses meandered through the grass, idly grazing side by side. Gilene shielded her eyes with one hand and made a slow pivot to survey her surroundings. "It's a good spot for a spirit to look out onto the living world."

It was indeed, and Azarion prayed his own spirit might enjoy the view as well when it came time to join his ancestors in the burial mound.

They hiked down the barrow's slope and completed their walk around its base, stopping when they came upon a withered bundle of herbs and flowers tied with a strip of yellow cloth embroidered in an intricate design of beads and horsehair thread. Gilene bent for a closer look but didn't pick up the flowers. "What is this?"

He thought he recognized the cloth, or at least the beadwork. "Offerings, mementos. That looks like my mother's stitchery. Tamura must have brought her here recently."

A niggle of guilt wormed through him. He'd been here only once since his return to the Sky Below, to see his father's bones laid out in the barrow and to leave an offering of his own to all his ancestors who had died and who now slept in this grave. He should have visited more than once. Should have brought Saruke here instead of relying on Tamura to do it. His sister had carried that responsibility, and others as well, on her own for long enough.

Gilene touched his arm. "I've always believed that talking to the dead is sometimes easier than talking to the living." She shrugged at his questioning look. "They listen better." She gestured toward their blankets and the remnants of their meal. "We need to return to camp. I'll pack everything and wait for you."

She left him in front of his mother's offering, and he listened as she whistled to the horses. Azarion knelt beside the flower bundle. Iruadis's bones lay inside the barrow, but Azarion liked to believe his spirit was out here, enjoying the wind and the smell of new grass alongside his son. Azarion closed his eyes and called up the image of his father when he last saw him, aged by the elements and diminished by illness but still powerful, still the respected *ataman* of a respected clan.

He kept that image in his mind as he prayed, first to Iruadis for guidance in pursuing his plan to retake the chieftainship and then to the pantheon of Savatar gods, especially Agna, for both mercy and favor. The wind caressed his ears, whispering its own supplications.

When he returned to the spot where he and Gilene had shared their food and conversation, he discovered their supplies packed away in the nearby satchel and Gilene stretched across both blankets, asleep in a pool of sunlight. He crouched down, making plenty of noise so as not to startle her when she opened her eyes and found him leaning over her.

She reached up with one hand to thread locks of his hair through her fingers. Azarion held his breath, stunned by her action and fearful he might ruin the moment with so much as a twitch.

"Did you pray?" she asked in a sleepy voice that set every nerve in his body to sparking. He nodded. Her touch was light as a moth's wings in his hair. "And did your gods listen?"

"I hope so." He bent lower, drawn helplessly down to her pale mouth. Still, she didn't move away.

Her fingertips traced a path across his face from cheekbone to cheekbone and over the tip of his nose. He closed his eyes when she repeated the action, this time going the opposite direction to journey across his eyelids before settling at the sensitive pulse point near his temple. When Azarion opened his eyes once more, he found her watching him intently, her eyes fathomless. They were so close now, he could feel the rise and fall of her chest as she breathed.

"I once thought I would always hate you, gladiator. That isn't true now." Her words set his heart to soaring, only to plummet it back to earth with those that followed. "I no longer hate you, and I will still never forget you."

He almost kissed her then, tethered to her by both desire and regret. Her eyes closed, black lashes soft on her cheeks, the fragile skin of her eyelids even paler than her mouth.

A chorus of whistles froze him in place. Gilene's eyes snapped open, and in a flash, she'd rolled out from under him and clambered to her feet. Azarion rose more slowly and joined her in her search for the source of the sound. A group of riders galloped toward them from the south, and Azarion recognized Tamura's smoke-gray mare in the lead.

Gilene reached for the satchel by her feet. "We've been gone a long time. They probably think we've come to a bad end."

He clasped her arm. "Gilene."

She turned to him then, her features once more set in the pinched visage she'd worn during their flight from the Empire. "Don't. Please. After all we've been through so far, together and separate, don't you think we both deserve some measure of peace?"

She twisted free and strode to her horse, leaving him to gather up the blankets. They saddled their mounts in silence and soon joined Tamura and her party in a leisurely ride back to camp.

Gilene was withdrawn the remainder of the evening, claiming the effects of too much sun when Saruke questioned why she seemed so listless. Once their household had eaten and settled down for the night, Azarion gathered up a blanket and saddle pad to take outside.

"Where are you going?"

Gilene stood behind him, wearing a thin shift, her slender feet bare.

"I thought you might wish to have the bed to yourself for tonight."

She hugged herself as if cold, though the *qara* still held plenty of heat created by the now cooling braziers. "I don't." She said nothing else, only dove under the covers of their shared pallet and pulled them up to her chin.

Azarion watched her for a moment before setting down his gear and undressing. He slid under the covers and lay on his back, counting the number of support poles in the *qara*'s roof. He and Gilene were more awkward now with each other than they had ever been, but he couldn't find it in himself to regret the day and his time with her. Given the chance, he'd do it again, only this time, he would ignore any visitors and kiss the fire witch's soft mouth.

He had started his third counting of the support poles, and was drifting off, when a pair of slender arms settled around his shoulders and tugged, coaxing him to roll to his side and into Gilene's embrace. She lay farther up on the pallet than he did so that his cheek rested against her breast and her chin grazed the top of his head. Her fingers combed gently through his hair.

It would be effortless to roll her to her back, push up her shift, and spread her thighs. He wanted her so badly, the desire made him dizzy. Instead, he concentrated on his breathing, on the feel of her hands in his hair instead of her warm body pressed to his.

She would accept his touch, his taking of her. He knew it by the languid sprawl of her limbs on his, the shallow rise and fall of her breast under his cheek, the changing scent of her skin. But he didn't want acceptance. He wanted enthusiasm, a passion for him that matched his for her. This embrace, as seductive as it was, came not from a place of lust but from one of solace.

So he settled harder against her and nuzzled the curve of her breast, content for now to listen to her heartbeat, rejoice in the knowledge she no longer hated him, and lament that such a change of heart wouldn't keep her in the Sky Below.

# CHAPTER THIRTEEN

S ummer had finally settled hard on the steppes, chasing away the rains that had lingered for weeks and turned the land into a vast quagmire. The relentless wet had left everyone and everything a soggy, miserable pile of foul-smelling wool. The people, the sheep, the *qaras*. They all reeked and were in desperate need of drying out. Only the horse herds and the wandering chickens escaped the stench. Today was the first dry day, and the wind galloping across the plains was finally dry instead of damp.

The new encampment the clan had set up lay a few hours' ride behind Gilene, and still she caught its stink on the wind. The green scent of sweet vernal was a welcome change.

A group of women and children, accompanied by a handful of archers, had left at dawn for a part of the steppe where one of the scouts had located a wide patch of wild strawberries not yet trampled or eaten by the horse herds. Gilene accompanied them, riding next to Saruke, who explained they'd cook for everyone while the women and children picked and gathered the berries.

They traveled for several miles, stopping when the scout who rode ahead whistled and waved to indicate the place where the strawberries grew. Tamura, lightly armored in a leather breastplate, vambraces, and greaves, rode up next to her mother. Even though Gilene had resided with their family for two months,

Azarion's sister remained guarded around Gilene, the suspicious light in her eyes undimmed.

"The six of us"—Tamura indicated the other five archers with a broad sweep of her hand—"will ride in the four directions to make sure we don't have thieves from Clan Saiga lurking in the grasses." She rode off, long braids bouncing against her back as the horse galloped toward the waiting archers.

When the foraging group reached their destination, they dismounted and fanned out, satchels draped across their shoulders, and bent to harvest the steppe's bounty. Gilene stayed behind to help Saruke set up a makeshift kitchen on the open plain. Soon flames coaxed out by fatwood and flint danced merrily under a large kettle filled with mutton fat.

She and Saruke sat side by side on a square of horsehide to keep their backsides dry and took turns placing flat rounds of barley cakes into the sizzling fat to fry. A bowl of butter sat nearby, alongside larger bowls of curds and hot, salty milk tea thickened with crushed barley.

Gilene handed one of the cooled cakes to Saruke. "Do you want to make more, or will these be enough?" Stacks of the cakes were piled up on a sheet of tin between them, glistening with fat and dripping with the butter spread on them. A few of the children lurked nearby, willing to brave Saruke and her long, accurate reach with a stick for the chance at snatching one of the treats.

"Oya!" Saruke snapped and waved the stick in a threatening sweep that sent the nimble youths bounding out of the way like startled hares. "Make yourselves useful and pick me some wild onion. I'll add it to the pot." They bolted away, part eager to help, part fearful of raising her ire.

She winked at Gilene and lowered her stick before taking

the offered cake. "This is good," she proclaimed after a few bites. "They won't complain, especially after hours with their backs bent over those berries."

Gilene wasn't so sure. Even though Saruke had made and rolled out the dough into individual cakes the night before, Gilene had been the one to fry most of them. The Savatar women would note it and no doubt criticize her efforts. As a possible *agacin*, she was treated in the most civil manner, given food to eat, a comfortable bed to sleep on, and shelter from the elements. But civility didn't translate to friendliness, and so far only Saruke had warmed enough to her to carry on a conversation that consisted of more than grunts, a few monosyllabic replies, and suspicious scrutiny. She might be an *agacin* according to those witnesses who'd seen her walk through the Veil, but she was not Savatar.

Saruke finished her cake and eyed the tin sheet holding the rest of the bounty. "Another handful will do it," she said. "Then we'll call the others back. A pack of them that size should be able to gather every berry out there in no time. We'll eat and head home." Her faded eyes swept the landscape. "We've wandered far today and are very close to Clan Saiga territory."

Gilene followed her gaze, seeing only the cluster of berry gatherers and the endless plume grass that grew as far as the eye could see. "How can you tell?"

Her companion audibly sniffed. "The smoke from their camp. They're down from the mountains earlier this year. There will be skirmishes over the best pasturelands."

In the time she'd been with the Savatar, Gilene had learned many things about the people of the Stara Dragana—mainly their love for fighting. "I thought the Savatar were united."

Saruke scooped curds into small cups and set them out near the tin of cakes. "In their hatred for the Empire, yes, but they still squabble among themselves. One clan against another for grazing and water rights. They marry each other's daughters and sons off to quiet the fighting, but it doesn't last long. The moment someone from Clan Marmot kills and eats a sheep belonging to someone from Clan Wolf, they start up again. Blood feuds, ritual combat. I sometimes wish the *agacins* would quench the Veil. Our warriors are restless pent up behind it. If they can't fight the Empire, they fight each other."

If Azarion's mother knew what Gilene did about Azarion's plan regarding the Empire, she might not wish for such a thing. Then again, Saruke might volunteer to ride alongside him in battle. The Empire had enslaved her son. She certainly had the motivation to heed a call to war against it.

"Karsas does nothing but drink and tup," Saruke muttered. "Useless leader, useless warrior. It's probably better the Veil stays up."

Her comment spurred Gilene to pursue a topic that had made her wonder since her meeting with the *agacins*. "Karsas betrayed Azarion, took the chieftainship from him through treachery instead of combat, yet Azarion says nothing of this to either council. Why? Wouldn't doing so make his claim stronger? Leadership of Clan Kestrel is his birthright. His reason for bringing me is to reclaim the chieftainship. Why not tell them what happened?"

They were out of earshot from the harvesters, but she took no chances, keeping her voice low. Karsas's wife, Arita, and their children were among those who picked, and while she observed that the marriage seemed more for political convenience than mutual affection, Gilene understood that loyalty was often commanded by more than emotion. She herself was loyal to Azarion. He was her way back home to Beroe. If she heard anything that might jeopardize his welfare, she'd tell him. That Arita would do the same for Karsas seemed probable. A memory of her time with

Azarion in front of his family's barrow, when he became something other than her adversary, teased her mind.

Saruke finished filling cups and turned her hand to pouring the milk tea. "Because he can't prove Karsas planned his capture and enslavement, and those who could bear witness to it because they were part of it are dead. Azarion is patient. He'll know the best time to make his accusations and take his revenge."

"I'd think it more justice than vengeance."

Was that a gleam of approval in Saruke's eyes? "Can it not be both?" she said and passed a cup of the milk tea to Gilene. "You defend him as fiercely as if you were his woman, though you are not."

Sharing the same *qara* day in and day out had made it difficult for Gilene and Azarion to maintain the lie that she was his concubine. Saruke was an observant woman, and it hadn't taken her long to understand their bond was built on something else. With a warning to keep what he said between them, he told her and Tamura the truth. Gilene sat next to him, listening and nodding as he explained their first meeting, his extortion of her help, her role as a Flower of Spring, and their escape from the Empire. He left out the part about Gilene's trickery with illusion and his own ability to discern it.

Tamura, who had treated Gilene with barely disguised disdain until then, stared at her with new eyes. "You're brave, and you saved my brother. My family is in your debt, *Agacin*." It was the first time she had addressed Gilene by that term. She still remained distant and suspicious, but the edge of hostility was gone.

Thereafter, Gilene slept alone in her own sleeping space not far from Azarion. At first, the change pleased her. Not once, in all the times they shared a bed, had he taken liberties with her, though she often woke to find him slumbering closer, an arm draped across her waist.

Likewise, morning sometimes saw her nestled against him, her head on his chest, his steady heartbeat a soothing lullaby in her ear. The first night in her new bed was a lonely one, though she'd never admit it to anyone, much less herself, that she missed his presence beside her under the covers, especially after his revelation about the empress's particular cruelties.

She understood his actions better now, that relentless push to reach his homeland and regain his place among his people, though it was at the cost of her own freedom. She didn't agree with it, and it didn't change her own determination to return to Beroe, but she no longer saw him as the enemy. Gilene had reached out that night and cradled him close, her soul aching over what he had endured at the Empire's hands. He lay heavy and peaceful in her arms, simply a man burdened by dark memory and lost time. The two of them were bound by a common past of subjugation and a resolve to overcome the damage it wrought.

Her thoughts turned to him more often during the day than she liked, but she couldn't chase them all away. More than once she'd caught herself mooning over his deft, patient handling of the horses in his mother's herds and how he tilted his head a little to the right before he laughed, even the way his long fingers curled around his teacup, or how the morning sun gilded his cheekbones when he sat outside to clip his beard short.

The suspiciously hopeful note in Saruke's voice made her back stiffen. "The sooner he's made *ataman*, the sooner I can go home." She glared into her teacup as if it refused to reveal some necessary secret.

Saruke sighed. "He can't claim the chieftainship until you

prove to the Fire Council that you are truly *agacin*." The hopeful note had turned to one of frustration.

"Was it not enough that I didn't burn to ash when they set me alight?"

The weeks that followed the Fire Council's decision not to declare her an *agacin* saw Gilene too busy to dwell on her prolonged stay on the steppes. She practiced her fire summoning, to no avail, and helped Saruke with her chores, which most often started before dawn and didn't end until right at sunset. Some of the household tasks were much like those she handled in Beroe; others were far different. She was on horseback as much as she was on foot and helped take care of the horse herds. She learned the basics of shepherding, complaining to Saruke at times that while the goats were entertaining, the sheep were dumber than rocks.

Saruke admonished her lightly with one of her bits of wisdom. "Better to have a dumb sheep that gives up warm wool than a smart rock that offers nothing to cold bones."

When they weren't shepherding, felting, weaving, cooking, or laundering, they were foraging—sometimes far beyond the encampment, like now, where wild strawberries, garlic, and onions sprang up among the plume grass.

Gilene fished the last barley cake out of the hot fat and dropped it on the tin with the others to cool. She and Saruke moved the kettle of oil away from the fire, replacing it with one filled with water. She stoked the fire with an iron rod, stirring the coals so they snapped and popped. The flames guttered a little, and a shiver of power danced down Gilene's fingers. Tongues of fire suddenly surged upward to embrace the pot before settling down.

Saruke leapt back, eyes wide. Gilene wrestled to contain her crow of joy. Her power was returning! More a trickle than a rushing river, but still there. Were she alone, she'd close her eyes, turn inward, and hunt for the fiery red thread she could always see in her mind's eye, one that wound through her in both flesh and spirit. Most often she resented its presence. Now, though . . . now she welcomed it.

She stirred the coals again, adopting a bored expression and ignoring Saruke's questioning look.

"Was that your magic?" she asked.

Gilene shook her head. "I think I just hit the right bundle of coals."

Doubt warred with excitement in Saruke's eyes. "Are you certain? Because if you can summon fire now, then we need to send a message to the *agacins*, and Azarion can challenge Karsas."

The last part of her statement made Gilene's heart stutter a little. Blood tanistry. The attainment of leadership through murder or war was no longer common in the Empire, but the steppe clans still practiced it. Karsas had avoided using it against Azarion and taken the coward's way, depending on others to rid him of the *ataman*'s son and clear the path for his own rise to the role of clan chieftain.

She took the chunks of wild turnips Saruke handed her and dumped them into the pot of boiling water. "Aren't you frightened he might lose in such a combat?"

Saruke's shoulders hunched as she tossed a handful of salt from a goatskin into the pot. "I just got him back after ten years. What do you think?"

They spoke no more of Azarion's plans as the foragers trickled back, their baskets loaded with wild berries. Women and children sported stained fingers and lips from eating the fruit as they picked. Gilene and Saruke passed out the barley cakes, bowls of curd, and cups of the still-warm milk tea. Another woman took over the task of boiling the turnips, and Gilene helped herself to the cache of berries.

They all flocked together in a rough circle, passing around the prepared food and drink. Lively chatter swirled around Gilene, who could understand only bits and pieces of the many conversations and relied on Saruke's translations to get an idea of what was said. In this, the Savatar—at least the women—were much like the women of Beroe in those topics that concerned them: difficult or kindly spouses, recalcitrant children, marriages and birth, death and war, the health of the livestock, the effects of the weather.

She would miss this once Azarion realized his ambitions and she left the Sky Below. These were not her people, not her ways, not even her language, yet here she could shed the burden of her duty as a Flower of Spring and simply be Gilene. An outlander, yes, and one whose blessing from Agna was still under a cloud of doubt, but no one here pitied her or lay the burden of their survival on her shoulders. Here, on the windy steppes, under a vault of blue sky, she could forget who she was and what waited for her to the west.

Conversation slowed to a trickle, then halted altogether at the rumble of fast hoofbeats. All six scouts who had accompanied their group to keep watch while they foraged bore down on them at full gallop, their horses' necks stretched long as they trampled a path through the grasses. The expressions on the scouts' faces as they rode closer made everyone stand.

Tamura reached them first, slowing her horse only enough to canter a circle around them.

"On your horses," she shouted. "Hurry! Clan Saiga raiders headed this way."

Had they been winged, the throng of women and children would have resembled a startled flock of birds taking flight. No one lingered to ask questions or demand details. Mothers gathered the youngest children while the older children retrieved the horses ground-tied nearby in a grazing herd.

Gilene helped Saruke douse the fire with the water used to boil the turnips. "What about our supplies?"

"Leave them," Saruke snapped. "If those Saiga catch any of us, it will cost the Kestrels a lot more in ransom to get them back than what a basket of berries or a couple of pots are worth."

They hurried to join the others and capture their horses. Only half their number had mounted when a high, triumphant cry sang on the wind. The low swale in which the group had foraged was surrounded on three sides by ridges. Neither high nor difficult to scale on horse or on foot, they nonetheless created a blind spot for those in the swale.

A line of horsemen slowly fanned across the top of one ridge, at least thirty, maybe forty—far more than the pitiful few who rode to put themselves between the Saiga raiders and the Kestrel women and children.

Tamura shouted over her shoulder, and Saruke hurriedly translated. "Hurry it up. We can't fight them all, but those on fast mares can outrun them while she and the others hold some of them off."

Gilene leapt to follow Tamura's order, then stopped. She was no warrior, no strategist or leader of soldiers, but even she could see their bid to escape the surrounding Saiga was futile. The six brave men and women trying to protect their clanswomen would die in the effort. She glanced at Saruke, who hesitated as well, her face white with fear. Not for herself but for her daughter whose straight back, fierce expression, and steady hands on the bow showed a warrior eager for a fight.

The Saiga warriors advanced down the slopes at a casual pace, their posture in the saddles revealing their surety of a successful capture of horses and hostages. Gilene grabbed Saruke's hand. "We can't outrun them. They're too many and too close."

Saruke shook her head. "What else can we do?" She tugged on Gilene's arm, pulling her toward the horses stamping and snorting as they sensed the tension in the air.

A plan took shape in her mind. A crazed one with about as much chance of success as outrunning the Saiga. However, if it worked, they'd all make it back to the encampment, with no one captured and no one dead. If it didn't, then the families of the fallen and the taken would have a ready source to blame in her. She would never see Beroe again if it did fail, and the thought made her pause for the space of a breath. So be it.

She wrested her arm free of Saruke's grip and grabbed the other woman by the shoulders. "Tell them not to run. Tell them to stay here. Together. To get off their horses and blindfold them with whatever they have."

Saruke gasped. "Are you mad?"

"Just do it. Tell them the *agacin* demands it."

She didn't wait to hear whether Saruke followed her instructions, but raced back to where she had doused the cooking fire. Voices argued behind her. She ignored them. All her attention centered on the pile of ash, and the tiny red spark that still glowed at its perimeter. No bigger than a bead, it had escaped the drowning from turnip water and gleamed bright and hot amid a bed of wet ash.

She crouched, her hand outstretched, palm down. The steppe, the women protesting her command, the steady drum of hoofbeats drawing closer—all faded as she stared at the jewel of hot coal and turned inward to listen to her magic.

The red thread was a stream now, still thin but unbroken. It spilled from the once empty well inside her, flowing through her veins in a steady current. Eager, waiting.

Fire magic was a harsh and unpredictable mistress, quick to turn on its wielder if not held in check by a firm hand. Gilene's life had been defined by controlling her birthright and suffering the consequences when she didn't. And now she'd be tested again, not by Savatar fire witches who demanded she prove her magic, but by Savatar warriors bent on raiding.

The tiny coal glowed hotter, brighter, bigger, until it surged up in a slender column of flame no bigger than a young willow branch. Unlike the god-fire of the Veil, it owed no allegiance to the Savatar and would readily burn any of them except the immune *agacins*. While the priestesses refused to recognize Gilene as one of theirs, this small flame obeyed its mistress. It shot through the space between her fingers, crackling in a merry dance that should have blistered her skin. Instead, more flames cascaded over her hand with a lover's touch, licking along her wrist and forearm, leaving flesh and clothing unharmed.

Gilene swept her arm in a graceful arc and whipped the fire across the ground, where it devoured the damp grasses in a shower of sparks and smoke that formed a circle around the now silent women and children. They watched her, eyes wide as she bent the fire to her will, feeding its hunger with the long grass, controlling its ravenous appetite with the magic she spun out in carefully measured strands.

The flames crackled low and close to the ground, the only hint of their presence to the approaching horsemen the telltale veils of smoke rising into the air. Gilene took her eyes off the fire long enough to find Saruke. "Tell them if they haven't yet blindfolded their horses to do so now or they'll lose them."

Saruke's rapid Savat broke the frozen tension, and more shuffling and horse snorts filled the air as the last of the horses had their eyes covered by torn bits of blankets, shawls, and the hems of tunics.

A trickle of sweat tickled the length of Gilene's back as the Saiga riders closed the distance, their casual pace speeding up until they hit full gallop. The whistling twang of an arrow loosed pierced the air, fired from the bow of one of the Kestrel scouts standing guard outside the fire circle. All six archers raised their shields as a thin volley of return fire spilled around them, arrows embedding in the ground around them and in the shields they held.

"A little closer," Gilene muttered. "Just a little closer." Patience, she reminded herself. Patience ruled fire. Not strength, not speed, and definitely not impulse.

The Saiga horsemen were almost on top of the defending archers when Gilene drew hardest on her magic. Were her power fully returned, the flames shooting up from the circle would have towered over them nearly as high as the Veil. Instead they created a wall only knee-high. Undeterred, Gilene incanted an illusion spell, and the flames exploded upward with the deep roar of an ancient draga's bellow.

On both sides, people cried out and horses whinnied as she shaped the flame into a colossal monstrosity of claws and teeth and glowing yellow eyes straight out of a Kraelian Book of Nightmares. The thing arched back before cannoning forward, its monstrous jaws snapping on a fiery bellow that sent the terrified horses of the equally terrified Saiga screaming and bucking as they fought their riders' control and lunged away from the horror threatening to either devour or burn them.

Gilene pitied the Kestrel archers, who cried out their terror and struggled to control their own maddened mounts, but there was nothing she could do for them. Outside the circle, all had to believe that an *agacin* of immense power had just raised a fire demon or some monster of equal horror and hurled it at them.

She fanned both flame and illusion with her magic until the last Saiga rider disappeared over the ridges, some now riding pillion with a compatriot, while their riderless horses bolted in the same direction, reins snapping behind them like angry vipers.

Once the Saiga were gone and the Kestrel archers paced their panicked mounts a farther distance back, calling out the names of those inside the circle, Gilene snuffed both the fire with a snap of her hand and the illusion with a softly spoken incantation. All that remained was a ring of blackened grass and the acrid smell of smoke.

Except for the occasional whicker from the horses and the ceaseless song of the wind, a heavy silence settled around her. Tamura, still shield-clad on her nervously pacing mount, wore an expression of wary shock. The same look was reflected on the faces of the other archers. Gilene's back prickled, and she pivoted to face the crowd inside the charred ring of grass.

Women clutched crying children or held the reins of blind horses with hands gone white at the knuckles. Their eyes were huge in their faces, some tear-stained, others pale with either terror or wonder.

A shudder racked Gilene, followed by a warning twinge along the underside of her arm. This magic she wrought was only a shadow of what she unleashed in the Pit each year, and the price she'd pay for it temporary. Painful blistering would ease over a couple of days with a soothing poultice. The red thread inside her still streamed and tumbled, undiminished by her careful use of its power combined with that of illusion. She might have cheered the triumph of her plan were she not being suffocated by dozens of Savatar stares.

She concentrated on Saruke. "Did that work? Will it give us enough time to reach camp before they come back?"

Saruke's smile slowly stretched across her face. "I think it worked fine, *Agacin.*" She bowed low, and as one, the crowd followed her lead. Gilene gasped, reaching out her hands in a futile bid to stop them.

When they straightened, many wore smiles similar to Azarion's mother. Saruke turned to them, hands on her hips. "You saw it," she said in trader's tongue. "We all saw it. She summoned fire."

Several nodded and one Savatar woman spoke up, also speaking in trader's tongue for Gilene's benefit. "We have to tell the Fire Council."

Gilene shook her head. She wasn't ready to face the *agacins* a second time. "It was only a small fire."

Saruke bent a doubtful scowl on her. "That was not a small fire."

"Trust me, it was," she argued. "If I'm to be tested again by the council, they'll know my power hasn't returned fully."

"But it's there." Saruke wouldn't be swayed. "Look how many of us saw you summon it!" Her smile returned. "You saved us, *Agacin.*"

A chorus of "Yes" and "Well done!" rose from the crowd, along with applause and cheering. Gilene squirmed inside, mortified at the unwanted attention. A blast of horse breath heated the back of her head. She spun and came face to muzzle with Tamura's horse.

Azarion's sister stared down at her, her imperious gaze challenging. She said nothing for long moments before swinging off the saddle to land lightly on her feet. She was of equal height to Gilene, leaner, harder, far more dangerous. Gilene fancied that if the Savatar allowed women to become *atamans*, this woman would rule a clan of her own.

Tamura bowed low like the others. Her features didn't lighten or smile, but her gaze was a little less suspicious, a little more admiring. "My brother will be pleased, *Agacin*."

A bubble of hysterical laughter filled Gilene's throat. The danger had passed for now, leaving the aftershock of relief to shatter her nerves. "Well, there is that."

Satisfied, Tamura barked orders that sent the crowd leaping to do her bidding. Blindfolds were removed from the horses, and children were placed in saddles. Those foodstuffs and supplies they originally planned to abandon were gathered up and loaded onto their mounts.

They traveled back to camp at a fast clip, cutting the ride time by half, unwilling to stop until they were within sight distance of the Kestrel encampment, where a wedge of warriors rode out to meet them.

Excited whoops and hollers filled the air. Gilene, riding in the middle of their group, next to Saruke, had never been happier to see the familiar sight of the Kestrel banner flags fluttering from the peaks of the subchiefs' and *ataman*'s *qaras* or the proud, handsome ex-slave riding toward them.

Tamura rode ahead, guiding her mount to cut across Azarion's path. He slowed, puzzlement flickering across his face. Gilene couldn't make out what his sister told him, but she could guess. Azarion sat even straighter in the saddle as Tamura punctuated whatever she said with flamboyant hand gestures. His gaze landed on Gilene riding toward him and stayed. Tamura turned to follow his stare until they were both watching Gilene like two hawks deciding who was going to eat the mouse. Azarion said something to his sister, who nodded, and then tapped his horse into motion.

The clan swarmed the returning riders, the roar of excited voices swirling around them as those who had been with Gilene recounted the tale of their escape to those who remained in camp. Reverent hands lightly touched Gilene's tunic and legs, the strappings of her low boots, as if by doing so, they could somehow touch her magic itself.

She was blessed multiple times by grateful husbands and fathers who didn't have to ransom their wives and children back. Some of the women removed brooches from their tunics and earrings from their ears to press them into her hands in gratitude. Gilene sought out Azarion as he slowly pushed his horse forward through the crowd. *Help me*, she mouthed to him.

He managed to extricate her and Saruke from the crowd with a few whistles and shouts before leading them to their *qara*. The people followed, and Azarion hustled them into the quiet interior. "They'll linger for a little while," he said. "Then go about their business."

"As they should," Saruke said as she crouched to start a fire in the *qara*'s main brazier. "Most of the day is gone, and there are people to feed as always." She gave Gilene another of her crinkly smiles. "Tonight, I cook something special."

She shooed them off with the admonishment that she couldn't work with people hanging over her, and Gilene dropped down to her sleeping pallet to remove her borrowed coat and hat. Azarion followed and crouched down in front of her.

Those bright green eyes, with their long lashes, searched her face. "Well done, *Agacin*." The pride and approval in his voice sent a warm glow spreading through her cold limbs.

She took up one of the felt slippers she'd been working on for Tamura. As Azarion said, there was business to tend to, and with Saruke working on their supper, she could see to this task. "It wasn't much, truly. It was your sister and the other archers who deserve the praise. They held their ground trying to protect us, even though they were easily outnumbered seven to one." Gilene recalled the six archers facing off against the Saiga warriors. Of the six, four had been women. "Savatar women are fierce warriors."

Azarion stroked her cheek. "As is this woman of Beroe. The entire camp is talking about the raid and how you chased off the Saiga. Your power has returned then?"

"Only a little." She stood and gestured for him to follow her to the cook fire. Azarion and Saruke watched, curious, as she waved her palm over the brazier's diminutive flames, making them jump. "This is the extent of my ability for now." She noted Saruke's confusion. "And this is how I can make the flames look bigger with illusion." Her short incantation turned the merry fire into a jet that shot toward the *qara*'s peak. Saruke scuttled back on a gasp; Azarion did not, and Gilene suspected he saw through this trickery as easily as he'd seen through all those she'd cast previously. "Your *agacins* may still not consider it enough to believe I'm one of them."

"If you show them this, how could they not?"

His absolute confidence in things never failed to surprise her. She admired his certainty, that focused will and careful strategizing, even when he had wielded it against her. There was much to be said for that kind of self-possession. "And if they do, will you then challenge Karsas for the role of chief?"

"Yes. It's long past time. Summer will end, and we'll be settled far into the east for the winter. I'll need to return you home before then." An odd intensity settled over his face, making an equally strange flutter tickle Gilene's insides. "That is if you still wish to go."

They stared at each other, Saruke forgotten. Had Azarion

asked this question a month earlier, Gilene would have thought him thickheaded. Everything she had done so far was an exercise in negotiation and tactics that would increase her chances of seeing Beroe again. Now, however, she hesitated to answer. Once, *wish* and *need* had been synonymous with each other. They were beginning to diverge. She frowned, unsettled by the notion. "I have to go. My family needs me. I have a duty to them and to Beroe."

A rare scowl darkened his features. "What is Beroe's duty to you, Gilene? You give the villagers everything, and they give you what? Their silence? Their secrecy? Their promise not to punish your family as long as you return to Kraelag each year? The clans would welcome you if you chose to stay. No Rites of Spring to suffer, no forced march to the capital or a night spent being used by a gladiator. You live easily among us now and, as an *agacin*, would be welcomed by any clan, not just Kestrel."

Saruke suddenly rose, her expression bemused. "Keep an eye on the fire while you talk. I need to borrow something from Odat. I'll return soon."

Her obvious bid at giving them privacy wasn't lost on either Gilene or Azarion. He watched his mother leave before turning back to Gilene. "She wants you to stay. You've been a good companion for her."

Gilene liked Saruke, with her nuggets of wisdom parsed out to any who listened, and she found the dour Tamura fascinating if not a little intimidating. They had made her sojourn among the Savatar not just bearable but enjoyable. The life of the Savatar was a hard one on the steppes, harder than life in Beroe if she discounted her annual trek to the arena, but she embraced it. Still, her duty lay to the west, though she now wished it otherwise. "I'm not Savatar."

Something in his expression made her breath catch. Despite her reluctant but growing affection—and attraction—for him, as well as his straightforward admiration for her, they were still captor and captive. Her resolve to return home hadn't changed.

She held still when he lifted her braid from her shoulder and ran his hand down its length in a slow caress. "You have a Savatar's strong heart. And you're Agna's handmaiden."

"Not yet. The council still has to decide that one, and I still have to pass their tests."

He snorted. "By now, the camp is buzzing like a hornet's nest with the news of you scaring away the Saiga. With as many people who saw you summon fire and have spread the word, I doubt there's a priestess among the council who will deny you the status."

She didn't possess his confidence, but so far he had been right in his assumptions. "What do you think Karsas is saying right now?"

A tight-lipped smile dipped in malice curved his lips. "I'm surprised my ears aren't on fire yet with all the cursing of my name I'm sure he's doing right now. He was certain you'd never regain your powers."

"You'll challenge him to combat?" Her stomach clenched as she said the words.

His fingers traveled along her braid as if it were a strand of prayer beads. "As soon as the *ata-agacin* declares your status."

She studied him while he stroked her hair, mesmerized by the action and by the heat of his gaze. "Your mother worries for your safety. I'm sure your sister does too." Did her voice just sound breathy?

His gaze intensified. "Are you troubled as well?"

She wanted to tell him no, but that would be a lie. Once, her worry would have sprung from the fear of not making it home to Beroe. No longer. Her concern for him was just as strong, but it had little to do with her chances of returning to her village, and Gilene inwardly flailed at the realization.

"Gilene?" He spoke her name as if in prayer.

"Yes," she said and gently pried her braid from his grasp.

He let her go, expression measuring, as if he peeled back layers of clothing, flesh, and muscle to look upon her spirit. "Even if I lose, I'll make sure you're returned home."

Gilene didn't pray. Gods were deaf, and life was short. She had better things to do than speak to those who didn't or wouldn't hear, yet she found herself silently beseeching the mercy of a goddess she refused to recognize for his continued welfare. Surely, Azarion's devout belief in Agna had earned him some small bit of divine providence.

She asked him a question, one that had nagged her over the days and weeks as he effortlessly settled back into the life of a Savatar warrior. "You've lived your life a slave for ten years and have found freedom once again. You've endured much to return to your people. I remember what you told me that day by the barrow. I understand your wish to reclaim all you've lost, but is this chieftainship worth the risk of losing your life to Karsas?"

That piercing gaze turned inward and away from her. "If Karsas ruled with merit, I wouldn't challenge him, but a lot has changed for my clan since I was sold, and none of it good. I truly believe I'll be a better *ataman* than him."

This was a man who would see his clan rise above all others in his lifetime. Gilene knew it in her gut. "I believe you'll not only be better than Karsas, but best of all the clan *atamans*."

His eyebrows rose, and a smile played across his mouth at her fervor. "I intend to be." Once more she came under the piercing stare. "If you stayed, you would be given a high place among Clan

Kestrel, a seat on the Fire Council, a bed in the *ataman's qara* for as long as you wish."

Something more lay beneath those words, an unspoken entreaty wrapped up in generosity. The odd flutter from earlier returned to dance beneath her ribs and tickle her heart.

Her family's fate rested in her hands, and while she couldn't recall any time where one of them offered her some escape from her own grim destiny, she knew herself incapable of abandoning them. She was Beroe's fire witch and the means by which they protected themselves from the Empire. It had always been so. That acceptance rankled even more in the face of Azarion's offer, but the guilt of abandoning others when she could save them would destroy her.

"I can't," she said, unable to hide the regret in her answer.

"Gilene . . ."

Tamura's entrance into the *qara* interrupted whatever he planned to say. The woman's eyes narrowed for a moment as she took in the scene of the two of them standing close together. Gilene stepped back, happy to put some physical distance between her and Azarion if for nothing more than to reclaim her ability to think and not just feel.

"Word has gone out," Tamura announced. "The entire camp knows about the *agacin's* deed. Riders have been dispatched to the other clan camps to tell the members of the Fire Council." A wide grin eased her hard expression. "We will celebrate tonight."

"Whatever for this time?" Even after weeks with the Savatar, Gilene was still flummoxed by the amount of celebrating they did, for everything from a girl's first bleed to a child's birth, to the recognition of some holy day.

Tamura eyed her as if she were daft. "Have you been outside

this *qara* since you returned?" At Gilene's "No," she snorted. "A mountain of gifts from grateful families will soon block the entrance."

Gilene gasped. "No! Send them back!" She grasped Azarion's forearm. "Please," she pleaded in softer tones. "No gifts. I did nothing to warrant them."

The magic she summoned had been nothing more than small grass fires enhanced with trickery to fool the unknowing Saiga raiders. But even had it been more, she couldn't accept the offerings. They were gifts in name only. Beneath their bounty and goodwill lay the expectation that she would do something similar in the future if the need arose. And she couldn't drain her magic for them. She wouldn't.

Fire magic wasn't limitless and the price to wield it steep. The light burn currently under her arm was the result of her building those small fires. Gilene conserved what she possessed not only to avoid the painful backlash of its use but also to ensure she had enough to make it through the Rites of Spring alive each year. If she helped the Savatar any more, she'd be unable to help Beroe when she returned, and that was where her first loyalty lay.

"No gifts," she repeated.

"Then you will insult these people in the worst way, *Agacin*," Tamura snapped.

Gilene glanced at Tamura's face, dark as a storm cloud, then back at Azarion's. His expression was far more enigmatic, as if he understood the reason for her refusal even if he might not agree with it.

"Unless you wish to offend every Savatar in this camp, you can't refuse the gifts, no matter how well-meaning." He must have seen the desperation in her eyes, because he covered her hand where it clutched his forearm. "Trust me. They won't assume your power is theirs to use at will."

With his assurances and no real choice in the matter, she reluctantly agreed to accepting the gifts and attending the celebration held in her honor that night.

Saruke's *qara* grew cluttered with numerous goods—pots and baskets, felted lap rugs and slippers, finely carved bone needles, and skeins of thread spun from wool and even silk. There were fur-lined gloves and tunics edged at the hem and cuffs with marmot fur. Bridles made of intricately tooled leather joined horse blankets striped in vivid colors. And these were just the items stored in the *qara*.

Outside, among the livestock and horses, the wealth of Azarion's family grew by several more goats, sheep, and a half dozen mares. The Savatar, to Gilene's quiet horror, were generous in expressing their gratitude. She only hoped they wouldn't hunt her down and punish her for her ingratitude when she left all of it behind with Azarion to return to her village at the end of the season.

Ten days after she built a monstrosity made of illusion and flame to frighten away the Saiga, the Fire Council once more congregated within the Kestrel clan's camp. Gilene was torn between dread and relief at the arrival of all nine of the *agacins* and their entourages. The wait had seemed interminable, highlighted by her own fear that she had burned out what little magic she managed to recoup, and the venomous looks Karsas cast her way anytime she was in his vicinity.

Those looks were broadcast to Azarion as well and either blithely ignored or returned with a stare that would freeze a hot coal in midburn. Gilene was far more intimidated by the *ataman's* obvious antipathy and strove to stay out of his way.

It was Tamura who escorted her to the *qara* reserved for the Fire Council's gathering and their testing of a handmaiden. Gilene's second trip to stand before the *agacins* was much like the first, made under the scrutiny of hundreds. Azarion stood near the entrance, his green eyes alight with both hope and faith. That look made the nervous sweat trickling down her back flow a little faster.

She and Tamura paused at the threshold, the hush around them a living entity that seemed to mock her. A woman appeared at the entrance to greet them, one of the nine priestesses Gilene remembered from the first council meeting.

"The Fire Council calls forth Gilene of Krael," she said in a loud, clear voice. She stepped aside and made a half bow.

Tamura nudged Gilene forward. "Good luck, *Agacin*," she whispered.

Gilene nodded, staring into the tent's black maw. She didn't dare glance at Azarion again to see his conviction in her success today. Her nerves were already stretched thin as it was.

The *agacins* were positioned as she remembered, in a half circle toward the back of the *qara* and facing the door. The *ata-agacin* stood at their center. An unlit brazier waited nearby alongside familiar items: candles, an oil lamp, a bundle of fatwood.

Gilene didn't know the fire priestesses' names. Such hadn't been shared during the first test of her powers, but she recognized their faces and their expressions, ranging from guarded expectation to outright disbelief.

She appreciated their skepticism. She had failed the first tests. She wasn't Savatar, and she didn't believe in, nor worship, the goddess Agna.

The *ata-agacin's* gaze scraped Gilene from head to foot. "We meet again, Gilene of Krael."

Gilene bowed. "Hopefully for a better outcome, *Ata*."

The priestess nodded. "Indeed." She pointed to the candles. "Show us as before. Light the candle."

She had done this during the first test with dismal results. This time, though, the red stream of magic flowed through Gilene's arms and down to her fingertips. The wick of each candle burst into life with a sizzle.

Every *agacin* sat a little straighter, and a few leaned forward, their doubt in her abilities burned away as quickly as the tallow coating the wicks.

The *ata-agacin* shared a speaking glance with her fellow handmaidens before returning her attention to Gilene. "Now the lamp."

Braced for failure even after the successful lighting of the candles, Gilene exhaled when the lamp's wick flared to life, the flames licking greedily at the oil. The shadows it cast danced along the *qara*'s felt walls as if in celebration of her accomplishment. The fatwood followed, burning to ash under her flame.

Whatever dubiousness regarding Gilene's power lingered with the *agacins*, it was gone now. They watched avidly as the *ata-agacin* pointed lastly to the cold brazier. "Light it."

This one required more power, and Gilene felt its drain as she concentrated on lighting the brazier. It roared to life with a burst of fire before settling down to burn the dried dung piled in the fuel bowl.

The *ata-agacin* raised an eyebrow. "Others say the flame you wrought to scare off the raiders was far greater than this. A wall of fire that turned into a draga." She might acknowledge the existence of Gilene's power, but by the look on her face, she wasn't particularly impressed with it.

"A bit of trickery," Gilene replied. "Fire isn't my only power." This time she incanted an illusion spell, raising a more epic sim-

ulacrum of the modest flames dancing in the brazier. A wave of
fire washed across the floor in a rushing tide, surging up the *qara*'s
walls and support columns to billow out across the roof.

The priestesses leapt to their feet, frantically gesturing to summon their own power and control the fire that threatened to turn
the *qara* into a roaring conflagration. They gaped, wide-eyed,
when Gilene abruptly ended the illusion with a single word. The
*qara* returned to its ambient gloom, with lamp, candle, and the
brazier flames cheerfully flickering away.

"What magic is this?" demanded one of the priestesses.

Gilene shrugged. "It's illusion. The draga that frightened off
the Saiga raiders was the magic of deception, not fire." She didn't
mention Azarion's odd and unexplained ability to see right through
illusion conjuring.

Another *agacin* scowled at her. "This isn't Agna's blessing."

"No, it isn't." The *ata-agacin*'s measuring gaze raked Gilene a
second time. Where before her regard had been one of faint dis-
missiveness, it was now that of cautious respect. "No *agacin* has
ever controlled illusion before."

"Maybe she isn't truly Agna-blessed."

The priestess reared back when the *ata-agacin* turned on her.
"No one controls fire without the goddess's blessing," she snapped.
"You speak blasphemy."

The other woman paled and raised her hands in a gesture of
surrender. "Forgive me, *Ata*." The other priestesses drew away
from her as if they feared whatever retribution the goddess might
visit on their sister would somehow spill onto them.

Gilene watched it all and wished herself anywhere but here,
before these rigid judges who would determine her worthiness
and, in turn, Azarion's ability to claim the chieftainship of Clan
Kestrel.

The *ata-agacin* returned her focus to Gilene. "Illusion isn't a blessing of Agna's." Her brow creased as her gaze turned inward. "But there are old tales, some spoken, others carved on the barrow steles. The ancient dragas used illusion to walk among us. It was once believed that draga blood spilled on sacred ground sometimes imparted its magic to those who lived on or near it." That piercing gaze snapped back to Gilene. "Where were you born?"

Gilene cast back in her memory for any mention by her parents or the village elders regarding something unique in Beroe's location but found nothing. She shrugged. "A village of no importance except for its dye exports."

Part of her wanted to howl with laughter at the idea she and the Beroe witches before her had somehow inherited magic from long-dead creatures that, until recently, she hardly believed ever existed. Yet another part of her wondered. No one could ever explain why a witch, with the ability to control fire and cast illusion, was born every generation to Beroe, in different families. What if her small, insignificant village was more than it seemed? And what if it explained Azarion's own unique talent for seeing through illusion? The *ata-agacin's* question of where Gilene was born made her pause as she recalled what he had told her when they sat together before his family's barrow.

*I was born in front of this barrow. My mother insisted on it.*

What lay in the soil under that barrow?

"Do you know something of the draga illusions, Gilene?"

Gilene's expression must have prompted the *ata-agacin's* question. Gilene wasn't willing to share her knowledge of Azarion's peculiar talent.

"No, *Ata*," she replied. "I know nothing of dragas or their powers." In that she spoke the truth and didn't look away from the *ata-agacin's* hard stare while the other woman delved deep for a lie.

After a tense moment, the priestess nodded. "How do we know these aren't simply candle flames with illusion cast over them?"

Gilene gestured to the items whose flames still burned due to her magic. "If you run your hands over those flames, you'll see their heat speaks true. And it's easy enough to prove. The raiders didn't discover my trickery because they didn't stay long enough to question it. Had they lingered, they might have figured out the fire they ran from was only a small one."

The woman's eyes narrowed. "I still don't understand why Agna would bless you. Do Kraelians even worship her?"

A shiver of apprehension cooled the perspiration gathered in the shallow valley of Gilene's back. There was real danger in this question. The *ata-agacin* didn't strike her as a zealot despite her chastisement of her fellow handmaiden. Still, the fervor of belief didn't always accept that some might not embrace it with the same enthusiasm. "I don't understand it either, *Ata*," she admitted. "I worship no god, Kraelian or otherwise, and unlike you, I pay a price for summoning fire."

The air in the *qara* grew noticeably heavier as the priestesses hunched toward her like crows over a carcass.

"What do you mean, 'a price'?" The *ata-agacin* moved closer to where Gilene stood, her watchful gaze curious and wary.

Gilene shoved back a sleeve of her tunic to reveal a burn scar under her forearm. A tug at the tunic's neckline showed another. "There are more," she said. "My back and legs. My ribs. One on my stomach. They appear after every summoning. Burns that heal quickly but scar when they do. The greater the summoning, the worse the injury and the scar." Her revelation garnered her a frown, but one more of confusion than disapproval.

"And yet you're blessed and walked through the Veil unharmed." The *ata-agacin* tilted her head, studying Gilene in a new way, as if she were an animal she'd never seen before. "Are your burns payment or punishment, I wonder."

Punishment? It was Gilene's turn to frown. Punishment denoted wrongdoing. What had she or the fire witches before her done to deserve such punitive consequences for wielding fire? "I don't understand."

The *ata-agacin* gestured toward the other priestesses. "Neither do we, though I have my suspicions."

Gilene hoped the *ata-agacin* intended to share them and not leave her puzzling over why she suffered injury when she was supposedly blessed by the Savatar fire goddess.

"Agna's blessing is given only to a few. It's an ungentle beast, tamed by belief and faith in the mother that created it. Those of us who receive the blessing are Agna's handmaidens. We're supplicants in her service. We believe." The *ata-agacin* paused, an unspoken message in her enigmatic gaze.

Gilene stiffened. She didn't recognize Agna, didn't worship her, and was most certainly not a supplicant. Was this why she was wounded after each summoning? Because she didn't believe? Didn't worship? Wasn't beholden? A blessing was a sanction, not a gift, and it was hard to be grateful to someone when you didn't even believe in them.

"Maybe the goddess doesn't see you if you don't see her."

"I can't worship something I have no faith in," Gilene protested. She'd gone too many years rejecting deities to suddenly embrace one wholeheartedly.

The *ata-agacin* shook her head. "No, you can't. So for now, you pay a price for the blessing." She gestured toward the *qara* entrance. "Wait outside. When we've made our decision, one of us will call for you."

Her abrupt dismissal didn't bode well, but Gilene didn't stay to argue. Outside, the sun shone bright in a clear sky, and while the curious crowd had grown impatient and diminished, Tamura and Azarion still waited.

Tamura bent for a quick peek into the *qara* before straightening to question Gilene. "Well?"

Gilene's eyes met Azarion's and stayed. "They're making their decision now. I passed their tests. The rest is out of my hands."

Tamura tapped her brother on the arm. "What will happen if they choose not to recognize her as one of theirs?"

Azarion shrugged. "Then I remain as I am. The returned son of the once-*ataman* Iruadis. Nothing more."

"And Gilene?"

Gilene refused to look away, hoping he read the message in her eyes. *You promised.*

"Gilene will return to the Empire."

His declaration literally made her wilt. Relief that she would return to Beroe in time. Disappointment over what she'd leave behind—days spent among the beauty of the Stara Dragana, acceptance among a people who saw her as something more than a useful sacrifice, and a driven man who enchanted her a little more each day.

Any more discussion halted when one of the *agacins* appeared at the entrance. "Come," she said. "The decision is made."

Gilene gave both brother and sister a quick nod before following the *agacin* inside the *qara*. Butterflies beat swift wings under her rib cage. She couldn't account for her dread of the priestess's decision. However they decided, she would still go home. She had fulfilled her part of the bargain with Azarion, yet she found herself knotting and unknotting her fingers, silently willing the council seated before her to accept her as one of their own.

The *ata-agacin* rose. The others followed suit. "Gilene of Krael," she said. "You aren't Savatar, yet you wield fire. You cast the magic of deception and don't worship any god known to your people or ours. Yet Agna has blessed you, resides within you. You aren't like us, yet you are as we are. The Fire Council recognizes you as a true *agacin*. Welcome to the Hearth, sister of the Flame."

# CHAPTER FOURTEEN

Saruke stepped back and swept Azarion with a critical look softened at the edges by pride. "You look like an *ataman*. They will note this when you stand before them."

For all that some *atamans* and subchiefs might admire his appearance, Azarion doubted any would be influenced by it in their decision regarding his challenge. "I don't think they'll care, *Ani*."

His mother sniffed. "They'll care. Don't think they haven't noticed how Clan Kestrel has dwindled. Clan Wolf is glad of it. They have risen because we're diminished, and they won't welcome your bid to reclaim the chieftainship. The others, though . . . they know better. All the clans need to be strong now. The Empire will find a way around the Veil in the west by encroaching from the east and overcoming the Goban. It's just a matter of time, and we'll be overrun by Kraelians and Nunari before we know it. All the Savatar are in danger. We can't afford to have someone as weak as Karsas leading us now."

She wasn't telling Azarion anything he didn't already know. His clan stuttered under the leadership of an inept *ataman*. Karsas had always craved power and prestige, and he was ambitious enough to plan his own cousin's enslavement to clear the way for his rise to clan leader. But he didn't know how to wield power once he possessed it, and the clan had suffered for it. It was long past time that Azarion take back what was rightfully his and save his clan.

Gilene stood just behind his mother. She wore the yellow sash of an *agacin* wrapped around her slender waist. It was a bright splash of color against the heavily embroidered tunic he'd given her to wear during her second test before the Fire Council. She still didn't know the identity of the generous benefactor. He no longer feared she'd give it back if she knew he'd been the one to gift it to her, but he wanted her to enjoy the outfit without wondering how she'd repay him for it or assume it had been given to soothe hostilities between them.

"Do you need me to stand with you?" she said.

"No. You'll be there as part of the Fire Council anyway. The *atamans* will approve or reject my challenge; the *agacins* will witness it and make sure the outcome is just."

A week earlier, the Fire Council had finally proclaimed Gilene an *agacin*. Tamura had whooped her glee at the announcement and made quick work of spreading the news throughout the Kestrel encampment.

They expected him to rejoice as well and put forth his challenge immediately. Instead, Azarion quietly escorted a shocked Gilene back to his mother's *qara* and served her multiple cups of tea until she stopped shaking. He then knelt before her and bowed over her hands. "Well done, *Agacin*," he said. Triumphant elation warred with a melancholy that constricted his breathing. He no longer had a reason to keep her in the Sky Below.

There had been much celebration that evening among the clan. Clan Kestrel could now claim an *agacin* in their midst, the concubine of the old chief's returned son. The people danced, sang songs, and toasted Gilene and the Fire Council.

*Atamans* and subchiefs from all the clans had arrived in an agreed-upon meeting spot unclaimed by any one clan and considered ground sacred to Agna. Here, the clans maintained a peace with each other long enough for the councils to meet and make decisions that affected the Savatar confederation as a whole. Today, he would stand before the leaders of all the clans, lay down his challenge, and pray they accepted.

Saruke gave his arm a last squeeze. "I'll get your sister. May Agna, and all the gods, bless you today, my son." She nodded to Gilene and exited the *qara*, leaving them alone within the glow of the brazier.

Azarion gazed at his newly recognized fire witch. She wasn't truly his and never would be. She belonged heart and soul to Beroe, but for this moment, he could indulge in the daydream. "You're *agacin* now, Gilene," he said softly. "One step closer to your return to Beroe."

Her head tilted to one side, her eyes reflecting only the shimmering light from the brazier. "And if they reject your challenge?"

"They won't. They can't. If they try, the decision will go to the Fire Council. The *agacins* defer to each other, and you support my bid. It is Agna's blessing. To reject my challenge is to reject the blessing." He reveled in the sudden bright glitter of admiration that entered her gaze.

"Sacrilege," she said.

He nodded. "Sacrilege."

She sighed. "Very clever, though never have I seen someone so eager to enter into combat."

"Combat is all I've known for a decade. I'm not afraid."

It wasn't an empty boast. He didn't fear a fight to the death with Karsas. In fact, he looked forward to it. That thirst for revenge had kept him alive, seen him through more battles than he could count as well as the vicious affections of an empress whose cruelty knew no bounds.

Gilene didn't possess that kind of cruelty, only a misplaced and unreciprocated loyalty to people who didn't deserve it. The ghost of a smile drifted across her mouth. "I can't imagine you afraid of anything, Azarion." The smile faded at his expression. "What?"

There was nothing of the Empire he wished to keep in either his home or his memory. Nothing save this resolved, enduring woman. "You don't address me by name often. I like the sound of it on your tongue."

He drew close, pleased beyond words when she didn't step back from his nearness. "*Agacin* who does not pray, I won't ask for your prayers before I face the *atamans*. Instead I'll ask for a kiss. One of luck." His fingertip brushed the underside of her chin. "Will you grant me that?"

There was a softness to her eyes and mouth that seduced him. "I'm an unlucky woman."

He traced the line of her jaw. "Not to me."

He slowly lowered his head, his heart thumping even harder when Gilene raised her face to his. Her cheek under his lips was smooth, giving, the skin over the bony ridge of her nose thin and fragile. Her eyelashes tickled his mouth when he brushed her closed eyelids, and a slow pulse beat at her temple. She was sublime, unweathered by the ceaseless wind that whipped across the steppe.

Even were she coarsened by years under the Sky Below's sun and breath, he'd still be drawn to her, find her beautiful. There was a brightness to her that shone from the inside, not of sunlight or the fire she wielded, but of the kind of light that winked off a sword blade.

Her lips were as soft as her cheek, her mouth welcoming as she opened slowly to him. He nibbled at her lower lip before teasing its surface with a sweep of his tongue and was rewarded for the caress with her startled inhalation. Despite her obvious surprise, she didn't back away but leaned forward even more, coaxing him with the angle of her body to do it again.

Azarion obliged her, settling his hands on the slight curves of her waist to draw her into his embrace before deepening the kiss. He made love to her with his mouth, reveling in the taste of her on his tongue, the feel of her lips pressed against his, the way her shallow breath drifted from her nostrils to fan across his beard.

The hands that unleashed fire pressed gently against his ribs, recalling a moment in a gloomy cell when her hesitant touch on his bruised, bloody body had offered succor.

Her soft moan set him alight quicker than any flame she might have summoned. One hand edged toward her tunic's hem, the other sliding upward to bury itself in the intricate knot of braids bound at her nape. He forgot about the councils waiting for him, his challenge against Karsas, even Karsas himself. Here, now, there was only Gilene in his arms and the grim realization that this magic was as ephemeral as the bright spark on steel.

The snap of the *qara*'s door flap signaled they were no longer alone. Azarion, reluctant to end the kiss, sucked on Gilene's lower lip a final time before straightening. He kept his arms around her, and she didn't pull away from him.

Saruke stared at them both, her face inscrutable. "It's time," she said. "The *atamans* call you to stand before them, my son, and state your challenge."

The *qara* erected to house both councils and witnesses was a large one set away from the other groupings of *qaras* that marked where

Clan Kestrel camped and where members of the visiting clans erected their tents. Multiple braziers heated the interior, and lamps cast a warm light on the occupants, who sat on blankets, furs, and pillows, awaiting Azarion's arrival.

They were the *atamans* of all the other Savatar clans, along with the subchiefs of Clan Kestrel. The *atamans* sat on one side, while the Fire Council, consisting of the powerful *agacins*, sat on the other.

Azarion gave Gilene a short bow. She returned it with a quick nod before striding to the side of the *qara* where the *agacins* sat and taking her place among them. She looked pale and serene. The only evidence of the passionate embrace they'd just shared was her lips, still rosy from Azarion's kisses.

Karsas didn't sit with the chiefs. Instead, he emerged from the shadowed periphery of the *qara* to stand beside Azarion. He spoke to Azarion, voice pitched low. "When I kill you in combat, I will return your body in pieces to your mother, and then I will hang your witch from the center pole of my *qara*."

Karsas's threat wasn't even a ripple on a still pond. Azarion had dealt with the like many times when fighting in the Pit. A tactic used to manipulate your opponent into reacting without thinking. Azarion ignored him in favor of studying the expressions of each *ataman*.

He recognized most of them, chiefs when his father ruled Clan Kestrel. Some bore a few more lines on their faces; others were so wizened and frail, they traveled from place to place in the Sky Below in carts instead of on horseback. Two looked close to his age, successors to their chieftainship either through birthright or challenge.

The *ataman* of the oldest clan, Clan Wolf, spoke first. "Azarion, son of Iruadis, child of Clan Kestrel, you stand before us. What is your claim?"

"I claim my birthright as *ataman* of Clan Kestrel." At his declaration, Karsas noticeably bristled.

"Clan Kestrel already has an *ataman*," Karsas snapped. "Chosen by the Ataman Council."

Azarion didn't waver. In the end, this was strictly a formality, a bid to gain permission from the other *atamans* to challenge Karsas in ritual combat for the right to assume the chieftainship. He addressed the council directly. "Only because I was sold to the Empire by my own clansmen at my cousin's bidding."

The crowd erupted into shouts, punctuated by Karsas's bellows of denial. Azarion waited for the chaos to die down and the councils to bring order. Once the *qara's* occupants settled, he continued.

"Karsas sits in my father's place for that reason alone. I have returned and with Agna's blessing." He nodded to where Gilene sat among the other *agacins*.

Karsas flung out a dismissive gesture in Gilene's direction. "She isn't even Savatar. A false *agacin*."

It was the wrong thing to say. Every *agacin* stiffened or frowned, affronted by the accusation.

Clan Wolf's *ataman* raised an eyebrow. "Not according to the Fire Council. They have claimed her as one of their own." He turned his attention back to Azarion. "We recognize your claim and the blessing, but it's only enough if Karsas agrees to step down and relinquish his place as *ataman*." He looked to Karsas. "Do you relinquish?"

Karsas crossed his arms. "No."

It was no less than Azarion expected and everything he'd hoped for before entering the *qara*. "Then I demand the right to ritual combat to reclaim the role from Karsas, son of Gastene."

A wave of whispers and murmurs rolled through the *qara* as the chieftains and witnesses gathered bent their heads to comment to each other.

The *ataman* of Clan Wolf settled a hard stare on Karsas. "Do you accept or decline, *Ataman* of Clan Kestrel? If you decline, you relinquish."

This time Karsas openly sneered at Azarion. "I accept."

"Then as the challenged, you may choose first blood or death."

A hush filled the *qara*. Karsas had no real choice despite the options given. If he chose first blood, he would survive, but the Savatar viewed such a choice as cowardly. He'd lose face with his clan, and the clan itself would lose even more status in the confederation. Sooner or later, he'd face another challenger and another after that, or else be found dead of some mysterious illness that struck no one else in his household.

Karsas was sly and murderous but not a fool. "I choose death," he announced.

Clan Wolf's *ataman* turned to Azarion. "Do you accept the terms?"

Finally. Ten years after hard struggle and patient resolve . . . "I accept," he said.

The *atamans* gathered closer together to discuss among themselves for a few moments. When they finished, they all stood. The *ataman* acting as spokesman turned to the Fire Council. "Does the Fire Council approve the challenge and the terms of combat?"

The *ata-agacin* stood as well. "We approve on both counts."

Azarion exhaled.

"You have today and this evening to make your sacrifices and appeal to the gods for their mercy." The *ataman* nodded to both Azarion and Karsas. "Tomorrow, at noon, you fight."

A huge crowd had gathered outside the *qara*, curious as to the meeting's outcome. Karsas shoved his way through the throng toward his *qara*, his face a thundercloud.

Azarion allowed the clans to swarm around him, answering their questions repeatedly as to what the *atamans* said and when the combat to decide the chieftainship would take place. The time for judgment regarding his ability to lead began now. Those who questioned him also gauged his behavior among them, deciding whether to remain neutral in this affair, offer him their support, or withhold it in favor of Karsas.

The light had waned by the time he returned to the *qara* where his mother, sister, and Gilene awaited him.

Tamura didn't waste time with questions. "You should practice after we eat. We can ride out from the encampment to a less crowded place. You can fight me. If you ask, I'm sure our uncle would sneak away to join us as well. It's been a long time since you've fought a Savatar, and you aren't as good on horseback as Karsas anymore."

Saruke hushed her and passed a wooden plate filled with food to Azarion. "I think his time fighting as a gladiator has prepared him well enough for this battle, on horseback or not."

"She's right, *Ani*," he said and accepted the plate with a nod of thanks. "I've ridden as much as possible since I came back, but ten years out of a saddle before that puts me at a disadvantage." He winked at Tamura. "The trick will be to get Karsas off his horse."

"Then we'll practice that," she declared. "I'll enjoy knocking you to the ground a few times. Revenge for when you pulled my braids when we were children."

They all laughed, even Gilene, and Azarion was grateful to Tamura, dour as she was, for keeping the conversation lighthearted. He'd have to be blind not to see the worry in her eyes or the fear in Saruke's. They had grieved his death once; they didn't want to do it again.

After supper, Saruke studied him and Gilene for a moment before ordering Tamura to accompany her to a friend's *qara* for a visit.

Tamura gaped at her. "Now, A*ni*?"

Saruke wrapped a shawl around her shoulders and strode to the *qara*'s threshold, an impatient scowl creasing her face. "Are you doing anything other than warming your feet by the fire?"

The younger woman grumbled but did as her mother bade. Azarion heard the two of them bickering as they walked away. He turned to Gilene, who dried the last of their dishware and set it aside.

"You brought me the luck I sought," he said. "I knew you would."

She refilled his cup with hot tea from the small pot simmering on the cooking brazier. "Is it luck? Tomorrow you fight to the death. It would have been better if Karsas had chosen first blood, don't you think? Your mother and sister fear for you."

"First blood for something as important as a chieftainship is a coward's choice. Karsas knew that. What respect he still has from the clan would be lost. To the death was the only real choice. Besides, first blood is too risky. I can give up a fair amount of blood and still win."

A grim smile curved her lips. "Only a Pit gladiator would say such a thing."

He scooted a little closer to where she sat. She reclined against a wedge of pillows, hands easy on the cup she held. She was beautiful. So grave, so composed. "Then you haven't lived with us long enough. The Savatar are fierce fighters."

One dark eyebrow lifted. "And unafraid of death?"

"Afraid enough to make them vicious in a fight." Karsas would be exceptionally hard to kill.

"Is Karsas a good fighter?"

Azarion shrugged. "I'll assume he's the best and hope otherwise."

Her brow knitted. "And he will be motivated."

"As will I."

He glided a finger down her tunic sleeve. She tracked its path with her eyes. Azarion wanted to kiss her again, but something about her demeanor—a hint of despair—made him hesitate. "I'll pray later tonight and make a sacrifice to Agna that she be my sword arm and the speed of my feet. Will her *agacin* keep me company while I do?"

"Don't you want your mother and sister there instead?"

"It will strengthen my challenge even more if the people see my *agacin* praying with me. That is how they see you."

"As yours or as an *agacin*?"

His finger slid over the knuckles of one of her hands. "Can it not be both?"

Her fingers fanned out, then briefly closed around his. Her dark eyes were bleak. "No, it can't."

# CHAPTER FIFTEEN

All of Clan Kestrel had gathered for the fight between Azarion and Karsas over the role of clan leader. People on foot and on horseback created a vast ring on an area of the steppe not far from the clan's encampment. Several members of the visiting clans had stayed as well to witness the combat, partly from curiosity or entertainment and partly to report back to their own clans as to who emerged victorious to rule Clan Kestrel.

Gilene stood at the very front of the makeshift arena next to Tamura. Saruke flanked her daughter's other side. Both women looked as grim as Gilene felt. Azarion had gotten what he wanted, the chance to challenge. That he might die in the effort to regain his birthright didn't seem to bother him. It scared her, and if the tight expressions on his mother's and sister's faces were any indication, it terrified them.

Across the stretch of grass, she spotted Karsas's wife and children surrounded by a retinue of his supporters. Arita wore a different expression from those who surrounded her, different from Tamura and Saruke. Hers was a bland facade, as if the confrontation about to take place held no more interest for her than watching sheep graze. Her children, a boy and a girl, neither of whom looked older than five or six, hugged her legs. Unlike their mother, they watched the gathering with wide, frightened eyes.

Gilene gestured to Arita with a lift of her chin. "What will become of Arita if Karsas loses?"

Tamura's arms crossed, her fingers digging into her upper arms. Time in the sun had burnished her skin to a golden brown, but now the color leached away, and her green eyes, so like her brother's, burned.

She glanced at Gilene from the corner of one eye. "It depends on many things. Arita and her children may return to her clan. She was Clan Eagle. They'd welcome her back simply for her value as a bride to another *ataman*." Such bitterness laced her words that Gilene's eyebrows rose. "Or she may choose to stay here if Azarion, as *ataman*, allows it." This time Tamura faced Gilene fully, that green gaze as piercing as a lance. "He may also wish to take her for his wife and name her children as his. It's been done before."

Something lurched inside Gilene, an unexpected and unwelcome pain. The memory of Azarion's kiss lingered in her mind and on her mouth. The brutal Pit fighter possessed many facets, including gentleness and passion. The thought of him sharing those with another made her nauseated and then annoyed.

Whom he chose or didn't choose as his wife was no concern of hers. His reason for bringing her to the Stara Dragana and her role in his rise in status were fulfilled. He was nothing more to her than the means by which she'd return to Beroe, just as she was no more than the means by which he'd regain his rightful place among his clansmen. None of that eased the ache in her chest. Her mind spoke reason; her heart refused to listen.

"It must be hard for her to witness this fight." She congratulated herself on the evenness of her tone.

Tamura shrugged and stared at Arita. A wistful look settled

over her features. "I don't know. Theirs was a match arranged by their families. Arita has always followed their commands above her own desires."

There was far more to the woman's comments than the surface meaning of her words, and the words themselves settled like stones in Gilene's belly. She followed Tamura's gaze. If Karsas had been the desire of Arita's family, who was Arita's desire? Had it been Tamura? She shook off her own jealousy over the idea of Azarion taking a wife, only to have melancholy take its place. If she interpreted Tamura's unspoken emotions correctly, how sad it must be to watch the one you love bind themselves to another and start a life with them, a life played out before you every day, with nothing to do but watch.

She wished she could offer some comfort or even a simple touch on the arm to let Tamura know she understood, but Azarion's sister was not a woman to welcome such an overt display of affection.

The crowd's raucous din diverted her attention. Both Azarion and Karsas traveled along a cleared path created by observers standing on either side. Each man rode a mare and was unarmored except for vambraces and whatever meager protection padded leather tunics and heavy trousers might offer. Both carried a sword sheathed in a scabbard tied to the horse's saddle instead of to the man himself.

The path opened up to the grassy arena where the two men would battle to the death for the title of *ataman*. They parted ways at its entrance so that Karsas circled to the left to pass in front of his wife and retinue while Azarion turned right and guided his mount toward the spot where Gilene stood with Saruke and Tamura.

A cheer from the crowd made Gilene look toward Karsas, who

had lifted his son to his shoulder. He raised a triumphant fist in the air, a signal to the crowd that not only would he remain *ataman* but also his son would inherit the chieftainship after him.

Azarion ignored the spectacle. He leaned down from the saddle to grasp his mother's hands with one of his and gave them a squeeze. She nodded once to him, a fierce tip of her head and an equally fierce scowl on her face proclaiming not only that she believed he'd win this fight but also that he better not disappoint her by dying. His lips twitched with the threat of a smile as he let her go to pause in front of Tamura.

His features softened, even as hers grew more severe. "Mura," he said gently. "When this is over, seek out Arita and offer her and her children shelter. The *qara* will be yours. And hers, if you wish it."

Tamura's lips parted. Made speechless by his statement, she could only gawk at him. She reached for him and gripped his fingers so hard, they turned red at the tips. "May Agna visit all her blessings on you today, Brother," she said fervently.

He squeezed her hand in return before letting go. He stopped in front of Gilene. "A blessing from a handmaiden, Gilene?"

She didn't hesitate. "Gladly given."

His eyes widened when she held out both arms to him. He lifted her so that she hung eye level in his embrace, his hands tight at her waist. She linked her fingers at his nape, offering a small smile when he gathered her close.

This time it was she who kissed him, an enthusiastic display of affection that made the crowd roar its approval and Azarion's mare dance sideways at the cacophony surrounding them. It was a kiss of desperation, of fear, and even of hope. Gilene ended it almost as quickly as she began it, leaving both Azarion and her gasping.

She cupped his face in her hands and gave him her most ferocious scowl. "Don't die, gladiator."

He stole a second kiss from her before resting his forehead against hers. "I won't, *Agacin*."

Saruke's smug grin when he set Gilene down was as much for her benefit as for the crowd's. Gilene pretended not to see. She ran her tongue over her lips, still tingling from the kiss. Azarion continued his navigation of the circle, touching the outstretched hands of the Savatar gathered there.

When the *ata-agacin* entered the arena, the people quieted until there was only the wind and the occasional nicker of a restless horse. "Come forth, Karsas, son of Gastene, and Azarion, son of Iruadis."

The two men rode forward until they stood on either side of the *ata-agacin*. The priestess raised both arms to indicate the opponents. "Savatar, before you stand the *ataman* of Clan Kestrel and the challenger to his title as chief. Azarion, son of Iruadis, has challenged, and Karsas, son of Gastene, has accepted combat to the death. Do you embrace the winner as your leader?"

As one, the clan shouted its acceptance. Karsas raised his fist again in another victory gesture. Azarion only gave a shallow bow in acknowledgment of the crowd's response.

The *ata-agacin* bowed her head and clasped her hands, her pose one of prayer. The other *agacins* followed suit, and Gilene mimicked their gestures, if not their praying.

She edged closer to Tamura to whisper. "He's very calm. Such peace must have served him well when he fought in the arena."

"He was the same as a child," Tamura replied in a whisper of her own. "Quiet, but also single-minded."

"And stubborn, I suspect." He would have to be to remain unbroken on the Empire's wheel.

Tamura chuffed and rolled her eyes. "Very. But he was never unkind in his pursuit of those things he wanted. The years as a slave have changed him in some ways."

Gilene sighed. "The Empire is a stain on the world. A wretched kingdom."

The Savatar paid her and Tamura no attention, their focus on the *ata-agacin* and the two men waiting to spill blood on the Sky Below.

Tamura's top lip twitched with a sneer. "Karsas is responsible for my brother's enslavement. I hope Azarion kills him and takes his head."

Gilene shuddered at the image her words conjured. "Kraelag trains its gladiators hard and often to fight well in the Pit. Azarion was the Gladius Prime. The best fighter with the most kills. The one the crowds made their bets on most, the one they all came to see. The favorite."

Her words dredged up the dark recollections of the Rites of Spring with its carcass-strewn Pit and blood-soaked sand. And here she was, a witness to another fight in another arena, resulting in another death. The consolation of knowing this fight was for a purpose beyond the entertainment of a bloodthirsty and bored audience didn't quell her horror.

Tamura suffered no such qualms. "Then let's hope those skills see him through today and he comes out of this combat the winner. Our people need him. My mother needs him."

Gilene nodded. *I need him.* The sentiment was unspoken, admitted only to herself and reluctantly at that. When had the man who was once only a means to an end become something more?

The *ata-agacin* finished her prayer and opened her eyes. She placed a hand on the neck of either horse. "To the victor, the clan," she proclaimed and stepped back into the circle's edge.

Though she tried her best to stay calm, Gilene's breathing quickened. The two men parted ways, each going to an opposite side of the circle only to wheel their horses around in preparation for a charge. They'd each unsheathed their swords. The slender, curved blades favored by the Savatar were perfectly designed for slashing attacks from horseback.

She shouldn't be afraid. Azarion was a renowned fighter, skilled in combat, and not just combat against men. The Empire pitted its fighters against animals as well—bulls, bears, lions, and wolves. Sometimes the men won, sometimes the animals did. Facing Karsas wouldn't even make Azarion break a sweat. Gilene, on the other hand, felt it trickle down her back and sides as fear gripped her.

She jumped when, with a bellow, Karsas charged first, sword flashing in the sunlight. Azarion drummed his heels into his mare's sides, and she raced toward the other horse. The ring of steel as the two blades met rose above the crowd's clamor.

Like his kinsmen, Karsas was an excellent horseman. Nimble and fast, he avoided Azarion's slashes by sliding half off his horse's back only to swing back up and wheel his mount around on a tight pivot to face his opponent again. His mare, used to such acrobatics, didn't so much as flick an ear when he sometimes dropped to the ground beside her, feet barely touching earth while he used her as a shield and vaulted atop her back once more after a charge.

Azarion was an adept rider, better than most Kraelian horsemen Gilene had seen, but he didn't possess his cousin's equine prowess. What he lacked there, he made up for in fast reaction, able to counter Karsas's attacks with lightning accuracy.

The two sparred with each other over several charges, neither managing to strike the other despite numerous attempts, equally matched in their abilities to dodge attacks. The crowd called out encouragement to its particular favorite, some throwing in suggestions for what to do next, others to spur them on to greater risks.

Another charge brought the two men close together in a pass.

At the last second, Karsas switched sword hands, bringing the blade down in a short arc that sliced a line across Azarion's chest and split the quilting of his tunic.

To avoid a deeper cut, Azarion lunged back, overcompensating in the movement, and tumbled off his mount. He sprang instantly to his feet but not before the mare galloped out of range for him to catch her.

Gilene clapped her hands over her mouth to stifle her gasp. Beside her, Tamura cursed, and near them Karsas pivoted his horse in a triumphant prance while he trilled a victory cry.

"He fell on purpose."

Startled by the comment, Gilene gaped at Tamura. "What do you mean?"

Tamura didn't answer, her gaze locked on the scene. Karsas trotted the perimeter, raising the crowd's avidity for the combat. Azarion jogged in tandem with his movements, always keeping his opponent opposite him until he stood with his back to Gilene, and Karsas faced them across the trampled expanse of grass.

Gloating at his obvious advantage, Karsas showed off his prowess with both blade and horse by leaping to a standing position atop his mount's back and spinning his sword in a fast circular motion that created its own shield wall as a defense against attack. It was a showy maneuver, effective in its intimidation against an enemy unfamiliar with Savatar fighting tactics.

Azarion didn't react, only held his ground and calmly observed Karsas's actions. To anyone watching, he was at a clear disadvantage—an armed man on foot facing an armed one on horseback—but Tamura's comment made Gilene wonder whether that was truly the case.

She didn't have the time to puzzle out the why of his action. Karsas dropped down neatly onto the riding pad and, with another victorious ululation, kicked his horse into a hard gallop straight for Azarion.

Azarion trotted closer to the center as if to meet the charge, then stopped, knees slightly bent, his sword held in a relaxed grip as Karsas raced toward him. The Savatar screamed and shouted.

*Get out of the way. Get out of the way!* Gilene shrieked the command inside her head. Beside her, Tamura was silent, taut as a bowstring.

Clods of dirt flew up from under the mare's pounding hooves, and Karsas lowered his body to her neck, streamlining both horse and rider until they resembled an arrow shooting straight for Azarion.

She did scream, as did Tamura, when Karsas's mare drew nearly abreast to Azarion. Karsas angled his body to the right and swung the sword in an upward arc, the move guaranteed to split his opponent open from groin to throat.

Had he remained in place.

The crowd gave a singular gasp when Azarion let go of his sword and dropped into a tuck and roll that carried him under the galloping mare's belly. The Savatar roared when the mare stumbled and a short spray of blood spattered the ground as Azarion sprang up on the other side, hands cupped under Karsas's left foot. He heaved upward, sending the startled rider flying off the horse's back.

Karsas hit the ground hard. His horse galloped several paces away before a Savatar caught her reins and brought her to a halt. Disoriented, the *ataman* staggered to his feet, still clutching his sword.

Azarion bolted toward him, a bright flag of blood cascading down his back on the left side. Gilene spared a quick glance at Tamura. "Why is he bleeding?"

Tamura shrugged, her eyes narrowed. "I don't know. I think the mare's hoof caught him when he rolled under her."

Azarion crashed into Karsas, arm slamming downward to smash the sword out of his hand. Karsas fell to his back, and Azarion followed, keeping enough of his balance to stay on his knees and pin his enemy down. He grabbed the other man by the ears, using them as grips to slam his head against the ground.

"Ten years," Azarion snarled. The open-palm strike he landed against the side of Karsas's head made the other man grunt and spit blood. Gilene's heartbeat thundered in her skull at the sight, at the sound of animalistic rage in Azarion's voice. "A slave to the Empire." Another blow, this time to the other side of Karsas's head. More blood to mingle with the crimson flow that spilled from the open wound on Azarion's shoulder to water the grass.

With a guttural roar, Karsas lunged upward, freeing one arm long enough to punch Azarion in the side and clip the underside of his chin with his head. Azarion fell away, only to spring to his feet. Karsas did the same, and the two men rushed at each other.

Lean and quick, with the powerful leg muscles earned from a lifetime of skilled horsemanship, Karsas used those strengths, landing a pair of kicks on Azarion in quick succession: one against his arm, another to his hip, followed by a knee to his groin. The last made the crowd groan as one.

Azarion never fell, never flinched, and Gilene noticed something in the violence of their match. He took the hits on purpose. Karsas had aimed for Azarion's knees and his ribs, vulnerable spots that, once broken, would have abruptly ended the fight. Azarion absorbed the kicks but twisted his body in such a way that Karsas's lethal strikes landed against his arm and hip. The groin hit might have taken another man down, but not a Pit gladiator. She'd seen some of the fights from a cell during the Rites. Strikes to the ribs, the liver, or the kidneys disabled opponents. Groin hits didn't.

While Karsas was fast, Azarion was equally so and also trained. It took the other man only a moment to realize Azarion had allowed the kicks to go through. He leapt back, but not quickly enough.

Azarion delivered a round of blows to Karsas's face and torso. Measured, swift, meant to bloody and bruise but not immediately disable, those blows spun Karsas one way and then the other, driving him back to where his sword lay in the grass. It became obvious to the crowd that Azarion was playing with his adversary the way a cat played with a rat.

Blood saturated Azarion's tunic from his shoulder to his hip, seeping from the wound made by the mare's hoof. He looked pale but undaunted by the injury as he swatted his cousin across the makeshift arena, eyes flat, expression murderous.

Karsas staggered, wiped a hand across his face that left a bloody smear, and lunged for his sword. He swayed on his feet, waving the blade in front of him with threatening swipes. "I am *ataman*," he declared before spitting out a gobbet of blood. "You are nothing but a Kraelian thrall."

Azarion halted and watched him for a moment before backing away to where his own sword had landed. He kept his gaze on Karsas and casually bent to grab the blade. A fleeting humorless smile played across his mouth when Karsas charged him.

Just as casually, he countered the attack, his years as a Pit fighter evident in the ease with which he handled the sword and fought his cousin.

Gilene steepled her fingers and pressed them to her mouth, hardly daring to breathe as Azarion and Karsas battled.

"I was enslaved, thanks to you," Azarion said. He caught Karsas across the chest, leaving a shallow cut that split the other man's leather tunic but didn't draw blood. "Beaten, raped, degraded."

"One," Tamura breathed in a soft voice. Gilene spared her a puzzled glance before turning her attention back to the fight.

Karsas's own swings were clumsy, his movements slowing. Exhaustion, mixed with fear, turned his features gaunt.

Azarion landed another cut, this one on Karsas's leg. Like the first, it was shallow. Unlike it, blood welled above the slash in the fabric. "Who else did you ambush or murder to keep your secrets and hold your power?"

"Two," Tamura said.

Others nearby turned to look at her. Realization dawned on Gilene, and her heart ached for the man who would likely find his justice but not his peace when this was over.

Another slash, this one across Karsas's abdomen.

Gilene joined Tamura. "Three."

A cut for every year Azarion had been enslaved because of his cousin's ambitions and his cowardice.

"Four."

Karsas cursed Azarion, calling him every filthy name in Savat as well as trader's tongue, bloody spittle glossing his lips. His eyes were wide, his stare frenzied and hate-filled. He no longer seemed to notice when Azarion cut him, painting him a little redder each time.

"Five." The crowd joined its collective voice to Tamura's and Gilene's.

A grueling, excruciating count that ground out in blood, sweat, and pain.

"Six."

Gilene prayed it would end soon. She felt no pity for Karsas, but his children stood across the field, their faces buried in their stoic mother's tunic. Justice and vengeance. The merciless speed of the first had become the prolonged savagery of the second.

At the seventh slash, she no longer counted out loud. By the eighth, she found herself praying, not to gods but to Azarion himself. "Finish it," she said under her breath. "Please."

As if he heard her plea, he altered his stance and struck with a sweeping arc of his blade.

"Nine," the crowd said in chorus, their voices lowered to a grim murmur.

A gout of blood spilled through Karsas's fingers, and he fell to his knees. Gilene closed her eyes against the sight of his entrails bulging from the gaping wound that split his gut. Azarion had nearly cut him in half.

She opened her eyes in time to witness Azarion end his cousin's suffering with a hard, clean slash that severed the man's head from his body. The head rolled in one direction as the body tipped to the side and hit the ground with a dull thud.

The silence that followed was deafening, broken only by Azarion's clipped voice. "Ten."

Keening cries of grief rose from the crowd but were soon drowned out by the triumphant roar of those who had sided with Azarion's bid to reclaim the chieftainship.

Gilene turned to Saruke, who stared at her son with tear-filled eyes. Her mouth trembled. "He lives," she said, as if still trying to convince herself that Azarion had come out the victor and the survivor of this bout.

Beside her, Tamura reacted in an entirely different way from Saruke, shouting her brother's name and chanting "*Ataman! Ataman!*" along with the rest of the clan as Azarion took a victory walk along the circle's perimeter, sword raised, his face gray. Blood coated his entire left side, but he paid it no heed as he recognized the clan's acceptance of his leadership.

He paused briefly before the newly widowed Arita and the

children pressed against her. Her expression was inscrutable when he leaned in and said something in her ear. Her features didn't change, though her gaze flickered toward Tamura before she gave a quick nod.

By the time Azarion had completed his victory walk and stood before the three women of his household, the crowd had gone riotous with celebration, passing flasks of fermented mare's milk between them and breaking into impromptu jigs, as if Karsas's headless body didn't sprawl before them in the bloodstained grass.

Gilene gathered around Azarion, along with Saruke and Tamura. Up close, he looked even more ghastly, and the serene facade he wore cracked under exhaustion. Pain darkened his eyes.

He grasped one of Tamura's hands. "Get me to the *qara* before I collapse," he said in a raspy voice.

His warning might have been a lightning strike at their feet. Gilene and Tamura each took up a place on either side of him and leaned close to offer support while Saruke cleaved a path through the gathering.

They made it to the *qara* without a moment to spare. Azarion took three steps past the threshold before dropping his sword and falling to his knees, bringing Gilene and his sister with him.

"Fetch a healer," Saruke snapped once Tamura gained her feet, and the younger woman bolted out of the *qara*.

Saruke and Gilene managed to coax Azarion up long enough to stumble to his pallet, where he crumpled, facedown, into the bedding.

His mother used a knife to cut away his gore-soaked tunic. "Drying cloths, quick," she commanded Gilene. "And there's a small green box in that chest." She pointed to one close to her pallet. "Bring it." Gilene jumped to do her bidding, returning with the items requested.

Saruke carefully peeled away the last strip of Azarion's tunic and tossed it aside. He grunted but didn't move. Both women gasped at the sight of the wound, a gaping slash with ragged edges that split a diagonal line across the shoulder blade and down his back. Blood welled from the wound to slide down his side and stain the bedding.

To Gilene, it looked life-threatening. "Is it very deep?"

"Deep enough that it'll need sewing." Saruke peered more closely at the injury. "I won't know much more until we clean him up."

She opened the box Gilene handed her and tilted its contents into her cupped palm. Gilene recognized the yellow powder. Her mother always kept a supply in her cupboard to help control fleas in the summer.

"How does the yarrow help?"

Saruke poured the powder directly into the wound. Azarion didn't move. "It stops the bleeding." She gestured for Gilene to pass her one of the cloths, which she folded and pressed to his flesh. Blood saturated the cloth, and she applied more until the compress lay thick and blood-spotted under her hand.

Gilene had set a pot of water to warm on the cooking brazier when Tamura returned with the healer, a tiny woman who looked more avian than human with her withered hands like bird feet, a nose that resembled a beak, and black eyes that saw everything. She crouched beside Saruke to inspect Azarion's injury.

Tamura joined Gilene at the brazier. "How badly is he wounded?"

Gilene stoked the coals before testing the water's temperature with her finger. Not warm enough yet. "Your mother managed to stop the worst of the bleeding, but she thinks he'll need stitching."

The idea of a needle puncturing his skin made her shudder. Her oldest brother had suffered through such a procedure when he was eleven. She'd never forgotten the sound of his screams. "I didn't know a horse's hoof could cut someone so badly."

The maneuver he'd executed to unhorse Karsas had been a risky one, dependent on perfect timing and speed to keep from being trampled. It had been an impressive display of Azarion's daring and prowess, but he hadn't come away from the feat unscathed.

Tamura gave an indelicate snort. "A horse's hoof can do a lot of damage, especially its edge. He's lucky the mare took him in the shoulder instead of the head. He wouldn't have survived otherwise." She and Gilene stared at each other, recognizing their mutual fear of Azarion's close call with death.

Gilene left the brazier to join Saruke and Vua, the healer, at Azarion's pallet. The healer was explaining that he would suffer fever from his injury and to dose him with both willow bark tea for the fever and bone broth for the blood loss.

She gingerly peeled back the compresses Saruke had used, careful not to dislodge anything newly scabbed. Azarion twitched but remained quiet. Gilene flinched for him.

Vua stared at the wound and frowned. "This is deep enough to need stitching," she said, echoing Saruke's earlier declaration. "I'll return with supplies." She replaced the compresses. "Keep a pot of water heated, and have more cloths ready." She rose and departed, leaving Gilene, Saruke, and Tamura gathered around their silent patient.

Gilene touched Saruke's arm. "What do you want us to do?"

Saruke ran her fingers through Azarion's hair. "Watch over him while I brew the tea Vua wants." She turned to Tamura. "See if you can find a family willing to part with some mutton bones. I used my last one two days ago for the soup we ate at supper. I need more to make that broth."

All three women startled when Azarion suddenly spoke in a raspy voice. "Tamura."

His sister bent down to him, the scowl on her face in contrast to the worry in her eyes. "Your years in Kraelag have rotted your brain," she admonished him. "I can't believe you were mad enough to roll under a galloping horse like that. I'd kill you myself for such idiocy if you hadn't nearly completed the task on your own." Her criticism lacked any sharpness.

Azarion's pallor was still ashy, and his lips pale, but he managed a small smile. "Skin me later. Go see Arita. Make it known to all who will listen that I offer her my protection before word is sent to her clan of Karsas's death."

She clasped his wrist in an affectionate squeeze. "Thank you, Brother," she said, before leaving with assurances to Saruke that she'd return with the mutton bones.

Saruke took her place at the brazier, sorting through a number of satchels in her lap and pouring some of their contents into the pot resting on the grate.

Gilene sat down cross-legged beside Azarion. "I won't ask you if you're in pain. It's a foolish question, considering." She waved a hand at his back. "Instead, I will ask, how can I ease your pain?"

His lips curved in a thin smile. "Distract me." His fingers brushed hers, and she captured them, bringing them to her lips for a brief kiss. "You didn't pray, but you brought me the luck I needed, as I knew you would."

"I wouldn't call that luck." She gestured to his back a second time.

"I won, didn't I?"

"Yes, you did."

She had watched the entire fight with her heart in her throat. That fluttering organ still slammed against her ribs with relief and terror, the first because he had indeed survived and defeated Karsas, the second because he lay on a pallet, his back split open. It might not be Karsas's sword that would kill him but Karsas's horse.

"I keep my promises, Gilene," he said.

Gilene blinked at him. What promise? It took her a moment to recall his vow to return her to Beroe once he became *ataman*. She squeezed his fingers. "Hush. We'll speak of it later."

His eyes closed. His fingers were dark against hers, browned by days in the sun. Hers were paler, with bony knuckles and broken nails.

They were an odd pair, the Savatar Pit gladiator and the Beroe fire witch.

Pair. The word sent a sharp pain through her chest.

They weren't a pair and never would be. His place was here, the new *ataman* of Clan Kestrel. Hers was to the west in a village full of secrets, cowards, and her vulnerable family.

"It's good to dream, though," she said aloud, her hands threading the same path through Azarion's hair that his mother's had taken.

"What did you say?" Saruke knelt beside her, a steaming cup in her hand.

Gilene blushed. "Nothing important." A tendril of steam uncoiled from the cup to tease her nose with the bitter scent of willow bark.

Saruke set the cup down. "Too hot for him to drink now. We'll let him sleep. The healer will return later and give the yarrow root a chance to work and his body a chance to rest." Her hand passed over his back, just above the compresses. "He wears the marks of the Empire carved into his skin."

The Empire carved into the soul as well as the flesh. Gilene held her tongue, sensitive to the sorrow in Saruke's tone. Azarion was luckier than most.

Kraelian slaves tended to lead short, miserable lives, and Pit gladiators' were even shorter and more miserable than most. That Azarion had not only survived the Pit for ten years but also gained fame in its savage arena was a remarkable achievement by anyone's measure. That he also escaped its cage to return home and reclaim his inheritance was a testament to his personal triumph over the forces that had sought to break him.

"He's fierce, Saruke," she said, hoping to reassure the older woman. "Clever and strong. Those scars are nothing to such a man. He's risen above them."

A thoughtful expression passed through Saruke's eyes. "You've grown to admire him."

Gilene looked away, unable to meet Saruke's gaze. Her emotions were in turmoil. Her feeling were stronger than admiration, and they made her want to weep.

While Azarion rested and allowed the yarrow root to work its power on the wound, Gilene stood guard at the *qara*'s entrance, turning away well-wishers and a steady parade of disgruntled sub-chiefs already lined up to jockey for positions of influence with the new *ataman*.

Tamura had returned from her foray through camp with a sack of mutton bones for Saruke to boil. She and Gilene helped Azarion sit long enough to drink the now cold tea Saruke had brewed earlier.

His face was still pale except for the pink flags of color on his cheekbones, and his eyes were glassy as he watched Gilene over the rim of his cup.

"You have fever now," she said. "I'm sorry you're in pain."

He shrugged, and his fingers went white around the cup. "I've dealt with worse."

The succinct reply made her sigh. She took his empty cup and brought back a refill for him when Vua returned, carrying a bag bulging with all manner of things.

She set the bag down and fished out the contents: more cloths, a carved box that held three needles and several lengths of catgut, prayer stones carved with mysterious runes that Gilene could only guess were blessings and beseechings, and a full flask of equally mysterious liquid.

Tamura frowned at the sight of it all. "Does he really need stitching?"

Vua sniffed. "Last I checked, Tamura, you were the warrior and I the healer." Satisfied with Tamura's thin-lipped silence after her chastisement, Vua faced Azarion. "Have you been stitched before?"

"Twice," he said, and Gilene wondered at his calm. She eyed the needles, remembering her brother's agonized shrieks.

"Then you know what to expect. I need you to kneel and keep your back as straight as possible so I can sew the wound proper and have the flesh knit right."

Azarion did as instructed and knelt, his spine straight, shoulders back, while Saruke set the bloodied compresses aside and settled behind him next to Vua. He took the short stick the healer handed him without comment before grasping one of Gilene's hands. "Don't fret, *Agacin*," he said. "Distract me instead."

Gilene cursed inwardly at the mistake of revealing her inner turmoil to him. He didn't need to see her worry right now. She stood and faced him, close enough that he was eye level to her sternum and he could lean his forehead against her if he chose. She gulped when he placed the stick crosswise between his teeth and gave Vua a nod to begin.

His fingers curled into Gilene's tunic as Vua and Saruke set to the slow and painful task of cleaning the wound. A low hum vibrated up from Azarion's throat when the healer made the first puncture and drew the needle and catgut through flesh. His teeth clenched on the stick. He crushed Gilene's tunic in both hands but made no other noise despite the obvious agony of the healer's touch.

Gilene framed his head in her palms, his sweat-soaked hair slippery between her fingers. Azarion pressed his forehead into her midriff, the stick in his mouth a rigid edge against her skin.

Except for the twitch of his wounded shoulder every time the needle punctured skin, he held still. Gilene massaged his scalp and spoke to him in trader's tongue, trivial things of little consequence to him but ones she hoped might provide the distraction he needed from Vua's painful work.

"My brother Nylan is married to the most foolish woman in all of the Empire, but she is kind, with a great heart, and loves Nylan more than anything, and that's saying something because he can be an ass sometimes. They have six children, all but one of them girls. I think Nylan saw his first gray hair after the third baby."

Azarion's hands clenched ever tighter in her clothing. Gilene stared at Vua's busy, bloody hands, willing her to work faster and end this suffering.

"My other brother, Luvis, remains unmarried, much to my mother's despair. He's promised her he'll seek a wife once our sister, Ilada, is safely married to a man who meets with Luvis's approval." She continued carding her fingers through Azarion's hair. "As particular as he and Ilada are about potential bridegrooms, I think he's found a way to avoid the marital trap without raising our mother's ire."

A lurch against her, and Gilene looked down at the top of

Azarion's head. Had that been a chuckle she felt from him or simply a pained cry muffled by her tunic?

The coppery scent of blood filled the *qara*'s still air. Gilene exhaled a slow sigh of relief when Vua tied off the last suture and cut the excess catgut with a small knife.

Her relief was short-lived when Saruke passed Vua a cloth saturated with a clear liquid poured from the flask Vua had brought. The astringent smell was the only warning before Vua pressed the soaked towel on the newly closed wound.

Azarion heaved forward with a tortured groan, hard enough to make Gilene stumble. She bent her knees and set her feet to hold steady. She could feel his heartbeat all the way into his scalp, a hard, fast thumping that matched his staccato breathing.

"It's almost over, Azarion," she crooned. *Please let it be over*, she prayed silently to any being that might listen and show mercy.

Saruke and Vua worked together to dry his back and shoulder before smearing a poultice of honey and herbs over the stitches. They swaddled his left side from shoulder to ribs, wrapping strips of woven cloth around his waist and under his arm before tying them in a knot at the top of his shoulder near his neck.

By then, his posture was no longer so straight, and he wilted into Gilene, his weight threatening to knock her over.

Tamura, who had guarded the *qara*'s threshold through the ordeal and glared murder at Vua the entire time, abandoned her post to help them lay Azarion on his stomach.

"Use a sop to get the tea and broth down him while he's on his belly," the healer instructed. She packed her supplies, accepted a payment of silver from Saruke, and bowed to Azarion. "It is right that the son of Iruadis leads Clan Kestrel. May Agna bless you, *Ataman*."

Once she was gone, Azarion called to Tamura, who crouched beside him. "Be my eyes and ears while I mend," he said. "Stay with Arita in the *ataman's qara* until I'm on my feet. She and her children can then come here."

She nodded. "What about Karsas's burial? The clan will expect one of us there."

"Attend in my name if I'm unable to go."

Gilene watched the interaction between brother and sister with a touch of envy. They were close, even after a decade of separation between them. Azarion trusted Tamura implicitly, and her belief in him was strong enough to be called faith by most. It was a reciprocal devotion Gilene wished she shared with one of her siblings.

Saruke left the *qara* not long after Tamura in search of more willow bark. "Keep watch," she told Gilene. "And give him the remainder of the tea when he's feeling a little better and won't retch it up. I'll return after I visit some of the women to trade supplies. I need to see a few of the subchiefs as well and assure them the new *ataman* isn't dead."

Alone with Azarion, Gilene used the time to shed her clothes and indulge in a quick sponge bath by the brazier. The rustle of cloth made her turn. She discovered Azarion had shifted and now faced her, his head pillowed on his arms, his green eyes bright as emeralds. The fever flush that graced his cheekbones had spread, and his skin was rosy from scalp to neck.

"You're very beautiful, *Agacin*," he said in a voice slurred with weariness.

She cocked an eyebrow and casually slipped her tunic back over her head. "The fever is affecting your eyes, I think, *Ataman*." She stepped into her trousers and slipped her feet into a pair of felt booties.

He didn't reply. By the time she padded to him with another cup of tea, he was asleep. She sat beside him, content to admire him stretched out on his pallet, the furs and blankets bunched at his waist, his back a white wasteland of thick bandages dotted with spots of blood.

The only sounds in the *qara* were the crackling of the coals in the brazier and Azarion's even breathing. Gilene was nodding off herself, caught in vague dreams of galloping across the Sky Below on a stolen horse with Azarion and a grotesquely headless Karsas in pursuit, when soft murmurings brought her fully awake.

Like her, Azarion walked in his dreams. He shivered with fever, and when Gilene felt his cheeks and forehead, he burned hot to her touch. She rose to soak a cloth in cool water so she could bathe his face. He jerked at the cold touch but didn't wake.

Gilene combed the tangled locks of hair away from his features. "You must wake up, Azarion. You need to drink."

His only response was a few more incoherent mutters before he said clearly, "Time to take you home, *Agacin*. In fact, it's past time."

His words made her stomach knot and her heart miss a beat or two. Gilene tried convincing herself it was excitement that sent her emotions tumbling off a cliff's edge. Why then did she feel like crying?

Azarion still hadn't opened his eyes, and he lapsed once more into unintelligible mumbling. Gilene stroked his head and face as she stared at the *qara*'s opposite wall, as if its felt expanse held all the answers to her questions and would reveal them if she just stared long enough, if she just blinked back the annoying tears that blurred her vision.

"I promised you, Gilene. I keep my promises." Another perfectly articulate statement amid the delirious mumbles.

"Shh," she said, gliding her fingers along the ridge of his cheekbone. "All in good time, *Ataman*, and then we bid each other farewell."

She said no more, fearful that, if she did, she'd choke on the words and the tears they inspired.

# CHAPTER SIXTEEN

The Sky Below stretched toward the horizon under a veil of golden sunshine. Summer still held sway over the steppes, and the plume grass swayed in a whispering swath as far as the eye could see.

Azarion guided his horse through the grasses. Tall and lush, they brushed the horse's belly and caressed Azarion's shins. Gilene rode beside him, occasionally swatting at the midges stirred up by the horses' passage through the grass.

They traveled west with an entourage of clansmen to Clan Eagle's encampment, where the leaders of more clans were gathered. Azarion's first act as *ataman* was to call for a gathering of the two councils and subchiefs of all the clans, asking that they meet in the largest clan's camp.

Clan Eagle was the largest clan, its wealth the greatest in the confederation, and its *ataman* once Azarion's father's best friend. Calling a confederation gathering in the Eagle camp was a great honor and allowed Erakes Ataman to bask in the temporary role of kingly host. Azarion hoped to benefit from that vanity and gain the *ataman*'s support of the plan that had first made Gilene's jaw drop in disbelief and would likely do the same to every *ataman*, *agacin*, and subchief who attended the gathering.

He was eager to reach their destination and dreaded their arrival at the same time. It marked the end of his time with Gilene.

He wished he had left her in the Clan Kestrel camp, far to the east and deep in the Sky Below's interior, but a promise made was to be kept. She had been patient but also unyielding in her insistence she return to Beroe as soon as possible.

His mare snorted and jerked her head to the side in a bid to avoid a quail startled into flight from the shelter of the plume grasses. The motion pulled hard on Azarion's healing shoulder, and he bit back a curse at the arrow of hot pain that shot down his arm to his fingers.

"If that didn't open your wound a little, I'll be surprised," Gilene said.

Azarion shrugged away the discomfort. "No harm done."

At least he hoped not. Vua would strangle him with a length of catgut if he managed to undo her work, and his mother would help her. Nor did he relish a repeat of the feel of a needle sliding through his flesh.

Eleven days had gone by since Azarion's fight with Karsas and his reclamation of Clan Kestrel's chieftainship. In that time he'd drunk enough willow bark tea and bone broth to float a fleet of merchant ships. The bitter taste of the willow bark still lingered on his tongue.

During his convalescence, he'd given up his place in his mother's *qara* to abide in the *ataman's* much larger one. It was a generous space, far too large for just him, Gilene, and Saruke.

As his concubine, Gilene was expected to join him, and she did so without protest. Saruke had arrived soon after, her cart filled with her belongings she'd taken from the smaller *qara*. That dwelling now sheltered Tamura; Karsas's widow, Arita; and Arita's two children.

He'd never forget the joy in his sister's face when Arita stepped across the threshold, her son and daughter in tow. The two women embraced, holding on to each other as if nothing else in the world existed around them.

Only when Azarion cleared his throat did they part. He nodded to Arita. "This is your home now for as long as you and Tamura wish it. I've gifted half of Karsas's herd to your family to appease them."

"Dower gift?" she asked, worry clouding her expression. It wasn't uncommon for a chieftain's widow to be claimed by her husband's closest male relative after the man's death, especially if she was still young. It raised his status among the clan, and the pretty Arita was not only a coveted prize but also a valuable asset for her clan and family. They would demand no less than half of Karsas's horses in exchange for relinquishing her to Clan Kestrel a second time.

"Not dower price," he said. "Adoption. You're Clan Kestrel now, as are your children, regardless of whether you remarry a Kestrel man." He doubted that would happen anytime soon.

Tears filled Arita's eyes. She sniffed them away. "I thank you, Azarion Ataman," she said and glanced at the grinning Tamura. "For everything."

While Saruke approved of Azarion's decision to invite Arita into their family, she chose not to stay with her daughter and Arita. Instead, she followed him and Gilene to the *ataman's* tent on the pretense of taking care of him while he convalesced, and no amount of reassurances that he didn't need the help changed her mind.

"It's a selfish thing," she admitted on the third day in their new abode. "I'm used to more peace and quiet. I'd forgotten just how noisy small children could be." She winked at Azarion. "Better Tamura deal with it than me."

The *qara* still held some remnants of Karsas's presence, a kind of vulgar opulence that reminded Azarion of the empress Dalvila's bedchamber but on a much more modest scale. He didn't welcome the comparison and asked Saruke to cleanse the *qara* of any dark will or malice still lingering there.

He would have been fine staying in his mother's *qara* with Gilene and sending Tamura to live with Arita in the more spacious tent, but the *ataman's qara* served two purposes. It was a family home but also the gathering place for the *ataman* and subchiefs to hold council and administer the affairs of the clan. Its size could accommodate a large group of people and served to impress visiting clan *atamans*.

"How much farther until we reach Clan Eagle's encampment?"

Gilene's question pulled him out of his reverie. She twitched one of her braids over her shoulder, its long length thumping softly against her back. He liked how the sun wove gold light through her dark plait. She wore the garb he'd given her. It was Tamura who had revealed him as the giver.

"What a stupid thing to keep secret," she had said, and flatly told Gilene, "What you're wearing is a gift from Azarion. You should thank him." With that, she gave an exasperated snort and strode away.

"Why didn't you tell me?" Gilene had glided a hand down one of her sleeves, her brow creased in a puzzled furrow.

"Because we were still adversaries then. You would have chosen to wear your rags over anything I might give you. Tell me I'm wrong."

She had laughed. "You're not wrong."

At the moment, she wore the yellow sash of an *agacin* wrapped around her narrow waist. It complemented her tunic.

"How much farther?" she repeated.

He swept a hand toward the gathering clouds in the distance.

"If the weather holds, we'll be there tomorrow afternoon. The *ataman* already has scouts following us."

Her eyes widened. She turned one way on the horse's back, her gaze sweeping the rolling landscape before turning the other way and doing the same. Except for a far-off stand of trees growing by a stream, the land was clear. "Are you certain? Where are they hiding?"

Azarion smiled. "You're assuming they're on horseback like us. These are Erakes Ataman's best runners. They lurk in the grasses, a good hiding place even for a tall man. Whatever we do is reported back to Erakes."

A day later and half a league from the encampment, an escort of twenty warriors met them and led their group back to a wide expanse of ground covered by what seemed like an eternal stretch of black felt *qaras*, their peaked roofs crowned with colorful family banners that snapped in the wind.

Azarion guided his horse closer to Gilene's. "Erakes will offer you a *qara* of your own during our visit."

A tiny frown marred her brow. "Why would he do that? Am I not your concubine?"

How he wished it were so in more than name and assumption. "You're an *agacin* first and will be given the choice of where you'll sleep." He was tempted to cajole her into staying with him. Not once had she slept in a different place than he since his return to the Savatar, and while he missed her next to him on the same pallet, he had grown accustomed to having her nearby.

Azarion stayed silent, hoping she'd refuse Erakes's offer in favor of sharing a *qara* with him. It lent more credence to her support of him as the new *ataman* of Clan Kestrel, but the choice was ultimately hers.

"I'm not interested in my own *qara*," she said. "I share one with you at home. There's no reason I shouldn't do so here."

It was a good thing he was an adept rider, or he would have fallen off his horse from shock. Gilene referred to the Kestrel camp as home. Azarion schooled his expression into a bland mask. She remained unaware of her very telling reference, only arching her eyebrows at his delayed response.

"As you wish," he said. He inwardly rejoiced at this small slip of the tongue, this peek into her thoughts. A hope he dared not nurture flared to life inside him. Would she change her mind? Turn her back on Beroe and stay with the Savatar? Stay with him if he asked?

Clan Eagle's population was easily five times greater than Clan Kestrel's. While all clan *atamans* were considered equal on council, an unspoken deference was shown to Erakes Ataman by the other chiefs. As the *ataman* of the biggest, wealthiest clan, he wielded considerable influence. His word might not be law, but it carried weight. Only the Fire Council equaled him in influence, a fact the *agacins* were quick to remind him of at every joint council session.

Now the camp had swelled to twice its size with the arrival of the other clan leaders and their entourages. Azarion and his group navigated a path through the encampment, passing curious onlookers who gathered to welcome the new *ataman* and the outlander *agacin* who accompanied him.

Erakes met them at the entrance to an enormous *qara*. The *qara* Azarion inherited from Karsas would have easily fit inside it with room to spare.

He, Gilene, and his retinue of subchiefs and Kestrel warriors dismounted to stand before Erakes. All save Gilene saluted him with flattened hands thumped over their hearts.

Erakes eyed them in silence before he suddenly grinned and yanked the taller Azarion into his arms for a rib-cracking embrace.

Azarion's healing shoulder and back spasmed. It took every bit of control he possessed not to instinctively hurl the *ataman* away from him.

"Stop!"

The entire camp froze at Gilene's exclamation.

Erakes's arms fell away. He turned to face the woman who dared shriek at him, and Azarion inhaled a grateful breath.

"Did you not know?" she said in slow, careful Savat. "Azarion Ataman was injured while fighting Karsas and is still healing."

Erakes's thunderhead scowl dissipated. His gaze swung back to Azarion, sweeping him from head to toe. "You look well enough. Where were you wounded?"

"Shoulder and back." Azarion gestured to Gilene with one hand. "I'm honored by the *agacin*'s concern for my health."

He hadn't missed the way Erakes's hand had dropped to his sword pommel at Gilene's protest, as if he'd been tempted to skewer her for such blatant impertinence. A quick reminder that she was one of Agna's handmaidens seemed prudent.

The wide smile Erakes wore earlier returned. "The affection of one of Agna's blessed is no easy thing to win. Killing Karsas was a far easier task." He offered Gilene a bow, acknowledging her status as a sacred *agacin* before all his clan. "Welcome to my encampment, *Agacin*. Clan Eagle is honored by your visit and that of Azarion Ataman."

She bowed in return. "I am honored to be here, Erakes Ataman."

Erakes ushered them all into his *qara*. Servants showed them to places where they could sit and rest in luxury. Numerous lamps ringed the dwelling, and the scent of roasting meat filled the air, making Azarion's mouth water.

The *qara* was a crowded place, filled with Erakes's family and servants as well as the *atamans* from the other clans. Each called a greeting to Azarion, along with congratulations on reclaiming his clan's chieftainship.

A finely dressed woman directed the servants with efficient ease. Azarion recognized her as Erakes's wife, though the *ataman* didn't introduce her to his guests.

He bellowed for wine, mare's milk, and food to share with the visitors. It was the start of a drawn-out process involving generous hospitality and hard-driving negotiation.

Gregarious by nature, and a hedonist with great appetites for food, music, drink, and women, Erakes was a shrewd negotiator and an ambitious clan chieftain—exactly the kind of man Azarion's plan might appeal to if presented the right way.

He would have to be careful. Iruadis himself had once said Erakes made for a loyal friend and a dangerous enemy. He was Savatar through and through, proud of his heritage and the land that birthed him and the many generations of his ancestors before him. His love for the Sky Below was superseded only by his hatred for the Empire.

He and Azarion swapped stories between them, including Erakes's recollections of growing up with Iruadis and the scrapes they got into as boys. Azarion, for his part, spoke briefly of his enslavement to the Empire and watched as Erakes's genial mood darkened. Azarion turned the conversation to a lighter subject before the *ataman* grew even grimmer. They bantered with the other *atamans* and subchiefs for the next hour about inconsequential things, each man measuring the other as either potential ally or adversary in future dealings. Nearby, Gilene sat among six of the nine *agacins*, carrying on her own conversation or listening to the *atamans*' conversations, her expression guarded and hawkeyed.

A servant girl approached Erakes and whispered in his ear. He nodded and sent her off before turning back to Azarion. "We have a *qara* for you and one for the *agacin* if she wishes it. Your sub-chiefs are welcome to stay with other families." He held his cup up to a servant for a refill of wine. "The last of the *atamans*, Tulogan of Clan Lynx, will arrive late tonight. We'll all get a good sleep and meet here again tomorrow once the sun has burned away the ground fog and hear what you have to say. Until then, I bid you all good evening."

They were dismissed and escorted out by more of the efficient servants. After declining the *qara* for the *agacin*, Azarion and Gilene followed one of the servants to a *qara* set near the camp's center.

Once inside, Azarion surveyed their surroundings, noting its many luxuries.

"This isn't nearly as big as Erakes's *qara*," Gilene said as she wandered the interior, pausing at various spots to admire the silk rugs that lined the floor and the elaborately embroidered hangings that graced the walls. "But it's certainly as opulent."

"It probably belongs to one of Erakes's subchiefs."

Carved stools joined plush backrests for those who preferred not to sit on the ground. Velvet coverlets in jewel colors draped pallets, and the lit candles smelled of beeswax instead of tallow.

"Does it appeal to you?"

The few belongings he possessed and those that became his at Karsas's death were basic by comparison. Clan Kestrel had never been as large or as wealthy as Clan Eagle, even at its height.

Gilene dragged a finger over a carafe made of delicate glass the color of milk with wispy tendrils of mist caught in the design. She waved a hand to encompass the interior. "This would appeal to anyone for a short while." She tilted her head to the side, a question in her eyes. "Do you not think it oppressive, though? It's all beautiful in its way, but it isn't the stars at night, and I feel as if I'd drown in silk and velvet by morning." Her expression turned pleading. "I don't wish to sound ungrateful of Erakes's generosity or that of the chief who allowed us the use of his home, but would you mind so much if we slept outside? It's warm enough, and the ground isn't muddy. And we can use our own blankets to keep from soiling these."

Azarion was tempted to pull her into his arms. Instead, he bowed. "As the *agacin* wishes. We'll sleep under the stars tonight and welcome the sunrise tomorrow."

She possessed a beautiful smile, one she showed far too seldom for his liking, and this time that smile was for him alone. They left the *qara*, fielding questions from those of both Clan Eagle and his own retinue; concerns the *qara* didn't meet with their approval and offers to provide them with something else to their liking.

Azarion assured them all he merely indulged the whims of the *agacin*, who wanted to stargaze and enjoy the warmer weather before the summer season faded to fall. Appeased, they left him and Gilene to journey outside the camp's periphery, opposite the horse herds, where the grasses were thicker but shorter, and the ground was free of horse dung. They stopped at the fire where his soldiers gathered for the night and took with them saddle pads and blankets for making a bed.

They were still close enough to the camp and its light to deter a visit from nocturnal hunters but far enough away to gain a modicum of privacy. The moon above them hung bright in the celestial black, creating shadows with razor edges on the Sky Below.

Gilene helped Azarion lay out the makeshift bed. Once finished, she dropped down to the bed, toed off her shoes, and lay supine atop the covers, face tilted up to the sky and the stars salting its expanse.

Azarion joined her, stretching out on his belly. He bent his arms to use as a headrest and rested his cheek on his forearms, content to watch the *agacin* watch the stars.

She spared him a glance from the corner of her eye. "Surely, you can't see the stars that way."

It didn't matter to him. She was prettier than the stars and gleamed more brightly, in his opinion. The sour look that had seemed permanently stamped on her features when they first met was gone now, in its place, the beauty of fortitude. This was how he wanted to remember her after she returned to Beroe, he and the Savatar only a vague memory in her mind. If she bothered to recall them at all.

"I've seen stars many times," he said. "I'm just glad to be outside."

She smiled. "Me too."

They lay in companionable silence for several moments until she spoke again. "Do you think the *atamans* will agree with your plan? More importantly, do you think Erakes will agree to it?"

He considered Gilene's question before answering. "I really only need Erakes. With his support, the other *atamans* will follow. He hates the Empire even more than we do. His first wife died a captive in a Kraelian brothel before he could rescue her."

Even in the darkness, he saw Gilene flinch. "My gods, I don't blame him. That poor woman." Her eyes glittered. "I think there must be no depth the Empire won't descend to in its cruelty."

"I'm counting on that hatred to sway him to my argument. He's the canniest of the *atamans* and doesn't turn away from a fight."

Gilene shifted to her side, her expression anxious. "Sacking the capital is a risky endeavor, Azarion, much like that mad tumble you took under Karsas's horse." Her lips quirked. "If I didn't know you better, I'd call you reckless."

He mimicked her position, feeling the stretch of taut skin over his sore shoulder. "But you do know me better now. What do you call me?"

"I think you're fishing for compliments," she teased.

"I'm asking for your honesty, which you've always so generously shared with me, even at its harshest."

She stared at him without speaking, and Azarion wondered what she saw and whether it pleased her.

"I would call you clever. Brave. Relentless in your pursuit of a goal. I don't know what defines a good *ataman*, but I think you will be one for your clan. They'll thrive under your leadership." She frowned then. "Should you live long enough."

Azarion reached out to capture a flyaway strand of her hair. "I've fought too hard to stay alive this long to suddenly embrace death."

The steppe wind chittered a faint laugh as if amused by his defiance.

"When we leave this encampment, it's a three-day ride through the Siraces Valley and another six days across Kraelian lands before you reach Beroe. It's a four-day return ride to the Kestrel camp. Will you not return with me, Gilene?"

He dreaded letting her go but had sworn to her he would. That oath didn't stop him from trying to convince her to stay.

Her eyes were so dark, no more than a play of shadows and the secrets she held close. "And what would I return as, *Ataman*? The concubine *agacin*?"

"You've seen the respect and regard all Savatar hold for the *agacins*. You're a handmaiden of Agna."

"I don't even believe in your Agna," she protested.

"And yet she chose you as one of hers. You don't have to stay with Clan Kestrel. Any clan would gladly welcome you into their midst."

Her face shuttered into an expressionless mask. "They are still strangers, people who know nothing of me nor I of them despite their honoring my role as Agna's handmaiden. Home is among those who love you."

Azarion rolled partially atop her, startling a gasp out of her.

He traced the line of her nose. "My mother has great affection for you. As does Tamura." She snorted at that assertion. He pressed on. "What if I said I loved you, fire witch?" Her entire body tensed under his, and her lips parted on another gasp. "Can that not be enough to convince you to stay and make the Sky Below your home?"

A lone tear trickled from the corner of her eye and slid into the hair at her temple. "You've wanted a great deal from me, *Ataman*. You want my heart as well? Have me abandon all I've known to stay here with you?"

He bent to kiss her right eyelid, then her left, the salt of her tears stinging his lips. "I'm a greedy man. I want all of you, heart, soul, and body. You already have all that I am. It seems only fair."

Deep down, he knew she'd refuse. Even if their relationship hadn't been founded on extortion, struggle, and captivity, she was single-minded in her devotion to a duty for which she'd never receive thanks nor recognition from those she saved year after year. If, as she said, home was truly among those who loved you, then Beroe wasn't her home. He didn't know whether to hold her in sympathy or shake her from frustration.

He couldn't regret asking her to stay. Soon they would part for good, and he was desperate to keep her.

"The same family awaiting you in Beroe willingly surrenders you to Kraelian slavers every spring so that you are raped and burned." His voice sounded harsh to his ears. She might love her mother and siblings, but she hated her fate. Azarion suffered no qualms in reminding her of that fact.

"Stay with the Savatar," he argued. "If I can convince Erakes that my plan is sound, has merit, and we unite to attack the Empire's capital, the Rites will end. No more Flowers of Spring to sacrifice. No more burning in the Pit. No worrying whether someone's mother, daughter, or sister will be tithed."

They stared at each other until Gilene sighed and raised her hand to trace Azarion's eyebrows with her fingertips. "That is a dream to hold close during the hard nights, but a dream it still is. Until you and the Savatar can make it a reality, I have to go back. I can't abandon my mother or my sister or any of the women who rely on me to protect them from the Empire. I will survive it. They won't. In my place, would you turn your back on them?"

She asked the question he'd hoped she wouldn't. It was the one he couldn't deny without lying, and he'd lied to her enough already. "No. I'd go back."

Her watery smile reflected in her gaze. "You risked everything to return to your people."

He moved so that he didn't crush her with his weight but could still feel the length of her against him. "Risked you as well." More words hovered on his tongue, difficult to express in a way that kept him honest but still conveyed his regret.

"Had there been another way to gain my freedom and regain the chieftainship other than abducting you, I would have chosen it. You can rightfully fault me as merciless and without compassion for your plight. I did what I did without thinking of your own circumstances. It was wrong, and though I can't regret bringing you to the Sky Below, I am sorry you suffered for it." He stroked her cheeks, loving the feel of her smooth flesh under his fingers. "That was no way to repay someone who only helped me. I don't ask your forgiveness, Gilene. I don't think I could give it were I in your place, but ask of me what you will, and I will do all in my power to fulfill it."

Gilene's tears had dried, leaving only the remnants of their silvery tracks on her cheeks. She stretched under him, long legs entwining with his. A procession of emotions crossed her features, quick as lightning flashes. Azarion wished he could interpret each one, but they were gone as soon as they appeared.

"You've promised to send me home. I know now you are an honorable man, and I believe you. I'd ask one more boon of you."

"Anything."

"Invading armies don't reserve their violence for their main target. The nearby villages and towns suffer it as well, their only offense their proximity to the city the army wants to destroy. If the Savatar succeed in reaching the capital, I ask that you remember Beroe and spare it. For my sake, and if not that, then to satisfy the wishes of an *agacin*."

Was that all? he wondered. Nothing for herself or material goods for her family? Azarion brushed a kiss across her forehead. "I should have known you wouldn't ask for silver or silk."

"Those won't do me much good when I stand in the Pit once more."

The harsh reminder of what awaited her in a few months' time made Azarion's stomach twist. He hated the idea of her going through such an ordeal again, but she wasn't his to keep, and her choice to return was hers alone. He could at least give her this one reassurance.

"I'll see to it the Savatar leave Beroe in peace." Her eyes closed in obvious relief. "Is that all, Gilene? Nothing more? I owe you much." He'd give her all of the Krael Empire if she asked him, if it meant she might live her days among the Savatar.

"One more thing," she said, and her smile was a sensual beckoning that drew him like a lodestone and set his heart to racing. "Show me what it is to truly be the concubine of Azarion Ataman."

She drew his head down to hers, and Azarion was lost.

## CHAPTER SEVENTEEN

The last time Gilene had lain with a man was during the Rites of Spring the year before Azarion revealed his knowledge of her illusion. Then, it had been a quick rutting against a cell wall. She had counted the number of thrusts—four in total—before the gladiator finished with her and stumbled to his pallet to pass out from exhaustion or drink or both. Gilene spent the remainder of the night sitting in a corner, keeping an eye on the snoring heap.

Her cellmate never woke when the guards retrieved her the next morning. She didn't remember his face, nor did she care about his fate.

Once more she lay with a Pit gladiator, but this time under the stars of the Stara Dragana instead of in a filthy cell, and she did so of her own free will. This man, once her adversary, would become her lover tonight, not her rapist. His face she'd remember, his fate she'd wonder about long after this interlude faded with time.

She kissed him, savoring the shape and feel of his lips as they slanted across hers. He rested heavy on her body, all lean muscle and wool tunic that tangled with her own garb as they shifted in their efforts to press closer to each other.

Gilene's hands slid into his loose hair, fingers tightening against his scalp as she swept her tongue over his lower lip in a wordless command that he open to her. With a soft groan, Azarion acquiesced and welcomed her, returning her deep caress with one of his own. He tasted of the berries the servants had passed around after dinner and the imported wine purchased from the trade caravans on the Golden Serpent.

Her blood sizzled through her veins as strong as the fire she sometimes summoned to her fingertips at the feel of his erection pushing against her, the shallow thrusts of his hips matching the deeper penetration of his tongue in her mouth.

They ended the kiss on a mutual gasp, and Gilene smiled at the desire glittering in his eyes; surely a reflection of her own wanting. Her legs parted wider, settling him even harder between her spread thighs. She caressed the outside of his leg with her ankle and calf, bending a knee so that her foot rode the back of his thigh. "Is the Gladius Prime as good at pleasing a woman as he is at fighting a man?"

The wind caught her question and spun it away, but not before Azarion heard. His answering laughter was part chortle, part snort. "That depends on whom you ask, *Agacin*. The best way to know is to find out for yourself." He punctuated his remark by nuzzling the underside of her jaw, planting a soft kiss there that made gooseflesh rise along her shoulders and arms.

She tilted her head, exposing more of her neck and the hollow of her throat to his caresses. Her hands busied themselves with shoving aside bits of his clothing, pushing his tunic up to expose his sides and back. His skin was hot beneath her palms, his muscular back flexing at her touch, skin twitching when her fingers glided over a ticklish spot along his ribs.

They exchanged numerous kisses, each one longer, deeper, more intense than the last until Gilene thought her heart would beat out of her chest. She stroked Azarion's arms, mapping a path over his back and shoulders, past the stitched wound inflicted by Karsas's horse, down the dip of his spine to his buttocks. His hips thrust forward in reaction to her grip, and he gasped in her ear.

She echoed the sound when his hand burrowed under her skirts to stroke every expanse of skin he could reach. "Too many clothes," he muttered.

Gilene heartily agreed and set to untying the laces that held his tunic closed at the neck. Azarion helped her, rising to shrug out of the garment before tossing it to the side. Bared to the waist, he knelt before her, bathed in moonlight. "Your turn," he said softly.

She sat up and pulled off her own tunic, along with her trousers. Her shoes joined the growing heap of clothing. He had seen her nude before, once as she bathed, another while she changed clothes. The burn scars she wore as souvenirs from her fire summoning weren't secrets to him. Even if they were, Gilene refused to hide behind her hands or her braids. Those scars were earned through tribulation and testaments to her will to survive, to offer mercy, and, in some small way, to throw the Empire's cruelty back in its face. She wasn't proud of the scars so much as she wasn't ashamed of them. They were simply part of who she was.

Azarion's eyes gleamed in the shadows, a dichotomy of bright and dark that obscured any emotion revealed there, but she heard it in his voice. "Agna blessed you with more than fire. I've never beheld a more beautiful woman."

The way he looked at her now only validated that assertion, for Gilene of Beroe was neither beautiful nor ugly, only an ordinary woman with an extraordinary power that had been her bane since the day it manifested. Azarion gazed at her as if she were the sun.

If anyone was Agna-blessed with physical beauty, it was him. Even when she thought of him as her enemy and wished down a gruesome fate on his head, a small part of her still recognized his allure even if her hatred of him made her immune to it.

She opened her arms. "I'm cold."

He moved with startling speed, wrapping her in his arms and tumbling them both to the pallet. Gilene laughed and kissed him. In no time he was as naked as she, huddled under the blankets, skin to skin. She touched him everywhere she could reach, stroking every plane and angle, bulge of muscle, and the stiff length of his cock where it pressed the inside of her thigh. He thrust into her hand, her name a drawn-out groan on his lips.

He, in turn, coaxed out gentle gasps and pleas for more of his touch as he caressed her breasts, suckled their tips into his mouth, and tracked a path with his lips that followed his hands from her throat and across her belly, pausing at every sensitive spot that made her shiver in his arms. He lingered at her thighs, and Gilene held her breath, both curious and apprehensive at this unfamiliar manner of lovemaking.

Azarion raised his head to meet her eyes. "Are you afraid? I'll stop."

She was anxious, but only because no lover had done this to her before. She wasn't afraid, not of this man's attentions or the exquisite way he played her body until every nerve thrummed and sizzled under her skin.

"I'm not afraid," she said. "Just unversed in this."

He smiled, his irises as dark as his pupils. "What I'm about to do doesn't require your skill, Gilene, only mine. This is for you to enjoy and for me to enjoy with you."

With that, he set to proving his words, his mouth and tongue a sweet torture that had Gilene lifting her hips and gripping Azarion's head as she panted his name on shallow breaths while she begged him to stop and then begged him to continue. The knot of pleasure fanning hot and bright in her belly spooled out with each caress like a thread from a ball of string, growing ever more taut until it snapped. Gilene's back arched under the force of her climax, and the guttural noises she made didn't sound human in her ears. Her knees clapped hard against Azarion's shoulders as she rode him through a tide of sensation that turned the stars blurry.

Azarion rose above her, a long, broad shadow that blocked out the sky. "Gilene."

Her name, only that, uttered in the tones of a temple worshipper. Gilene curved her legs over his back and twined her arms around his neck. "You are mine," she said in a ragged voice. "I am yours."

He sank into her with a sigh, his thrust deep. She gasped at the feel of him slowly filling her, his body heavy as hers stretched to accommodate his girth. Every muscle, inside and out, clenched against his partial withdrawal, and he shuddered in her arms.

Gilene didn't count the number of thrusts this time or turn her mind away from the moment. Instead, she reveled in it and willingly gave up her body and her heart to the man who made love to her under the open sky of the Stara Dragana.

He came inside her with a harsh moan and a shiver that racked him from head to foot. Gilene held him close, savoring the heat of his orgasm, the way his muscles flexed and his back went rigid before he settled on her, skin slippery with sweat, breath hard and uneven in her ear.

They lay entwined, with the blankets twisted around them, binding them close. Azarion hooked an arm under Gilene's hip and rolled them both to their sides. His mouth looked lush in the moonlight, swollen from her enthusiastic kisses and his pleasuring of her body. Satisfaction warred with anticipation in his gaze.

"Unless you say otherwise, there'll be no sleep for either of us tonight," he said.

She grinned and traced a meandering line across his collarbones, stopping for a moment to paint an invisible swirl in the hollow of his throat. "Is that a promise or a threat?" she teased.

"What do you want it to be?"

Gilene pretended to consider the options for a moment. "You always keep your promises, so a promise then."

A shadow passed through the depths of his eyes. "There are promises I wish I'd never made." His voice was as grim as his expression had suddenly grown.

She knew to what he alluded. He had promised he'd return her to Beroe, and her belief in him, slow to grow, didn't waver now. Her own sense of loyalty, however, did, and that scared her. He had offered his heart to her, and Gilene knew Azarion well enough by now to understand he didn't make such a momentous declaration as a platitude. It was a gift beyond price, one she would hold close when she returned to the capital in the spring. One that tested her resolve to return at all.

His cheek was warm under her hand, the unwelcome tears heavy in her throat. "I can't say it," she said. "No matter that I want to. If I do, I will falter, and I can't falter."

He captured her hand to plant a quick kiss on her palm and pressed his own hand to her chest. "It's all right, Gilene. You say it here."

Grateful that he didn't try to further persuade her from her chosen course, Gilene hugged him, allowing a few tears to trickle down her face before she blinked the rest away. In little time, her sadness was forgotten as Azarion made good on his promise and showed her that not all Pit gladiators were simply butchers or rutting beasts.

He made love to her through the remainder of the night, pausing for short stretches of time to rest but never sleep. They talked or simply caressed each other in silence while the moon above them made its slow descent. When the sun crested the horizon in a blade of fiery light, and the sky slowly lightened from black to indigo to lavender, Gilene sighed and gazed at Azarion's peaceful features, hoping to memorize each line.

"Do you trust Masad to accompany me home to Beroe?" It was a question she'd considered when Azarion had first outlined his plan for returning her to her village.

He nodded. "Yes. He might not agree with a decision or a plan, but he serves the *ataman* faithfully. He'll do as I instruct, even if it means taking an *agacin* away from the Sky Below."

Azarion had surprised her with the details. Masad would cross the steppe and Nunari territory at its narrowest passage to deliver her to Beroe. Once Azarion and his subchiefs completed negotiations with Clan Eagle, he'd return home to the Clan Kestrel encampment. His trusted captain, however, would sneak away in the small hours with the outlander *agacin* and guide her back to Kraelian lands. She spun a lock of his hair around her finger. "Part of me wishes it were you who will take me back to Beroe. The other part is glad it won't be."

The rising sun gilded the lower half of his body, turning the blankets and pelts that covered him a deep shade of gold. In that moment, he seemed both man and statue. He sighed, a hollow sound. "It's better that Masad deliver you instead of me. I might well break my promise. He won't."

It was one of the many things Gilene respected about Azarion, the self-awareness of his nature and his willingness to accept it and act according to those traits both weak and strong. She watched the sunlight creep up the blankets, a relentless timekeeper that showed no mercy to those who tried to capture moments and hold them still. "We have to meet with Erakes soon, don't we?"

"Yes." Azarion stroked her back. "There's no guarantee he'll agree to my plan, especially when it's one in which the Savatar start a war with the Empire." His gaze turned piercing. "If he does agree to it, I will do all in my power to see that Beroe is spared any attack from the Savatar who may pass it by on their way to Kraelag."

The sun had topped the horizon by the time they rose, dressed, and rolled up their belongings to return to their borrowed *qara*. Someone had entered earlier, leaving behind a tray of food and a basin of still-warm wash water.

Azarion gathered the subchiefs who accompanied him outside the entrance to Erakes's *qara*. He acknowledged each man with a quick nod.

The *ataman's qara* was nearly full once again when they entered. Erakes sat on an elevated pallet, a tall backrest draped in white fur behind him, reminding Gilene of a monarch's throne. A coterie of subchiefs and a pair of *agacins* stood in clutches close by. Gilene nodded to her sisters of the Flame, who nodded back but didn't invite her to stand with them.

Azarion stood before Erakes, his subchiefs in a half circle behind him. Gilene took up a place at its periphery, close enough to hear the exchange between the two *atamans* but far enough away to remain out of the discussion itself.

Erakes sat at ease, one arm draped across a bent knee. The fragrant smoke of incense scented the air, along with the steam of freshly brewed tea. Two servants passed tea to the meeting's attendees before fading into the *qara's* shadows.

"You've called a confederation council, Azarion Ataman." Erakes took a swallow of tea from his cup before continuing. "Karsas was a lazy *ataman*, content to grow fat on the tributes of his clan and sire children. You, I think, are like your father. Iruadis was never content to grow old behind the Fire Veil."

Azarion bowed. "As his friend, you knew him better and longer than I did, Erakes Ataman. He was a man of ambitions and dreams. I am like him in the first, but I prefer practicality over dreams, and the Savatar have sat too long behind the Veil, dreaming of their greatness on the Sky Below."

Gilene caught the murmurs and shifting of the chieftains as they whispered among themselves over Azarion's remark.

One of Erakes's eyebrows rose. "I'm listening," he said.

It was the opening Azarion wanted, and Gilene hoped he was as good an orator as he was a fighter, that his natural charisma and sound pragmatism would appeal to Erakes.

"I was a slave of the Empire for ten years," he said, addressing the entire group. "A gladiator of the Pit, the Gladius Prime." More murmurs swirled throughout the *qara*, along with a few approving whistles. If there was one thing the Savatar admired, it was a skilled warrior. Azarion had proven himself to be such, not only in Kraelag's arena but on the steppes as well.

"While I was a slave, I heard the truths and rumors of the Empire, how it wants to expand its reach, how it uses the Nunari to test the strength of the Veil, to find its weakness so that one day they might collapse it and bring their armies onto our lands."

"The Veil will never fall!" one *ataman* declared. "Our *agacins* won't let it happen."

Azarion's gaze settled briefly on the pair of *agacins* standing near Erakes before he turned to give a short nod to Gilene. "Agna's handmaidens are indeed powerful, and the Veil is strong, but it protects the Sky Below on one side only. There is no Veil to the east."

"No, but there are the Gamir Mountains," Erakes said. "They're almost as good at protecting us in the east as the Veil does in the west."

"That may have been the way of it in the past, Erakes Ataman, but no longer." Azarion paused to pin each *ataman* with a piercing look. Gilene held back a smile. He was good at this, very good. Every eye was riveted on him, every man leaning forward to hear his next words. Even Erakes had straightened against his backrest, his body no longer half slumped in casual repose. "Raiders from the Gamirs descend into Goban farmlands, destroy the crops, kill or steal the livestock, and burn the homesteads. They've collapsed some of the iron mines and cut off access to others."

Erakes shrugged. "We all know this. I've sent my men, as have the other *atamans*, to aid the Goban and drive back the raiders. It's the risk of living where they do."

"Did you know it is Kraelian weapons and Kraelian horses the raiders are using to attack the Goban? Or that the raiders themselves are often Kraelian soldiers disguised to look like Gamir tribesmen?"

That raised an outcry. Judging by the sudden consternation on Erakes's face, Gilene guessed this information was new and caught him by surprise. "How do you know this to be true?"

"Because I fought alongside and against Pit gladiators who once served in the Kraelian army. Men of high place who fell from favor when they incurred the wrath or displeasure of their commanding officer or a nobleman of more power." Azarion paced a little in front of Erakes, every step tracked by his enraptured audience. "The Empire is secure in its belief it's impervious to attack from outside its borders. They don't bother with secrets, and these men were free with their knowledge while they trained or waited to fight in the arena.

"We all know there are four Kraelian garrisons perched alongside the Serpent, each about nine leagues from the base of the Gamir Mountains on the other side of Goban lands. Three are manned by battalions, the fourth—the largest—by a legion. Together, they can march as many as eight thousand men across those mountains and onto Goban territory. They haven't done it yet because it's too easy to pick them off in the narrow passes."

Erakes waved a hand, unconcerned. "But for what purpose? The Goban are numerous enough to hold their territory if the Kraelians try such a thing, and the Empire won't empty out its garrisons just to conquer farmers and their crops."

"No, but they'll do it to stop a people who can field an infantry, and they'll take control of the iron the Goban bring out of their mines. They'll do it if it means they can conquer Savatar land without breaking the Veil."

An expectant hush settled even deeper onto the *qara* as Azarion continued. "The Krael Empire is long-lived because it's long-thinking. It devours its neighbors by slow degrees instead of immediate attack. It's the predator that waits in the cave, the spider at the center of the web. Ever patient, never merciful." Gilene shivered at the picture his words created. "The Empire puts it about that its garrisons protect the traders who travel the Serpent from the bandits who plague the route. The traders know these bandits are Kraelian soldiers who rob to line their pockets and fill the garrison coffers."

Another *ataman* spoke up. "If that's so, why don't the caravans quit traveling the trade road?"

"Because what they lose in these robberies can be made up elsewhere in profit. To abandon the Serpent altogether would see them exiled from the Trade Guild, also controlled by the Empire, and their riches dwindled to the scrapings left by the established free traders."

"What would you have the Savatar do?" Erakes motioned to a nearby servant for a refill of his tea.

"The Empire won't stop with four garrisons. They'll build four more and four more after that and the roads to reach every one of them. While the Gamir raiders destroy Goban crops and hold the mines, the Goban people will fight them and starve while doing it, far too busy staying alive to worry about a Kraelian garrison with a legion of soldiers being built right under their noses. Once the Empire gets a foothold in the mountains, we will be at war, and we will lose." Azarion's tone sharpened even more. "They outnumber us ten to one and can field both infantry and cavalry in great numbers. All they'll need is a foothold and time, and the Sky Below will fall to the Empire from the east just like the plains of the Nunari fell in the west."

The silence hung heavy as every person in the *qara* held their breath and he waited for Erakes's response. Erakes stared at Azarion a long time, and Azarion stared back. Gilene wondered who might blink first.

Erakes didn't blink, but he did speak. "What do you propose?"

A collective sigh ran through the *qara* as everyone exhaled and exchanged low-voiced commentary between them. Azarion didn't relax his guard. He could claim victory for the first part of his bid in convincing the most powerful Savatar clan that his concerns were worthy. The more difficult part remained: convincing them that attacking the Empire first was not the plan of a madman.

"We sack Kraelag," he replied.

Outraged shouts joined disbelieving laughter, but he remained stoic in the face of ridicule, his gaze never moving from Erakes, who didn't join in the mockery. Instead, the *ataman* waited until the noise subsided before speaking, a glower darkening his face. "You, more than any of us, should understand what a foolhardy thing that would be to do. You're neither an idiot nor mad, Azarion Ataman. This much I know; so why suggest something that would only result in the senseless deaths of thousands of Savatar?"

Gilene had asked him the exact same thing.

Kraelag was a fortified city with thick walls supported by watchtowers, ramparts, and deep ditches. The standing army defending it numbered in the thousands and could be called forth in a matter of hours if needed.

She'd seen the massive catapults waiting between the curtain walls, their munitions of giant stones and the architectural wreckage of old ruins piled into heaps beside them, waiting to be hurled onto an invading force. The Savatar were a nation of horse soldiers versed in cavalry tactics. Sacking Kraelag required siege warfare.

"Because we want the Empire to think its capital is besieged. They will call up not only their closest legions but also those from the garrisons that ride the Golden Serpent."

Erakes's eyes narrowed, and now he stood to pace, one hand stroking his beard in thought. "They'll leave the garrisons manned by only a few." His eyes gleamed in the dim lighting. "Vulnerable. Easy to destroy."

Azarion nodded. "Yes. We split the confederation forces. Half to ride to Kraelag from the west. We'll have to cross the plains and possibly fight the Nunari along the way."

"Or gain them as allies. They've never rested easy under the Empire's yoke," Erakes said.

"Hope for the best but prepare for the worst. Just as the Kraelians are greater in number than we are, the Savatar are greater in number than the Nunari. That they won't expect our incursion into their territories will also work in our favor."

A wolfish grin replaced Erakes's glower. "While the Empire panics and sends more of its soldiers to defend the capital, our eastern forces join with the Goban to sack the closest garrisons and take control of those stretches of the Serpent."

The blood raced through Gilene's veins as she listened to the two men flesh out the plan Azarion had hatched while he waited for the Fire Council to proclaim her an *agacin*. No wonder he had been so patient all that time. He had planned this strategy in detail, prepared to argue for its validity. The moment he was made *ataman*, he'd taken action.

Their battle plans roused her excitement. Anything that cut a wound in the Empire's hide made her smile, but she also knew that the course Azarion wanted the Savatar to take meant a path of no return and open war with the mightiest, cruelest empire that ever controlled the world known to men.

"We don't have the men, the time, or the supplies to lay siege to Kraelag," Erakes said abruptly.

Azarion shook his head. "No, we don't. And truth be known, we don't need to. We just need to keep the Kraelian armies busy defending her long enough that our eastern forces can do their work. Then we flee back behind the safety of the Veil."

"Cut off their grain supplies," Gilene volunteered into the pause.

The weight of numerous stares suddenly pressed down on her. She ignored it to focus on the man whose judgment would decide how all this might end.

"What do you mean, *Agacin*?" Erakes moved closer to her.

"Kraelag stores its grain supplies in granaries at the harbor of Manoret on the mouth of the river Oret." She knotted her fingers together, uneasy beneath so many doubtful stares. "Dyes, linen, and silk are kept there as well. My family are dyers. Each month we deliver our dyes to Manoret for shipment. Those granaries are the capital's main food supply. Any siege would be short if the city faces starvation, no matter how strong the walls."

Azarion's slow smile was cold and calculating, and Gilene shivered at the sight. "And the more desperate might well just open the gates for us."

Erakes's gaze held a glitter of suspicion. "You are of the Empire, *Agacin*. Why would you betray its weakness to us?"

She bristled. "Because the Empire is a blight, its capital a maggot feeding on a corpse. I've witnessed its savagery firsthand and the joy it takes in the misery it inflicts on its citizens as well as its slaves. Ask Azarion Ataman. He knows of what I speak. You must be loyal to something in order to betray it. I owe the Empire nothing, least of all my loyalty."

Erakes stared at her a moment longer before turning to Azarion. "If she returns to the Empire, she could reveal our plans."

Azarion shrugged. "To the Empire, she's an unknown village woman. They won't believe her."

Still unconvinced, Erakes returned to scrutinizing her while addressing Azarion. "Have you seen these granaries?"

"I have. When the gladiators were sent to fight in other cities, we shipped out of Manoret. They're well guarded but not impenetrable. The soldiers guarding them are equipped to fight off thieves, not armies."

Erakes slowly pivoted, his gaze sweeping the *qara* and its occupants, before returning to Azarion. "I agree that the Empire grows more dangerous by the day and that the Veil is no longer the surest way to protect the Savatar. Your plan is risky. If it succeeds, we'll be fighting for Savatar sovereignty and doing so on two fronts. If we fail, we'll be fighting for our lives. Those are hard choices for the Ataman Council to make."

Gilene hugged herself and tucked her hands under her arms to hide their shaking. If the clans united, they'd make a formidable enemy. If the Savatar allied with the Goban and possibly the

Nunari, the Empire would quake before them. Maybe, just maybe, it would then be far too busy staving off attacks from the steppes to indulge in the barbarous rituals associated with the Rites of Spring. A tiny flame of hope flared to life inside her.

"War is never an easy choice," Azarion said. "Do I have your support in this?"

Silence greeted his question, and Gilene's heart plummeted to the floor until Erakes offered his hand to Azarion and the two men clasped forearms.

"The council must decide together, but I lend my voice to yours. Clan Eagle stands with Clan Kestrel in this." He turned to the other *atamans*. "What say you? Are we in agreement?"

A chorus of enthusiastic ayes answered him. Gilene laughed aloud when Azarion suddenly pulled her into his arms, a wide grin curving his mouth before he kissed her long and hard to celebrate his first victory in this risky, dangerous endeavor. Gilene hoped it wouldn't be his last.

After several toasts of tea and mare's milk, she excused herself from the gathering to catch a few hours of much-needed sleep in the borrowed *qara*. She didn't hear Azarion return, waking only briefly to feel him slide under the blankets to curl against her.

"Stay with me, Gilene," he whispered in her ear.

"I can't," she murmured, still half-asleep.

"I will conquer all of the Empire to bring you back."

She tucked herself deeper into the warm cove of his body, taking pleasure in the feel of him next to her. "Just survive," she said and squeezed his fingers where they notched with hers. "That's all I ask."

"Swear you'll do the same for me," he urged.

"I swear."

Sleep overtook her once more. She awakened later to the pleasurable caress of Azarion's hands on her body and his lips on her

GRACE DRAVEN

skin. This time Gilene straddled him, her hand spread across his chest where the pounding of his heart made her palm pulse with each beat.

He rested inside her, softening with each sated breath he took. Like sunlight, like all light, firelight was kind to him, enhancing the beauty of his features and the color of his eyes. He watched her with a contemplative gaze.

Gilene slid her thumb across his lips. "What troubles you?"

"Have you ever wondered if what the Beroe fire witches do in the arena only makes things worse for them and Beroe?"

She tensed. The movement tilted her hips enough that Azarion slipped out of her. His hands tightened on her waist, and his green eyes darkened.

Something in his tone made her wary, and his words started a sick feeling in the pit of her stomach. "What are you saying?"

"The Empire holds the gladiator fights to entertain the crowds. They hold the Rites of Spring to gain the gods' favor. Every Flower of Spring burned is a gift to them, the fire itself like wine. Entertaining the people in the seats is secondary. Entertaining and pleasing the gods is first and foremost if the Empire wants to maintain its power and control."

He wasn't telling her anything she didn't already know, but the way he phrased it made her skin crawl. She imagined deities quaffing fire from chalices while they devoured the dead of the arena like pieces of rotten fruit. "Go on."

He looked away, as if deciding how to say what he wanted or even if he wanted to say it at all. His hands stroked her sides, and his expression was both wary and pitying. Every warning instinct inside Gilene surged to the forefront.

"I've seen you wield the fire the guards start on the pyre," he said. "How you make it grow and surge and burn hotter. I've seen you build an illusion of the flames, creating rivers and lakes of more fire to fill the arena floor. You even turn yourself into one of those flames to escape the Pit without anyone the wiser."

"Except you."

He didn't smile at her grim quip. "Gilene, for all that your fire and illusion keep the Flowers from suffering agonizing deaths and allow you to run away so you can return home, they only spur the Empire to make the ritual greater every year."

She gasped. "That isn't true." He held her in place when she tried to climb off him, his words like blows from his fists.

He winced at her distress but was relentless. "Shh. Listen to me. Listen." She stilled, and his features grew blurry in her vision. "The people praise the spectacle, certain the gods are among them and approve the sacrifice. Your control of fire, and the illusion you create from it, makes it act in ways fire doesn't act on its own." He stopped, allowing time for his words to sink in.

A terrible revelation rose inside her. "The people see divine intervention, the presence of the gods among them."

"Yes."

She covered her mouth with a hand. Wretched sounds of grief still escaped past the barrier of her palm. What had she done? What had Beroe done these many decades? In trying to save itself, it had only made things worse for everyone subject to the tithe: itself, other villages, every family with a daughter who dreaded the coming of spring and the knowledge they might have to give up that child as a sacrifice.

Azarion's arms slid around her and gathered her close against him. She sobbed in his arms, drenching his skin. He stroked her back, her hair, and her arms, and planted soft kisses on her temple and cheekbone. "I'm sorry I hurt you," he whispered in her ear. "Forgive me."

She continued to cry for several moments while he held her in silence. When there were no tears left, she squirmed out of his embrace to snatch a cloth from a table holding the washbasin and blew her nose until her ears rang.

Azarion watched her from their tumbled nest of blankets, his face pale, green eyes dark with anguish. Gilene returned to the bed and knelt in front of him. "There's nothing to forgive," she said. "They're hurtful words, but that doesn't make them less true, and I needed to hear them. I wish all of Beroe could hear them."

"This would be a very crowded *qara*." His gentle teasing made her smile, and he reached out to tuck a strand of her hair behind her ear. "It's just a guess based on what I observed, Gilene. I could be wrong."

She exhaled a tired sigh and shook her head. "I wish I could believe you were, but it makes too much sense to deny. The Empire does demand more tithes. More women stand with me each year."

She scraped her palms across her damp cheeks to dry them, her thoughts racing. "What am I to do? I can't just let the women burn next to me, hearing them scream as their flesh melts off their bones. And how would I escape the Pit if I didn't create the illusion of more fire?"

"Don't go," Azarion said. "Stay here with me on the Sky Below."

"That's a wish, not a solution." She rose to clean up and dress. A bubble of tears still lodged under her ribs, making it hard to breathe, but she didn't succumb to it. The time for weeping was done. She needed a clear head to plan. She studied Azarion where he still reclined in their bed.

His mouth was set in a thin line, his visage dark. "Spring will be the best time to attack Kraelag. The Empire won't expect us to march our forces while snow is on the ground and the rivers are frozen." He captured her hand when she returned to him. "Moving an army across winter landscape is slow and difficult. Gilene, I can't guarantee we'll reach Kraelag in time to stop the Rites of Spring. Even if we're standing before the gates, it may not be enough to save you and the others from the immolation."

Gilene saw it in his eyes. Desperation. Fear. Fear for her and what she faced. She squeezed his fingers. "I'm not afraid," she lied.

"I am," he snapped. His expression shuttered, and he stood to yank on his clothing. "You're determined to go back."

She looked away. "What else can I do?"

He came to stand before her. "You can stay here! You're an *agacin* now."

Gilene chuckled, a humorless sound. "A concubine *agacin*."

He was an *ataman*, an unmarried one with alliances to forge. His people would expect him to marry.

"Be my wife," he argued. "Treasured and beloved."

That bubble of tears threatened to burst inside her. Gilene closed her eyes. "Stop, please. Your words only make it harder."

"I don't want it to be easy, Gilene!" He gripped her arms to give her a light shake. "I want it to be so hard, you'll change your mind." He kissed the bridge of her nose. "I understand your devotion to your family, though I think they and the entire village are cowards. What they demand you do for them, what they expect you to do for them . . . it's cowardice, and I can't find sympathy for them. Are they really worth your sacrifice? Your suffering?"

"You're about to go to war. Will you ask these questions of every Savatar warrior who follows you?"

He scowled. "Your village elders have enslaved their fire witches for how many generations?"

"For as long as any of us remember," she said in a small voice.

Azarion's scowl turned even more ominous than before. "Release me from my oath to leave Beroe untouched by the Savatar. It deserves a razing as much as Kraelag."

"No it doesn't. The village isn't full of evil people, just a lot of frightened ones with families. Would you not put Tamura and Saruke before your clansmen's sisters and mothers?"

He raked his fingers through his hair. "How does anyone answer that question until they're forced to?"

"They don't, not if they can help it." How she wished she didn't have to answer it now. Or ever.

Gilene caressed his jaw. "Wife of a chieftain," she said, wistful. "I would rise up in the world."

Azarion leaned his cheek into her palm. "And I would be made exceptional by the union, *Agacin*."

"You already are, Azarion Ataman. The ancestors for whom your mother has so much reverence would be proud of her son."

"And yet I still can't change your mind." She shook her head, and he growled low in his throat. "You're a stubborn woman."

She smiled at his accusation. "It's why I will prevail."

Her words made him pause, and he stared at her until the heat of a blush crawled up her neck to her cheeks. "Of that, *Agacin*, I have no doubt."

Once they were both dressed, he ushered her out of the *qara* and across the camp where everyone had gathered around the Ataman Council to hear an abbreviated explanation of Azarion's plan.

Erakes was as good an orator as Azarion, and in no time he had incited his warriors to such an eager state for battle, they were ready to mount their horses and ride for Kraelag in that moment to take on the Empire single-handedly.

"What happens now?" Gilene asked, leaning against Azarion's side as they stood at the crowd's periphery.

"The *atamans* will return to their clans and do as you've seen Erakes do: inform the clan what's to happen. We'll then meet with the Goban people to offer an alliance. I'd be surprised if they refused. They're the ones most vulnerable to the Empire right now." He kissed the top of her head. "I promise I will do all in my power to make sure we reach Kraelag by the equinox."

Gilene held on to the promise of that hope with both hands. The coordination alone for such a task was monumental with no guarantee of success. Even if the clans of both peoples agreed to ally themselves, their chances of failure were equal to, if not greater than, those of victory.

"Do you truly believe it's worth so much chaos and death?" She knew his answer, knew he'd asked this question of himself many times before she did.

His voice never wavered. "Down to my soul, *Agacin*. I've been a slave of the Empire. Never again will I be so, nor will my people, not if I have any say in the matter."

That evening, the people celebrated around a communal fire. There were wrestling matches, drinking games, dancing, singing, and trysts made in the swaying shadows of the concealing plume grass. Gilene and Azarion joined in the revelry, determined to enjoy this last night among the free-spirited Savatar who had taken her into their midst, and though they didn't see her as one of their own despite her magic, they welcomed her and treated her well. She was both *agacin* and Azarion Ataman's concubine—a potent combination of power and influence. Given time, the Savatar would accept her fully. This she knew. There was, however, no more time.

Her coupling with Azarion later that night bore the hallmarks of desperation and silent farewell that left him dour and her grief-stricken. At dawn, his entourage thanked Erakes for his hospitality and departed for the Clan Kestrel encampment with promises to host the *ataman* of Clan Eagle there soon.

They were a day and evening into their return when she, Azarion, and Masad left their party to turn back toward Clan Eagle's camp and the narrow passage that took travelers through the Veil and over the sliver of Nunari territory into the boundaries belonging to Krael proper.

"Don't linger," Azarion instructed Masad. "The Savatar respect the rule that *agacins* are free to choose the clan and camp of their preference, but some may interpret that rule differently for Gilene and keep her trapped here."

Masad nodded. "We'll ride hard, travel at night, and rest during the day."

His words conjured up an unpleasant memory for Gilene. "No sleeping in barrows," she said. "Ever again." The *tirbodh* gave her a puzzled look and then a shrug.

Azarion nudged his horse to stand alongside hers. His face was set, his lips thin and drawn tight against his teeth. "Should you have second thoughts, don't hesitate. Masad will lead you back to the Sky Below without question."

They stared at each other as the *tirbodh* guided his own horse away to allow them privacy. Gilene reached out with a shaking hand, stricken when Azarion drew back from her touch.

"Don't," he said, and his voice was harsh. "If I touch you, I won't let go."

She breathed back the tears gathered in her nose and throat, making her eyes ache. "Goodbye, gladiator. Our bargain is met. Good luck." If she said his name, she'd fall apart.

He didn't suffer such weakness, and her name was a prayer on his lips. "Farewell, Gilene of Beroe."

He turned his horse and galloped back to where their camp

slept under the moon's waning light. Gilene followed his shadow until it blended with all other shadows, and the sound of hoof-beats faded, leaving only the wind's dirge in their wake.

She guided her own horse to where Masad waited, and offered him a watery smile. "Beroe waits, Masad. I've been long away."

The villagers' ecstatic relief at seeing her ride into the village alongside Azarion's uncle was short-lived. The miller's wife saw her first and raced down the street toward the house of the most senior village elder. Soon the street was filling with people, all calling her name as if she were a conquering hero returned to them in splendor. They stared at Masad, wide-eyed and wary of the fierce-looking warrior riding beside her as their horses ambled slowly down the main avenue toward the house Gilene shared with her mother and sister.

"You're welcome to stay as long as you like, Masad. We can feed you and put you up in a bed. The hearth keeps all the rooms warm enough."

He declined her offer. "I'm needed elsewhere, *Agacin*," he said. His gaze swept the crowd gathered nearby, unabashedly watching them. He lowered his voice. "Are you certain you won't come back to the Sky Below?"

No, she wasn't at all certain, and maybe one day, she would go back. But, like him, she was needed elsewhere. "Maybe one day," she said. "Not today."

He bowed, wished her well, and rode out of Beroe as quickly as he had appeared, the look in his eye a worried one.

That worry wasn't without basis. Once the initial celebrations over Gilene's return had ended, the villagers' relief at having her back had soon turned to resentful suspicion. She looked none the worse for wear for her sojourn in the Stara Dragana, and in no time the questions of what happened to her became poisoned with the taint of accusation. Even her family eyed her askance at times, though none of them dared to ask the questions she saw in their faces. Had she truly been abducted? Or had she fled only to change her mind and return to Beroe out of guilt or because she had no other place to go?

As witnesses to Azarion tossing her across a horse's back and racing through the capital's streets, her brothers had at least zealously assured any who asked that she'd been an unwilling captive. Her mother and Ilada, though . . . Gilene had caught the dubious expressions on their faces more than once during the long wax and wane of the winter season.

She returned to the tasks that had always been hers when she lived in Beroe—helping her mother and sister with the household chores, working in the dye houses. It didn't take long for her hands to stain green once more. The rhythm and pace of the village was as familiar to her as her own reflection. Sleepy and slow in winter, always with an undercurrent of dread as everyone anticipated the coming of spring and the arrival of Kraelian slavers.

Gilene shared nothing of her knowledge regarding Azarion and his plans, and offered little about her time among the Savatar, even when her mother and Ilada pressed her for details.

"You've become so secretive, Gilene," her mother fussed, giving her dish towel an annoyed snap as they worked together washing and drying the supper dishes one evening.

Gilene shrugged away the complaint. Her mother's irritation didn't bother her, nor did the speculative stares of her siblings or those of the villagers when she moved among them.

Her role as Beroe's annual savior had made her an outsider years earlier—among the villagers and within her own family—

and she felt the isolation even more now, only this time, it was she who held herself apart.

She missed the Sky Below with its open spaces, its horse herds, and black *qaras*. She missed Saruke with her odd bits of philosophical advice. She even missed the dour Tamura, whose devotion to her mother and brother and to Arita was a thing of beauty to behold.

Most of all, she missed the man she once thought she'd sworn to hate and ended up loving. Every night, when she closed her eyes, Gilene pictured his fierce, elegant face, and the emptiness inside her yawned wide and deep.

Beroe had been her birthplace and where she'd grown up, but she no longer belonged here. Coming back had been a necessity. The distance between her and her family stretched even wider now, but they were still her family, still at the mercy of the village elders, who wouldn't hesitate to use them in forcing Gilene's cooperation to act as a tithe.

Azarion had been right to call them all cowards. They were, and that cowardice had perpetuated a terrible assumption, one she had strengthened for the last five years. She prayed the Savatar and their allies would win the day, claim victory, and end the Rites once and for all. No more tithes, no more bleak duty to a place that used her guilt and her shriveling affection for her family as chains to trap her. Maybe this time, when she wielded fire, it would be in the service of other saviors.

# CHAPTER EIGHTEEN

Azarion blinked away the sweat that dripped into his eyes, wishing for a blizzard or even just a quick squall of snow flurries to cool the air. Snow still lay on the ground this early in spring, and nighttime frost iced everything before the sun rose to melt it away. It might still be cold to someone in everyday clothing, but harnessed in the encompassing armor of a heavy cavalryman, he roasted under the pale sun.

He sat his horse amid four thousand Savatar heavy cavalry occupying a low rise that gently sloped toward the walled capital of Kraelag. The land between the city and this hill had not yet been plowed for planting, and it stretched flat and clear for at least a league. On the opposite side, the Kraelian army had amassed several legions of soldiers. A Savatar scout had returned the previous night from reconnoitering the enemy.

He had bowed to Erakes, Azarion, and the other four *atamans* gathered together in Erakes's crowded war *qara* along with the captains who would command the squadrons of archers supporting the heavy cavalry. "*Atamans*, from what we saw, the Kraelians are three times our number at least. Four thousand cavalry, four thousand light infantry, and twenty-five thousand heavy infantry. A general named Mal Vornak leads them."

Erakes turned to Azarion. "Do you know him?"

"By name only. He's a seasoned commander and led the Kraelians to victory against the Prathics and the Oseks. With almost forty thousand men at his disposal, this will be a battle hard-fought."

Erakes shrugged. "We knew that when we planned this attack."

Everything leading to this confrontation had been hard-fought for the Savatar. They had used winter to their advantage, guiding their tough horses over snowy terrain and rivers frozen so solid, they didn't crack under the weight of the thousands of riders who traveled them like roads to cut the distance it took to reach Kraelag.

When the weather was kinder, they trekked twenty-five leagues in a day, a grueling pace no Kraelian horse could handle but that the steppe ponies conquered with ease. They subsisted on the brittle grasses browned by cold and buried under snow while the Savatar themselves lived off fermented mare's milk and whatever game they could hunt in the harsh depths of winter. By the time Krael recognized the danger to its capital, the steppe clans were nearly at Kraelag's gates.

The standing army assigned to protect the capital was drawn from a ring of garrisons that surrounded the rich farmlands and rivers that kept Kraelag's citizens and its vassal towns and villages fed. Azarion suspected Mal Vornak had ordered every one of them emptied and their soldiers marched immediately to the capital. So far Krael was doing everything Azarion and the other *atamans* had hoped.

Three leagues away, the vulnerable Manoret Harbor with its valuable granaries had fallen to a squadron of Savatar, who now held it. No doubt a messenger dispatched by a desperate Kraelian harbormaster had reached the capital with the news. Azarion didn't think the man lived beyond his telling of events. The last thing those in power in the capital wanted was for its populace to learn they might starve behind the walls.

With the inclusion of Nunari clans that had turned renegade

against their Kraelian masters, the Savatar horde had swelled in number, though, as the scout predicted, the Kraelian army they were preparing to fight outnumbered them at least three to one.

The Kraelian army advanced toward the Savatar force. This day, Azarion expected they'd water the soil with blood instead of rain.

At Erakes's signal, the Savatar beat war drums and blew the slender, dog-headed horns whose trumpeting sounded like a cross between an enraged woman and a howling wolf.

The Kraelian army continued to advance with infantry at the center and cavalry on the wings. At a series of shouted commands, they paused and re-formed into a hollow square, lined twelve-deep on all sides, before continuing their march.

Erakes, more experienced than Azarion in large-scale combat, grinned at the sight. "Smart man. He's re-formed his infantry to keep from being outflanked, but at the cost of mobility."

All around them, the Savatar heavy horse waited, eager and impatient to engage their enemy. Beyond the Kraelian line, Kraelag shimmered in the spring sun, a corrupt jewel waiting to be shattered.

Azarion studied the hollow square. "If we send the heavy horse in first, we may not be able to break the line. There are too many of them."

Erakes nodded and sent up a series of signal whistles, calling the captains to his side. "Send in your archers," he told them. "Surround the square and rain down arrows until the Kraelians can't see the sky above them. Draw out their cavalry from the wings." He turned to Azarion. "Prepare your heavy horse. When their cavalry draws closer to us, you'll attack."

Azarion left his commander's side to gather his forces in readiness. He caught a glimpse of his fierce sister galloping past him, first arrow already nocked into place as she raced with the other Savatar light cavalry toward the Kraelian line.

In no time the sky had turned black with the hail of arrows as Savatar archers harried the square's perimeter, shooting straight into the line or up in the air where the arrows fell from above like sharpened rain, pinning arms and shoulders to shields and feet to the ground.

Mal Vornak ordered his skirmishers to attack the archers, but they were driven back to hide behind shields by the relentless Savatar arrows. As Erakes predicted, the Kraelian general ordered his light cavalry to engage the archers.

Azarion timed the maneuver, counting as the Kraelian light cavalry chased the retreating horse archers ever closer to the main Savatar force. He wheeled his mount around and bellowed to his captains, "Make ready!" Armored riders atop barded horses formed their lines, couching the long, heavy spears meant to puncture enemy lines in a frontal charge.

As the horse archers galloped past the heavy cavalry, Azarion called out again. "Ride forth!"

The thunder of hooves and war whoops from the Savatar deafened him as they charged into the pursuing lines of Kraelian light cavalry, spears lowered. Azarion lurched backward on his horse, nearly sliding off as the animal struck breast to breast against another horse. Equine squeals joined the screams and shouts of men fighting and dying on the field.

Azarion turned the spear into a battering ram, using it and the sword he carried to cut, stab, and bludgeon his way through the melee of Kraelian and Savatar fighters until his blade coursed with blood, and he and his horse were painted crimson in gore.

He fought off gauntleted hands that tried to rip him from the saddle, and lost his favorite dagger when he plunged it into a soldier's neck. The fountain of blood erupting from the wound temporarily blinded him in a hot tide, and he barely dodged the blow of a hammer against his helmet.

The blaring howl of the horns signaled the heavy cavalry's retreat, and his men gathered together to gallop back to the main force, passing another wave of horse archers who returned to harass the Kraelian infantry.

The hours of slaughter and bloodshed wore on as the sun traveled its path across the sky. Unplanted fields were littered with the corpses of Kraelian and Savatar soldiers and their horses. The ground crackled underfoot from the wood of thousands of spent arrows.

That evening, in the Savatar war camp, Azarion stood outside his *qara* and peeled off his blood-caked armor, letting each piece drop to the ground. He swiped a hand across his face, succeeding only in smearing more blood on his skin. He was drenched in sweat, the splatter of entrails, and horse shit. The Savatar had won the day, and while he was pleased with the outcome, he didn't dare call it a victory. They had to get through tomorrow and a sunrise that would surely reveal the arrival of reinforcements from outland Kraelian garrisons.

The light of a nearby torch revealed the approach of a visitor. A tall shadow solidified into his sister. Like Azarion, she was filthy and bloody, with dark shadows painting the skin under her eyes. Still, she gave him a triumphant grin and raised a flask in offering.

Azarion sat in the dirt and invited her to join him with a wave of his hand. She settled next to him and passed the flask. Her braids had come unraveled, and her dark hair spilled over her shoulders to drag through the dust in a tangled mass. "It was a good day," she said.

He took a swallow of mare's milk before passing the flask back to her. "It was a bloody day, and we aren't any closer to breaching the main gates."

She shrugged. "But we're still here, still ready to fight tomorrow, and a lot of Kraelian dead are fertilizing those fields right now." Her side-glance was puzzled. "Besides, didn't you say in council we didn't need to actually breach the city? Just keep the garrisons focused on it long enough for our eastern forces to capture the Gamir section of the Golden Serpent and destroy those garrisons?"

That had been his plan, the one he repeated numerous times, first to Erakes and the other *atamans*, then to the Kestrel clan, and finally to the Goban. Sacking the city wasn't the primary goal, though Gilene's idea of capturing the granaries and holding them ransom to avoid a long siege worked in their favor.

Gilene. Azarion sighed and pinched the bridge of his nose, between thumb and forefinger in an attempt to lessen the pressure of a headache blossoming behind his eyes. A day didn't go by that he didn't think of her, a night that he didn't ache to have her next to him while he slept. His worry for her gnawed incessantly at him. Were the autumn and winter not taken up by planning for this battle, he might well have succumbed to the overwhelming temptation to ride for Beroe and fetch her back.

It would have been easier to let her go and let her be were she returning to a peaceful life, instead of a wretched one.

"What troubles you, Brother?" Tamura regarded him steadily, her green eyes, so like his own, bright in the torchlight.

He stared in the city's direction, its walls and towers hidden by trees and shadow. "The equinox is upon us tomorrow. The Empire always celebrates it with the Rites of Spring."

A strong hand gripped his forearm, and he glanced down to see Tamura's slender fingers, with their broken, dirty fingernails, clutching his vambrace. Sympathy softened her hard features. "Do you think the *agacin* is in Kraelag?"

He shrugged. "I don't know yet. I sent two scouts to find out. I'd hoped to hear from one or both tonight."

As if fate heard him and chose to humor his concern, a man entered the pool of light and bowed to Azarion. "Azarion Ataman, I have news."

Azarion stood, his exhaustion forgotten as his stomach somersaulted in anticipation of the scout's words. Tamura stood with him, a comforting hand on his back. "Tell me."

"The Rites of Spring will be observed tomorrow. Those women who were tithed as sacrifices will burn at midday."

Tamura's flattened hand seized into a fist, gathering Azarion's tunic tight in her grip as he lunged forward, ready to bolt through the camp and over the bloody fields, straight into enemy territory so that he might scale the walls or beat down the gates with his fists and retrieve the woman who had captured his soul and held it willing hostage.

"Her trial is not yours, Brother," Tamura hissed in his ear. "She will survive it. You won't if you run into the arms of Kraelians waiting to hack your head from your shoulders!"

The scout edged away from the pair, wary of Azarion's reaction to his news and Tamura's snarling warnings.

Azarion shook her off and exhaled a shaky breath through flared nostrils. Gilene would survive the fires tomorrow, but what about after, with the city under siege and no doubt closed to any who would enter or leave it now except the armies? His gut churned at the thought of what she might be enduring now, in a cell with a gladiator still raging from a day's fighting in the arena, blood still hot and his lust high.

He closed his eyes, hands fisted at his sides so tight, his knuckles turned white. Tamura's words—"She chose this, Azarion. She knew what awaited her"—did nothing to ease the fury boiling inside him. Gilene was so close, but she might as well have been trapped on the moon for all that stood between them.

Azarion sent the scout away with a short thanks. He didn't return to his seat next to the meager fire he'd started earlier, choosing instead to pace, his weariness burned to ash.

Tamura reclaimed her spot and watched her brother while she drank. "Hold your anger, nurse it, fan it until you can taste it on your tongue and smell it in your nose, but don't waste it on some fool rescue attempt that'll see your head on a gate spike for the Kraelians to jeer at when the sun rises."

He halted to glare at her. "Would you follow this advice if it were Arita in Gilene's place?"

She gave a humorless chuckle. "You ask that as if I'd have a choice in the matter. I wouldn't, and neither do you."

Azarion growled and resumed his pacing. His sibling was annoyingly correct. Dawn and battle couldn't come soon enough. He would hack his way through every Kraelian soldier and breach the gates alone if necessary to get Gilene out of Kraelag alive.

He spent the remainder of the evening with the other *atamans* and commanders, going over last-minute plans for the following day. The stars mocked him from on high, reminders of a better night when the fire witch of Beroe whispered his name in a loving voice and welcomed him into her arms and body.

At dawn he'd fight; at noon she'd burn. If the gods were merciful, neither would die.

# CHAPTER NINETEEN

The catacombs below the city hadn't changed in the year since Gilene had last walked across their floors. Still squalid and fetid, they welcomed her and the newest crop of Flowers of Spring into their labyrinth to await the immolation most of the capital had turned out to watch.

Rumors ran rife throughout the city, filtering down even to these depths, of savage steppe nomads who threatened Kraelag and fought the Kraelian army on the wide expanse of untilled farmland that stretched north of the capital's main gate. Still no one seemed concerned. No one fled the city or hid in their houses. Even the emperor and empress remained in residence and planned to attend the Rites. All believed the powerful Kraelian force would annihilate, or at least drive away, the horse clans, and such a clash would not interfere with the popular Rites of Spring.

Here, under the city, no hint of the warfare taking place beyond Kraelag's walls reached them—if one didn't count the rumors. The Flowers, isolated in the large, damp holding cell, awaiting their deaths, caught threads and whispers of the events outside.

Gilene tried not to listen too closely or dwell too long on the idea that Azarion rode among the ranks attacking the Kraelian armies. She still believed he lived, and he had fulfilled his second promise to her: spare Beroe as the Savatar rode into the heart of the Empire. The village still stood, though others weren't so fortunate.

There were differences as well, good and bad. Unlike the previous spring, this one was much colder, and the women huddled together in small groups for warmth and comfort. More of them crowded the holding cell, but none had been subjected to the attention of the gladiators the night before. The catacombs were uncommonly silent and empty, no vulgar shouts or comments from imprisoned fighters taunting the guards or each other, no threats from the guards themselves. The few assigned to the women were restrained, as if the events outside the city walls occupied their thoughts most.

Gilene crouched alone in one corner, her hands tucked under her arms to keep them warm. She took note of each woman in the cell. They varied more in age this year, from old to just beyond childhood, and it was the last that made her stomach lurch. The guilt that always sat heavy in the back of her mind regarding her role in these Rites threatened to overwhelm her. Her reasoning told her they were condemned to die, that the only help she could offer was the mercy of instant death instead of the horrific torture the Empire planned for them for the entertainment of the arena crowd.

Azarion's words, that Beroe's deception might have increased the popularity of the Rites, still made her bleed inside, and her soul, weighed down by what she must do, told her reasoning to kindly shut up.

Most of the women didn't pay her any mind, warned away by her grim demeanor or too focused on their own misery and fear to worry about anyone else's. Gilene wanted it that way. She still regretted the brief conversation she'd had with the prostitute Pell the previous year. Distance meant the deaths didn't cut as deep. Her interaction with Pell still haunted her these many months later.

One woman, however, didn't do as the others did. A small creature no older than Gilene and as delicate as a bird, with large eyes, a full mouth, and a strong jawline, stared at Gilene. That scrutiny never wavered even when Gilene scowled at her.

She leaned her head back against the damp wall and closed her eyes, listening to the quiet conversations around her.

"I was supposed to be married next month."

"Do you think the horse clans will break through the gates?"

"If they do, it won't be to save us."

"Will the gods hear our prayers?"

Gilene's eyes snapped open for a moment, and she stared at the cell bars. *No*, she thought. *They are deaf and blind, and without mercy.* She didn't share the thought. Hopelessness already reigned supreme here. She closed her eyes again and listened.

"I miss my family."

"So do I."

Gilene didn't miss hers, at least not the one in Beroe. They'd waved her off with the same presumption from previous years. This was her place; this was her purpose. A few of the villagers had even looked happy to see her go, as if the months on the Stara Dragana hadn't been spent as a captive but as an escapee. To these villagers, such dereliction of duty deserved punishment, and a return to Kraelag as a Flower of Spring was hers.

She had refused her brothers' offer to wait for her after the Rites were over. She didn't want their help any longer and would find her own way out of the city, injured or not. Their lack of argument or insistence they wait had frozen her heart against them a little more.

"You gather spirits around you like bees to a flower," a voice said close to her.

Gilene abandoned her grim recollections and opened her eyes

to find the bird woman crouched next to her. "What are you talking about?"

The other woman gestured at the space they occupied. "This cell is crowded with the dead."

Considering that every woman in here, except Gilene, would burn in the Pit in a few hours, Bird Woman was right. She waited to hear what else her odd companion might say.

"They began arriving the moment you entered. One or two and then a stream of them. All women. Except my father, of course." She cocked her head to the side. "Can you not feel them?"

Gilene straightened away from the wall. She felt nothing but the cold and the itchy coating of dirt encrusting her skin. A sudden thought occurred to her, and she glowered at her unwanted visitor. "You're a shade speaker, aren't you?" At the other woman's nod, she scooted away as if a sudden foul odor had wafted up between them. "Go away."

Gilene believed in ghosts. After a night spent in cursed Midrigar, she'd have to be willfully blind not to. What she didn't believe in were shade speakers.

They were charlatans of the worst sort who made their living off the grief of those who'd lost a loved one by offering to communicate with the dead. She doubted any of them had ever seen a shade, much less spoken to one. If they did, they'd outrun a frightened deer as they fled. Even the Empire didn't recognize them as true sorcerers and left them alone.

She startled when the bird woman suddenly grasped her arm in a grip whose strength belied her small size. "Listen to me," she hissed, before casting a quick look over her shoulder to see if anyone else heard her. "One of those women has a message for you."

Gilene yanked her arm away and scooted back on her haunches. Her fingers tingled at the perceived threat, her magic coursing hot through her veins. Restored to its full strength over the winter, it flowed under her skin, a vast pool of power she conserved for just this day. "Go away," she all but snarled.

The bird woman remained undeterred. "I speak for the dead, not the living. Whether you choose to believe or not is no concern of mine. I've done what they asked." She stood and brushed off her skirts. "Pell wishes to tell you, be brave. All is forgiven."

Her words might have been arrows shot from a Savatar bow at close range. Gilene gasped and surged to her feet. "What did you say?"

Bird Woman backed away, her farseeing eyes the color of dull steel. "I've delivered my message," she said, voice soft once more. "Treat it as you will." She picked a path back to the spot she'd occupied earlier, and this time she cast her gaze on the tiny window high above them where the sun streamed through.

Her knees shaking, Gilene resumed her seat before she fell. She wouldn't weep, though she breathed in pained staccato pants. She didn't want to believe the shade speaker, but her mention of Pell convinced her of the truth of her words.

Were the ghosts around her those of the women who had burned in her fires? She had never asked for forgiveness for her part in their deaths. She didn't feel she deserved it. However fate chose to judge her after she died, it would weigh her intentions against her actions and decide her punishment. She expected no less and hoped for no more.

A woman's wails suddenly filled the cell, yanking Gilene out of her melancholy. "I don't want to die! I don't want to die! I don't want to die!"

A chorus of shushing noises and more strident commands to be quiet fell on deaf ears as the woman worked herself into a frenzy. Gilene marched toward the screamer, prepared to shake her into silence. She didn't get the chance.

A catacomb guard sprinted down the hall, keys jangling on his hip. He slammed into the bars at a run, rotted teeth bared in a snarl. "Shut your racket, ye stupid cunts!" He grasped the key ring attached to his belt and pulled a key from it to unlock the cell door.

Gilene shoved the two women closest to her toward the back wall at the last second, narrowly avoiding the biting kiss of the whip as the guard flung the door open, whip arm already arcing toward them. The whip's serpentine leather split the air with a warning crack. The screaming stopped.

"Unless you're sucking my cock, you keep your mouths shut," he commanded. "If I hear so much as a cough out of any of you, I'll drag you out, fuck you in the hallway, then strip the skin off your back with this here toy. Understand?"

No one answered him. Satisfied, he coiled the whip and retreated from the cell, slamming and locking the door behind him.

Gilene watched him leave, keeping her tingling hands hidden in her skirt. Hatred boiled inside her. Her fire burned the wrong people. That guard and those like him deserved to stand in the Pit and beg for mercy.

The silence continued once he'd gone, his threat vile enough to keep the most terrified Flower of Spring mute, until the shade speaker spoke. "Before I die, I'd like very much to see that weasel hanged by his whip."

Enthusiastic ayes accompanied a few gasps and bursts of swiftly muffled laughter. The murderous humor served to break the tension if not the gloomy fear filling the cell. Gilene eyed Bird Woman with newfound respect.

She made to return to her spot in the corner, when a commotion broke out at the far end of the corridor where the guard had gone. He returned, ahead of a crowd of silhouettes that seemed to jostle and tumble around each other as two more guards on either side of them pushed and shoved them toward the cell where the Flowers waited.

The guard opened the gate and, to Gilene's horror, herded at least a score of frightened prisoners into the already crowded cell.

The new additions ranged in age from baby to grandmother. Mothers clutched nursing infants to their breasts while adolescent girls cradled siblings on their hips. All were female, all terrified, and, if they were brought here, all condemned.

Some sobbed while others stared around them in mute, wide-eyed terror. Sick to her soul at the sight, Gilene approached one woman who didn't cry or look to be on the verge of fainting. She clutched the hand of a small girl who clung to her skirts and sucked her thumb.

"You can't be part of the tithe," she told the newcomer, hoping she was right. Certain she wasn't.

The woman hugged the child close. "We weren't. Not at first. Then soldiers came and brought us here."

Gilene frowned. Soldiers, not slavers. So much was different this year from the last. Still grim and horrible but also changed, and she very much feared the arrival of the attacking Savatar had brought about that change. "What did they tell you?"

The woman took a shuddering breath. "The armies needed the favor of the gods, and such favor demanded more Flowers for the Rites."

Magic, scorching, eager to burst forth, tumbled through Gilene's blood. Was there no quenching the Empire's thirst for killing?

She thought of Azarion, a slave of the Empire who embraced its brutality to survive. His people clashed with the Kraelian army outside Kraelag's walls and died in the fields outside the gates.

Another voice spoke up, this one from the original Flowers brought to the capital. "The Empire is more afraid than everyone thinks. Afraid of the horse clans, so it will sacrifice more of us."

An idea took shape in Gilene's mind, inspired by a resolve as cold as the magic inside her burned hot. Enough. She'd had enough. Enough deception, enough guilt, enough bitterness. She would no longer protect Beroe's cowardice, not even for the family who took her for granted and accepted her fate long before she ever did. Her gaze slid over the crowded cell, packed to the walls now with terrified women and children whose only crime was to be born as citizens of an empire that would see them die agonizing deaths.

She made shushing noises until the quiet murmurs of conversation halted and she could be heard by all while speaking in a softer voice. "Who among you knows anything about these catacombs? Such as a way out that isn't through the main passage?"

Gilene had always walked out of the maze of hallways through the main entrance, but she'd been one woman with the benefit of an illusion spell to aid her. Getting a large group of people out without being noticed required another plan.

Bird Woman raised her hand. "I do. There's an even lower level than this one that can be reached through a storage chamber. It's from when the first capital stood, when it was still just a fortress. Three tunnels lead outside the walls. Two are impassable, full of rubble. The third is narrow, and you have to crawl in places, but you can get out of the city that way."

One of the other women spoke, her tone and expression both hopeful and suspicious. "Are you certain?"

A shadow passed over the shade speaker's features, a grief blunted but not gone. "My father was once a Pit gladiator imprisoned in the catacombs. He told me."

Gilene wondered whether such knowledge had been passed on while the woman's father was alive or if she spoke to his shade the way she'd spoken to Pell's. "If I could get us out of this cell, could you lead everyone to the tunnels and out of the city?" At the other's nod, a spark of hope ignited.

"You don't have a key!" one not-so-helpful voice chimed in.

"No, but I know of a way to get it. We'll have to work together, and I'll need one of you to scream as loud as you can." Her gaze settled on the woman whose shrieking had brought the guard and his threats in the first place. She bowed her head and hunched her shoulders, doing her best to make herself as small as she could.

"That will bring the guard back," another woman said.

Gilene nodded. "I'm counting on it."

A tall woman, of similar height to Gilene, sporting vibrant red hair streaked with gray, stepped forward. "I'll do it. The gods know I've had plenty of practice with that worthless husband of mine." She grinned.

The woman who warned of the guard's return frowned at Gilene. "Why don't you scream instead of her? This is your idea."

"I don't have a strong enough voice." And she needed it in working order to invoke her illusions. She glanced at the redhead. "Scream as loud as you can. When the guard arrives and demands to know who's making noise, I'll say it's me."

"What will you do?" Bird Woman stood in front of her now.

"What I should have done a long time ago." Gilene gestured to the hallway beyond the cell's bars. "Which way to the tunnels?"

Bird Woman pointed straight down the hall. "Two cells past these and then to the right. A short passage leads to a row of storerooms. At least it did then. The last one takes a person to the tunnels."

"Is it guarded?"

Bird Woman paused, as if listening. "No."

Someone in the crowd protested. "We'll die if we try to escape!"

Bodies moved out of the way until Gilene had a clear view of the frightened speaker, a young girl, no more than fourteen. She stared at Gilene, face pale with terror.

Gilene wished she could offer something more encouraging to buoy the girl's courage. But there was only hard truth to cling to if they had any hope of making it out of the catacombs alive.

"We will die if we don't try. If we stay in this cell and do nothing, we won't see the sun set today." The girl blanched even more and whimpered. "I wish I could tell you otherwise."

The redhead came to stand next to the shade speaker. "What do you want us to do?"

Gilene's heart beat hard in her chest. Fear, resolve, even a sense of relief. These women and children might survive today. She would not, but she would die knowing that at this Rites of Spring, she helped people to live instead of to die.

"Remember your instructions," she said. "Most important, back well away from the door, no matter what." She pretended not to see the curious looks those peculiar words inspired. She turned to Bird Woman and the redhead. "I'll get the key. Once I have the door open, lead the others to the tunnels. I'll take up the rear and hold off any guards who might give chase." She didn't have much hope they'd follow her next directives, but she had to try. "If you face a guard or guards at the storerooms, you will have to kill him. He can't get away. You can't just injure him. He'll warn others. You kill him. Or them. Whatever it takes."

The redhead's stare raked her. "And you plan to guard our backs? By yourself? You don't look like a warrior. How do you plan to hold off a couple of Kraelian guards?"

Magic burned under her palms, eager, waiting. "You'll know soon enough."

Gilene glanced at the movement of the shadows created by the sunlight spilling across the wall. It grew brighter with each passing moment. It wouldn't be long before midday arrived and a retinue of guards came for the sacrificial tithes. She nodded to the redhead, whose first shriek made everyone wince and clap their hands over their ears. The small children and babies, frightened by the noise, added their voices to the cacophony.

The woman even rattled the cell bars for emphasis, all the while wailing at the top of her voice, "Let me out! Let me out! I'll die in here! Let me out!"

As Gilene had hoped, the guard who had threatened them earlier returned, rounding the corner of the corridor, his face savage, the whip already half-unfurled. Gilene waved the women back and took the redhead's place at the bars. She lowered her head and whispered a spell under her breath before raising her head again to meet the guard's furious gaze. Shocked gasps rose behind her.

What had been simple rage instantly changed to feral lust. Gilene's illusion spell had done its job, transforming the plain mask she wore to a visage of breathtaking beauty, even through the layer of grime covering her.

She rattled the bars as the redhead had done. "Please," she cried out in her most plaintive tone, hoping to coax him closer. "I can't stay in here. Just a moment in the hallway. I'll do anything."

He couldn't unhook the key ring off his belt fast enough, fingers fumbling as he cursed his clumsiness. "A moment, no more.

And I'll put that mouth of yours to better use than screaming me deaf."

The whip unfurled at his side as he unlocked the cell door and pulled it open. His bleary-eyed glare swept the cell's occupants. "The rest of you stay there and keep quiet." With that, he grabbed Gilene's arm and yanked her out of the cell, slamming and locking the door behind her.

Several gasps echoed in the hallway, and Gilene prayed no one would give away their plan. She had kept her part of it mostly secret for just that reason. She stumbled after him as he led her toward the center of the corridor, the grip on her arm unyielding. He finally stopped and turned to face her.

It took every bit of control she possessed not to lurch away from him. She'd helped cover cesspits cleaner than this man. He didn't let go of her arm but dropped the whip to free his other hand so he could unlace the placket at the front of his breeches.

"Aren't I lucky that the stupidest one in the cell was also the prettiest. Too bad you'll burn later, but I'll make good use of you now."

The startled squeak he emitted when she suddenly stepped closer to him would have made Gilene smile if her skin wasn't threatening to peel itself off her bones and flee of its own accord. This close, and his reek nearly made her pass out. She rested her hands on his shoulders and smiled into his eyes.

"Today you will burn with me."

The fire had surged against the cage of her will for so long now, it needed no coaxing to surface. She simply let it go, and the magic of flame burst out of every pore, enveloping her and the guard in a conflagration that doused the floor, ceiling, and walls around them in a tight radius before roiling back toward its source and its victim.

The guard died instantly, that surprised squeak the last sound he made before Gilene's fire immolated him in a flash of heat and light, leaving him nothing more than a pile of ash and charred bones at her feet once the flames died around her. She bent to retrieve the key ring, glowing hot but not yet melted. To any other but a fire witch, the metal would have fused into her palm.

Gilene blew gustily on the key ring to cool it before kicking aside the cremated ruins of their jailer. She cast her illusion spell once more, returning to the nondescript appearance the other women recognized. They pressed themselves against the cell's back wall as she drew closer.

She had felt nothing except triumph when she killed the guard, but the sight of her cellmates' terror made her cringe. "I mean you no harm," she assured them and held up the smoking key ring. "You must hurry if you want to get out of here."

She used the still-hot key to open the lock and swung the door wide, stepping to the side so as not to block or intimidate the fearful women. The shade speaker and the redhead were the first to walk across the threshold, both encouraging the others to follow. They were an interesting pair standing together, the fragile-looking bird woman with the big eyes that saw the dead, and the statuesque redhead with the fearsome gaze that reminded Gilene a little of Tamura.

The shade speaker waved them all out, gave Gilene a low bow of thanks, and hurried away toward the passage she claimed led to the tunnels. The red-haired woman paused. She, too, gave Gilene a quick bow. "May the gods remain merciful to us all this day, fire witch. Thank you."

A sudden thought occurred to Gilene, and she caught the other woman's arm. "If . . . when you make it out of the city, and if you face the steppe warriors, tell them you are all of Beroe. That

Azarion Ataman keeps his promise." At the other's confused expression, she shook her arm for emphasis. "Just do it. Don't forget."

The redhead's eyes narrowed. "You aren't coming."

"Not yet. Remember, I need to stay behind and take care of any guards so you can reach the tunnels in time." Gilene offered a rueful smile. "And now you know how I can hold off Kraelian guards by myself." She gave the woman a light push. "Go on. You can't linger."

She watched until the last woman disappeared into the passage's clot of shadows. If fate was merciful, they would escape the city unharmed to return to their families. If it wasn't, they'd die in those narrow spaces or beneath a hail of Savatar arrows. Gilene had either saved them from death in the Pit or sent them all to their deaths beyond Kraelag's walls.

The ash and bone pile that had once been a man was now nothing more than a soot mark on the floor's wet stone, trampled by the feet of fleeing women. The bones lay scattered in every direction, and she took a moment to kick them all into a corner where none could see them unless they actively searched.

The catacombs' hush thrummed in her ears, occasionally broken by the cheers of the crowd as they enjoyed bloodshed with their breakfast in the arena above her. Gilene ventured farther down the corridor's run, past the empty gladiator cells to the stairs leading to the street level and another less squalid passageway dominated by arches and columns.

Kraelian guards called it the Last Journey or the Last Walk. Gladiators marched down its length, prepared to fight to the death, and the Flowers of Spring were carted the distance in a cage pulled by horses. At its end, a pair of gigantic doors stood closed and barred, guarded by Kraelian soldiers. On the other side, the roofless arena known as the Pit, with its baying spectators, waited.

Scuttling noises at the end of the hallway sent her sprinting to a shallow alcove, where she squeezed herself into its space.

A pair of guards appeared, their shadows stretched across the walls where the torches cast sickly coronas of light. They paused, and from her hiding spot, Gilene clearly heard two sharp inhalations.

"Are you seeing what I'm seeing? Those fucking cunts got out somehow!"

A second voice joined the first. "Where's that fucker Molt? I'll kill him if he's drunk in a corner again!"

The sound of running feet warned her they drew closer. Gilene held her breath and stepped into the hallway. The two guards almost stumbled in their surprise. She darted past them, into the passage the women had taken earlier.

"Catch that bitch!"

She reached the hall's end before it forked in two directions, and waited. Her pursuers rounded the corner, their features promising murder when they caught her. Magic surged through her, a beast leashed on a fragile tether. For a second time, Gilene set it free.

Torches, mounted on either side of the hallway's entrance, flared bright, their flames stretching toward Gilene as if pulled by a lodestone. At a hand gesture, flames exploded out of the torches, white-hot flares erupting off the twisted wicks as if they'd been dipped in draga blood instead of tallow.

Fire danced in mimicry of Gilene's hand motions, filling the tunnel with a bestial roar. The guards shouted and turned to run, only to be cut off by a barricade of flame. A final slash of her hand through the air, and the fire consumed the two men in one bright gulp, leaving nothing behind but soot.

Torches guttered and died, plunging the hallway into a thick blackness scented with the caustic odor of cremation. Gilene leaned against the passage wall with a shudder. The urge to retch almost overpowered her. She clenched her teeth against the impulse and pulled the neckline of her tunic up over her nose to breathe. After days in the company of slavers and guards who didn't care whether the Flowers of Spring had food much less a bath, she didn't smell particularly sweet, but it was better than the sting of charred human flesh in her nose.

She allowed herself a moment to shiver in the darkness before straightening away from the wall. The Pit awaited her.

No one stopped her as she ascended the stairs from the catacombs to the Last Walk. She wore the illusion of an old male servant. It stood her in good stead as she navigated her way past armored guards, the occasional blood-splattered gladiator, and the beast masters transporting half-starved wolves and big cats to the upper levels. There, the condemned creatures were kept until sent into the Pit. Her heart stayed lodged in her throat, certain someone like Azarion would see past her spellwork and call out a warning to others that something strange was afoot.

She shuffled along until she came within sight of the great doors that opened to the arena. She waited for a lull in traffic before darting behind a stack of wine barrels. From this vantage point, she could watch the doors while staying hidden.

A beast master with his bevy of apprentices and servants surrounded a wagon loaded with a large cage that housed a monstrous bear. The creature paced in the confining space, emitting the occasional roar as it hurled its big body against the bars. Pity for the unfortunate animal strengthened Gilene's resolve. Animals in cages, people in cages, all to satisfy the Empire's unending bloodlust.

*Enough*, she thought. Enough.

She noted the garb the apprentices wore—rust-colored robes with a yellow insignia patch sewn at the shoulder. The patch denoted at which training school the apprentice studied and his rank among the students.

Gilene abandoned her illusion of the old man for that of an adolescent boy dressed in the apprentice's robes. She waited until the bear wagon stopped at the doors before leaving the shelter of the barrel stack.

The guards unbarred the doors and heaved them open to reveal the colossal expanse of the arena, with its screaming crowds and blood-soaked sand. The wagon rolled forward at the beast master's shout to the driver. Its entourage walked beside and behind it. Gilene jogged to catch up, playing the part of tardy apprentice but keeping enough distance so the true apprentices wouldn't notice her behind them. The guards thought nothing of it and waved her through with hardly a glance before pulling the doors closed with a creaking thud.

The crowd's roar bludgeoned her ears, the scent of gore strong in her nose. A surge of spectators packed the narrow walkways that led to the arena's seating as well as to the outer ring of hallways encircling the structure where food, prostitutes, and favors could be purchased. Here, it was easy to disappear into the chaos, and Gilene took advantage of it to part ways with the beast master and change her illusion yet again.

Illusion magic wasn't an endless well, and the effort to invoke and hold another disguise grew ever harder. This, however, would be her last.

The spectators inhaled a collective breath soon punctuated by appreciative whistles when a solitary woman of startling beauty crossed the bloodstained sands toward the platform built of dried kindling and the bodies of the dead. Garbed in robes the colors of twilight, with flowers woven in her dark hair, she shimmered in the sun, the epitome of spring.

Gilene didn't falter under the weight of their avid scrutiny nor stumble as she climbed the grotesque hill of dead men and animals to reach the immolation pillar prepared for the Flowers of Spring set to burn for the crowd.

She pivoted slowly so that all the arena might see her, before halting to face the pavilion where the emperor lounged in shaded splendor to view the events. The chair beside him was empty. Where was the empress?

A voice rippled across the arena, rising above the crowd's murmurs. "Burn! Burn for us, Flower of Spring!"

The audience took up the call, their chant rising ever louder until it was a one-word bellow. "Burn! Burn! Burn!"

Confused guards approached the platform, pausing at times to look around them for the wagon full of women they expected to arrive instead of this single girl. They stopped and edged back when Gilene lifted her hands. Fire ignited in her palms. The crowd roared its approval, demanding more.

Gilene turned her focus inward, to the ebb and flow of magic purling through her body and her spirit. She spooled it out slowly, reining in the surges of power so that the flames dancing merrily in her palms spilled through her fingers to splash across the platform and ignite the kindling. The planks beneath her feet vibrated with the cheers from her audience. The guards sprinted away.

This immolation would be her final one, the last desperate effort to end the Rites once and for all. She would burn up and burn out, use every last drop of magic inside her, fuel it with her life force until she was drained of both. Far better this than years of pain and slow disfigurement and a duty to pass on this hideous burden to another Beroe fire witch.

The flames grew, bursting upward with a roar that rocked Gilene back on her feet under a scorching wind. She stood within a whirlwind of fire that twisted and spun like a frenzied dancer. Power spilled out of her with every pull of her will, building layer upon layer until the entire floor of the arena transformed into a fiery lake. This was no illusion, but true fire, and it surged toward the arena's lower tiers in a wave of blistering heat.

Cheering changed to screaming as people closest to the arena floor abandoned their seats and fled up the steps to the higher levels.

Strength flowed out of Gilene like blood from a wound. In previous years she would have abandoned her place atop the pyre and fled the arena as an illusion of flame herself until she reached the questionable safety of the catacombs. Not this time. This time she stayed.

The fire climbed the high walls and hopped over, licking at the fleeing crowd as its flames galloped up the steps, grotesquely sentient in its movements as it consumed more and more of the arena.

Gilene's vision blackened as she poured her life force into her magic and nurtured the beast devouring the Pit. The flames had reached midway and seemed to slow. People jammed together in a tightly packed ring that huddled along the highest tiers. They began shoving each other to make room, and bodies tumbled down the steps and into the flames, their shrieks instantly lost in the inferno.

The seating, carved from stone, turned black and scorched, and anything cloth or flesh that succumbed to the fire was reduced to char. Still, it wasn't enough. Gilene snarled her frustration, and the fire leapt briefly in response, swallowing an entire section of the arena up to its highest point.

Tears filled her eyes only to evaporate instantly. For the first time since her magic manifested, she truly prayed.

"Agna, hear this woman you have named handmaiden. Your children die before the gates of Kraelag, and the Empire would burn its own to defeat them. I ask for your strength, not your mercy, because I can't do this alone. Make my death not a vain one, nor the deaths of those women who died here before me. There is vengeance, and there is justice. This is justice."

She didn't wait for an answer, didn't hope for some celestial recognition of her pitiful cry for help. The gods weren't deaf. They simply didn't exist, not even the one Azarion so fervently worshipped.

Gilene called on the tattered threads of her strength to make the fire hotter. Her lungs burned and her chest hurt, as if her heart struggled to push the blood through her body.

The arena seats drowned in fire, its spectators gone or immolated. She hated those who attended the Rites, hated them for slaking their thirst for agony and death under the guise of religious fervor. She would die unburdened by guilt over their demise.

A stray thought flitted across her bleary mind, of plume grasses murmuring in the wind while a Savatar *ataman* twined her hair through his fingers and kissed her lips with the passion of a lover and the reverence of a votary.

The fire was dying, as was she, when the sense of being watched overcame her. She peered into the flames surrounding her but saw only the hazy outline of the burning arena. Her eyelids were heavy, and an anvil rested on her chest, crushing her breastbone and making it so very hard to draw breath. Still that feeling of being observed didn't lessen. Gilene closed her eyes and gasped at the image filling her mind.

A woman, but not just a woman. This was something else,

something so vast and ancient, Gilene's spirit shied away with a whimper. She comprehended an ever-changing face whose eyes were the gathering of stars and whose body was woven of sky and meadow. The being was all that was both supernal and earthly, all that was young and old, frail and vigorous. Eons of time had passed through her fingers, and her fluttering hair reminded Gilene of a horse's mane.

"The Great Mare," she whispered.

The goddess tilted her head in a curious gesture. Mountains shivered in response. "You called me, handmaiden. I have heard you."

"Agna." Gilene tried to lift her hand and touch the hem of the goddess's gown, but she lacked the strength. "Help me," she said on a weak sob. "Make it all stop."

The goddess stared at her for what might have been a moment or a year or a century. Gilene shuddered at the sudden rush of possession, a surge of otherness that filled every part of her being. She fell to her knees, helpless before the onslaught, feeling every thought, every memory and emotion picked apart, examined, and judged.

When it was done, she fell forward and retched. Her empty stomach brought nothing forth, but the weakness was gone, as was the crushing pain in her chest. She raised her head, wondering whether her eyes were truly open or if she only beheld the goddess of the Savatar in the throes of a dying dream.

"Stand, Gilene of Beroe." The goddess's command usurped Gilene's will, and she didn't so much stand of her own accord as she was lifted to her feet. Agna's shifting features reflected a divine wrath. "There is vengeance, and there is justice," she said, repeating Gilene's words. "This is *both*."

Power, unlike any of the feeble magic Gilene commanded,

struck her with the force of lightning bolts, sending her body into a convulsive dance even as her spirit splintered under Agna's touch.

Gilene, who was no longer Gilene, but the crumbling avatar of an angry goddess awakened by an unbeliever's desperate prayer, screamed in triumph and despair.

# CHAPTER TWENTY

Azarion wrenched the spear free from the impaled Kraelian fighter just in time to block another's sword strike with the haft.

A thunderous snap followed by a bellowed "Look out!" from a nearby warrior made him and his opponent look up to the terrifying sight of a stone the size of a cart hurtling toward them from above.

Azarion leapt out of the way, skidding through the battlefield's churned mud. A hard strike to his leg made his toes go numb for a moment before shooting pains ricocheted from his shin to his thigh. A spray of mud shot skyward before pelting him in a rain of droplets, and the ground shook under his feet.

The rock had grazed him as it fell, denting his greave hard enough to pinch skin and cloth at its crease. He was lucky, far luckier than the Kraelian fighter he had fended off moments earlier. The man hadn't dodged as fast as Azarion and paid the price. All Azarion could see was a boot and part of a leg, bent at a strange angle, under the boulder.

He glanced at the ramparts where the long-armed skeletons of catapults suddenly rose above the walls. Around him, men and horses from both sides fled the field. His squadron of heavy horse, however, hadn't yet noticed the danger. They engaged the Kraelian infantry in a vicious battle, the gleam of bright steel flashing under the morning sun as they fought each other with sword and spear.

Azarion clambered to his feet, half limping, half running toward his mount and the men under his command. "Fall back!" he shouted. "Fall back now!"

Too late. A second booming snap followed by whistling heralded another hail of crushing shrapnel, this time a mix of stones, broken wood, and nails that ripped into the clusters of fighting men and horses. Human screams joined equine squeals of agony as death fell from the sky.

Azarion covered his head and raced for his horse, stopping once to drag a wounded Savatar fighter with him. When he looked once more toward his mount, it lay in the mud, dead.

Trumpets sounded from the horde perched on the low rise above the city, and soon a swarm of horse archers descended onto the field, despite the danger from the lethal catapults. Azarion shoved the man he helped toward the rider bearing down on them. She stretched her arm out as she rode past, and the soldier grabbed hold, swinging himself up behind her, the horse never slowing pace.

The light cavalry swooped in, rescuing those in the heavy cavalry either injured or without their horses. Azarion leapt onto the back of Tamura's horse as she nearly ran him over to save him. They raced back to the safety of the Savatar camp, where the catapults' range couldn't reach.

Azarion met Erakes at the entrance to his *qara*. "If we want to breach those gates or take down the rest of the infantry, we have to destroy those catapults."

That the Kraelians had employed the catapults in their defense of the capital didn't come as a surprise; still, Azarion had hoped they'd wait until the Kraelian ships arrived from the east and it no longer became necessary to engage the ground forces already defending Kraelag.

Erakes, still in half harness from his own earlier foray onto the field, motioned him inside the tent. He scowled at Azarion. "Number of casualties?"

Azarion shrugged. "It's anyone's guess. I'd say I've lost half my squadron. If we send in the other ones, the same will happen to them. Krael is willing to crush its own men in the effort to stop us. Heavy horse is useless against catapult fire."

Erakes paced, stroking his beard in thought. "The archers can still do plenty of damage and keep the Kraelians pinned in that square of theirs. They're mobile enough and fast enough to avoid the worst of the catapult's projectiles. And remember, we don't need to breach the gate. Not today. Not this battle. The treasure inside is worth warring over but not worth a defeat. We just need to fight long enough for the Kraelian ships to arrive with their eastern garrison soldiers."

"Or until our supply of arrows runs out."

They had brought with them a massive baggage train consisting of hundreds of horses loaded with thousands of arrows. An infantry's best defense against horse archers was to simply wait them out until the archers used up their arrows. Erakes had made certain such wouldn't happen with the baggage train in reserve.

They were interrupted from discussing more by a soldier. "*Atamans*," he said. "You need to come see this."

They followed him out of the tent, riding to a part of the ridge where they had a clear view of the battlefield and the city's defended gate. The Kraelian forces were shouting, cries of "Death to the savages!" carrying over the batter of sword flats on shields. The commanders spurred their horses up and down the lines, raising their arms in victory and encouraging the shouts to even greater volume. While a number of Kraelians kept an eye on the ridge, most watched their leaders or tilted their faces up to the city ramparts.

Erakes watched the tableau for a moment before shrugging. "They just sent us into retreat by hurling giant rocks at us. Of course they'd be celebrating. Why do we need to see this?"

Azarion barely heard the question. He'd followed the direction of the soldiers' gazes to the top of the city walls. The ringing that started in his ears almost drowned out everything else as his gaze caught on a diminutive figure standing at the ramparts, gleaming bright and golden in the sun. Black fury erupted inside him, along with a hatred so deep, it had etched itself into his bones.

He pointed to the figure. "That is Empress Dalvila on the ramparts," he said in a voice gone guttural. He guided his new mount down the ridge's slope, not waiting for Erakes's reply. "Find me the best archer and have them meet me," he shouted to the soldier who had brought them here. "Not the fastest. The most accurate."

The man bolted back to the Savatar encampment. Erakes trotted down the hill, catching up with Azarion, his features avid with the possibility of a quick victory. "Cut off the head, kill the snake?" he asked. "What about the emperor?"

Azarion didn't care about the emperor. Given enough time, the empress would dispatch with him. His gaze stayed riveted on Dalvila as she called down praise to her commanders. Defiant, flamboyant, she buoyed her troops' morale with her reckless disregard for her safety. She stood partially shielded by the rampart walls but still vulnerable to a well-aimed arrow.

"The Spider of Empire," Erakes remarked. He grinned at Azarion's quick, surprised glance. "You didn't know that's what she was called? Herself has many names outside the capital. Most not complimentary."

"They aren't complimentary inside the capital either," Azarion muttered.

He tried to contain his impatience as they waited for the archer to appear, and prayed Dalvila wouldn't leave the ramparts before then.

The rhythmic thud of hooves signaled the archer's arrival. She gave Azarion and Erakes each a quick bow. "You asked for the best archer, Azarion Ataman. That's me."

He waved her to follow him farther down the ridge, sheltered among a cluster of stone outcroppings where Savatar scouts kept watch and reported back to the commanders.

"They're too far away, Azarion," Erakes argued. "Even for the best archer."

Azarion ignored him. He pointed to where Dalvila stood. "Can you shoot her from here?"

The archer dismounted and eyed the ramparts, squinting and pacing a short distance one way and then the other. She nocked an arrow and drew back the bowstring to take aim. More pacing and squinting had Azarion clenching his jaw to keep from hurrying her. Finally, she lowered the bow and shook her head. "They're a good distance away, and she's a small target. I'd have to just about stand on the field's edge to guarantee a hit. I'll never get an arrow in the air before I'm dead."

"Impossible then?"

She shook her head again. "No, just improbable."

"Try anyway."

The archer bowed. "As you wish, *Ataman.*"

"Azarion, she better get that arrow in the air now."

Erakes's warning made him whip around. The empress was leaving the ramparts.

"Fuck!" he snarled before slamming his heels into his horse's sides. The animal leapt forward toward the open field. He spotted an abandoned shield on the ground, leaned from the saddle, and snatched it up before slowing his horse to a walk. He kept the shield in front of him, a guard against Kraelian arrow fire.

The Kraelian war chant faded away as the soldiers wondered why a lone Savatar rode to the edge of the field to pace his horse before them. The empress paused, staring over the ramparts.

"Come on, bitch," Azarion murmured. "Come back to the edge." Behind him, the archer waited. He'd found a way to capture her attention. Now he just needed to keep it.

He pulled off his helm. He'd been beardless when he escaped from Kraelag a year earlier. The one he wore now was neatly trimmed, but it still obscured some of his features and altered his appearance. Distance would also make it difficult for her to see his face clearly, but Dalvila was familiar with more than his face. She'd seen him fight in the arena and fuck in her bed. She knew his body language, and he counted on that now, helmless and alone as he stared at her from the edge of the field.

She lunged for the rampart. From where Azarion stood, she was too far away for him to make out her expression, but her one word, venomous and bubbling with loathing, pealed across the battlefield.

"YOU!"

Azarion wheeled his horse around and raced back toward the outcropping. The empress's shrieks blistered the air. "Kill him! Kill that gladiator!"

He flattened against the horse's back, making himself as hard a target to hit as he could while they raced for the safety of the Savatar lines. The stretch of a bowstring and muffled *thwump* of an arrow fired sounded close by. His archer had taken her shot.

Dalvila's shrieking halted abruptly. Azarion dared not look

back as more arrow sounds filled the air, only this time aimed at him.

He galloped past the shielded outcropping before swinging around to where Erakes and the archer waited. "Did you hit her?"

The archer blew out a breath. "Yes, though I'm not sure it was a kill shot. I couldn't tell if I got her in the chest or the shoulder. The shot knocked her backward, out of sight."

"It's chaos on the ramparts." Erakes pointed to the city. "Look."

People raced to and fro along the battlement walls. There was shouting and plenty of arm waving. Below, where the Kraelian army stood in formation, the commanders shouted for order. "Hold the line! Hold the line!"

Erakes leaned from the saddle to clap Azarion on the shoulder. "That was either good strategy to damage morale or personal retribution useful to all of us." He saluted the archer. "Impressive shot. From what clan do you hail?"

She grinned. "Saiga, Erakes Ataman."

"I'll sing your praises to Insaza Ataman when I see him."

The archer's smile widened even more. She bowed to him and to Azarion as he paused in front of her and waited until Erakes was out of earshot before speaking. "I'm in your debt, archer."

"I don't know if I succeeded, *Ataman*."

"You did," he said. "And you'll be rewarded. You honor your family with your bravery and your skill." He made sure to learn her name before he spurred his horse to catch up with Erakes.

It would be too much to hope that the arrow had killed Dalvila outright. Azarion could hardly believe it managed to hit her at all. His need for revenge against the woman who had debased him in ways his mind still shied away from was blade-sharp, though the archer's arrow had blunted its edge a little. With any luck, whatever wound it made would poison and kill the Spider of Empire.

They returned to the camp and had barely come out of the saddle when another scout arrived with different news.

He gave a quick salute. "I have news, *Atamans*. We've captured a group of women and children fleeing the city. They made it outside the walls but were caught trying to reach the river. All of them say they're from Beroe. That Azarion Ataman keeps his promise."

The blood still singing through Azarion's veins from his brief confrontation with Dalvila rushed even faster through his body. Gilene. Those were Gilene's words. The scout's eyes widened, and he took a hasty step back when Azarion stalked him. "Where are they?"

"Just outside. Riders brought them here when they mentioned your name."

"This has been an eventful day," Erakes said and followed Azarion and the scout to where a small crowd of Savatar clustered around a ragged group of women and children. They held on to each other for support, their faces bleached of color, eyes rounded with terror as they stared at the fearsome nomads surrounding them. None wore illusion. Gilene didn't stand among them. The tiny hope that flared to life inside him at the idea she might be here, in his camp, died.

Azarion approached carefully, hands at his sides, body relaxed. It would do him no good to scare them more than they already were. "Who speaks for you all?" he asked in a quiet voice.

There was a long pause, in which no one moved, before a tiny woman with big eyes and a generous mouth stepped forward. She folded delicate hands in front of her and lifted her chin before addressing him. "I do." She spared a quick glance behind her. "I think."

"Who told you to say you were of Beroe?" He knew. Knew in

his gut but wanted to hear this woman say it. He didn't get his wish.

A graying redhead stepped up alongside the petite woman. "She never told us her name. She was a Flower of Spring like us. She gave me the message before we escaped the catacombs."

Secretive, suspicious Gilene. That wariness had served her well on numerous occasions. "Was she tall with dark hair?" *And beautiful. The most beautiful woman ever born.* Those words Azarion kept to himself.

The tiny Kraelian woman answered this time. "Tall, yes, but with light hair and blue eyes." Awe altered her expression. "She can wield fire."

His eyebrows shot up. Her powers had replenished then over the winter months. He knew they would, but that she had revealed them to those who would recount what they witnessed had been either an act of desperation or one of dark resolve. Neither lessened his worry. "She isn't among you."

"She stayed behind to face any guards who would follow us. If she escaped, we didn't see."

Erakes spoke up this time. "How did you escape?"

The Kraelian paused, reluctant to answer. "There is a tunnel forgotten by all. My father told me about it. It leads from a storeroom in the catacombs to the city's outer curtain wall. You can't see the entrance because of the wall's angles and the growth of bushes there. It was barricaded. The barricade has collapsed."

A rush of bitter laughter rippled up Azarion's throat, and he clamped his lips shut to keep it from escaping his mouth. What he wouldn't have given during his ten years of enslavement to learn of that tunnel.

An insidious voice entered his thoughts. *But would you have met the fierce agacin?*

Fate was a vicious taskmaster of cruel, arbitrary humors, but every once in a while, it granted a boon in its own twisted way.

He glanced at Erakes, whose eyes glittered, before returning his attention to the Kraelian. "You all made it through."

She nodded. "Aye, though some spots are narrow and low. We had to crawl in places, one behind the other."

Erakes grabbed his arm and pulled him to the side out of the women's earshot. "Six armed Savatar. That's all we need to get inside. Three to kill the soldiers manning the catapults and destroy the devices, three to kill the guards at the main entrance and open the gates."

It was the perfect solution to victory without catastrophic losses to the Savatar horde. It seemed fitting that it was a Flower of Spring who handed them the means by which to sack Kraelag.

He might have celebrated more if Gilene were among the women who escaped. Maybe he could follow the tunnels as well.

Erakes must have read his thoughts. "You're too big, and you know you can't be the one to go in there. Your place is here with the warriors you lead."

It was a stray thought, nothing more. A temptation to torture him while he stood with Kraelag in sight and Gilene so far out of his reach. Azarion sighed. "We step up our arrow attacks, keep the army and the guards on the ramparts occupied while the six sneak into the city."

Erakes gestured to the Flowers of Spring. "What do you want to do with them?"

Azarion eyed them for a moment. Children among the women, and the women themselves both older and younger than what the Empire usually required of its sacrificial tithes. They were desperate, fearful. The Empire had demanded more sacrifices in the hopes of earning the gods' mercy by virtue of number. "Keep them here for now. They're safer with us than trying to flee into the forest, and we don't need one of them to regain a sudden loyalty to the Empire and run back into the city with tales to tell."

"We could just kill them." He grinned at Azarion's glare. "I'm jesting, *Ataman*. We owe them a debt, not death, and your *agacin* would never forgive us if we did such a thing."

Erakes gave instructions to have their captives-turned-guests housed and fed and given blankets to warm them. He and Azarion gathered with their captains in Erakes's *qara* to plan based on the new information offered by the Flowers. They had little time. The first volley from the catapults had taken everyone by surprise, but it wouldn't be long before the Kraelian heavy infantry used the Savatar's retreat to march forward and retake the ground Erakes and Azarion's forces had claimed in the fighting to reach the gates.

When they were finished, he once again sought out the Kraelian woman who had acted as the escapees' mouthpiece. He found her standing not far from where the others huddled around a fire, her back to them as she stood on the remains of a tree stump and surveyed the battlefield where dead men and dead horses lay strewn. She didn't turn when he came to stand beside her, and her voice held a far-away quality, as if his presence was nothing more than a vague interruption of her contemplation.

"When your battle is over and the fields replanted, the crops that grow there will whisper the names of the dead. Most don't stay, but those who linger will speak to the living when the wind blows and the rain falls."

Another time, and a worm of unease might have crawled across Azarion's skin at her words. Now, he barely noted them. "The fire witch. How was she when you last saw her?"

Her focus turned from the far place to settle on him. "Are you Azarion Ataman?" He nodded. "She was well. She burned a guard to gain the keys that opened the cell door." She cocked her head to one side. "You know her better than the others do."

He liked to believe he knew her best. "Yes."

Her round eyes gleamed for a moment. "I'll pray for you both that she survives to return to you."

"She doesn't believe in the gods."

The Kraelian woman's smile enhanced the strong line of her jaw. "That's all right. Most of us don't."

He had nothing else to ask her that wouldn't be a repeat of his earlier questions, so he left her to her odd notions of crops and spirits and returned to the camp's center. He found the six Savatar who volunteered to sneak into the city standing outside Erakes's *qara*, among them a familiar and beloved face.

"Why did I know you'd be one of the six?" He scowled at his sister.

Tamura tied her braids into a knot at the back of her head, shoving a pin into the mass to hold it in place. She wore an unapologetic grin. "You would have been shocked if I weren't."

She and the other five had removed anything on them that shone or might catch the sun's glare. Their long tunics were gone, replaced with short leather doublets and tighter breeches. They had set aside their bows and quivers full of arrows, carrying instead a myriad of short knives that made them lethal but didn't hinder them as they traversed tight spaces.

Erakes eyed the six with satisfaction. "You all understand what to do?" At their nods, he said, "May Agna be with you then."

Amid half-hearted protests and empty threats to emasculate him if he didn't let her go, Azarion embraced his sister until her back cracked. "Be careful," he whispered in her ear. "For my sake and our mother's as well." He set her away from him, and she shook like a wet dog before glowering at him.

A solemn affection softened the glower. "If I find Gilene, I'll bring her out of there. I swear it."

She saluted before turning on her heel to follow her companions through the camp to where their horses waited to carry them to a rendezvous point. From there, they would go on foot to reach the vulnerable entrance described by the Kraelian woman.

The Kraelian army, its ordered lines broken at first by the catapult volleys and the empress's shocking injury, had quickly re-formed. Shields staggered by the perimeter's soldiers formed a shield wall against direct arrow hits. The interior fighters followed suit, raising their shields above their heads to create a roof against the storm of arrows the Savatar would fire into the sky so that they fell down in an arc on the formation.

The sun had not yet centered itself in the sky when the catapults on the ramparts fired more shrapnel into the air, this time to land on the edges of the Kraelian formations where the Savatar light cavalry circled, darting in and out on fast horses to fire directly into the shield wall.

Azarion's reduced squadron of heavy horse was broken up and re-formed under the remaining three squadrons. They stood at the edge of the encampment, waiting for the signal that the catapults had been disarmed.

He stared at the city walls, fancying that, if he just looked a little harder, he could see through them to the arena where Gilene stayed behind. What had she been thinking not to escape with the other women? She'd been brave to protect them in a way they couldn't protect themselves from any who might pursue them, but she could have followed once they were no longer pursued.

"Why, Gilene?" he said under his breath. "Why did you stay?"

The moment Tamura and her group opened the gates, he'd be

the first to charge through. He cared nothing for looting or pillaging or burning the buildings. All he wanted was his *agacin*.

The horses and warriors around him grew restless with the waiting, and the armor and barding they wore grew ever hotter in the sun as it approached midday.

An inhuman wail suddenly split the air and set the horses to whinnying and rearing. Below the Savatar encampment, the Kraelian line rippled with a collective shudder, and the shield walls wavered. Horse archers clutched the manes of their mares and abandoned their arrow shots to stay in the saddles and control their frenzied mounts.

It was an unearthly sound, vast and piercing. Another followed, and every man and woman around Azarion gasped and covered their ears. The horses went berserk, many of them throwing their riders before bolting away, either into the forests or to the rolling hills behind the Savatar encampment.

Azarion instinctively raised his arms to cover his face as a colossal whirlwind of fire suddenly blasted up from the center of the city on an invisible concussion wave of pressure that made his ears pop. The air around him sucked in toward the city, bowing nearby trees, before exploding outward, shattering the city's outer barbican walls.

The damage the catapults did was nothing compared to the catastrophic destruction of masonry debris and wood shrapnel flying through the air. The Kraelian formations collapsed, obliterated by a howling gale that hurled them about like leaves in an autumn storm.

The monstrous column of fire expanded, and within the gaps of the broken walls, Azarion saw people running and screaming as they fled before the onslaught of what was surely holy retribution.

This fire moved with purpose. Fast, destructive, it devoured everything before it as it spun through the city, leaving conflagrations in its wake. Kraelian soldiers still alive and mobile ran into the wood or vainly sought to capture horses racing past them. The Savatar fled the field as well, their mares stretched low to the ground as they strove to outrun whatever monstrosity had just erupted from the center of Kraelag and turned it into fiery rubble.

When his horse fought him hard enough to nearly buck him off its back, Azarion dismounted and jogged farther down the slope leading to the deserted battlefield, ignoring the warning cries of his people behind him. His frantic gaze swept the path his sister and the other Savatar had taken, praying they hadn't yet made it to the city when it literally exploded before everyone's eyes.

The heat radiating off the burning city kept him from drawing closer. Every tree, bush, and weed nearest Kraelag's periphery had been reduced to blazing silhouettes.

Flames spiraled out of the moving whirlwind, hideous and graceful. Azarion squinted against the heat and light as the last of the Savatar archers raced past him for the uncertain safety of the camp.

That vortex of fire drew Azarion closer, despite the burn and the pain of blisters erupting on his exposed skin. A face coalesced in those flames, beautiful and terrible to behold. That face collapsed into the conflagration only to re-form once more, this time with a different woman's visage. It did it over and over again as the twisting maelstrom turned Kraelag into an inferno.

A chorus of voices rose behind him, and he turned to hear what they said. Savatar lined the slope, calling out to the whirlwind.

"Agna! Agna!"

Azarion pivoted back to stare at the bright, destroying beacon with its many changing faces. The Great Mare, creator of all the Savatar, the goddess of fire. She had manifested before Kraelian and Savatar alike and changed the world in the span of an indrawn breath.

His wonder changed to horror. He knew now why Gilene stayed. Only an *agacin* could call down the fire goddess. What had she done to capture the attention of a deity? What had she sacrificed?

He shouted her name, but the hot wind barreling off Kraelag shredded the sound. He called out again and again until he was hoarse and tasted blood at the back of his throat.

The spiraling column halted in front of the remains of the city gates. Behind him, every Savatar dropped to their knees in supplication.

"Gilene," he said in an almost soundless whisper, and this time, the goddess heard him.

A sliver of fire separated itself from the main column and floated across the littered battlefield to where Azarion knelt in the drying mud. He stayed on his knees, mesmerized. The entity stopped a short distance from him, close enough that he felt the heat it generated but not so close that he would burn from its proximity.

The splinter changed, taking on the face and form of a woman, and Azarion groaned at the sight.

Gilene, made of flame now instead of flesh, stared at him with eyes the color of luminous gold coins. She raised a hand, outlining his form in a loving caress that sent ripples of heat over the grass to buffet his face and arms.

Grief threatened to suffocate him. He'd found her again, but she was forever lost to him now. No longer a handmaiden of Agna but part of the goddess herself.

"Gilene," he said once again, and this time it was a prayer more than a name.

Her smile, wistful and sad, danced across her mouth. "I can

say it now," she said in a voice that crackled like burning wood in a hearth. "I won't falter." Again her hand caressed the air in front of him. "I love you, gladiator. Always." She floated back a little, leaving a scorch mark in the dirt. He reached for her, and she darted back even farther. "Farewell."

He leapt to his feet, reason scattered as he lunged to capture her, only to embrace empty air. She drifted away again, and this time she no longer pulsed with living flame. Instead, she faded, bit by bit, until there was nothing more than a single spark that winged away and finally disappeared from sight.

As if the goddess had bided her time until her handmaiden said goodbye, the giant column of fire suddenly collapsed, cascading down to a sheet of flame that flared twice before winking out completely. It was over.

Azarion stared with dry eyes at the smoking ruins of the once great city of Kraelag and her shattered walls, her battlefield a graveyard of charred bodies.

The Savatar had won. His place as *ataman* of his clan was secure. He and Erakes would return home as heroes.

There was much to celebrate. And far more to grieve. He closed his eyes, remembering the *agacin* whom he loved and who loved him in return. "I will not falter," he said and turned his back on the city to trudge toward the camp. He had Tamura to find, hopefully alive and unharmed.

"I will not falter," he said once more and climbed the slope to where the Savatar awaited him, wearing expressions of awe, reverence, and pity. They parted before him, a few reaching out as if to touch him before drawing away.

"I will not falter."

If he said it enough, he might not break.

# CHAPTER TWENTY-ONE

Gilene dreamed of fire and awakened to rain. Cold droplets splashed onto her face. She blinked her eyes open to watery splashes of gray and green. The deep smell of dirt and new leaves filled her nose, and an unpleasant wetness ran the length of her body, chilling her to the bone.

She shivered and curled in on herself, gasping as every muscle screamed a protest at her movements. Rain sheeted down on her, serenaded by faraway thunder. That she was outside in the elements was obvious, but where was outside?

As her vision cleared, the gray became a stormy sky above her and the green a cluster of bushes and small trees, their leaves bedecked in jewels of rain droplets. She lay in the mud, saturated to the skin, with a lone snail sheltering under a leaf to keep her company. More shivers racked her, and she sneezed. The exhalation made her cry out, and tears of pain joined the rain sliding down her cheeks.

Her memories were hardly more than blurry images and remnants of emotion—mostly fear. Two, though, emerged clear as the water droplets decorating the surrounding foliage: Azarion kneeling at the edge of the battlefield, his face red and blistered; and the goddess he worshipped, vast and powerful, her quicksilver visage both terrifying and glorious to behold.

"Agna," she whispered, and the thunder answered with a distant rumble.

She held up a trembling hand, surprised to see that, except for streaks of mud and a few broken fingernails, it was unchanged. Agna had been merciful to her handmaiden. Gilene had been sure when she walked into the arena alone, she would die. When she became the goddess's avatar, that certainty hadn't wavered. She was, after all, a frail human holding the power of a deity inside her for a brief time. That her body didn't burst and her bones didn't shatter from acting as Agna's vessel was nothing short of extraordinary.

She still felt as if she'd been trampled by a team of oxen and then run over by the wagon they pulled, but she was alive. Not for long if she stayed here, wet, cold, and hiding under a clump of bushes.

Standing was a grueling affair, accomplished with a slow ascension from her side to all fours, then to her knees, and finally to her feet, where she yawed from side to side like the ships that docked at Manoret. She embraced the trunk of a young tree next to her with the zeal of a lover and took in her surroundings.

Nothing looked familiar, but with the cobwebs clouding her mind and a veil of rain covering the landscape, she could easily be standing in her brother's garden and not recognize it. How she had even gotten here was a mystery.

She wiped more rainwater from her eyes. A muddy road stretched not far from where she stood, leading toward a cluster of buildings in the distance, their rooftops almost indiscernible in the steady deluge. A town or village. Shelter.

She glanced down at herself. The frock she wore was tattered and stained, with burn holes dotting the skirt and sleeves. Mud caked her entire back and right side, and somehow she'd lost one shoe. Agna might have carried her handmaiden from the ruin of Kraelag, but she hadn't exactly dropped her into the lap of luxury.

Gilene plucked at her soiled skirt and took a cautious step away from the tree, then another, until she tottered onto the road.

She made it a dozen steps before she fell. Weak, disoriented, and sick to her stomach, she didn't move. Hours might have passed as she lay there and let the rain wash over her. She slept, only opening her eyes at the sound of a donkey's bray and the rolling of wagon wheels.

A face, solemn and pretty, hovered over her. "My gods, Gilene?"

Gilene blinked. She knew this face. The free trader's niece. Halani of the soothing hands and magical potions that stopped pain. She smiled, drifting away on welcome warmth as Halani lifted her head out of the mud.

"Uncle, come quick! Help me!"

She woke briefly when someone held a cup to her lips. "Drink," they said, spilling a trickle of cold water into her mouth. She winced as she swallowed, certain glass splinters lined her throat. She fell back against a pillow, exhausted by that small effort, and fell asleep.

Images plagued her dreams. A bear trapped in a cage, Kraelag swallowed up in an inferno of god-fire, Azarion's desolate gaze as she bade him farewell. These and more flashed through her mind's eye, wraiths no more substantial than the ghosts of Midrigar, and just as miserable.

The next time she wakened, the sky above her was domed, painted, and familiar. She'd been here before, in similar circumstances.

"How do you feel, Gilene?"

Gilene sought the source of the voice and discovered Halani sitting cross-legged next to her feet. "Halani?" The word came out as a croak, but the other girl smiled, pleased.

"You remember me. That's good." She tucked away the ball of yarn she'd been winding and stood. "Don't say anything else. You've been down with fever and a cough for almost a week. I've a warm pot of tea waiting for just this moment. I'll be right back."

Good as her word, she returned with a cup filled nearly to the brim with tea flavored with herbs and honey. She helped Gilene sit up and propped the pillows behind her so she could drink. "Do you need help holding the cup?"

Gilene shook her head, determined to hold her trembling hands steady and manage the cup herself. Why fate had determined that this particular woman would end up being her nurse, not once but twice, she couldn't fathom. "I'm sorry you're playing nursemaid again. I promise I didn't plan it that way." She sipped the tea, closing her eyes in delight at the flavor.

Halani laughed. "I physic everyone in this caravan, Gilene. One more makes no difference." She brushed a hand across Gilene's arm. "Besides, I'm so pleased to see you again, even if it was under such strange circumstances."

That was putting it lightly. Gilene sipped more of her tea before speaking. "Where did you find me?"

"On the trade road outside Wellspring Holt. What happened to you?"

That was an answer requiring more energy and discretion than Gilene currently possessed. She handed the cup back to Halani. "I will tell you," she said as she slumped back under the blankets. Her eyelids felt weighted with stones, and the trader woman faded in her vision. "I promise."

It was a promise easier made than kept, and the story she told was as much fabrication as truth. "I ended up a Flower of Spring, taken by the slavers and separated from Valdan. I don't know where he is now, or if he's dead or alive." Tears welled in her eyes, honest ones that made that particular lie sincere.

Halani's mother, Asil, patted her shoulder in sympathy. "But you got out of the city before it burned! Did you see it burn?"

"Wait, Mama," Halani said. "In good time."

Gilene smiled. The childlike Asil remained as sweet-natured and enthusiastic as ever. "Another tithed woman knew of a way out of the catacombs. We managed to overpower our guard and escape." Applause greeted Gilene's statement. "I still have no idea how I ended up outside Wellspring Holt." That was partly true. Her memories after she told Azarion goodbye were a blank wall.

Hamod blew a perfect smoke ring into the air. It floated toward one of the trader children, who laughed and slipped her hand through its center like a bracelet. He pointed the pipe stem at Gilene. "Your husband was a capable sort. A good hunter, and I suspect an even better fighter. You'll find him again. Or he'll find you."

Gilene very much hoped he was right.

Spring passed into the first days of summer as she regained her strength. The caravan plied their wares on the trade roads and the Golden Serpent as well. She remained with the trader band through her convalescence and, at Hamod's gruff invitation, after that.

"You're welcome to stay. You do your part and help the other women," he said. "We have enough to feed you."

Beroe was no longer home, and her obligation to it and her family finished, at least in her opinion. She had lived her life in service to them, a service inherited instead of chosen. Gilene had accepted her lot and did her best to fulfill the role, even as the resentment ate her up from the inside.

Now, she had no reason to stay, no duty to embrace. Kraelag

had been obliterated, a city turned into a char heap by a deity who had burned every building to the ground and turned the sands of the arena floor into glass. There would be no more gruesome Rites of Spring.

While she was grateful to Hamod for his offer, she didn't plan to stay with the caravan permanently. As soon as she was well enough to travel on her own, she'd find a way to return to the Sky Below and seek out the man who had made her see there was more to life than dreary sacrifice.

Gilene shared Halani and Asil's wagon, though like most in the caravan, she slept outside on clear nights. One night, when the ache of missing Azarion gnawed at her, she had a particularly vivid dream. Agna of the changing faces loomed over her as she slept. Lightning danced down her hands to her fingers, illuminating the spiderwork of veins under the skin. Gilene caught her breath as the goddess pressed her palm to the spot just above Gilene's navel.

"No more pain for my name's sake, handmaiden. No punishment for summoning fire. We see each other now, you and I. You and yours have my protection."

Gilene woke with a gasp loud enough to startle half the camp awake. She apologized, citing a dream as the culprit. Her hand fluttered over her belly. Was it a dream? Or a memory of that time between time, after she walked as Agna's avatar and before she woke up in the mud in a woodland outside Wellspring Holt?

She pondered the dream memory every day after that but, like her magic, kept it to herself. The traders welcomed her among them, accepting her as one of their own. She didn't want to compromise that acceptance with stories of visitations from goddesses.

One early-summer evening, Hamod made an announcement that set free a horde of butterflies in Gilene's belly.

"The Goban have invited all traders, Guild and free, to their solstice market. Since the Trade Guild no longer controls the Golden Serpent, we'll have access to the Goban tribes and the Savatar clans they're allied with, which means access to their silver as well." He grinned as the other traders cheered.

Busy with the task of washing the supper dishes, Gilene swayed on her feet, made light-headed by Hamod's announcement. Could it be? Had fate finally decided to show her some small favor and put her on a path that might intersect with Azarion's?

There was no guarantee the Kestrel clan would be there, but she refused to relinquish the hope bursting inside her. It would take longer to reach the Sky Below by traveling the trade route, but she wouldn't have to choose the more dangerous option of traveling it alone to reach her goal.

"Gilene, are you well? You've gone pale. Do you need to sit down?" Even after weeks of recuperation and assurances from Gilene that she was now fine, Halani still hovered over her.

She was alive and whole and bore no additional scars from her summoning that last fire. Agna had been merciful to her apostate handmaiden.

Gilene put away the last dried dish in its chest and flipped the towel over her shoulder. The smile she gave Halani felt like it stretched from one ear to the other.

"I feel good. Just happy with your uncle's news. I've always wanted to visit the east beyond the Gamir Mountains."

Halani nodded. "I as well. With the Trade Guild's hold on the Serpent now broken, we can trade beyond the usual routes." She wiggled her eyebrows. "And I hope the Savatar are at the market. I've always wanted to see the steppe nomads firsthand. I hear they're beautiful to behold on horseback."

An image of Azarion chasing the wild mares across the pastures of plume grass rose up in Gilene's mind. *They are*, she replied silently. *They are glorious.*

Summer in the lands of the Goban was a gentler season than what it was in the Stara Dragana to the west. The barrier of the Gamir Mountains blocked the fierce winds and kept the temperatures warm but not scorching along the populated territories that hugged the great trade road known as the Golden Serpent.

The high holy day of the summer solstice had brought traders of every kind to peddle their wares at the vast market set up in the tumbled remains of a Kraelian garrison. People flooded in from every town and city in a ten-league radius, while others had traveled for weeks from the western hinterlands to attend the market. A sprawling tent town, ringed by caravan wagons, had sprung up overnight, surrounding the market.

It was the first of its kind, the creation of an opportunistic group of traders, both free and ex-Guild who saw a chance to make a sizable profit without the restrictions of the Guild or the stranglehold the Empire had once placed on the trade route.

Hamod stood next to the makeshift shop his caravan had erected, surveying the tide of humanity parading past him with a satisfied smile.

He turned to the two women nearby, busy with restocking their tables and quoting prices to curious browsers. There were teas and furs to sell, carvings and small knives, silk ribbons and purses, and hats stitched with feathers and jewels.

"What do you think, eh? We've never done so well in a day when we were banned from trading on the Serpent."

Halani nodded. "I suspect many free traders think the same thing, though you've made no friends with the Guild traders."

He snorted. "I won't lose any sleep over that one." He eyed Gilene, who stood next to Halani. She carefully measured dried tea into linen pouches before marking them with a quill dipped in ink. "The east all what you hoped it would be, Gilene?"

Gilene didn't shift her gaze from her task, but she did smile at the caravan leader. *Not yet*, she thought. Not quite yet. Since their arrival, she'd given herself a neck ache and blurry vision as she searched the crowds for any hint of a Savatar clansman or clanswoman. She'd even walked the entire market twice without any luck. "It's very promising so far," she replied out loud.

The sight of an acquaintance caught Hamod's attention and he was off, striding through the crowd to make himself known and likely do his best to swindle the person out of a purse of coins.

"I think all of the Empire and the lands beyond are here," Halani said. "I've never seen so many people in one place."

Gilene filled the last bag with tea, made her mark, and set down her quill. She grasped Halani's hand in hers and gave it a squeeze. "Or so many thieves either." She snatched back a canister of tea leaves from a boy with quick fingers. He moved on to his next mark with only a brief shrug her way.

The Krael Empire convulsed at the loss of its physical and spiritual capital. The Savatar who attacked it had returned to the steppe without further fighting. There had been no looting or pillaging of Kraelag. Everything of value had been burned or melted. The Empire itself had not fallen, but the cracks in its armor were widening as vassal territories reclaimed their autonomy once they realized their master wasn't invulnerable.

Everyone assumed the emperor had died in Kraelag's inferno,

though there were more than a few conjectures that his wife might have taken that golden opportunity to rid herself of her co-ruler.

Empress Dalvila had been wounded by a Savatar arrow but survived and currently hid behind the walls of her summer palace while her empire teetered on the brink of collapse. Gilene had no doubt a wake of vulturous Kraelian nobles gathered to swoop in and take control.

As the caravan trundled its way toward Goban, Gilene had thought of Azarion constantly and *prayed* to Agna that he would be at the market.

Halani interrupted her contemplations with a tap on her arm. "Can you watch the tables? I've started negotiating with a trader out of Palizi for a shawl I know Mama will love."

Gilene shooed her off. "Of course. Go on, and good luck!"

She was in the middle of a transaction with a customer when Halani raced back to their booth, eyes shining with excitement. "I just heard. Several of the Savatar clans have arrived."

Gilene's heart instantly took up the hard beat of a war drum. She blinked at Halani, afraid to believe the news. "Are you sure?"

The other woman nodded so hard, the pin holding her braid coiled at her nape fell out, and the braid tumbled down her back. "They're roaming through the market now. Word is their chieftains are honored guests of the Goban chief who controls this territory." She stood on tiptoe and craned her neck to stare above the crowd, as if a Savatar might suddenly pop up amid the crowd, astride their horse.

A loud whistle made both women look to where Hamod motioned for Halani to join him and a group of traders surrounding an item covered by a square of indigo silk.

Halani groaned. "Probably another statue Uncle wants me to

look at. I'm better than he is at spotting a fake. I'll have to leave you again for a moment."

"It's all right. See to your uncle. We'll switch places when you return."

The moment Halani came back, Gilene planned to escape the trade stall she worked and find the Savatar encampment. Was Azarion here? Did he walk these crowded streets? Would she sense his presence even if she couldn't see him in the throng of people? Her heart raced and her hands shook so hard, she abandoned the task of measuring tea.

He thought her dead, consumed by Agna's possession. Did he mourn her? The thought made her cringe.

An odd prickling along her back warned her she was being watched. She made a show of straightening the tables, all the while casting quick glances into the crowd to find the source of that regard.

Her gaze lit and stayed on a dark-haired woman with a dour face. The woman's eyes went wide when Gilene met her gaze, and she mouthed Gilene's name as if she didn't believe what she was seeing.

"Tamura," Gilene said.

Azarion's sister was too far away to hear her, but judging by her reaction, she'd read Gilene's lips.

"Azarion! Come quickly!"

Tamura bellowed so loudly, it set dogs to barking, goats to bleating, and children to crying. The steadily moving traffic that wove a maze through the market halted, and people stared at Tamura slack-jawed.

She ignored it all and repeated her brother's name in that same booming voice.

A ripple of movement in the crowd, and Azarion burst into the gap that had opened around Tamura, sword unsheathed, ready to do battle.

Gilene clenched her teeth to hold back her gasp. He'd aged in the months since she'd last seen him. Still handsome, still commanding, he looked haggard, weary. Bleak. He wore leather armor over a long, sleeveless tunic that highlighted his muscular arms. The summer sun hadn't yet done its work in darkening his skin to the nut brown she remembered, but his green eyes were still as vivid. His hair had grown past his shoulders, and sunlight highlighted the silver filaments sprinkled in the long locks as well as in his beard.

He swept the crowd with a single glance before turning to his sister, confused and exasperated. "What? What is it?"

Tamura pointed to where Gilene stood behind the line of tables. Azarion followed the direction of her gesture and froze.

A muscle worked in his jaw as he continued to stare at her. Gilene drank in the sight of him like a woman dying of thirst who'd just been handed a cup of water.

She remembered their conversation in a *qara* on the eve of their separation.

*Be my wife. Treasured and beloved.*

This time if he asked, she could say yes.

He passed his sword to the now grinning Tamura. The slow, hesitant step he took toward Gilene quickly transformed to a ground-eating stride. People leapt out of the way before they were shoved aside.

He stopped in front of her, the table a flimsy barricade between them. Gilene could hear him breathe—arrhythmic pants, as if he'd sprinted up the side of a mountain without stopping. His hands curled into fists, the knuckles turning white.

Such agony in that long, silent gaze. Such disbelief. Gilene trapped a moan behind her teeth.

"I thought you were dead," he whispered, voice cracking on the last word. "I saw you fade to nothing, consumed by Agna."

It took two tries and a little throat clearing before she could reply. "I think I was consumed. So much power, Azarion. I can't describe it." She stared at him, willing him to believe she was real and not some simulacrum of the fire witch from Beroe. "Agna brought me back. I woke on the road to Wellspring Holt, sick and witless. Hamod's trader band found me and nursed me back to health. I traveled with them here, hoping I'd find you again."

Staring at his handsome face, with its elegant angles and lines of sorrow, became as difficult as gazing upon Agna in all her vengeful majesty. Gilene dropped her gaze to hide the tears threatening to spill over her lashes.

"Wife of my soul," he said, and this time his voice didn't shake but held all the command of the Savatar *ataman* who had led an army against the Empire and won. "Look at me."

His words sent an arrow of euphoria straight through her chest. Still, she couldn't look up.

"Look at me," he repeated in the same tone. His fingers curled around her jaw to lift her chin.

She dragged her gaze to his, the drumming of her heartbeat making her ribs hurt. He leaned over the table, mouth hovering just above hers, eyes blazing with joy.

He shoved the table out of the way and pulled her into his arms. He raised his hand to drag a thumb gently across her lower lip before following its path with his mouth. Gilene sank into his embrace, kissing him back as fiercely as he kissed her. The market surrounding them faded as she reveled in his touch, in this reunion she never dared hope for since they went their separate ways at the boundaries of the Sky Below almost a year earlier.

Azarion kissed her until she was light-headed from lack of air. When they finally parted, they both gasped for breath.

His green eyes were soft now, but no less intense as he searched her face. She was reminded of their first true meeting, in the tenebrous confines of the catacombs on the eve of an immolation, when she avoided his gaze and prayed he wouldn't recognize her.

He must have remembered the same meeting. His lips tilted in a faint smile. "*Agacin,*" he said reverently. "I know you."

# ACKNOWLEDGMENTS

Writing a book is a solitary endeavor. Polishing and packaging one, a team effort. My sincerest thanks to the following amazing people who helped me bring this book across the finish line:

Anne Sowards, editor extraordinaire; Mel Sterling, principal beta reader and eleventh-hour rescuer; Aria Jones, principal beta reader; Julie Fine, beta reader; DeeAnn Fuchs, beta reader; Pilar Seacord, beta reader; Ilona Andrews, who taught me the suspense of the countdown; Sarah Younger, agent badass; Arantza Sestayo, cover artist; Angelina Krahn, copy editor.

# ABOUT THE AUTHOR

**Grace Draven** is a Louisiana native living in Texas with her husband, kids, and a big doofus dog. She is the winner of the RT Reviewers' Choice Award for Best Fantasy Romance of 2016 and a *USA Today* bestselling author.

## CONNECT ONLINE

gracedraven.com
facebook.com/gracedravenauthor
twitter.com/GraceDraven

Ready to find
your next great read?

Let us help.

**Visit prh.com/nextread**